CW01207796

The DRAGON of ANGUR

Sinclair Forrest

Illustrations by Giles Robson

Bloomington, IN Milton Keynes, UK
authorHOUSE®

AuthorHouse™
1663 Liberty Drive, Suite 200
Bloomington, IN 47403
www.authorhouse.com
Phone: 1-800-839-8640

AuthorHouse™ UK Ltd.
500 Avebury Boulevard
Central Milton Keynes, MK9 2BE
www.authorhouse.co.uk
Phone: 08001974150

This book is a work of fiction. People, places, events, and situations are the product of the author's imagination. Any resemblance to actual persons, living or dead, or historical events, is purely coincidental.

© 2007 Sinclair Forrest. All rights reserved.

No part of this book may be reproduced, stored in a retrieval system, or transmitted by any means without the written permission of the author.

First published by AuthorHouse 3/7/2007

ISBN: 978-1-4259-4757-6 (sc)
ISBN: 978-1-4259-4758-3 (hc)

Printed in the United States of America
Bloomington, Indiana

This book is printed on acid-free paper.

CONTENTS

Prologue		1
Chapter 1	Gastelois De Bois	10
Chapter 2	The New Dolmen	20
Chapter 3	Sylvia D'Arass	37
Chapter 4	Vraicer T'loch	47
Chapter 5	An Unexpected Problem	59
Chapter 6	The Magician of Sersur	75
Chapter 7	A Nocturnal Visit	89
Chapter 8	The Flight to Piltdown	102
Chapter 9	Piltdown - 'Stone-Ears' Meade	122
Chapter 10	Mannequin De Perrelle	141
Chapter 11	An Unexpectedly Useful Encounter	150
Chapter 12	Equinox	165
Chapter 13	Diggings in the Darkness	178
Chapter 14	A meeting at Mont Mado	196
Chapter 15	Plottings at Sunset	208
Chapter 16	The Geonnais Communists	216
Chapter 17	A Chanting of Levitations	230
Chapter 18	A Betyle for the Kerions	245
Chapter 19	A Day Best Forgotten	260
Chapter 20	The Vial	268
Chapter 21	A Breach of Rules	280
Chapter 22	A Dolmen in the Doldrums	302
Chapter 23	A Festive Island	321
Chapter 24	The Contest	334
Chapter 25	Shenanigans on the Seashore	356
Chapter 26	Trial and Tribulation	369
Epilogue	A Hougue for Hugo	408

------- 0 -------

THE ISLAND OF ANGUR

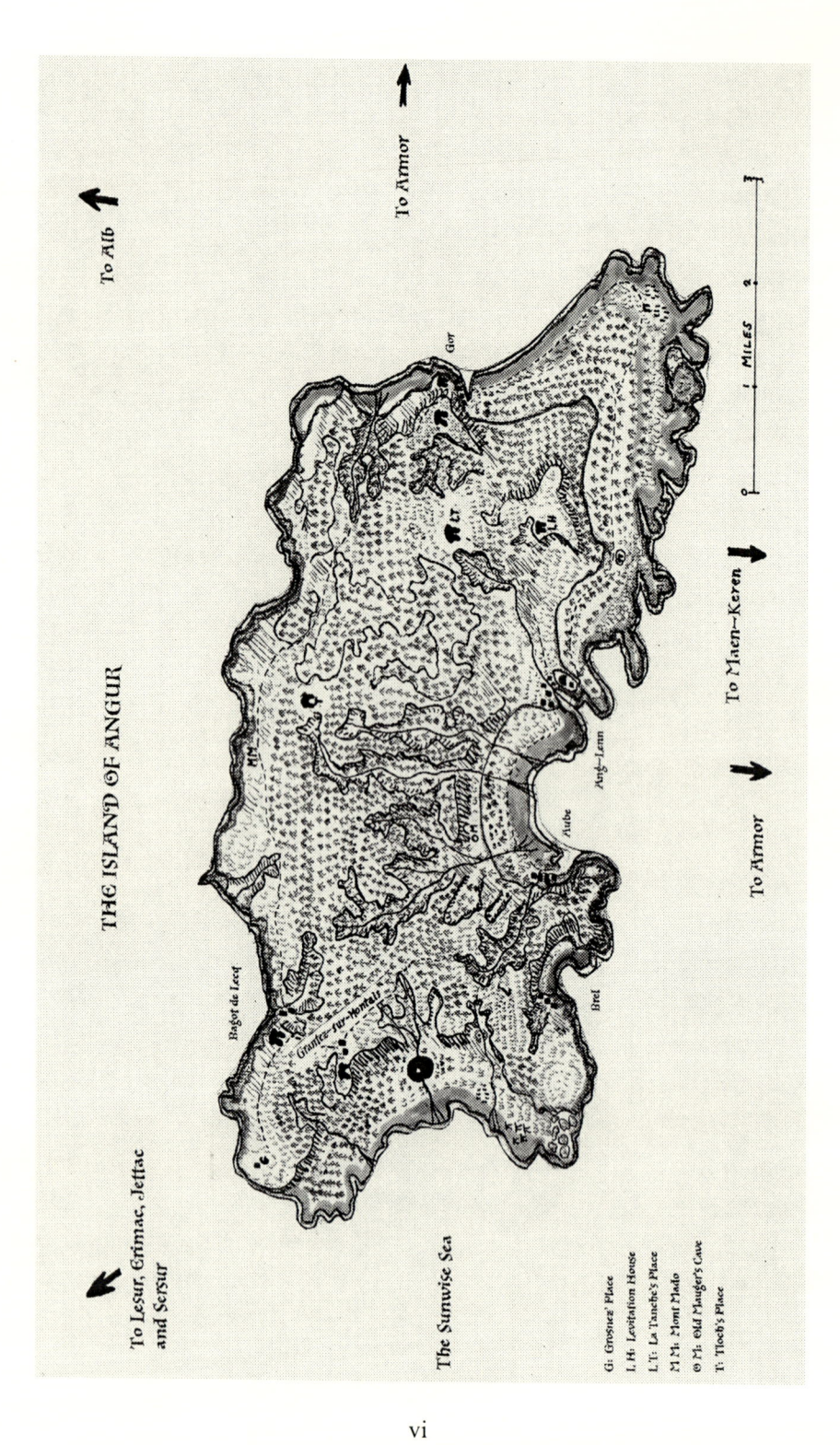

G: Grosnez' Place
I.H: Levitation House
L.T: La Tanche's Place
M.M: Mont Mado
O.M: Old Mauger's Cave
T: Tioch's Place

PROLOGUE

OLD MAUGER

Old Mauger lay on his belly at the edge of the marsh, smoking contentedly in the shade of an ancient tree. The sound of breakers reached his ears from a not-too distant shore, accompanied intermittently by the screeching of seagulls wheeling overhead, while around him the marsh muttered its way through the hot afternoon, fanned by a cool, leisurely breeze from the sea.

Old Mauger was much given to thought these days, particularly when the weather was so fine and he could while away an afternoon in dreamy reflection of bygone days. He had neither the inclination nor indeed the energy for any form of physical activity, and just liked to dwell on the past and the eventful moments of a dragon's long life. He thought often of his father, dead for eighty years, who had lived on the treacherous south-west point of the island. There he had warned seafarers of the proximity of dangerous reefs by sending up a pillar of smoke by day and a column of fire by night. Old Mauger always sighed when he thought of this, for it reminded him of how his father had met his end - if only those smugglers had not been so careless!

Then he would sometimes think of the strange bearded man dressed in a striking iridescent robe who had visited the marsh many years before. He had carried a long wooden staff carved with strange symbols at whose meaning Old Mauger could scarcely guess, and around his neck there had hung a finely-wrought crystalline vial, which had glowed with a soft yellowy-green light from the liquid it contained. After some words of explanation, he had produced a small turtle shell that had been concealed within the folds of his robe. He had presented it to the dragon, instructing him to guard it well and never to part with it unless asked for it by one attired like him and wearing a similar vial of glowing liquid. Then he had departed and Mauger had never seen him again. Nor had anyone like him come to ask for the shell, and it still lay in a dark recess at the rear of Mauger's cave in the cliffs bordering the northern edge of the marsh.

He yawned and shut his eyes. Rich green and soft golden light filtered through the gently waving leafy canopy of the nearby tree and wove intricate patterns on his eyelids, some of it seeping through to register on his sleepy brain. Feminine chatter dimly reached his ears, gradually growing louder as the owners of the voices drew nearer. Old Mauger knew who they were – a group of old women who regularly came down to the marsh ponds to wash their clothes. Sometimes he helped them, but he knew that they would not have need of his hot breath today: the weather was too fine.

The women greeted him when they arrived, and he returned their greeting, his deep booming voice echoing across the marsh.

He rolled on to his back and listened to them for a while, but gradually their chatter and the splashing of their washing became fainter and more distant as he slowly drifted off into a peaceful slumber, smoke rising lazily from his broad nostrils.

* * *

The Sun was beginning to set as the small leather-hulled boat approached the high cliffs of the island of Angur's rugged northern coastline. The small, lone figure pulling on the oars was not in the best of humours, as a freak wave had removed the craft's rather flimsy sail earlier in the crossing from the neighbouring island of Lesur, necessitating the completion of the journey by rowing. In these waters, this was an arduous activity at the best of times; today it was particularly difficult, not to mention unpleasant, as the wave's onslaught had left the boat half-full of seawater and its hapless occupant drenched. He had neglected to bring a bailer with him and had soon given up trying to use his hands, as this had proved rather futile. So the water remained in the boat, making it sluggish and difficult to control, with all the handling prowess of a cattle-trough!

Wet and miserable, and endlessly cursing his bad luck, he had had no choice but to carry on. It was with considerable relief, therefore, that he eventually reached the base of the cliffs. Pulling into a narrow cave, he moored his boat alongside the two others already there. He thought about draining it, but decided that that could wait until later. Right now all he wanted was to change into some dry clothes and get something to eat.

The DRAGON of ANGUR

Piton Le Malin hated the climb from the cave to Grosnez' home. The tortuous pathway snaking up the cliff face was strewn with loose stones and gravel, and his feet were constantly slipping as they tried to retain their grip. The cliff-side offered a few projecting roots and Piton made frequent use of these as handholds. There were no such aids on the other side of the path, only a precipitous drop straight into the sea. To make matters worse, vision was becoming increasingly difficult in the deepening twilight.

Piton struggled upwards, muttering to himself. When eventually he did reach the top, he had to sit down for a few moments to get his breath back. Although it had been a warm day, the air was now somewhat chilly and, despite a degree of heat generated by his recent exertions, he felt rather cold, his condition not helped by the fact that he was still wet through from the soaking he had received earlier. Shivering, he got up to walk the hundred yards or so to Grosnez' front door.

The mound covering his master's stone house was black against the darkening sky. Smoke was issuing from a hole in its summit. *Good*, thought Piton, *a nice fire to drive away this confounded chill.* He reached the heavy oaken door and knocked.

A tall, lanky individual with a pointed black goatee beard and piercing eyes opened it. "Ah! Piton, mon vier," said Grosnez Chatel. "Come in, come in."

Piton was only too glad to comply and followed the black-garbed figure along the short passage leading to the living area. From there, the smell of roasting meat wafted to his nostrils and his mouth watered as he contemplated dinner. They emerged into the living area, a drystone-walled circular chamber off which opened a number of smaller chambers. A log fire was burning in the central hearth of the main room, the smoke drifting up towards a hole in the apex of the corbel-vaulted stone roof, and on a spit straddling the fire a wild boar was being steadily roasted. On seeing this, Piton licked his lips in anticipation.

"I expected you back earlier," said Grosnez. Then, for the first time noticing the other's bedraggled state: "What happened? You fall overboard, you?"

"I was lucky not to! A bloody great wave attacked the boat and took away the mast and sail. I had to row all the way back, me."

"Aw, what a pity!" said Grosnez unsympathetically. "Get changed, and then we'll have a drink before we eat."

Grosnez Chatel

Piton thought that this was an excellent idea and disappeared into one of the side chambers to change. In due course he came out, freshly attired, and walked over to the fire to warm himself, standing close to it and rubbing his hands together vigorously. Grosnez handed him a clay drinking-vessel half-filled with the former's rather excellent home-brewed beer. Piton gratefully took it in both hands and noisily gulped down some of the refreshing liquid.

Grosnez slowly turned the handle of the spit while prodding various parts of the boar with a long flint knife, its juices sizzling as they dripped on to the fire. "Ah! It's done," he said. "While we're eating, you can tell me about your day." He stared at Piton with cold, hard eyes. "I trust you have some int'resting news for me." There was a slightly threatening tone to his voice.

Piton swallowed nervously. "I do, Grosnez, I do."

"Good." Grosnez cut off a piece of the boar and handed it to his servant. Then he hacked off a larger chunk for himself. "Well?"

Piton settled himself cross-legged by the fire and bit off a mouthful of meat. "As we thought," he began, chewing noisily, "Old Mauger has the turtle shell."

"You certain, you?"

Piton nodded. "I went into *The Quivering Crapaud* to see what I could find out, and I saw this old man I thought I recognised. It turned out to be Tourvel Le Crochon."

Piton Le Malin

"Ah yes!" I'd forgotten that was living in Lesur now." He filled his clay jar with more beer from a hide flagon and then put the flagon down beside him.

"You remember how he used to love to gossip, that one," said Piton, reaching over for the flagon and then pouring some of its contents into his jar. "Well, he's just as garrulous as ever - especially after a few drinks. I bought him a beer and then went over and introduced myself, hoping he'd remember me. He did."

"That would claim to remember anyone who bought it a beer," remarked Grosnez sarcastically. "Go on."

Piton cut off some more meat from the boar and took a mouthful. He swallowed it quickly when he saw the look of impatience on Grosnez' face. "Well, I started off by chatting about old times and gradually worked my way around to Old Mauger; I'd remembered that time past Tourvel used to spend a lot of time with him."

"Indeed!" exclaimed Grosnez, nodding. "I recall him going to visit Mauger on a number of occasions."

5

"We talked about Mauger for quite a while, and I made sure that Tourvel didn't run out of drink so he wouldn't dry up. Then I brought up the matter of the shell. I fed him the story we'd agreed upon, us."

"That we had one ourselves and suspected the existence of another?"

"Yes." Piton took a large swig of beer and swallowed it noisily, wiping his mouth with the back of his hand. "I described 'ours' to him and asked him if he'd ever seen one like it. He had to think about it for a few moments, but then he said that he had - in Mauger's cave!"

"Excellent!" said Grosnez. Then he began to stroke his chin, his face assuming a pensive look. "Although I'm a bit surprised he told you so readily; you know how valuable that shell is."

"Aw but Grosnez, he was pretty pissed by that stage, him. He would have given away anything."

"You have a point there, you," admitted Grosnez, nodding. "And of course he may not have a clue about its value. Did he say anything else?"

"Not much - just that he recalled that the shell was lying somewhere towards the back of the cave."

"I see." Grosnez hacked off a piece of the boar, tossed it to Piton and then cut off a piece for himself. "So," he said, contemplating the slice of meat in his hands, "the problem now is Old Mauger."

"I know, Grosnez, I know."

"He's in our way. We can't get at the shell with him there."

"Aw but he's a nuisance, him." Piton scratched his head with a greasy hand and frowned pensively.

"We'll have to get him out of the way, Piton. We can't let a ruddy dragon interfere with our plans, aih!"

"How do we do that, Grosnez?" Piton looked at the other.

"I don't know, but he'll have to be r'moved."

"But he's pop'lar, him."

"Pah!" Grosnez spat into the fire. "I don't care about *that*. We've got to get rid of him."

Piton stared into the hearth, his eyes flickering with the reflection of the firelight. He did not like what he assumed to be going through his master's mind. "I don't know, me," he said at last. "The people won't like it.

The DRAGON of ANGUR

"I trust you have some int'resting news for me"

"The people can go to Sersur!"

"But Grosnez, if we kill the bloody beast, we'll have an uproar."

"Piton, mon vier!" Grosnez looked at his servant reproachfully. "Who said anything about killing him?"

"I... I just presumed that's what you were getting at, you."

"No, no, not at all! I do have my reputation to think of. We just need to get him away from the cave - long enough for us to get the shell. The question is how?"

"Aw but that's a good question, that!"

They both gazed into the fire. A log shifted slightly, sending up a small shower of sparks. There was a sputtering sound as some fat dripped from the remains of the boar on to the glowing wood.

"However it's done, it will have to be done with subtlety," mumbled Grosnez.

There was a long pause, the silence broken only by crackling and spitting noises from the fire and by an owl hooting intermittently outside.

"I have an idea!" exclaimed Piton suddenly, his voice triumphant in the manner of one who has ideas all too rarely.

Grosnez stared at him. "Well?"

"As you know, it's the High Elder's Flint Jubilee this year."

"Yes, yes. What of it?"

"Well, mon vier, as you also know, they're planning all sorts of cel'brations for him." Piton was hardly able to contain his excitement. "That means contests."

"True. Go on, go on." Grosnez did not see what the other was driving at and was becoming impatient.

"Well, we persuade the Elders to have a sort of dragon-hunting contest, the object of which will be to drive Old Mauger from the marsh and chase him as far away as poss'ble. Then, while he's out of the way, we can go into his cave and get the shell." He looked at his master for approval while adding: "Of course, the Elders will have to get his agreement and they'll have to make sure that he doesn't come to any harm."

Grosnez contemplated this for a few moments. Then he nodded approvingly. "Aw but Piton you've the basis of an excellent idea there, you." He popped a piece of meat into his mouth and chewed it slowly. "But I don't think the contest should start at the marsh.

The whole thing should be held well away from there to ensure we're not seen and to give us more time."

"You have a point there, you," agreed Piton.

Grosnez stood up, scratched the end of his rather large, hooked nose and vigorously rubbed his bony hands together with glee. "By Teus!"[1] he exclaimed. "I'm going to be so powerful, me."

---

1 The *Teus* was the god of wayfarers, a benevolent spirit of huge stature clothed in white, who protected nocturnal travellers against evil spirits and other terrors of the night by sheltering them under his cloak until the danger had passed.

CHAPTER ONE

GASTELOIS DE BOIS

The boat that approached Angur from the south-west one fine evening during the Third Moon of the Season of Lengthening Days was a moderately large, broad-beamed affair with a high prow and a single, square, leather sail that flapped noisily in the stiff breeze. Ahead, the granite cliffs of the headlands dominating the island's south-western coastline glowed red as if set on fire by the rays of the sinking Sun, their rocky ramparts sheltering the bays and coves at their feet.

On board were eleven men, two of whom were not involved with the running of the ship. These latter were sitting near the stern, large hide bags at their feet, and were talking of their recent visit to Armor, the country lying to the south of the group of islands of which Angur was the largest.

One of the men was in his mid-thirties, tall, but slightly too thin for his height. Unusually for an inhabitant of Angur, his hair was fair, and this, together with his stature, made him stand out from the crowd. Grey-blue eyes sparkling from sharply-incised features and a high forehead spoke of a keen intellect, and he had the assured air of one who possessed great knowledge and was in a position of some authority. He wore a brown, knee-length hide garment secured around the waist by a thick leather belt, while his feet and legs below the knees were enclosed in woollen boots wrapped around with leather thongs tied behind the calves. A long cloak of a finely woven, emerald-green cloth was fastened around his throat with a circular, polished flint clasp.

His companion was similarly attired, except that his cloak was dark blue. He was a couple of years younger than the other, and was a short, slightly burly individual with a round, friendly face and short-cropped black hair. His brown eyes possessed an almost permanent twinkle, and when he spoke, his voice had a sort of sing-song quality that fell easily on the ear.

"Well, Gastelois," he was saying, "I thought your talk on suitable types of rock for capstones went down very well."

Gastelois de Bois looked over the side of the boat at the water frothing past the hull and shrugged his shoulders. "Could've been better," he said. "I'd have preferred more time, but with so many speakers I suppose that just wasn't possible." His accent was cosmopolitan, the result of much time spent in other lands, and only rarely lapsed into that of his native island. He sighed: "No doubt they'll want me back next year to speak on some other subject, or on the same one again."

"Come on, Gastelois, it's not that bad," chided his companion. "You know you enjoy it. Anyway, maybe they'll give you longer next time. After all, you have been going there for the past five years."

"That remains to be seen, Thière." Gastelois glanced at the other and then returned his gaze to the water. As one of the most highly esteemed members of the *Venerable Brotherhood of Dolmen Builders*[2], a position signified by the flint clasp on his cloak, he was

---

[2] Dolmen – literally 'table stone' – a structure of large stones known as *megaliths*. The simplest form is a stone chamber formed by a single capstone supported by three or more uprights or *orthostats*. More complex variants are the *passage-dolmen* and the *gallery-dolmen* (see below).

very much in demand at conferences on megalithic construction (the building of structures using very large stones), and his advice on this subject was much sought after. But there was usually so much to be discussed at these meetings that even he had to have his time limited. He was also Angur's chief dolmen-builder, having inherited the position from his late father, Arbreur Le Bois, who had taught him the trade.

"At least we had good weather." Thière de Guérin, chief dolmen-builder of Lesur and fellow member of the Brotherhood, leant back and stretched. A more retiring and self-effacing man than his companion, he very rarely spoke at the conferences, preferring instead to let others play a more active role.

"That's true," said Gastelois. "I think it's going to break soon, though." He pointed to the western horizon where a large bank of clouds was building ominously, their tops tinged yellowy-orange by the gradually sinking Sun.

Thière followed Gastelois' outstretched arm and nodded in agreement. "You could be right, mon vier. We may see rain by the morning."

As the boat ploughed steadily through the waves towards Angur, sea foam hissing past its flanks, the two men talked further about the conference from which they were returning. This one was held every spring at the megalithic centre of Carnac, near the south-west of Armor. This year's had been very stimulating, and a number of novel ideas had been presented pertaining to the erection of dolmens and the single standing stones known in that part of the world as *menhirs*. The high point had been a visit to the south central region of Armor to see a brand new dolmen of immense size, which had recently been completed. Known as *Le Grand Dolmen*, this had taken the visitors' breath away by virtue of its architect's use of huge stones and its unprecedented size. Some sixty feet long and twenty wide, it measured a good ten feet from ground level to the undersides of its four enormous capstones, the largest of which weighed nearly ninety tons.

"I bet their priests had fun getting those up," Thière remarked of the capstones.

"The thing is, they managed it." Gastelois shivered and drew his cloak more tightly around him. With the approach of dusk, the air was turning chilly. "I doubt our lot could pull off such a feat."

"Mmm," mumbled the other, and then lapsed into contemplative silence for a few moments before saying: "It would be good if I could build something that big in Lesur."

"Why don't you?"

"Apart from our priests being very nearly as incompetent as yours, the Elders would never sanction it."

"Why not?"

"Too expensive."

The boat was by now passing the headland known as *Le Mont Noircissant*, so called because tradition held that it always appeared dark irrespective of the weather or the time of day. To its east lay the large crescent form of the Bay of Aube, which occupied the central part of Angur's south coast, tree-cloaked slopes rising behind it to meet the edge of the high plateau that formed the bulk of the hinterland.

The vessel's destination, the island's chief settlement of Ang-Lenn, lay on the far side of the bay, near the shore on sandy flats below the southern edge of the plateau. It was really quite large, especially considering the norm for the day, and was more like a small town than a village. On the southern side of the settlement, a tidal inlet with direct access to the sea provided a safe anchorage for boats, as well as a haven for a few timber thatch-roofed buildings supported by stilts to keep them clear of the water even at the highest tide. These belonged to fishermen, and all manner of fishing paraphernalia was usually visible piled on the parapet that ran around each house at floor level, while the men's boats were moored to the stilts.

On the eastern side of the inlet, the land rose up to form a steep-sided eminence, known as *Le Ville Mont*, or The Town Mount, which stood like a rocky island parted from the main Angurian plateau to its north, its cliffs revealing the reddish-pink granite of which it was composed. By virtue of its colour, this granite had found favour (with those who could afford it) as a building material for special structures such as dolmens, and it could be seen gracing quite a few of these around the island.

The top of the eminence had two distinct summits, and was almost entirely wooded, with the exception of just a couple of areas. The first of these was the northern summit itself, which had been cleared of vegetation to provide space and material for the construction of the large, round, wooden edifice that now occupied the site. A truly venerable building, now showing its age to a considerable extent, it was the Assembly Hall for the equally venerable members of the Assembly of Elders when they met to discuss matters of island government.

The second treeless area lay to the south of the first on a lower part of the hilltop, and, unlike the site of the Hall, was concealed from the sight of anyone lower down by the woods enclosing it on three sides, the fourth abutting against the rocky mass of the southern summit. Nestling in the shadow of the granite cliff that formed the northern face of this was a building of somewhat dilapidated aspect known as *The Granite Cabbage*. This was a hostelry reserved solely for the use of the Elders, and, as well as looking after their 'spiritual' needs, also provided them with accommodation while they were in session. Like the Hall, it was long past its best and its walls, partly built of stone and partly of wattle-and-daub, leaned nearly as much as some of the Elders did, while its thatched roof was in places almost as free of straw as many of their heads were of hair. To those of an enquiring mind, its name was rather interesting, and referred to a legendary tall-stalked cabbage plant of great size that was supposed to have grown somewhere in the area now occupied by the Assembly Hall.

According to legend, it had possessed magical healing powers, but if ever it were to be removed from the ground it would turn to stone. One night, a couple of greedy individuals, hoping to get rich by exploiting the plant's properties and either ignorant of or not believing the consequence of its removal, had uprooted it under cover of darkness and had carried it to their boat, planning to sail over to the island of Lesur with it. But halfway across, the plant had suddenly turned to granite, trapping the two rogues where they sat, the great increase in weight promptly sinking the boat and taking them to a watery grave.

The inlet to the immediate south of Ang-Lenn was for a while hidden from the sight of those on the approaching vessel by the largest of three grass-topped, tidal islets that jutted from the sea ahead of them. Eventually, however, as the boat carefully navigated around the jagged rocks forming the islet's southern tip, the entrance to the inlet came into view. A few lights were already burning in the fishermen's residences and in the town beyond, and, as the craft nosed into the inlet, its occupants could hear the babble of voices coming from the large building which stood close to the inlet's northern end.

The DRAGON of ANGUR

"The *Vraic*[3] appears to be as lively as ever," remarked Gastelois, nodding towards the building.

The Old Vraic and Coracle was generally considered to be the best pub in Ang-Lenn. This was not altogether surprising in view of the fact that at that time it was the only one that was actually open in the settlement, *The Cracked Capstone* having collapsed two months before, *The Lamplighter* undergoing refurbishment, *The Priest and the Potter* still under construction (labour disputes having delayed its completion), and *The Side Chamber* having closed pending an inquiry into certain dubious activities indulged in by its clientele.

A somewhat ramshackle edifice orientated east-west, the *Vraic* gave the distinct impression of having been built in a number of stages, with the later ones added with no great thought as to how they might relate aesthetically to what was already there. Situated near the western end of the town's main square, it consisted, in essence, of a large gallery-dolmen[4] of traditional form, its walls composed of massive granite uprights and its roof comprising eight capstones of impressive size. Whilst not as spectacular as the aforementioned *Grand Dolmen*, it was nonetheless an imposing structure, but the purity of its original design had been tainted by the wooden 'lean-tos' that sprouted wart-like from its longer northern and southern sides, the dilapidated drystone one tacked on to its western end, and the flimsy-looking portico, also of wood, that framed its eastern entrance.

"Just think, if it hadn't been for *our* Elders," said Gastelois, nodding towards the building, "we might not have one of the best pubs in Angur."

"Indeed so," said his companion, who knew its history.

One of the most ancient buildings in Ang-Lenn, the *Vraic* had not always been a pub. It had in fact started life as the Elders' original Assembly Hall, but with government committees and departments proliferating with the passing of time, the Elders had eventually decided that it was too cramped and therefore they needed more space. Whether this was actually the case, no-one had ever managed to find out, but the end result was that a brand

---

[3] Vraic (pronounced vrake) – the local name for seaweed.
[4] Gallery-Dolmen – a megalithic structure, rectangular in plan, walled with orthostats and roofed by capstones, and divided into an antechamber and a main chamber.

new hall, in the shape of a splendid wooden roundhouse, had been erected on the Town Mount – to the great detriment of the public purse.

This of course had left the dolmen without a *raison d'être*, so to speak. Soon after its abandonment by the Elders, the good people of Ang-Lenn had held a meeting and had quickly decided upon a use for it, a use they deemed far better (on the basis that you could not have too much of a good thing) than its original purpose. The Elders had been consulted and had voiced no objections (apart from one or two grumblings from those concerned with planning matters), whereupon the townsfolk had promptly set about converting the building into a pub, renaming it *The Old Vraic and Coracle*.

Their boat safely moored amongst some others tied up at the inner end of the inlet, Gastelois de Bois and Thière de Guérin went ashore. The Town Square was already dim in the deepening twilight, but the two men could clearly hear the leaves of the trees around it rustling in the evening breeze and the babbling of the brook which ran through it from north-east to south-west, passing close to the southern side of the pub before entering the inlet.

In the gloomy interior of the *Vraic*, where alcoholic odours prevailed and the steady drone of voices filled the air, the regulars were supping beer or cider out of pottery drinking-vessels, discussing the day's business and occasionally making jokes at someone or other's expense. As the two dolmen builders walked in, some species of argument appeared to be in progress between two of the men leaning against the bar counter, which ran in front of the wall facing the entrance.

"But I don't see that that matters, me," one of the two was saying. He was a powerfully built man with thick-set features who sported a particularly mature, red beard and whose eyebrows seemed to be trying to rival said facial growth for bushiness. The part of his face not protected by hair exhibited a leathery, weather-beaten skin that told of a working life spent regularly exposed to the elements. His accent was a particularly strong version of the local one, sounding even thicker on this occasion by courtesy of the fairly substantial quantity of alcohol he had consumed since coming into the pub.

"Of course it does!" retorted the other, a smaller, thinner individual whose somewhat timid aspect belied his underlying boldness. "Clarry, you can't just sail into someone else's waters and fish there without permission."

"And why not?" Clarry Le Brocq boomed, glaring at his companion. He was a garrulous individual with a voice like a foghorn and a mouth big enough to take one. He invariably spoke before he thought and this, allied to a temper of almost legendary quickness, regularly landed him in trouble of one sort or another. Which was precisely what had happened earlier that day.

"I could give you a good many reasons," answered the other, whose name was Pierre La Roche, "but I won't bother as you never listen. You could have chosen a safer spot, though, especially the way things are at the moment - I'm not surprised you ran into trouble with those Sersurians."

"But I was fishing there and minding my own bus'ness when..."

"Yes, Clarry," interrupted La Roche, "but you were fishing too close to Sersur, and you damn well know what a delicate issue *that* is just now."

Sersur, the fourth largest of the islands in the archipelago, lay to the north-north-west of Angur and to the east of Lesur. The steep cliffs that bordered it on all sides gave it a decidedly formidable aspect, while the dark, impenetrable forest that occupied a good part of its central plateau region lent it a particularly brooding atmosphere. Most of the other islanders avoided it like the plague, believing its inhabitants to be distinctly surly and unfriendly, if not downright belligerent. There was invariably some species of dispute going on between the Sersurians and the inhabitants of at least one of the other islands, (although to be fair to the former, they were not always the instigators), the one in progress at the present time being concerned with fishing limits. The Sersurians had recently demanded the extension of their fishing territory, claiming that that worked jointly by Lesur and its two small neighbouring islands, Erimac and Jettac, was far too big for the latter's needs, while their own was too small to feed their rapidly growing population. This did not wash with the other islanders, who knew perfectly well that the Sersurians had more than enough food as things were, and quite rightly saw the latters' demand as nothing less than an attempt at territorial expansionism.

A delegation of worthies with vested interests in the matter had gone over to Sersur from Lesur to try to sort things out amicably, but as 'amicable' was not in the average Sersurian's vocabulary where disputes were concerned, their efforts were inevitably doomed to failure from the outset. The Sersurians had given them short shrift and had sent them back home, refusing their pleas to be reasonable and drop their demand, or at the very least modify it somewhat. So the situation was currently at stalemate, and unlikely to change until one side started making concessions.

It was not altogether surprising, therefore, that the worthy Le Brocq had hardly been welcomed with open arms when a party of Sersurians had discovered him fishing rather close to their island earlier in the day, and, although he would never have admitted it, he had been lucky to escape unscathed.

"I hope you'll show a bit more sense next time, you," La Roche told him. "But I suppose that's expecting too much."

"In trouble again, Clarry?" said Gastelois, smiling. He and Thière had arrived at the bar in time to overhear enough of the argument to gather what it was about.

Le Brocq belched and turned around, glowering, but when he saw who it was, his countenance softened somewhat, for there were few people on Angur who did not have time for the island's skilled and amiable dolmen-builder. "Ah, Gastelois! Those bloody Sersurians!"

"Let me get you a drink," offered Gastelois. "Another beer should help heal your wounded pride."

Clarry accepted and Gastelois nodded towards the landlord, who had just returned to the bar after looking for something in the *Vraic's* store in the drystone lean-to at the back of the pub.

"Ah, Gastelois! You're back, you!" said the landlord, coming over to him with a broad, welcoming smile on his face. Boileau Le Gobel was a rotund individual with a permanently flushed face, bright, sparkling eyes and a warm, friendly manner. "Ah, Thière, it's good to see you again, too," he greeted the Lesurian. "Did you have a nice trip?"

"We did, thank you. Most interesting."

"That's good!" said Le Gobel, starting to fill a couple of drinking vessels for the two dolmen builders, one with beer for Thière and the other with cider for Gastelois.

"I'll buy these two characters one as well," said Gastelois, nodding towards Clarry Le Brocq and Pierre La Roche.

"Right." Boileau handed Thière the first drinking-jar. "Oh by the way, Gastelois, the Elders have been looking for you."

"Yes?" He reached into the leather pouch slung from the belt around his waist.

The landlord nodded as he took the half-dozen limpet shells Gastelois had produced from his pouch as payment for the drinks. "I don't know what it's about, me, but they've been asking where you were."

"But they knew I was in Carnac," said the other. "Honestly!" He sighed in exasperation. "Oh well, I'd better see them in the morning. You don't mind if we stay here for the night?"

"Not at all, not at all," said Boileau. "You know you're always welcome."

Gastelois thanked him. "Fine. Now we can relax and enjoy our drinks. We've had a long day." He turned to Clarry and, with a sidelong wink at Pierre, said: "Now Clarry, mon vier, let's hear all about your latest adventure."

CHAPTER TWO

THE NEW DOLMEN

Despite the earlier threat of rain, the following morning dawned bright and sunny. Gastelois and Thière were up with the sunrise, as the latter wished to make an early start for Lesur. Boileau Le Gobel provided them with a good breakfast of shellfish and hunks of bread, washed down with liberal measures of the *Vraic's* best ale and cider.

They were about halfway through breakfast when a slightly dumpy teenage girl of moderate height wearing a brown, finely woven knee-length dress entered the pub and walked up to their table. Bright greyish-blue eyes gazed out of a round suntanned face liberally blessed with freckles and surmounted by a mop of tousled ginger hair.

"Ah, hello, Lène!" said Gastelois, looking up and greeting his half-sister with the pet name he had used for her since she was tiny. He got up from the table and gave her a brotherly bear hug.

Marie-Hélène de Bois freed herself from the embrace and sat down at the table with them. "I heard you were back," she said in her soft, mellifluous voice. "Did you have a good trip?"

"Pretty good," said Thière. "Gastelois spoke very well at the conference." He smiled at Marie-Hélène, who dropped her eyes, blushing.

"Oh, it wasn't *that* good," said Gastelois modestly. "Can I get you anything, Lène?"

"No thanks. I had breakfast earlier." She gazed admiringly at the other.

Since the death of Arbreur Le Bois, their father, a few years previously, Gastelois had assumed the paternal role. She always looked up to him and went to him for advice, which he gave willingly and the best that he could.

"What's in those?" she then asked, pointing at the two bags reposing on the floor next to the table.

"Dolmen plans," said Gastelois.

"Yes," confirmed Thière. "We were given some very interesting ones this time."

"Sylvie would love to see them," said Marie-Hélène.

"Oh, does she know I'm back?" said Gastelois, his heart quickening at the mention of her name.

"I don't think so. We've been wondering when you'd get back, but I haven't seen her for the past couple of days." She paused for a few moments before adding: "But I'll tell her as soon as I can."

Gastelois nodded slowly. He knew he could not stop her, even if he wanted to. Sylvia d'Arass and he were close friends, perhaps closer than he dared to admit, sometimes even to himself. Marie-Hélène was aware of their feelings for each other and did her best to encourage the friendship in the hope that it would develop along more romantic lines. There was, however, a slight complication that was likely to stymie the fulfilment of her teenage dreams – Sylvia was already spoken for. Even so, because she wanted the best for Gastelois, she continued to hope and dream.

The two dolmen builders finished their breakfast and then all three of them sauntered down to the inlet so that Thière could board the boat that would take him home. The craft in question was the one that had brought them back from Armor. It was in fact a Lesurian vessel, but it had stopped at Angur en route to Lesur to let Gastelois off. Rather than continue in the dark and brave a nocturnal crossing, the crew had opted to stay in Ang-Lenn overnight and to set off in the morning.

Gastelois and Marie-Hélène said goodbye to Thière and watched as the boat was rowed out of the inlet and into the open sea, where there was sufficient wind for the crew to rely on the sail alone.

"Don't worry, Lène," said Gastelois, noticing the wistful expression on Marie-Hélène's face. "You'll see him again soon – he's coming over for the Jubilee."

"But that's *ages* away," she grumbled.

"It'll be here before you know it."

As they gazed after the slowly receding stern of the boat, a familiar figure emerged from one of the inlet buildings and began to tend the fishing net draped over its parapet. He glanced over towards the pub and, noticing the dolmen builder, raised his arm in greeting. Gastelois waved back, then, leaving Clarry Le Brocq to work on his net, he and Marie-Hélène retraced their steps to the pub, stopping on the way to chat with another fisherman who, it turned out, wanted some advice on alterations he was planning to make to his house.

When they reached the *Vraic*, Gastelois and Marie-Hélène parted company; she hurrying off doubtless to find Sylvia to give her the news of his return, he going back into the pub.

By now, the place boasted quite a few early morning customers. Three of these were sitting at a table close to one end of the bar, and as he stood nearby talking to the landlord when the latter was not serving, Gastelois caught snippets of their conversation. After a while, this took quite a bizarre turn, and he found himself listening intently in spite of himself.

"I tell you they were bones." The speaker, a round-faced individual with a ruddy complexion two shades short of apoplexy, was clearly adamant that the objects in question could not possibly have been mistaken for anything else.

"But where did you see them, you?" asked one of his companions as he lifted his beer jar to his lips.

"In the tub, Jean," said the first. "They were piled in the tub!" He gulped down some of his own beer, nearly choking in his excitement.

"The wash-tub?" enquired the third man, a craggy type with tousled hair.

"Yes," spluttered the first.

"But François, what was Edouard doing with bones in his tub?" asked the one called Jean.

"That I don't know, me," said François. "I didn't like to ask."

The other two nodded, as if agreeing that asking would not have been the thing to do in the situation in question.

René, the one sporting the tousled hairstyle, frowned, then said: "But whose bones were they?"

"They were Rondel's," said François.

"How d'you know that, you?" asked René.

"Aw, but they had his bloody name on them!"

The three men fell silent for a few moments. Then Jean asked: "I pr'sume they were Rondel's ancestors?"

"I b'lieve so," said François, nodding.

"That was careless of him, aih!" said René. "Leaving the ancestors' bones in someone else's tub."

The DRAGON of ANGUR

"Aw, but I don't suppose Edouard would be too bothered by that, him," remarked François.

"Why's that, then?" queried Jean.

"Well, they weren't *his* ancestors," replied François, "so they would be fine for making the soup!"

Gastelois smiled and drank some of his cider. He could not begin to imagine what Edouard was doing with Rondel's ancestors' bones in his wash-tub, but he was sure that there was probably some rational explanation.

* * *

He stayed in the *Vraic* until almost midday, there being no point in leaving earlier to see the Elders as it seemed to take them ages to get going in the morning. Whether this was due to their advanced years, their somewhat excessive lifestyle, or a combination of both, no one was sure. In fact, when they were in session, members of the general public were permitted to see them only in the afternoon, and it was a measure of Gastelois' status that he was one of the very few who could visit them virtually whenever they wished.

He climbed the path that led up the western side of the Town Mount, passing through the occasional copse of trees. The lower slopes below the rock face of the escarpment that flanked the upper part of the hill had once been thickly forested, but the number of trees had been greatly reduced over the years due to the demand for timber for Ang-Lenn's buildings, as well as for boats and other items. Every so often, he glanced down to his right to where the waters of the inlet shimmered in the midday sunlight, lapping against the stilts of the fishermen's houses and the hulls of those of their boats moored there.

The path levelled out as he reached the thickly wooded area between the northern and southern summits. He followed it into the trees to where, a short distance ahead, it met another track running from north to south. There he turned left, following this path through the trees as it sloped gently upwards to emerge a few hundred yards later into the clearing of the northern summit.

Ahead, resplendent in the midday sunlight, stood the great rotunda of the Assembly Hall in all its decaying grandeur. It was an old building: its circular wall leaned at precarious angles, while the surface of its conical roof of logs and thatch resembled that of the sea on a rough day. Holes were to be seen everywhere, and much of the wood making up the structure was dangerously rotten. It was long overdue for replacement, as Gastelois himself was continually telling the Elders, but this would be expensive and as a result was being put off for as long as possible. Most people confidently expected the edifice to fall down at any moment, and some were in the habit of looking up at it every morning just to see whether it was still standing.

He walked up to the Hall, and when he reached its entrance, he hailed the edifice's attendants. One of these presently appeared, a thin, lanky specimen who would not have looked out of place holding up runner beans. It blinked as it emerged into the sunlight from the dim interior of the Hall.

"I've come to see the Elders," stated Gastelois.

Beanpole squinted at him: "Ah, Gastelois! I haven't seen you for a while," he said in a bored voice.

"I've been away." He nodded towards the building. "Are they inside?"

"No, I'm sorry, they're not here yet."

Typical, thought the dolmen builder. "You mean they haven't started?" The tone of his voice was more that of a statement than a question.

Beanpole shook his head. "No. They had a late night last night. Amongst other things, they've been trying to r'solve how to spend this year's defence budget and they've also been consid'ring the r'newal of *Angur Boat's* licence." He smiled reassuringly: "I expect they'll be along soon, though."

Gastelois dreaded to think how the defence budget would be allocated, and as for *Angur Boat*, the sooner the running of the round-the-island coracle service was awarded to someone else the better. He grunted. "It's them who want to see me." Then he shrugged his shoulders. "I've no idea why."

"You can wait inside if you like. I'm sure they wouldn't mind."

Gastelois shook his head. "No. Thanks anyway, but I'll wait out here."

Beanpole nodded and went back inside the Hall. Gastelois seated himself on the grass a short distance from the entrance and contemplated his surroundings. It was not done for members of the public to go into the Assembly Hall before the Elders, and although Gastelois himself could have got away with so doing, he did not like to abuse his position by taking advantage at every opportunity of the perks it afforded him.

The Hall commanded a superb view westwards over the inlet and the Bay of Aube beyond nestling in the embrace of the southern side of the Angurian plateau, which curved southwards at the west end of the bay to form the dark, rocky headland of Le Mont Noircissant. To the north of the inlet, the buildings of Ang-Lenn sprawled inland around the northern end of the Town Mount, occupying the flat land that separated this from the wooded southern slopes of the plateau. On its eastern side, it overlooked the extensive lowland area of marsh, dune and deciduous forest that lay to the east and south-east of the town; a wild, virgin area largely untamed by man.

Gastelois looked to his left, to the dense copse of trees that grew between the Hall and *The Granite Cabbage*, blocking his view of the latter. As the Assembly was in session, he knew that the Elders would be residing there, and would therefore come along the path that wound through the trees from the *Cabbage* to the Hall when they deigned to make a move in that direction. Gastelois watched the spot where the path emerged from the trees for a few minutes, but he neither saw nor heard any sign of the Elders. Tutting in exasperation, he gave up and contemplated Ang-Lenn and the bay instead.

On the far side of the bay, he could see some of the rooftops of Aube, Angur's second largest settlement, but the rest of it lay hidden by the forest of oak and alder that reached almost to the shoreline. His own house lay on the outskirts of Aube, snug against the hillside overlooking the settlement and sufficiently clear of the treetops to afford a fine view over the bay. As his eyes rested on it, he hoped that his meeting with the Elders would not drag on as he was looking forward to getting home after the Carnac conference.

Then, looking to the south, across the surface of the sea shimmering in the midday sunlight, he could just about make out the long, low form of the island of Maen-Keren brooding darkly against the sky. Lying approximately halfway between Angur and Armor, it was almost as big as the former in area, but much lower; at no point did it rise more than a hundred feet above sea-level. Although its environment was generally pleasant, its gentle topography consisting predominantly of areas of grassland interspersed with forest and isolated stands of trees and bushes, and expanses of coastal sand dune, and a good living could be made from the sea, it was not permanently inhabited. Those who fished the waters around it or among the pools and inlets littering its rocky coastline did not like to linger for long.

The island's name meant 'stone houses', and judging by the ancient, time-scarred ruins that huddled silently around the highest point of the island and lay scattered over other parts of it, with some weed-covered walls disappearing into the depths of the waters lapping its shores, Maen-Keren had once been host to some stable, sedentary population. Although long gone in the flesh, it was popularly believed that the ghosts of this people patrolled the crumbling remains of their buildings, exacting a horrible revenge on those who dared trespass on to their property by dragging them down into the dark, sunless caverns that local wisdom held to exist deep under the island, there to imprison them for all eternity. It was therefore a place to be shunned; its waters fished only because of their bounty and the island itself only to be alighted upon if absolutely unavoidable.

There were those, of course, who were not bothered by such tales, and Gastelois was proud to count himself one of their number. In fact, since he was a small boy he had visited Maen-Keren several times and explored its enigmatic ruins. He was intrigued by them and longed to know who had built them and when. He sighed. Perhaps such knowledge would forever be denied him.

He studied the Bay of Aube for a little while, a haven of tranquillity on this fine spring day, occasionally glancing in the direction of *The Granite Cabbage* for any sign that the Elders might be returning, but none was evident.

The Assembly of Elders effectively (or ineffectively, depending on your point of view) governed the island of Angur, and basically consisted of sundry priests, chieftains and the presidents of the various committees that tried, with varying degrees of success, to run the place. These were some of the oldest, wisest and most experienced members of the population. At least that was the general theory - apart from age, which was generally ascertainable (admittedly with difficulty where some of the Elders were concerned), the degree of wisdom and experience was, in quite a few cases, highly questionable.

Presiding over this motley crew was the High Elder, a hereditary position based on matrilineal descent and held for life. Some erstwhile bearers of the title had evidently taken the latter point very seriously, and had gone on for rather longer than was perhaps desirable for the good of the island, clinging to the mortal coil when they should have been enjoying the company of the ancestors.

The present incumbent, Cou-Cou La Tanche, was proving to be particularly tenacious in this respect. A decidedly wizened and decrepit individual long in his dotage, he was as overdue for replacement as the hall in which he sat, but despite his age and apparent condition, there was as yet no indication that he was about to join the ancestors.

Directly under the High Elder was the High Priest, Haut-Maître Hacquebuttier Le Grandin. Appropriately enough, in some people's eyes, for someone who was in charge of the islanders' spiritual well-being, he was also the President of the *Trade and Licensing Committee*, which controlled, amongst other things, the production and distribution of Angur's alcoholic beverages.

Cou-Cou La Tanche

Ang-Lenn and the island's six other settlements each had its own priest, who was a senior member of the Angurian priesthood, and these seven ancient specimens also sat on the Assembly with Le Grandin.

Next there were the headmen of the seven settlements, one of whom served as Chairman of the Assembly for a period of two years. These individuals also made up the *Defence Committee*, with the headman of Ang-Lenn being the president. This was the only committee all of whose members sat on the Assembly, the others being represented only by their presidents with, at best, one other.

Amongst these other committees, there was the *Pouquelaye and Earthworks Committee*, which concerned itself with planning and development matters ('pouquelaye' being a local term for dolmen), and the *Marine and Land Exploitation Committee*, which looked after Angur's food supply and generally all aspects of fishing and farming locally. Sometimes referred to as the 'Surf and Turf' committee, it was more frequently called the 'Sod it and See' committee due to its somewhat cavalier attitude and the tendency of its policies to miss more often than they hit.

Keeping a wary eye on his colleagues was Gaston Corbel, the President of the *Financial Strategies Committee*, who bemoaned the likely excessive cost of each and every new project and proceeded to bleat about the probable resulting drain on the strategic reserve – a huge pile of limpet, ormer and other currency shells stashed in a large cavern somewhere in the bowels of the Town Mount.

Finally, there were two individuals, selected annually from the population, who respectively represented the island's fishermen and farmers.

The Assembly met for Major Sessions and Minor Sessions. Each of the former lasted for a lunar month and took place four times a year, around the periods of the winter and summer solstices and the spring and autumn equinoxes. The solstices respectively marked the transition from the Season of Shortening Days to the Season of Lengthening Days and *vice versa*, while the equinoxes marked the two season's mid-points.

During the Major Sessions, new laws were drafted, existing ones sometimes repealed or amended; serious grievances from members of the public dealt with; and trade with the neighbouring islands and with lands further afield reviewed. The Assembly also discussed the island's food situation, considered major building programmes and generally dealt with all important matters relating to Angur and its inhabitants.

Outside these meetings, Minor Sessions were held every second week during which those of the Elders who were not otherwise engaged, or had not forgotten what day it was, met for one or two days (depending on how they felt at the time) to consider routine items of government.

Apart from these occasions, the headmen of the settlements could be contacted in their respective abodes and the priests either at the communal dolmen attached to each village or at one of the island's two main ritual centres.

The committees, on the other hand, were rather more difficult to approach, preferring to conduct the bulk of their business behind closed doors and presenting the results of their deliberations as *faits accomplis*. They met at a variety of different times and there was not much in the way of collaboration or liaison between any of them.

The Elders were at present a few days into the Spring Equinox Major Session. When the equinox itself occurred they would take a break for the associated festivities. As they were being slower than usual about getting started on this particular day, Gastelois came to the conclusion that some especially awkward problem must have occupied them late into the previous evening. He hoped that they would not be much longer, as he was beginning to get fed up with waiting; in any case, he was keen to find out exactly what it was that they wanted to see him about.

He did not have much longer to wait, however. He became aware of a low, confused muttering emanating from the trees on his left. It appeared that at long last *The Granite Cabbage* had disgorged its august clientele, and so Gastelois stood up, looking towards the wood in anticipation.

Sure enough, a line of predominantly ancient and doddering wheezers presently lurched into view, slowly negotiating the path through the trees. They eventually emerged from the wood, aiming in the general direction of the entrance of the Hall. Gastelois was intrigued to see that the High Elder was not in his usual position at the head of the procession - in fact, he was nowhere to be seen at all. He had probably overdone it in *The Granite Cabbage* and had been left there to dry out.

The man actually at the head of the procession, a rather less doddery individual than the majority of his companions and not quite so advanced in years, spotted the dolmen builder and hailed him: "Ah! Gastelois! You're back, you."

"Yes, Gaetan, that I am. You wanted to see me about something?"

"Aw but yes, aih!" Gaetan Le Sterc, Headman of Ang-Lenn, President of the *Defence Committee* and the current Chairman of the Assembly of Elders, reached him. "Where've you been, you? We've been wondering where you were."

"Carnac - the annual megalithic conference. I told you before I left."

"Did you?" Le Sterc favoured Gastelois with a look of some surprise. He had obviously forgotten. "Anyway, you're back now, which is all that matters. Come inside. There's an aspect of La Tanche's Flint Jubilee we wish to discuss with you. He's away in Sersur at the moment seeing if he can do anything to help resolve this fishing limit bus'ness that's been going on over there."

"I wondered where he was," said Gastelois. "I presume de Richolet's gone with him?"

The other nodded.

"Thought so," said Gastelois.

Albert de Richolet was the current President of the *Marine and Land Exploitation Committee.* Perhaps surprisingly, because of the possibility of a conflict of interests arising, he was also the current representative on the Assembly of the island's fishermen. He had been re-elected to this position annually for longer than anyone could remember, and there were those who were suspicious that his continual re-election involved certain underhand dealings or 'arrangements'.

De Richolet considered himself the best and most important fisherman in Angur (although Clarry Le Brocq would have had something to say about the former), and therefore indispensable in any negotiations to do with fishing disputes. For him not to have accompanied La Tanche to Sersur would, certainly as far as he was concerned, have been unthinkable.

Gastelois waited until the chairman and the other Elders had all entered the Assembly Hall and then he followed them in.

Its dimly lit interior smelled dank and musty, and the maze of pillars - tree trunks cut to size - supporting its conical roof gave you the impression of entering a thick, gloomy forest. The primary source of illumination was a large circular hole in the roof's apex, but its effect was to a great extent negated by the ancient and gnarled oak that grew directly below it, blocking off most of the light. The problem could have been easily solved by the removal of the tree, but this could not be done as this particular ligneous growth was held to be sacred, although nobody could ever remember why.

Additional illumination was provided by lamps burning animal grease or fish oil (depending on which fuel was to hand) and attached to some of the pillars. Only a few of these were ever lit at any one time, however, as the smoke and the smell from them tended to hang about in the Hall for quite a while before dispersing. Besides, it was just as well that the whole lot was never alight at the same time, as the fire risk would have been considerable.

The Elders seated themselves on the benches that rose in tiers on either side of the gangway that led in from the entrance. These benches formed a semicircle facing the aforementioned tree. In front of the oak, there was a wooden dais on which reposed a high-backed chair hewn from a single block of pink granite. This faced the Elders and was occupied by the High Elder himself whenever he was present. It was always somewhat cold, damp and distinctly hard, this chair, and was probably at least partly to blame for the High Elder's rheumatism, not to mention his piles, but then that was the price you paid for being top man of Angur.

Le Sterc occupied the seat when Cou-Cou La Tanche was not present, and he now settled into it, shifting uncomfortably as his rear end made contact with the cold stone.

To one side of the space between the dais and the tiered benches stood a low wooden platform. This was reserved for members of the public when they addressed the Assembly. It creaked ominously when Gastelois stepped up on to it and directed his attention towards the chairman, ignoring the seated sages to his left. Some of these were watching him, but most were mumbling among themselves about this matter or that matter, or about nothing in particular.

"Well, Gastelois," began Le Sterc, "I won't waste your time with any preambling, so I'll get to the point. As you know, it's La Tanche's Flint Jubilee this year, and so we'll be holding cel'brations around Midsummer. We're arranging, among other things, a number of contests. These will be open to people from outside Angur as well as to our own pop'lation. We've got quite far with our plans already, in fact."

Gastelois wondered just how far they had got, but he was certain that their plans were not as far advanced as the chairman wanted him to believe they were.

"One of the contests was only suggested to us a few days ago," continued Le Sterc. He scratched his grey hair and then examined his fingernails. "It's really a rather good idea. Basic'lly, it's a dragon-hunting contest."

"A *what?*" demanded Gastelois, staring at the chairman incredulously.

"A... A dragon-hunting contest," repeated Le Sterc, a little taken aback by the dolmen builder's reaction.

"That's what I thought you said. And where, pray, are you going to get the dragon from?"

"Er.. Old Mauger," said Le Sterc.

"Old Mauger!" Gastelois stared in disbelief at the other. Had the Elders gone completely off their heads while he'd been away?

"Yes, mon vier, but don't..."

"Who on earth came up with such a hare-brained scheme?" Gastelois interrupted him. "I've never heard such a ridiculous idea in all my born days. I..."

"Gastelois, Gastelois," said the chairman soothingly, realising why the other was sounding so upset. "Don't worry, he's not going to come to any harm. We all love him as much as you and everyone else. Look, we're going to explain everything to him and ask his permission."

"I should hope so too. And while we're on the subject, you might explain it to me."

"Look, as I've said, Mauger won't come to any harm," said the chairman, doing his best to put Gastelois' mind at ease. "We're as concerned about his safety as you are."

"Then why hold the contest?"

"It'll be good for the island."

"In what way, pray?"

The other Elders had by now stopped mumbling among themselves and were watching Gastelois with growing interest. Outbursts of this nature were rare from him, but on this occasion he was definitely not in the best of humours. Few on Angur knew that the dragon had, some years back, saved Gastelois' life.

"By attracting people of high standing to the island," said Le Sterc. "Look, why don't I let Etienne explain." He nodded towards the assembled Elders. "Etienne?"

A grey haired, rather nondescript individual of advanced years and average build and stature, whose main distinguishing feature was a particularly hairy wart sprouting from the right side of his nose near the tip, got slowly to his feet from his place in the second row, gave a slight nod of his head to Le Sterc and then turned to face Gastelois.

Etienne de Crochenolle was the President of the latest committee to come into being, the recently created *Tourism and Immigration.* As he now explained to Gastelois, it had been specially formed in time for the High Elder's Flint Jubilee, its initial aim being to coordinate all the arrangements for that event. Apart from the involvement of local people, it was confidently expected that large numbers of visitors would arrive in the island from overseas to take part in the celebrations, news of the impending joyous occasion having been spread far and wide. These people would have to be housed and fed for the duration of their stay on Angur and the organising of this was just one of the many items on the new committee's agenda.

Then there were the contests, the aforementioned dragon hunt being the latest. It was reasoned that the better, in the sense of interesting and challenging, the contest, the better, in the sense of desirable, the class of person it was likely to attract. And, as de Crochenolle reminded Gastelois, it was current policy to tempt a few well-to-do, and therefore socially acceptable, people to the island every year in the hope that they might stay permanently.

The *Tourism* president concluded by describing what would happen in the one involving the dragon: "We hold a contest in which the partic'pants shoot soft-tipped arrows dipped in different coloured dyes at Old Mauger as he flies past, and we award a prize to him who scores the most hits."

"What sort of prize?" demanded Gastelois, who had been listening to de Crochenolle's monologue with an increasingly suspicious look on his face.

"Res'dency in the island and a fam'ly dolmen to go with it," said Le Sterc, taking the words out of his colleague's mouth.

It now dawned on Gastelois why the Elders had wanted to see him. "A dolmen, aih? Well, well, well!" He stared hard at Le Sterc. "And supposing Old Mauger doesn't want anything to do with this scheme of yours - what then?"

From the expression that came over Le Sterc's face and also de Crochenolle's, it was abundantly clear that neither of them had thought of that possibility. The chairman shifted uncomfortably in his chair and looked at the *Tourism* president as if expecting him to provide the answer, but that worthy just shrugged his shoulders.

"Aw, but I don't think that'll be a problem, that," Le Sterc then decided.

"Why not?"

"Aw, we'll have a chat with him. We can arrange it so that he leaves the scene of the contest before things get out of hand. Then we'll hold a cel'bration for the victor, and Mauger can return to his home afterwards."

Gastelois shook his head slowly "I don't know. It all sounds pretty dubious." He shrugged his shoulders. "But then, it's up to you. As long as the dragon doesn't get hurt." He paused for a few moments, gazing up at the roof of the Assembly Hall. Quite frankly, he rather doubted that Old Mauger would go along with the Elders' plan, and for that reason he was now a little less concerned about the dragon's well-being than he had been initially. He looked at Le Sterc and said resignedly: "All right, what d'you want me to do?"

"Well, Gastelois, we want you to build the dolmen for the lucky winner."

Gastelois smiled knowingly. He had half suspected as much. He said nothing, letting the chairman elaborate.

"Nothing too large or special, mon vier; just a normal fam'ly dolmen."

"I see," said Gastelois. "Where?"

"We're not sure yet, but prob'bly somewhere in the east. We'll let you know as soon as poss'ble. But for now, we'd like you to consider the building of the dolmen - what kind of stone you're going to use..."

"That depends on where it's going to be," interrupted Gastelois.

"True, true. But you can think about the design of the thing, get some plans pr'pared."

"I take it," said Gastelois, a slight frown creasing his features, "that, as this is for a special occasion and there's a deadline to meet, I'm going to have more cooperation from Planning than has sometimes been the case in the past."

Le Sterc looked at the Elders. "Branleur!" he called.

A tall, somewhat emaciated specimen with long, straggly brown hair sitting next to Etienne de Crochenolle got shakily to his feet, his right hand pushing down on the stout walking stick he invariably had with him. Branleur de Bitte was the President of the *Pouquelaye and Earthworks Committee* and one of the most powerful of all the Elders, despite a physique and a general demeanour that might have led you to conclude the contrary. In fact, he was one of the prime movers and shakers of the Assembly.

"Gastelois," he began in a tremulous voice, peering hard at the dolmen builder, "we are here to make sure that every erection will be something of which all Angurians can be proud. Too many shabbily constructed eyesores have sprung up in the past, them." He pointed his stick shakily at the other while speaking, as was his habit when he wanted to emphasise what he was saying.

"You mean like that new building..."

"Submit your plans and we'll give it due and proper consideration," said de Bitte, interrupting him. He sat down and muttered something to de Crochenolle, who nodded slowly as if in agreement.

Gastelois frowned in their direction and then looked at Le Sterc.

"You'll do it, then?" asked the chairman, a hopeful tone in his voice.

"Build your dolmen?" Gastelois assumed a pensive air for a few moments. "Yes, I will. But first hadn't you better sort things out with Old Mauger? We're rather jumping to conclusions at the moment."

"We'll see him tomorrow." Le Sterc stood up. "Now, I think it's time for lunch."

The other Elders, who had begun to show signs of wearying of the proceedings, immediately perked up at the mention of lunch and started talking noisily. Gastelois was about to leave the Hall, but the chairman called him back.

Now what? thought Gastelois at the sound of his name. He turned and looked at Le Sterc.

"I'd appreciate it if you'd have lunch with me in the *Cabbage*. We can talk further about all this over some good food and a few ales."

Gastelois accepted the invitation. After all, it was not just anyone who was invited to eat with the Elders, and he was, he had to admit, beginning to feel a little peckish. Besides, it would be interesting to discuss this rather dubious contest at greater length.

CHAPTER THREE

SYLVIA D'ARASS

It was late afternoon by the time Gastelois finally left *The Granite Cabbage* and made his way home to Aube. In the course of their discussions in the pub, Gaetan Le Sterc had asked Gastelois for his assistance in selecting a location for the prize dolmen, re-iterating the Elders' preference for the eastern side of the island. During his walk home and into the evening, Gastelois tried to think of a suitable site.

Although he had a number of female friends, of varying degrees of closeness, he lived on his own, having so far not found anyone unattached with whom he was prepared to settle down, a state of affairs his friends frequently urged him to rectify. They half suspected that he valued his privacy too much to want to share it with anyone else, although they lived in hope.

Hope at the moment was pinned on Sylvia d'Arass, Marie-Hélène not being the only one who could see the especial closeness between Gastelois and the raven-haired Iberian. She was the daughter of a venerable and much-respected dolmen builder from that part of the world and of whom Gastelois had formed a high opinion, although he had never had the pleasure of actually meeting him. Dolmen building was in the family's blood and Sylvia had taken a keen interest in her father's work from an early age. An artist of no mean talent, she had decorated the interior of a number of Iberian passage-dolmens[5], completing the most recent one not long before arriving in Angur.

Not surprisingly, she and Gastelois got on extremely well and greatly enjoyed each other's company whenever they met.

If questioned on the subject, Gastelois was adamant that their relationship was purely platonic, which was just as well as, regrettably, the delectable Sylvia was married – to none other than Albert de Richolet.

The latter had met her whilst on a visit to her homeland a couple of years previously. It was not exactly clear how he had acquired her, but he had evidently traded something – or someone – for her. Interested observers and gossip-mongers were at pains to point out that de Richolet's first wife, who had accompanied him on the trip, had not come back with him and conclusions had been swiftly reached. There was nothing unusual about a man having more than one wife, but number one's continued absence from Angur gave rise to much speculation as to her fate. De Richolet himself was always careful not to be drawn on the matter, dismissing any enquiry by saying that she was spending time with relations in

---

[5] Passage-Dolmen – a megalithic structure, in which a passage leads into a main chamber of varying design off which may open one or more side chambers. The passage and chamber are commonly walled with orthostats and roofed by capstones, although drystone walling may be employed as well. The main chamber is sometimes roofed with a vault of oversailing stones or corbels, a technique known as corbel-vaulting. The whole may be covered by a mound or cairn known as a tumulus.

Armor 'for family reasons' and that he wasn't sure when she would be back. He would then quickly change the subject. Of course, the longer she 'stayed away', the more difficult it would become for him to keep this story going and the more the gossipers and speculators would be able to nod their heads knowingly.

Gastelois' friends found it hard to accept that someone like Sylvia was saddled with such a windbag of arrogant pomposity as de Richolet. Apart from his character failings, which to them were glaringly obvious, he was at least twice her age, being nearly fifty while she was the younger side of twenty-five. The fact that he was very wealthy and able to convey the air of someone of great importance probably explained how he had been able to prise her from her family in the first place, in addition to whatever trade arrangements there had been. There was always the possibility, however, that one day she and de Richolet would part company and then her and Gastelois' obvious fondness for each other would have free rein to blossom into something deeper – one could but hope!

During the course of the evening, Gastelois considered a number of possible sites for the new dolmen, but after much deliberation rejected each of them in turn, every one being unsuitable for one reason or another. Eventually, he decided to go to his local pub for a few drinks before he retired to bed.

* * *

The Prancing Pouquelaye was, if not by any means the largest or most imposing pub in Angur, certainly one of the oldest. It was named after an ancient dolmen on the site, which had actually been incorporated into the fabric of the pub. 'Pouquelaye' was of course a local term for dolmen, but the 'prancing' part of its name referred to an old legend that described how this particular dolmen was wont to dance in the light of the full moon and, on occasions, even go for a swim in the nearby inlet that connected Aube with the open sea.

Of course, no one had actually ever seen the dolmen perform either of these feats, although there were quite a few who, after imbibing one jar too many, swore that they had seen it dancing.

Gastelois left his house and walked down the sloping main street of Aube to where *The Prancing Pouquelaye* stood by the settlement's harbour at the end of the tree-lined inlet. He could see the firelight from the hearths of the houses on either side of the street flickering through their windows as he passed them, the strands of seaweed used as curtains waving gently in the slight sea-borne breeze.

Apart from its age, *The Prancing Pouquelaye* was nothing particularly special. It consisted of a wattle-and-daub roundhouse nearly thirty feet in diameter with a conical thatched roof sporting the obligatory hole in the apex to emit smoke from the central hearth below. A few large standing stones, set into the curving wall at regular intervals, provided support for the rough-hewn wooden beams that spanned the interior of the building where wall met roof and from which animal-grease lamps hung, swinging gently in the breeze wafting through its few, seaweed-curtained windows.

The old dolmen itself consisted of a large capstone supported by three massive uprights, forming a recess some nine feet wide, seven feet deep and six feet in height jutting out from the main circle of the building directly opposite its entrance. The wooden counter of the bar stood across the open end of the dolmen, a gap at one end providing access to the chamber behind.

On one side of the pub, halfway between the entrance and the bar, a low side cell was set against the interior wall. Formed by two stone uprights spanned by a capstone, it was long enough and wide enough to take two people lying down next to each other.

From the din emanating from its interior, Gastelois could tell that the pub was pretty busy, a not unusual state of affairs for this time of day. He entered by the main door and made his way to the bar opposite, acknowledging several greetings from people sitting at the numerous, rather haphazardly-arranged tables as he did so.

The landlord, an especially jovial fellow by the name of Gaston Le Remplieur, had seen Gastelois enter and had begun pouring a jar of his favourite tipple before he had taken many steps towards the bar.

"There you go, mon vier," he said, pushing the brimmed jar of cider towards Gastelois when the dolmen builder reached the bar.

"Thank you," said Gastelois, smiling at the other. The landlord's rather cherubic face seemed even ruddier than usual. Maybe he had been sampling some new brew.

"You've been away, you?"

"Yes. I went to Carnac for the annual megalithic conference."

"Ah yes!"

Just then, someone bumped into Gastelois, making him spill some of his drink. He turned around to see a large, well-built individual with dark, straggly hair swaying unsteadily before him, the jar in his right hand held at an angle that threatened to decant whatever quantity of liquid still remained in it.

Louvel Le Soulard stared at Gastelois for a few moments without saying anything, glazed eyes trying to focus as they regarded him from a complexion that was even ruddier than Le Remplieur's. Then he belched.

"Sh.. shorry," he stammered apologetically and swayed alarmingly. One of the pub's regulars, standing just behind him, reached out to steady him, fearing that he was about to topple over.

"Aw, but he's got a few aboard, him," said another, watching him warily. "He may have problems making port tonight!"

At that precise moment, Louvel went cross-eyed, let his jar slip from his grasp, and then crashed unceremoniously to the clay floor where he lay, snoring loudly.

The landlord leaned over the bar. "Put 'im in the usual place," he sighed, contemplating the prone figure on the floor, the shards from the broken jar lying scattered nearby.

"But the unwashed one's already in there," pointed out one Henri, who had been standing nearby.

"I, I'd forgotten about that," said Le Remplieur. "Put 'im in anyway. A spell next to Morpion Le Crasseux might sober 'im up quicker!"

"Sorry about that, Gastelois," said the landlord as Henri and his brother, Charlot, dragged the inert form of Le Soulard to the side cell where he could sleep off his drunken stupor in peace until woken by a bucket of cold water at closing time – unless the malodorous stench emanating from the aforementioned Le Crasseux roused him first. Although used by a variety of people from time to time, this compartment had become known as 'Le Soulard's Chamber' as he was its most frequent occupant.

"No problem," said Gastelois. "I didn't spill much."

"I'll top it up for you anyway," said Le Remplieur, taking the other's jar. As he handed back the replenished vessel, a new arrival in his pub caught his eye. "Ah," he said, looking past Gastelois, "someone's 'ere you might want to see, you."

Gastelois turned round. A slender, olive-skinned woman in her mid-twenties was gliding gracefully over the floor towards him, her oval face, framed by long, black, flowing hair, broadened by a warm, welcoming smile.

"Sylvia!" exclaimed Gastelois. He put his jar down on the bar and, beaming broadly, walked towards her, arms outstretched to embrace her.

"I heard you were back," said Sylvia d'Arass as they hugged. "I've just been up to your house, and as you clearly weren't at home I thought I'd probably find you in here." Her voice was soft, gentle, the accent not of these parts.

"And here I am," said Gastelois. "Cider?"

"Yes please."

Gaston Le Remplieur was already pouring it. "Albert's in Sersur," he said, winking at the dolmen builder as he finished filling the jar and handed it to Sylvia.

"So I gather," said Gastelois flatly. He knew precisely what the other was implying. "Shall we go over there?" he then suggested to Sylvia, nodding towards a free table some distance from the bar.

He led the way to the item of furniture in question. Sylvia d'Arass sat down and parted the long strands of black hair from her face with her slender fingers. She smiled at Gastelois as he took the seat on the other side of the table, placing the jar of cider in front of her. He smiled back, looking into the dark, liquid pools of her eyes. She returned his gaze, holding it, unblinking.

"So," she said. "I hear you had a good trip." She sipped her cider slowly, gazing at him over the rim of her jar.

"Yes, thanks. It wasn't too bad." He took a drink from his own jar. "I've got some plans back at the house which I think you'd be interested in."

"Dolmen plans?"

Gastelois nodded. "Yes. The majority are from Armor, but there are two or three from other areas."

Sylvia's eyes lit up: "I'd love to see them." She looked enquiringly at him, waiting for the invitation she was sure would come.

"Well, how about in a little while, after we've had a couple of drinks."

"This evening?"

"Why not?"

A good reason why not entered the pub just at that moment. A thin man of slightly taller than average height accompanied by a slender woman of similar stature walked through the main doorway, a boy aged about ten trailing reluctantly behind. They stopped and surveyed their surroundings. The man motioned towards a table right next to Gastelois and Sylvia's and then, after exchanging a few words with his wife, he went to the bar while she and their son made their way over to the table.

Gastelois' heart sank when he saw them. "Pierre-Juste!" he hissed at Sylvia in a low voice.

She turned round and saw the woman and the boy heading in their direction. "Not to mention Marguérite and Armand-Juste," she added in an equally low voice, turning back to face him. "And they're coming over here!"

"We'd better be polite," said Gastelois, resignedly.

"Good evening, Gastelois. Fancy seeing you two in here." The voice was as far back as it could possibly be. Sylvia was ignored in the greeting.

Gastelois got up. "Good evening, Marguérite. Hello, Armand-Juste." He gave a slight nod of his head towards them and then resumed his seat.

The woman was a good three or four years older than Sylvia and, although undeniably elegant, could not hold a candle to her as regards facial attractiveness. Her steely grey eyes were too narrow, the lips below the slightly aquiline nose too thin, the complexion sallow. She wore a seemingly permanent expression of superiority, emphasised by the way she held her head back, nose in the air.

She sat down on the far side of the adjacent table, deliberately choosing this position so she could observe Gastelois and Sylvia. The boy sat on the stool next to her. Armand-Juste had inherited his mother's narrow eyes and thin lips, but his nose was fuller, fleshier, the nostrils rounder. The size of these particular nasal openings could not be entirely blamed on genetics, however. They had grown broader than they would otherwise have done as a result of Armand-Juste's predilection for picking his nose, in which particular nasty habit he now proceeded to indulge.

"Stop that!" commanded Marguérite, knocking her son's hand away from his face.

"I'd have thought you'd have beaten that habit out of him by now, Marguérite," said Sylvia smugly. Gastelois smiled at her.

Marguérite's face coloured and assumed a patent it's-none-of-your-business expression.

Just then, her husband returned with three jars of drink, two large and one half their size, which he put down on the table.

"Thank you," said Marguérite, taking one of the larger jars and passing the smaller one to her son. "Say thank you to your father, Armand."

"Thank you, Papa."

"I hope that's not alcohol, Pierre-Juste," said Sylvia, nodding towards the jar whose contents the boy had begun to gulp noisily down his throat.

Pierre-Juste de Richolet favoured her with a disdainful look and sat down opposite Marguérite. Albert de Richolet's son by his first wife, he had little time for his stepmother and there was not a lot of love lost between them. Despite his father's assertion that his mother had departed of her own volition to spend time with relations in Armor 'for family reasons', he blamed Sylvia for having turned Albert's head and did his best to cause problems between them whenever he could. She, for her part, considered him to be an obnoxious, arrogant twit and refused to let herself be riled by his petty jibes.

On the other hand, she was not above making the odd underhand or sarcastic comment herself if she thought the occasion demanded it, the remark about the alcohol being a case in point. She was a woman of strong will and more than capable of standing up for herself, which Gastelois greatly admired.

"I've just been given an interesting project," he said in a low voice.

Although there was little chance of him being heard above the general hubbub of conversation in the pub, he was mindful of Pierre-Juste and Marguérite's proximity and the last thing he wanted was his business being broadcast to all and sundry. The male de Richolet was quite adept at gossiping and disseminating information about people, but his abilities paled into insignificance compared to those of his wife. For gossip mongering, rumour-spreading and general muckraking, she had few equals.

"Oh, what's that?" asked Sylvia in equally hushed tones.

"The Elders want me to build a new dolmen as a prize for the winner of a dragon-hunting contest that'll feature as part of La Tanche's Jubilee celebrations."

"Not Old Mauger!" said Sylvia perceptively.

Gastelois nodded: "'Fraid so. But don't worry," he went on, seeing the concerned look on her face. "The idea is that the contestants will shoot soft-tipped arrows soaked in coloured dyes at him, the winner being the one who scores the most hits."

"And he gets a new dolmen for his troubles?"

"Yes, and residency in the island to go with it – the contest will only be open to foreigners, would you believe!"

"I see. And what does Mauger think about this?"

"Don't know. The Elders haven't asked him yet. They're seeing him tomorrow and they want me to go along too." He took a long draught of cider, smacked his lips in satisfaction and put the jar back down on the table. "I've got to decide on a suitable location for the dolmen, as long as it's somewhere in the east."

"That shouldn't be too difficult," observed Sylvia.

"Harder than you might think."

"You'll find just the right spot – you always do." She took a sip of cider, giving him a wide smile over the rim of the jar.

"I'd like you to do the interior paintings," said Gastelois, smiling back at her.

She frowned. "Michel Langlois won't like that."

"Tough," stated Gastelois emphatically. "He's not the only decent artist around." He took a quick drink of cider before adding: "And I know some would question the use of the word 'decent' in his case."

"Well I'd love to," said Sylvia, beaming even more broadly. "What about the dolmen's design?"

"Haven't really thought about that. The Elders only told me about this today." He drained his jar. "They don't want anything too elaborate or expensive, though."

"Typical!" exclaimed Sylvia. "And yet they'll waste a beachful of shells on some extravagant project that nobody wants, such as that huge new midden pit they've commissioned for Ang-Lenn's rubbish." She drank some more cider.

"Indeed! And they've called in some so-called 'experts' from Alb to advise."

"Which will make the whole thing even more expensive."

"Yes," agreed Gastelois. "But when did any of their projects come in within budget?"

"And I suppose you could come up with something better," a sneering voice suddenly broke into their conversation.

"No more than you could, Pierre, but then I don't pretend to be an expert," retorted Sylvia.

Gastelois had wheeled round on his stool as soon as Pierre-Juste had started to speak. *How long had he been listening to their conversation for?* he wondered. *Had he overheard anything about the dragon contest and the new dolmen?* Gastelois was sure it wasn't common knowledge yet. True, he had just told Sylvia about it, but he knew it was safe to do so – she would not go and blab the news to the first person she met.

"Actually," de Richolet was saying, "I have been asked to assist with the planning of the town midden."

"That should be right up your street, dealing with rubbish," remarked Sylvia. "You certainly talk enough of it!"

The other glared at her and was on the verge of uttering a particularly damning remark at Sylvia's expense when Marguérite took hold of his arm and pulled him round to face her.

"Leave it!" she said, her eyes narrowing as she caught sight of the smirk on Sylvia's face. "She's not worth the bother."

"You ready for another one?" asked Gastelois, ignoring Marguérite.

"Why not," said Sylvia. "I'll come up with you."

"Fine. Once we've got the drinks, I must tell you about the Iberian artist I heard at the conference. He gave a fascinating talk about the use of colour in dolmen carvings."

CHAPTER FOUR

VRAICER T'LOCH

The weather continued fine the following day, but the great dark forest that occupied a good part of the central plateau area of Angur was as gloomy as ever. Ancient and mysterious, it was generally shunned by the island's population, who believed the old legends that told of strange beings lurking in its sombre, shadowy depths.

But deep in its heart, in a small crepuscular clearing, stood a strange house within a circle of moss-covered standing stones.

Octagonal in plan, this building consisted of massive granite uprights which sloped inwards from bottom to top and supported the roof: a single enormous capstone. There were no proper windows, only the gaps between the stones and a circular, two-foot-wide hole cut into the roof permitting light to enter the interior.

Stranger still, there was no normal door. Entrance was effected via a secret trapdoor in the ground just within the surrounding forest. This gave access to a subterranean tunnel which terminated beneath another trapdoor in the building's floor.

Smoke was at present rising from the hole in the roof indicating that the edifice's equally strange occupant was in residence. This was Vraicer T'loch, an enigmatic magician of formidable powers whom people rarely saw and who lived as solitary a life as he could. He was not a native of Angur, and no one knew exactly when he had first arrived on the island nor from whence he had come. It was rumoured that he hailed from a fabulous island far away across the *Sunwise Sea*, an island that had met with catastrophe in the dim and distant past. The 'Vraicer' part of his name derived from his great attraction to seaweed - 'vraic' of course being the local name for this. T'loch used it in his magic rites and practices; his bed was composed of it; the walls of his house were decorated with intricate tapestries woven from it; and when he wished to meditate, he suspended himself upside down over a slow-burning fire of dried seaweed to which were added certain powders in mind-enhancing proportions, and let the smoke and warmth from this bathe his body.

And that was precisely what he was doing at this particular moment. As he hung there, suspended from a beam in the roof and swinging gently to and fro, the ends of his long black hair perilously close to the smouldering contents of the hearth directly below, he let his mind drift until it seemed to be free of his body. Now he could see far; he could see everything he wished to. An image formed itself: a group of generally doddery old men grunting and wheezing as they made their way along a sandy path by the sea. There was a rather younger, fitter-looking person in the group, and he seemed to be engaged in earnest conversation with its leader.

T'loch concentrated harder. *Excellent!* he thought. So the Elders *were* seeing the dragon today. But what was this? Who was this goblin-like specimen furtively sneaking along behind them? *Ah, of course!* T'loch smiled. Things were progressing at a goodly speed, and exactly according to plan, too...

The DRAGON of ANGUR

Now he could see far; he could see everything he wished to

* * *

Old Mauger had decided to take his afternoon nap in his cave. He had just settled down in front of the pile of polished jadeite axes and other treasures that he had accumulated during his long life and was beginning to doze off when a distant mumbling and muttering reached his ears.

His eyes opened slowly and he peered myopically out of the entrance to his home, his vision slightly obscured by the smoke drifting up from his nostrils. He blew his nose to clear away the vapours so that he could see better. His sight improved and gradually a group of figures came into focus, moving slowly and carefully through the marsh towards him. *So soon?* thought Mauger. *That was quick!* He had not expected them for at least another day or two.

There was a loud splash as yet another of the Elders lost his footing and tumbled into one of the marsh pools, and the party came to a halt for the fourth time since they had entered the paludal area. Their efforts to rescue their soaked colleague were rewarded with howls of derisive laughter from the washerwomen attending to their laundry not very far away.

"Show more respect, you!" cried one of the sages, nose twitching in a bright red face.

The good women tried to control themselves, but it was not easy when faced with the spectacle of a group of old men, short in the sight and impaired in the balance, four of whom had so far fallen into the marsh.

"What're you doing anyways, you?" called one of the laundresses.

"We're going to see the dragon," returned Gaetan Le Sterc, casting an anxious eye over the Elder who had just been retrieved from the water.

"He'll be asleep, him. It's time for his afternoon nap."

"I can't help that," said Le Sterc, somewhat irritably. "We have to see him on a matter of urgent importance."

The woman shrugged her broad shoulders and wiped a thick, fleshy arm across her forehead. "That's up to you, then. But he won't like it."

With that, the women returned to their laundry, chattering amongst themselves with much sniggering and cackling, punctuated by the occasional look in the Elders' direction.

The DRAGON of ANGUR

As for those worthies, they continued their progress towards Mauger's home, eventually halting at the base of a steep scree slope that lead down from the mouth of a cave some twenty feet up the face of the cliff bordering the marsh. The dragon watched them through half-closed eyes.

"Well, here we are," said Etienne de Crochenolle, stating the obvious.

"D'you want me to call him?" asked Gastelois, looking up at Mauger's snout which was protruding from the cave entrance.

"If you like." Le Sterc shrugged his shoulders. It didn't really make any difference to him who got the dragon's attention as long as someone did.

The dolmen builder cupped his hands around his mouth and called the dragon's name, repeating it twice.

Old Mauger pretended not to hear. He wanted to give the impression that he was asleep.

Gastelois tried again. No response. The protruding snout did not stir - the smoke issuing from its nostrils the only sign that its owner was actually alive.

Gastelois turned to the Elders' chairman: "I suggest we both try."

Le Sterc nodded. Both men hailed the dragon, calling his name at the top of their voices. Mauger decided to show some sign of stirring and so emitted a groan. The two men looked at each other and then called the dragon again. The latter let out a loud sigh.

"We might be getting somewhere," observed de Crochenolle.

"Mauger! Mauger!" called Le Sterc. "We want a word with you."

The dragon slowly poked his head completely out of the cave and said in as drowsy a voice as he could: "I'm tired. Let me sleep."

"We just want a quick word with you, that's all."

"Who's *we?*" asked Mauger sleepily, knowing full well who it was.

"I'm Gaetan Le Sterc of the Assembly of Elders. With me are the other Elders and Gastelois de Bois."

"Ah, Gastelois!" muttered the dragon and repeated the name to himself a few times: "Gastelois, Gastelois, Gastelois." He yawned noisily, and then said in a bored voice: "What do you want, then?"

"We want a favour."

"I'm in no mood for favours," returned Mauger. "Let me sleep."

"We'll leave you alone in a moment, Mauger, just as soon as we've had a chance to tell you what we want."

There was what seemed an interminable pause. Then: "All right, I'll listen." The dragon opened his eyes a little more and regarded the group myopically. *Amazing that only four of these old fools had fallen in the marsh. Quite amazing!*

Le Sterc proceeded to explain how they intended to hold a number of contests to celebrate the High Elder's Flint Jubilee, adding that these would benefit the island's reputation abroad, as they would be open to foreigners as well as Angurians. Although the Elders had a number of ideas for these competitions, they felt that they did not have enough, and so they were grateful for any new suggestions that came their way. Somebody had recently suggested one that the Elders considered to show great promise: a dragon hunt.

"A *what?*" demanded Mauger, his booming voice echoing across the marsh, all trace of sleepiness gone from it.

Le Sterc shifted uncomfortably from one foot to the other and glanced nervously at Gastelois, who was trying to restrain a smile.

"A... A... dragon, er, hunt," repeated Le Sterc nervously.

"And what has *that* got to do with me?" Mauger flared his nostrils, and a large quantity of smoke rose from them.

The Elders' chairman looked even more uncomfortable. His colleagues' eyes, although rather glazed as a result of their lunchtime excesses, were fixed upon the cave and the long smoking snout protruding from it.

Le Sterc cleared his throat: "Well, er, you're a dragon, aren't you?"

"That is what they tell me." Mauger blew a cloud of smoke at one of the Elders, who was promptly seized by a fit of violent coughing.

"Well," continued Le Sterc, "we would like you to take part in the contest and..."

"*Me?*" interrupted the dragon. "Who d'you think I am? I have absolutely no intention of being hunted or attacked in any

The DRAGON of ANGUR

way at all." He let out a tremendous roar which had all the Elders quivering in their shoes before it died away. Mauger restrained a chuckle. He was enjoying himself immensely.

Le Sterc had broken out in a cold sweat. This was proving harder than he had expected. He turned to Gastelois: "How do I persuade 'im?"

The other shrugged his shoulders. "I don't know. I did warn you. Anyway, you haven't told him anything *about* the contest. Maybe if you can convince him that he's not going to come to any harm..."

The chairman nodded slowly. "M.. Mauger... M.. Mauger," he stammered. "L.. Let me explain."

"Please do. But I would be grateful if you'd get on with it." He yawned noisily. "I do want to go to sleep."

Le Sterc then explained what the object of the contest would be. He added that if at any stage Mauger became fed up with the proceedings, he could just leave of his own accord. If, however, he did stay to the end, he would be able to return to his home as soon as the contest was over.

"I still don't like it," said the dragon when Le Sterc had finished. "One could still get hurt. Anyway, what's in it for the winner?"

"Res'dency in the island and a fam'ly dolmen to go with it," the chairman told him in a somewhat pompous voice.

"Supposing the winner already lives here?"

"Ah, this partic'lar contest will only be open to foreigners."

Old Mauger nodded slowly. He had suspected as much. No self-respecting Angurian would stoop so low as to consider taking part in something that might endanger the well-being of the local dragon. "And this dolmen," he went on. "I suppose that's why friend Gastelois is here?"

"Yes," said Gastelois. "They want me to build it. I'm also here to ensure that this thing is arranged properly. I certainly don't want you coming to any harm."

The dragon believed him. He was very fond of the dolmen builder, and knew that he had his best interests at heart. "Come up here, Gastelois. I'd like a word with you."

The worthy de Bois promptly scrambled up the loose surface of the scree slope leading to the dragon's home and entered the cave, squatting down beside the long snout, which Mauger had drawn back from the entrance.

"This is fun, isn't it?" whispered Old Mauger.

Gastelois looked at him: "Putting the wind up the Elders?"

"Yes."

"I must confess to rather enjoying the proceedings myself."

They were both silent for a few moments, and then the dragon asked in a low voice: "How risky d'you think this contest'll be?"

Gastelois shrugged his shoulders. "I'm not sure," he said, speaking equally quietly. "But I think it'll be safer if you insist on limiting both the number of contestants and the number of arrows each of them will be allowed to fire, as well as the length of time each contestant has in which to try to drive you away. I'll do my best to draw up a set of rules that'll ensure fair play. And I think that you should give up and leave the area as soon as reasonably possible after the start of the contest - just to be on the safe side."

"You think I should agree to it, then?"

The other shrugged his shoulders again. "It's up to you. They can't force you to take part. But I don't think you'll come to any harm, if we're all careful. After all, it is only a contest - it's not as if people were out to kill you." He looked pensive. "I would like to know who came up with this idea, though."

"You mean you don't know?" Mauger sounded surprised. Gastelois shook his head.

"The Elders haven't told you?"

"No."

"But I presume that *they* know - or at the very least Le Sterc does."

"Oh yes, I'm sure they know."

"And they won't even tell *you!*"

"Apparently the fellow wishes to remain anonymous."

The dragon snorted. "That doesn't surprise me. Probably scared the people will lynch him if they find out."

Gastelois laughed.

"*I* know who it is," stated Old Mauger matter of factly.

The smile vanished from Gastelois' face. "*What?*"

"Yes. Grosnez Chatel."

"Grosnez!"

"Indeed so."

A puzzled expression came over Gastelois' face. "Why would *he* want to suggest contests to the Elders? I didn't think he was interested in that sort of thing."

The dragon said nothing.

"But how did you know it was him?" Gastelois went on, staring at the creature. "I mean, how did you find out?"

"Someone told me. In fact, I probably knew the Elders were coming to see me before you did."

"You mean, you knew about the dragon hunt?"

"Not exactly. I knew there was going to be a contest of some description and that I would be involved in some way or the other."

"But who told you?"

"Ah, that would be telling," said Old Mauger, a mischievous glint in the eye facing the dolmen builder.

"Mauger! Come on! I'm not going to blurt it out to all and sundry," remonstrated Gastelois.

"I'm just winding you up," Mauger reassured him. "It was Vraicer T'loch."

"T'loch?"

"Yes. He contacted me in my sleep – he does that quite a lot – said that you and the Elders would be coming to see me about some contest that Grosnez had suggested to them as part of these silly jubilee celebrations. He said that the contest would involve me and that I should agree to take part, but beyond that he didn't say anything else about it." The dragon yawned noisily and then emitted a cloud of smoke.

Gastelois coughed as the cloud enveloped him.

"Sorry," apologised Mauger.

Gastelois looked pensively at the dragon for a few moments. Then he asked: "Are you going to do it, then?"

The dragon sighed. "Take part? I suppose so. It'll probably be very inconvenient, but on the other hand it could be fun." He lapsed into silent reflection for a couple of moments. Then: "I could even *win* the contest - I mean, if nobody succeeded in... if nobody beat me, I would be the winner, wouldn't I?"

"Mauger! I..."

"Then I would have my very own dolmen." He chuckled. "Now that would be rather nice!"

"I trust you're having me on," said Gastelois, favouring the dragon with a suspicious look.

The other chuckled again. "Perhaps I am, perhaps I'm not," he said enigmatically. "Anyway, when exactly will this contest be? I gather the Jubilee celebrations will be taking place around Midsummer."

"Yes, but I've no idea exactly when the individual events will be. And I don't think the Elders have either."

"I'd be very surprised if they have even the vaguest notion. Well, I suppose we'll find out - soon enough."

Gastelois nodded. "Right then, I'll tell them that you'll take part in the contest, provided, of course, that we can come up with a decent set of rules."

"Yes."

"Good. Then maybe they'll give me more guidelines for this dolmen than they have so far."

"Ah yes, the dolmen." The dragon nodded his head slowly. "I shouldn't waste too much effort on it, if I were you."

Gastelois looked somewhat mortified. "My dear Mauger! I do have my standards to keep up."

Old Mauger chuckled. "I suppose you do." He was silent for a moment, as if thinking about something. "Well," he said eventually, "I'll leave the rest to you. I'm going to get some sleep now." Another pause. Then: "Oh by the way, when you leave, make sure that *you* walk a little to one side of the Elders."

"Aih?" Gastelois gave the dragon a puzzled look.

"Just do as I ask." The creature winked mischievously at him.

"All right then."

Gastelois bade Old Mauger farewell and made for the cave's entrance.

"Oh, one last thing," said the dragon suddenly.

"What's that?" asked the dolmen builder, turning around and looking at him.

"Give Sylvia my love."

The DRAGON of ANGUR

Gastelois smiled. As he left the cave and scrambled down the scree slope, he thought about what he had just learnt. Grosnez was up to something; of that he was certain. The question was: what? Upon reflection, he decided not to say anything about this to Le Sterc or his colleagues. When, therefore, he rejoined the others, he merely informed them that all was well and that plans for the contest could go ahead.

"Thank goodness for that!" exclaimed Le Sterc, breathing a sigh of relief. "Let's be off, then. I'll buy you a drink in the *Cabbage*; you deserve one."

With that, the Elders began to make their way back across the marsh. Gastelois kept well to their left, pretending to be interested in some species of plant life that was to be found growing near the edges of the still, brackish ponds abounding in the area. He wondered what naughty act the dragon was going to perpetrate.

Suddenly, there was a tremendous bellow and a jet of flame shot from the mouth of Mauger's cave, scorching the ground immediately to the right of the group of old sages. Such was their alarm at this that four promptly fainted, five fell into a nearby pond and the remainder only just stayed standing themselves. In fact, it was a wonder that none of them suffered heart failure. Gastelois had to suppress a desire to chuckle as he helped Le Sterc and the others who had not fainted or fallen in the water attend to their stricken colleagues.

A raucous laugh resounded from the cave, and Le Sterc shot a venomous look in that direction. Gastelois smiled. The dragon might be getting old, but he certainly was not losing his sense of humour.

* * *

The goblin-like creature waited until the Elders had left, then furtively stole away from the marsh and headed northwards as fast as his spindly legs could carry him. Grosnez would be very pleased to hear his report. Oh yes Grosnez would be very pleased with him...

* * *

Vraicer T'loch smiled a satisfied smile as he swung gently over the smouldering fire of seaweed. All was going according to plan. He could see Piton Le Malin hurrying to give his master all the latest news about the dragon contest. One of these days that little twerp was going to get himself caught; he was always snooping about and eavesdropping on other people's conversations, one of his particular specialities being hiding in the branches of the old tree in the Assembly Hall and listening in on the Elders' meetings.

T'loch took a deep breath of seaweed smoke and slowly exhaled it. His mind shifted to Grosnez Chatel's residence. He could see its owner sitting on top of the mound that covered his home, staring out to sea. Wasn't it fortunate that Grosnez was so greedy – the fellow was playing right into his hands.

Yes, things were proceeding very well. Grosnez would soon be getting everything that was coming to him, and not before time.

T'loch withdrew his mind from the Chatel residence. *Now,* he thought, *for the next stage of my plan...*

CHAPTER FIVE

AN UNEXPECTED PROBLEM

That night, Gastelois stayed up late trying to think of a suitable location for the Elders' prize dolmen. Despite having exercised his brain on the matter for some time now, the ideal spot was still eluding him. He was not helped by the fact that his brain wanted to dwell on the question of what Grosnez was up to. Whatever it was, Gastelois was sure that it was some species of dastardly scheme – where Grosnez was concerned, it could hardly be otherwise.

Eventually, he decided to take a break from his ruminations and instead sketched out some ideas for the plan of the new dolmen in charcoal on a piece of cowhide. While he was working, he managed to get through quite a few jars of his own cider, which he produced from apples growing on trees near his home.

It was well past midnight when he finally decided that he was too tired to continue with either drawing dolmen plans - none of those sketched so far filled him with any enthusiasm - or thinking about where to build the thing, and headed for his bed. He wondered whether a spell on the plane of dreams would give him the answer to the latter question.

Gastelois had found in the past that he would sometimes dream the solutions to problems that were plaguing his mind. This particular night turned out to be just such an occasion, and when he awoke the following morning, early as was his habit, he knew the ideal spot for the dolmen. He was sure that he'd have no difficulty in persuading the Elders to accept his choice - he doubted that they themselves would have come up with one - and he aimed to put it to them before the morning was over.

It had been a rather strange dream. He had followed a tall, thin man, facially indistinct, wrapped in a dark cloak through a blurred, misty landscape to a patch of gorse and bracken near a stand of trees. The man had indicated this area with a sweeping motion of his right arm. Then he had led Gastelois to a nearby headland overlooking a col upon which stood a familiar, moundless gallery-dolmen below which lay an equally familiar seaside settlement, boats bobbing gently in its harbour.

He lay in bed for a while, thinking first about this dream and then about things in general. He had a slight hangover and as a result he resolved to go easier on the cider in future. Having sorted out the problem of where to put the dolmen, he would now be able to concentrate on its size and design. His time would obviously be limited, and no doubt his resources would be too, but, as he had told the dragon, he had his standards to maintain, and he would therefore do the best he could within the constraints imposed.

He duly got up and fixed himself a light breakfast of bread, goat's cheese, and seaweed tea. After that, he tidied his house, checked some plants growing outside, and then set off for Ang-Lenn and the Elders.

He made his way down the sloping main street of Aube, cordially greeting those residents he encountered as he passed through, in due course reaching the settlement's harbour at the end of the tree-lined inlet that connected it with the sea. A couple of fishermen were tending their nets by the water's edge and looked up as he approached.

"Morning, you," greeted one of them.

"Morning, Raoul," returned Gastelois. "Looks like it's going to be a fine day."

"That it does," said the other. "Busy day?"

"Looks that way, Pierre," said Gastelois. "Got to see the Elders."

He did not elaborate and the fishermen knew better than to be too inquisitive.

Raoul, instead, said: "I wonder what they'll do with the defence budget this year. I b'lieve they're supposed to be discussing it at this session."

"They won't use it for what we really need, that's for sure," said his companion bitterly. "They know we need an air-sea rescue dragon, but they'll waste it on something useless."

"Well, we'll find out soon enough," said Gastelois, smiling. "Good day."

With that, he left them loudly discussing the Elders' failings as they worked on their nets, and headed off along a path leading away from the harbour and the inlet. The path cut through the trees and emerged on to the Bay of Aube, where it followed the crescent of the bay just above high tide level towards Ang-Lenn. As he walked, some quite radical concepts began to form in Gastelois' mind with regard to the design of the prize dolmen. He hoped that the island's planning department would go along with these, especially considering the reason for the dolmen's birth.

He looked to his right and his eyes settled on a rather large coracle moving slowly across the calm, deep blue waters of the bay in the direction of Ang-Lenn. Somewhat longer and broader than the usual vessel of its type and therefore capable of carrying rather more people, it appeared to be almost empty in relation to its capacity. Gastelois could see only six people in it and at least four of these would be crew. But knowing the identity of the vessel, he was not surprised in the slightest.

Angur Boat was supposed to run a regular service around the island, calling in at all the coastal settlements. The company's interpretation of *run* and *service* did not, however, accord with most people's understanding of the words, and this had led to much dissatisfaction amongst those who did not have their own coracles and relied on its boats to get from one village to another.

It was hoped that one day the Elders would grant the licence to another outfit, but it was thought unlikely that they ever would, particularly as the last time this was tried the result was a strike and no service of any kind for more than a month.

Gastelois sighed. *Oh well, one day*, he thought as he continued on his way.

* * *

Vraicer T'loch swung slowly over the smouldering embers of his seaweed fire. It had been a tiring night. The fact that he was adept at insinuating himself into the dreams of others did not make the process any the less exhausting. Still, it had been a success. Gastelois would build the dolmen in just the right place.

* * *

Gaetan Le Sterc's relief at Gastelois' arrival was palpable. Acting on instructions, the attendant Beanpole had shown the dolmen builder straight into the Assembly Hall and had announced his presence, interrupting one of the Elders who was in full flow giving forth on the matter of *Angur Boat's* licence renewal.

"Ah, Gastelois! Good to see you again," Le Sterc greeted him, ignoring the protestations of the pontificating Elder. The debate

Sinclair Forrest

on whether to renew the licence in question was now in its fourth day and showing no sign of reaching a conclusion. It had become rather heated, to say the least, and the chairman was glad of an excuse to break away from it.

"So," he went on, "have you come up with a site?"

Gastelois nodded. "I think so," he said as he stepped on to the wooden platform and faced the chairman, who was again ensconced in the High Elder's seat. "On the headland overlooking Gor."

"Aw but that's ideal!" exclaimed Etienne de Crochenolle enthusiastically. "A nice spot in the country, but conveniently near to a settlement."

A number of the other Elders muttered their approval. Le Sterc was relieved that Gastelois had come up with a location, as it saved him and his colleagues the trouble of having to find one themselves.

"That seems fine," he said, agreeing to the dolmen builder's choice.

"And have you decided yet exactly when you're going to hold the contest?" asked Gastelois. "Is it going to be actually on Midsummer's Day, or before then?"

La Sterc shrugged his shoulders. "Aw but that we haven't decided yet."

Gastelois let out an exasperated sigh. "Well, I would like some idea of when I'm supposed to have this dolmen ready for."

"Yes, we appreciate that, mon vier," said Le Sterc. "But we've still to sort everything out – arrange things in the order we want them." His face assumed a pensive expression. "I think it will either be on Midsummer's Day itself or on the day before."

"Right," said Gastelois. "I'll contact my assistant and we'll look over the site. I should be able to let you have my ideas on the size and design within a few days."

"Fine," said the chairman. "Nothing too big or elaborate, though. We can't afford to spend a fortune."

Gastelois nodded. He thought about reminding the Elders that they still owed him for the last dolmen he had built for them, but decided against it. So, without further ado, he bade them farewell and made his way out of the Hall, leaving them to resume the main business of the day.

* * *

"What container? What're you talking about, dolt?" Grosnez Chatel glared at the spindly specimen cringing before him.

"A c. container of some, er, l.liquid," stammered Piton. "I saw Tourvel again... er, this morning. He's come over to Angur for a few days to see his... er... brother. Apparently that's been taken ill."

"Yes, yes. Get on with it! I'm not interested in Tourvel's brother. The container, fool, the container!"

Piton swallowed. "I... I saw him go into *The Old Vraic and Coracle*, so I followed him in. I th.thought he m.might be able to tell us more about the shell, so I bought him a drink and joined him. While we were talking about the shell, he mentioned this, er, container of liquid."

"What sort of liquid?"

Piton swallowed. "One that, er, glows, Grosnez." He had so far been reluctant to impart this information to the other for fear of ridicule.

"So, a glowing liquid," he said somewhat sarcastically. "What of it?"

"W.Well, it s.seems we, er need it."

"Why? What for?"

"The, er shell is no good without it Grosnez."

"*What?*" Grosnez advanced menacingly on his servant. "What're you saying you?"

Piton gulped, backing away from the lanky frame towering threateningly over him. "I.It s.seems that we can't use the sh.shell unless we have this l. liquid."

"*What?* You mean that shell is useless on its own?" Grosnez continued to advance on his hapless servant.

The latter nodded, continuing to back away, his eyes fearfully regarding Grosnez'.

"Well, did he tell you why this liquid's so nec'ssary?"

"No." Piton's back suddenly encountered stone - the circular wall of the main chamber of Grosnez' home - and his retreat was thus cut off. "He just said that the shell's useless without it, but he didn't know why."

"And there's some in some form of container?"

Piton nodded again.

"Well, did he tell you anything about this container?"

The other shook his head. "No. But he did think that it might... that it might be somewhere on this island."

"Somewhere on this island!" roared Grosnez. "Fantastic! I have no intention of searching all of Angur trying to find a container of some strange liquid that glows." He suddenly thrust his face close to Piton's, assuming an expression even more menacing than any he had exhibited so far. "I trust you're not having me on."

Piton swallowed. "Wh.Why should I want to do that, Grosnez?"

"I don't know. Just a thought." He turned and walked away from his servant, lapsing into silence for a few minutes. "Well, we'll just have to find T'loch," he declared eventually. "If anyone knows more about this, he will."

"But how 're we going to find T'loch?" whined Piton.

"By looking for him, dolt!"

"But..."

Grosnez tutted irritably. "I heard the other day that he's in Lesur, so we'll start by looking there." He paused for a moment. "But it's a bit late in the day now, so we'll go tomorrow. In the meantime, I want to see La Cloche. You can stay here and think about what you 're going to cook me for supper."

* * *

Vraicer T'loch took a deep breath of seaweed smoke, exhaled it slowly, and smiled a satisfied smile. So they were under the impression that he was in Lesur and were going to look for him there. That was fine by him. A little nocturnal journey, and he would be on that island waiting for them. There would be no problem about arranging a meeting...

* * *

Clychard La Cloche, head of the Angurian branch of the *Dolmen and Granite Workers' Union* (D.G.W.U.), was a small, fat man of middle age with a prominent potbelly that spoke of too much indulgence in the island's alcoholic brews. He was almost bald, had ears that stuck out and seemed too large, and his piggy eyes, which rarely looked at you directly, gave him a decidedly shifty aspect.

The DRAGON of ANGUR

Clychard La Cloche

It was rumoured that he had attained his current prestigious position by somewhat suspect and underhand methods, but so far nobody had been able to prove anything. Moreover, he had shown himself to be a shrewd and capable negotiator, and his members were quite happy to have him as the head of their union for as long as he continued to benefit them.

He was at present pacing up and down inside the large dolmen that served as the local branch's headquarters. Situated not very far to the east of Ang-Lenn, on the headland of *Le Mont Tubelin* overlooking Angur's south coast, it was known as *Levitation House,* after the method employed by the priests to assist with the moving of megaliths. It had an entrance passage some eighteen feet in length leading into a spacious main chamber of roughly oval plan with internal compartments separated by tall, vertical slabs, arranged along the inside of its walls. The structure was roofed by huge capstones, the largest of which weighed nearly twenty-five tons, and the whole edifice was covered by an oval mound of rubble some twenty feet high. This was stepped in two tiers, each tier being faced with large granite blocks. One of the most impressive dolmens in Angur, it had been built by Arbreur Le Bois, and the classical simplicity of its design had led those who knew about such things to conclude that it was his masterpiece. It had not originally belonged to the D.G.W.U., having been built for someone else, and it was not clear how it had come into the union's possession. Double-dealings were suspected, but again no one could prove anything.

Grosnez Chatel was with La Cloche, and had just told him about the mysterious substance reputedly vital for the proper use of the turtle shell. The two men had been 'associates' for some considerable time and had, between them, concocted not a few scams which they had perpetrated on the good people of Angur.

Grosnez was leaning against one of the granite uprights forming the walls of the main chamber, his right cheek warmed by the heat from a nearby animal-grease lamp, one of a number that attempted, with moderate success, to illuminate the chamber's interior. His eyes were following the union chief's somewhat agitated pacing.

La Cloche stopped abruptly, turned and faced Grosnez: "You're absolutely certain about this, you?"

The other nodded. "I don't see why Piton should lie to me."

"No, indeed."

"He knows what would happen to him if he did."

"I dare say you've made that clear to him on a number of occasions."

"That I have." A malicious grin twisted Grosnez' features as certain memories came back. "But to return to the matter in hand: we need that liquid."

La Cloche nodded and his face assumed a pensive expression. "We'll have to find it, that's all." He looked up at the underside of the huge capstone above him. "But where do we start looking?"

"Well, I'm going to Lesur tomorrow with Piton to see T'loch. I'm led to b'lieve that he's there at the moment, and if anyone knows about this liquid, whatever it is, he does."

"It's worth a try, although there's no guaranteeing that he'll tell you even if he does know – you know what that's like!" La Cloche frowned. "But I hope you're successful. Nothing must stand in our way."

"No," agreed Grosnez. "Absolutely nothing."

The DRAGON of ANGUR

* * *

It was still dark when Grosnez kicked his confederate out of bed early the following morning. The unfortunate Le Malin remained asleep until he hit the stone floor, the impact jarring him painfully awake. Nursing his bruised posterior, he looked up in bewilderment at the lanky frame towering over him.

"Up, fool!" ordered Grosnez. "There's no time to lose!"

"What's happening? What's going on?"

"If you recall, we're going to Lesur. Now hurry, or you won't have time for any breakfast before we leave." As Piton got shakily to his feet, Grosnez added: "And I suggest you eat well to build up your strength; if there's not enough wind you'll have to row, and I don't want to take all day to get there."

With that he went off to prepare breakfast, as he did not have time to wait for Piton to do the honours while the latter tried to come to terms with being awake long before his body thought he should be. Rueing the day he had had the misfortune to get involved with his master, he struggled into his clothes, grumbling constantly. He hoped that the trip to Lesur would be easy; he knew very well that Grosnez would not help with the rowing.

* * *

Gaetan Le Sterc and Ernaud de Langetot, the Chairman of the Lesurian Assembly of Elders, were sitting in *The Granite Cabbage* enjoying some food and some much-needed ale. They were on their own, despite the fact that a number of Le Sterc's colleagues were also in the pub. It had been a particularly harassing morning, not helped by an earlier than usual start necessitated by the amount of business on the day's agenda. De Langetot had rarely had to sit through such a fraught meeting of the Angurian Assembly, although he had experienced far worse in Lesur. All both men wanted to do now was relax, which very probably would have been difficult had they sat with the others, who doubtless would have pressed them for their opinion on this point or that point arising from the morning's proceedings.

These had revolved around the festivities to be held in honour of the High Elder's forthcoming Flint Jubilee. De Langetot had come over for a couple of days to discuss Lesur's role in the celebrations, as the High Elder had insisted that that island (and indeed the other islands) be involved. Cou-Cou La Tanche himself was still safely out of the way in Sersur, supposedly discussing fishing limits, but more likely enjoying the hospitality of the ruler of that island, an elderly lady of great cunning and daring known as 'La Blanche Dame', who had a quite formidable reputation in local politics. She and La Tanche got along very well, and there were those who were certain that their relationship was rather more than just political. It was to be hoped that Albert de Richolet, who, as President of the Marine and Land Exploitation Committee, had accompanied the High Elder to assist with the negotiations, was allowing La Tanche and La Dame at least some privacy.

Gaetan Le Sterc drained his beer jar with remarkable speed and let out a deep sigh of satisfaction. "Aw, but that was good, that! What a morning, aih?"

His companion nodded. "Certainly was." He shifted his massive frame in his chair and settled himself into a more comfortable position. "But I think we got somewhere, mon vier."

"Aw yes, I'm inclined to agree with you." Le Sterc snapped his fingers in the direction of the bar to indicate that he wanted a refill.

De Langetot finished his jar. "So at least we now 'ave a number of things finalised, although the way things were going at one point this morning, I really thought we were going to get absolutely nowhere."

"I know what you mean. I wish that Gaston Corbel wouldn't keep sticking his oar in just when we think we've got something worked out. He's a ruddy nuisance, him!"

The Lesurian agreed, thanking the barman, who had just placed some fresh jars on their table. "I was r'lieved to 'ear that you're getting somewhere with the music. Cel'brations without music aren't proper cel'brations, them."

"Indeed so," said Le Sterc. "I'm glad *The Rolling Capstones* have agreed to come – that'll keep the young people happy. They'll have to make extra room at *The Rock Bottom* to accomm'date all the fans." He paused while he took a drink. "But I'm partic'larly looking forward to hearing Pierre Rocher de l'Isle's latest composition – the one we've specially commissioned for the Jub'lee – I'm sure that will be well worth waiting for."

"Judging by what I've 'eard of 'is efforts, it certainly should be."

"Mmm, he's performed in Lesur a few times, I seem to recall." Another pause for another mouthful. "By the way, how's your new concert hall coming along?"

De Langetot swallowed the mouthful of ale he had just imbibed. "*La Rocque qui Sonne*? Pretty well. What's taking the time is getting the acoustics right. Ev'ry time Thière positions a stone, the musicians 'ave to check it." He drank some more beer. "It isn't proving pop'lar with everyone, though."

"How d'you mean?" asked Le Sterc, giving him a puzzled look. Surely no one could object to a brand new, state of the art concert hall.

"Well, there's this chap 'ocart who lives not very far away. 'e reckons the music will be too loud and will cause a disturbance of the peace. 'e's threat'ning to break the place up if it does."

"It'd be amusing to see him try."

"Yes." The Lesurian drained his jar and placed the empty vessel on the table in front of him. "So let's r'view things. What do we 'ave so far? A beer-drinking contest between our two islands - that'll attract a lot of entrants; the Sersur - Angur coracle race - La Dame's agreed to that, as I said; a lev'tation contest to see which team of priests can lift 'n' move the 'eaviest block of granite. Where d'you intend to 'old that one, by the way?"

"Not sure yet," said Le Sterc. "But somewhere safe where there's plenty of room."

"Very wise." The other took a long drink. "Yes, very wise. These lev'tation contests can be very dang'rous them, partic'larly as 'alf the contestants 'aven't a clue what they're doing."

"I know what you mean. We once considered banning them completely but the opp'sition from the priests was too strong, so we had to relent."

"Protecting their own int'rests. Doesn't surprise me." De Langetot stroked his black beard pensively; its bushiness made his face seem even broader. "I recall a contest a few years ago in Lesur. Two teams tried to move a large men'ir at the same time. Nothing 'appened for a while, and then the thing went on a rampage around the 'arbour, sinking sev'ral boats and narrowly missing Philoche du Tus's. That was on it at the time, and for months after 'ardly ever ceased giving forth on the idiocy of the partic 'pants."

Le Sterc smiled. He knew du Tus very well and had no difficulty imagining the scene. He drank some beer and stared contemplatively into his jar. Then he went pale. "That story's just reminded me of something I meant to mention this morning – Corbel's interruptions distracted me and it slipped from my mind. Rumour has it that Leoville de Vinchelez is threat'ning to unveil his latest invention."

Ernaud de Langetot's bushy black eyebrows shot up with extreme rapidity. This de Vinchelez lived in the north-west of Angur and fancied himself as something of an inventor. He produced all manner of strange devices which he thought would be of great benefit to the good people of the island. Once they had experienced them for themselves, however, the good people invariably thought otherwise!

Leoville de Vinchelez

"Can't 'e be stopped?" The Lesurian's face was registering alarm.

"Unfortunately not. La Tanche is all for private enterprise. We tried to stop him once before, but our dear High Elder interceded on his behalf, saying that one day Leoville might produce something that would really ben'fit the commun'ty. So whatever he plans to spring on us will be sprung."

"Mother of Earth 'elp us!" exclaimed de Langetot.

Le Sterc swallowed a mouthful of beer. "Well, as long as he keeps it away from the other festiv'ties, we should be all right. I shudder to think what might happen if it interfered with the lev'tation comp'tition or the dragon contest."

The DRAGON of ANGUR

De Langetot nodded. "I agree. I don't think Old Mauger would be too 'appy 'im, if that idiot caused a problem."

The other finished his ale, smacked his lips in satisfaction and assumed a pensive air. "You know," he said after a few moments, "I'm not sure whether that dragon thing will be a fitting climax to the cel'brations after all."

The Lesurian chairman shot him an anxious look. He wondered whether his friend was serious. Was anything better really needed? What with, among other things, a beer-drinking contest, a boat race, hazardous feats of levitation, a dragon contest, and Leoville de Vinchelez loose on the scene, the whole area was going to be dangerous enough. Was it wise to try to top that lot with some other, no doubt even more deadly, event? He shuddered at the thought.

* * *

Piton Le Malin was exhausted. He had completed the crossing to Lesur in what he thought was a reasonably quick time, despite having had to row against a head wind for a good part of the journey, but of course Grosnez was complaining that he'd taken too long. Was his master never satisfied? Glaring daggers at his back, Piton followed him along the seafront of Lesur's main town, Lennac. They were heading for *The Quivering Crapaud*, arguably the most popular pub in the town, which they deemed the best place to start their search for Vraicer T'loch. If he was not there, there were four other ale houses in the settlement that they could try.

The *Crapaud* stood at the north end of town, its main entrance facing the sea. It was a rather ramshackle wooden roundhouse, riddled with woodworm, whose conical roof was losing its thatch like a man going bald, leaving an increasing number of holes through which wind and rain could attack the interior. The pub's name alluded to the opinion the locals traditionally had of the inhabitants of Angur. The crapaud was a species of toad found on that island, and Lesurians had long held the view that your typical Angurian was a spineless, sycophantic toady, so it is not difficult to see how the pub came by its name.

These days, however, the 'Quivering' part of the title could just as easily have referred to the fact that the whole place had a tendency to shake alarmingly every time the wind blew with anything greater than moderate force. It was perhaps surprising that nothing had so far been done about the increasingly decrepit state of the building, but then again Lesurians habitually left things until the last possible moment, especially if there was likely to be an element of cost involved.

The *Crapaud* was fairly busy when Grosnez and Piton walked in, it being around midday and the majority of its regulars who habitually went there for lunch already ensconced in their customary places. Distracted by the sound of the door opening and closing, a few of the customers glanced round to see who had entered and shot them looks that verged on the suspicious. Piton appeared a little put out by this reception, but Grosnez ignored it and strode up to the bar. While they waited for their beer, their eyes swept the pub for the one they had come to find.

At first they couldn't see him. Then Piton suddenly grabbed his master's arm and pointed to one of the log pillars that supported the roof. Standing behind it, so that it partly obscured him from their view, was Vraicer T'loch, a jar of beer in his right hand. He appeared to be on his own.

"Come on," muttered Grosnez, and they went over to join him.

T'loch was wearing a long grey cloak which completely enveloped his very tall, lean frame. He was taller even than Grosnez, who considered himself above average, and Piton always felt quite dwarfed in his presence. His long black hair framed a sallow face whose most notable features were the piercing, steely-grey eyes that seemed to look into the very depths of your soul, the bushy black moustache and the long, flowing, equally-black beard. As regards his age, you would estimate it to be near forty. Nobody knew for sure, however, and there were those who swore that he always looked the same, that he never seemed to get any older. It was whispered over jars of beer in dark corners of dingy pubs that he had discovered some magic elixir that kept him eternally young.

T'loch looked up as the two men approached him. "Ah! Grosnez Chatel and my little friend, Piton. How are you both?" His voice was rich, deep and sonorous, the accent foreign. He certainly could not have been mistaken for a native of these parts.

Grosnez did not look directly at him. He was well aware of T'loch's powers and abilities and he always felt distinctly uncomfortable in his presence. His eyes shifted around nervously. "I'm sorry to bother you, mon vier," he began in a low voice, "but it's a matter of some urgency."

"Go on." T'loch stared unblinkingly at the other.

"I'm planning to do something for our High Elder's Flint Jub'lee - a magnificent display of, er, magic."

"Oh yes?" T'loch did his best to keep any hint of scorn out of his voice.

"Yes, mon vier. I have some ideas, but I need some special liquid for the high point of my display."

"What sort of liquid?"

"One that glows."

"I see," said T'loch. He took a drink of his beer, not once removing his gaze from Grosnez' face. "It must be years since anyone asked me about the liquid that glows. You must indeed be planning something extra special. Tell me, how did you hear of it?"

The other shifted uncomfortably. "An old friend of mine whom I hadn't seen for a long time visited me recently," he lied, avoiding direct contact with T'loch's eyes. "We were talking about my display for the High Elder's Jub'lee and he suggested I use this magic liquid he'd heard about on his travels. He thought there was a container of the liquid somewhere on Angur, but he had no idea where." He looked hopefully at the other: "We were wondering if you might know."

"I might..., but then again, I might not," said T'loch enigmatically.

Grosnez frowned. He had feared that T'loch might be difficult, and it now looked as though that was going to be the case.

"Just suppose I do know and I tell you, what guarantee do I have that you won't use it for some nefarious purpose? You tell me that you're planning a display of magic for La Tanche's Jubilee, but I have only your word for that. Goodness knows what you might get up to with such a powerful substance - your reputation isn't exactly untainted."

Grosnez thought about this for a few moments. Then he said in a somewhat servile voice: "But, mon vier, even if I were to misuse it, I'm sure your magic is infinitely superior to mine and you would soon put me in my place."

T'loch permitted himself a smile. "You flatter me," he said. "And you do have a point." He glanced into his beer. "There is one problem, though."

"What's that?"

"Believe it or not, I don't know where the container in question is."

Grosnez tutted irritably. It looked as if he had wasted his time.

"But I do know someone who does," T'loch went on, mentally chuckling to himself as Grosnez breathed a huge sigh of relief. "And I am prepared to let you in on the secret - us magicians must stick together, eh?"

"Yes, yes," agreed Grosnez. "We must stick together."

"Right then. We'll go somewhere quiet where we can continue this conversation in peace; this place is too noisy." He looked around furtively. "Besides, pubs have very good ears."

CHAPTER SIX

THE MAGICIAN OF SERSUR

"Sersur!" Piton Le Malin's voice shrieked in panic. "I... I... d... don't want to go *there*."

"Well, if you want to get hold of that liquid," said T'loch matter-of-factly, "I'm afraid you're going to have to."

The three of them were sitting at a square wooden table in the main living-room of a small shack on the harbour front a couple of minutes' walk to the south of *The Quivering Crapaud*. Said dwelling belonged, according to T'loch, to a friend of his who was presently out, that worthy having a standing arrangement with T'loch that the latter could use his home if he so wished whenever he was in Lesur.

Grosnez broke off a hunk of bread from the loaf on the table, bit off a hefty chunk and noisily swigged some beer to wash it down.

"You're not afraid of Sersurians, you?" he asked scornfully, his mouth still half-full.

Piton started to mumble something, but T'loch cut in: "Don't worry. Verman Clouet lives on Little Sersur. The majority of the population live on the main island, and very few of them venture south across *La Coupée*. Little Sersur has a reputation for strange goings on – mysterious sounds and ghostly lights in the night – and these keep your average Sersurian well away. In reality," he looked reassuringly at Piton whose face was registering alarm at the prospect of meeting mysterious sounds and ghostly lights, "these odd happenings are merely old Verman's harmless experiments and nothing to worry about."

Piton looked relieved.

T'loch drank some beer and then helped himself to a couple of the oysters that constituted the main dish of their lunch.

"Mmm, I've noticed weird lights coming from there from time to time," said Grosnez. "And Clouet," he went on, grabbing a particularly juicy-looking oyster just as Piton was about to take it, "he knows where we can get hold of this container?" He fixed T'loch with a penetrating stare, having by now overcome his earlier reluctance to meet the other's gaze.

"I believe he does," said T'loch, staring at the other with equal penetration. "Yes, I'm sure he must. It's a long time now since it was buried, but he's old enough to remember." His eyes assumed a misty, far away expression. "Yes, he's old enough," he muttered distantly.

"Good," said Grosnez, slurping noisily as he relieved yet another shell of its oyster. "How do we find him?"

"Easily enough," said T'loch, refilling his clay jar with more beer from the large vessel on the table. "But you must follow my instructions carefully."

* * *

The journey over to Sersur was accomplished in good time, helped by an ebb tide and a stiff north-westerly breeze which allowed them to rely on sail power rather than Piton having to row. From Lennac they sailed past the west coast of Erimac, a couple of boats bobbing gently in the sparkling waters of the little harbour lying in front of the three small, round fishing huts nestling at the foot of the grassy slopes rising up to the island's central plateau. With seagulls screeching overhead, they then tacked south-east between Erimac and the green, vegetation cloaked hump of Jettac to aim for the west coast of Sersur.

* * *

After they left, T'loch remained in his friend's house, sitting quietly at the table, resting his head on the fingertips of his long, slender hands that were held together as if he were praying. When his friend came in some time later from the entrance behind him, he gave no immediate indication of noticing.

"Ah, Tourvel," he then said quietly, without looking up, "I didn't think you'd be too long."

Tourvel Le Crochon walked round to the other side of the table and sat down opposite T'loch. He was a rather ordinary-looking, elderly individual of average height, with no especially distinguishing features. "Yes, I got my bus'ness attended to quickly." His Lesurian accent was particularly thick. "That Jean Corbeau is easy to deal with, 'im."

"Good," said T'loch. He disengaged his hands and looked up. "Grosnez and Piton are on their way to Sersur to see Clouet. Verman will send them to Alb, to Piltdown for further directions."

"That should be fun for them," said Tourvel with a chuckle. "That poor Piton should enjoy going *there*."

T'loch nodded. "Indeed. But we have to be careful. Grosnez may be consumed with greed and envy, but he's no fool, and I suspect more capable than some of us realise. There are things in that part of Alb that he must not get his hands on."

* * *

The steep, granite cliffs of the west coast of Sersur loomed ahead, glowing red in the afternoon sunlight. The little boat sped along under full sail, the waves slapping noisily at its hull. Piton was ensconced at the stern, hand on the tiller, while Grosnez sat amidships facing him, his back hunched against the breeze and the spray that broke over the bows.

They sailed past Brecq, a small, flat-topped island inhabited only by shags and gulls lying just off Sersur's west coast about halfway between its northern and southern tips, and then Piton steered south-east. They were to land in a sandy cove on the western side of La Coupée, the nearly three-hundred-foot high narrow ridge of rock that connected the main island of Sersur to Little Sersur. As they neared the beach and Piton clambered past him to take the leather sail down, Grosnez turned and glowered at the practically sheer wall of vegetation-cloaked cliff facing him. This side of La Coupée may have been less formidable than the eastern side, but it still presented a daunting prospect to anyone wanting, or having, to climb it. At least it was a fine spring afternoon, so there was plenty of light.

Piton was glad that they were not arriving at night. He was only too familiar with the whispered tales of ghostly funeral processions that reputedly crossed La Coupée after dusk. Coming to this place by day was bad enough, but the mere thought of those things believed to take place during the hours of darkness sent nervous shivers tingling down his spine.

The boat hit bottom and Piton jumped out, the sea splashing up around his thighs. He drew a sharp intake of breath - despite the warmth of the day, the water was cold. He heaved on the bow rope to pull the vessel ashore. Needless to say, Grosnez did nothing to help, staying aboard until it was sufficiently clear of the sea so that he could alight without getting wet. Although Piton was by now well used to this behaviour, it still annoyed him.

He took down the mast, adroitly rolling the sail around it before laying them both in the base of the boat. Then, following Grosnez' orders, he dragged the craft up the beach and under cover of some rocks clear of the high water mark, where they hoped it would remain adequately concealed from prying eyes.

"Right", said Grosnez. "Let's get a move on. We've no time to waste." He strode off towards La Coupée with Piton following a few paces behind, muttering oaths beneath his breath at his master's expense.

As they approached the base of the rock face, they noticed that a narrow path cut into it wound sinuously up to the top where it emerged at the north end of the ridge. Piton's heart sank when he realised this, as traversing the legendary narrowness of the summit of La Coupée was an activity he did not relish.

The climb up, however, proved no worse than that Piton regularly had to undertake at home between the cave where their boats were moored and his master's cliff-top residence – and that was one he had often done at night, sometimes under a clouded sky with no moon or even starlight to aid visibility.

When they reached the top, a trifle hot and breathless after the climb, they stopped to survey their surroundings. Piton flopped down on the grass and fearfully looked around him, half-expecting to be set upon at any moment by a band of bloodthirsty Sersurians who, he was certain, would have no qualms whatsoever about tossing him over the edge.

Grosnez rested for a few minutes himself, but, keen to move on, was soon on his feet again.

"Come on," he said, grabbing his companion roughly by the scruff of his neck and hauling him to his feet, "I don't want to hang around here all day."

"Aw, Grosnez!" protested Piton.

"Well, I can always leave you here for some Sersurians to find." His face twisted into a leer: "You'd like that, wouldn't you?"

Piton needed no further encouragement. After anxiously glancing northwards at the main plateau area of Sersur, its central forest just as gloomy and foreboding as that on Angur, he began to follow his master across La Coupée.

The ridge ran in a southerly direction for about one hundred feet, curving gently down towards the mid-way point and from there gradually rising for the remainder of its length. Although never less than a couple of feet wide at its narrowest, the steep cliff face on its west side and especially the vertiginous drop on its eastern one made traversing the ridge a decidedly nerve-racking experience for those not used to it and who lacked a good head for heights.

Grosnez was not one of the latter and strode quickly across. From the safety of Little Sersur, he looked back at his servant, who was still on his way across.

"Come on!" he called impatiently.

"I'm coming, Grosnez. I'm coming!" squeaked Piton in reply as he tottered momentarily on the ridge. Regaining his balance, he hurried across to join his master.

"I didn't like that!" he declared, his heart thumping in his chest.

Grosnez ignored him. He nodded towards the dirt track nestling between grassy banks and leading away from La Coupée. "According to T'loch," he said, "we follow this track until it forks, at which point we take the left fork. Then we go along a lane until we come to a right turn by a menhir." He paused briefly. "Let's go."

They headed along the track, leaving La Coupée behind. They were both glad of their fur jackets for, although the spring sun was still quite warm, a chilly breeze had arisen with the waning of the afternoon and the approach of evening.

The further away from La Coupée and the main island of Sersur they got, the more relaxed Piton became and the less frequently he glanced behind him, although he remained apprehensive about meeting Verman Clouet. He started to enjoy the beauty and tranquillity of his surroundings, peering through the gaps that occasionally opened in the banks to reveal fields where sheep, goats or aurochs grazed contentedly.

Before too long they reached the aforementioned fork and went left as instructed. The right-hand one led to a cluster of wooden roundhouses, smoke rising from the top of their conical thatched roofs as fires were lit as the day grew chillier. This was the only village on Little Sersur and Piton was relieved to observe that none of its inhabitants appeared to be out and about. He was not sure what sort of reaction his and his master's presence would elicit.

The lane they were now walking along wound this way and that as it meandered around and between outcrops of grey, lichen-covered rocks half-hidden in clumps of yellow-flowered gorse. It was also rising slightly, but it soon levelled off again while at the same time becoming straighter. Piton then noticed a large and particularly malevolent-looking specimen of aurochs chewing on some gorse in the field to the left of the track and uncomfortably close to their route. It snorted when it saw the two humans and began to stamp a front hoof on the ground, simultaneously fixing them with a baleful stare.

"Gr.. Grosnez," began Piton in a whining voice.

The other ignored him. "Ah! That must be the menhir." He nodded towards a large granite standing stone a short distance ahead to the right of the track. "Come on!" he called as he strode towards the menhir. "That beast won't harm you."

Piton was not so sure. He began to walk slowly past the aurochs, almost falling over the bank bordering the opposite side of the track so intent was he on keeping as far away from the animal as possible.

The latter glowered at him, snorting regularly, head lowered, emphasizing the massive shoulders. Suddenly it gave forth a fearsome bellow, causing Piton to trip over a stone in panic and sending him sprawling on to the hard, dusty surface of the track.

As his hapless servant slowly got to his feet, Grosnez laughed heartily: "That was a good one, that!" he said, chuckling.

"I don't think that was funny," said the other, brushing himself down with his hands.

Grosnez did not respond, but walked on, still chuckling. He turned right at the standing stone and headed down another track.

Piton, keen to be clear of the aurochs, hastened to catch up with his master. Glancing up at the grey form of the distinctively shaped, ten-foot-high menhir as he walked past it, two cup-shaped hollows about two-thirds of the way up the side facing him caught his eye, and these together with a crack in the rock running down from them and a slight ridge below this and almost at right angles to it, like a nose and a mouth, gave him the impression of a face watching him. Still nervous after his encounter with the aurochs, he hurried on.

The DRAGON of ANGUR

The track at first gradually, but then more steeply, descended into a coastal valley. To the left, the grass and gorse-covered slope, interspersed with the occasional tree or small copse of trees, rose gently upwards towards the skyline, while to the right it fell more steeply towards the forested valley floor.

After running more or less straight for a few hundred yards, the track began to turn to the left, following the curve of the valley slope, now steeper, rockier and more sparsely covered with vegetation as the valley opened out as it approached the coast. A little further round the cliff face, the track came to an abrupt end and Grosnez and Piton found themselves on a wide, rocky platform at the mouth of the valley.

They looked around. A couple of seagulls screeched loudly overhead and waves crashed noisily on the rocks below. The salty tang of a stiff, sea-borne breeze ruffled their hair and assaulted their nostrils.

"There should be a door or entrance here somewhere," said Grosnez, studying his surroundings. "Aha!" he exclaimed. "There it is!" He pointed towards part of the cliff face, near the end of the platform.

Piton followed the other's outstretched arm to where what appeared to be a granite lintel supported by two upright monoliths jutted out from the cliff. They walked towards this and found that the stones framed a low, heavy-looking oaken door. Grosnez strode up to it and rapped loudly on it with his right hand.

Almost immediately, the ancient door creaked noisily open, seemingly unaided. Grosnez and Piton waited. No one appeared and only darkness beckoned from inside. They looked at each other. Piton's heart was thumping in his chest.

Grosnez stooped and peered into the blackness. "Hello!" he called. "Anyone at home?"

Nothing.

Grosnez called again. Suddenly he noticed disembodied flames flickering ahead of him and quickly realised that these belonged to torches illuminating a stone-lined passage. He frowned. Strange how they had suddenly appeared as if lit by magic. He smiled at the thought. *Magic, of course!*

He turned to his servant: "Come on, Piton," he said brightly. "Let's go in and meet the venerable Clouet."

Piton looked doubtful, but knew better than to argue. Reluctantly, he followed his master's bent form as the latter stooped to negotiate the doorway.

The low, narrow passage they found themselves in was rather reminiscent of that in a typical passage-dolmen, as its walls were built of large stone uprights, although the roof, as far as they could make out, seemed to have been carved out of solid rock. Illumination was provided by animal-grease torches set into the spaces between every three uprights on the left side of the passage. They had a way of spontaneously bursting into flames as Grosnez and his servant approached and self-extinguishing once they had passed them that spooked Piton comprehensively.

The passage suddenly curved sharply to the right, then to the left before running straight again. A few yards further on, it began to heighten and they were able to proceed without Grosnez having to stoop. At the same time, they noticed that some of the megalithic uprights of the walls bore decorations, single and double spiral motifs not native to the islands. Piton had no idea what they meant, and if Grosnez knew, he was not telling.

Then, almost without warning, the passage opened out into a large octagonal chamber whose sides leaned gradually inwards as they rose up to disappear into the gloom above. The ceiling was not visible.

A fire burned brightly in a hearth in the centre of the chamber, the flames occasionally springing up and simultaneously turning pink or blue for no apparent reason.

Alcoves filled with clay jars of varying shapes and sizes were set seemingly haphazardly into the walls, while other jars reposed on a couple of wooden tables standing on either side of the hearth and a little way from it. Piles of stone tablets lay on the floor along with a few coiled up, knotted ropes, with some more tablets propped up against the walls.

Apart from the fire, additional illumination was provided by torches, similar to the ones in the passage, set into the walls above some, but by no means all, of the alcoves.

"C.. come in! C.. come in!" a rather frail sounding voice suddenly croaked, echoing feebly around the chamber so that it was difficult to pin-point its source. There was a sizzling sound and blue flames leapt up in the hearth. "Vraicer said you'd be coming."

"Verman?" called Grosnez, glancing around. "Verman Clouet?"

"The same," croaked the voice. The blue flames died down. More sizzling. Pink flames. "D.. do forgive me. I wasn't expect.. expecting you so soon."

A thin, white-cloaked figure, almost spectral in its aspect, then appeared from the other side of the hearth, bending slightly forward as it seemed to glide slowly over the floor towards them. The long fingers of its right hand were closed around the top of a particularly knobbly stick while those of its left held on to two small, leathery pouches. The hood of the cloak was down, revealing a high-domed head from which a mass of grey, almost white hair erupted uncontrollably to cascade on to the shoulders. The face framed by this hirsute jungle echoed the thinness of the body it surmounted: long and bony with a pointed nose and an equally pointed chin. The eyes were bright, almost unnaturally so.

As Verman Clouet approached Grosnez and Piton, the gliding motion became a shuffling one. He transferred the pouches to the hand in control of the stick and stretched out his left arm, beckoning them.

"W.. welcome. W.. welcome to my humble abode." He turned slowly around. "C.. Come!" He began to retrace his steps, shuffling back towards the far side of the hearth.

The other two followed him. Piton was somewhat unnerved by his general appearance, but Grosnez was totally unfazed. He led them round to three rather rickety-looking chairs arranged facing the hearth and motioned them to sit down in the outer two, carefully lowering himself into the centre one.

"Right," said Clouet, letting his stick drop on to the floor next to him. "How can I help you?" He stared into the blazing hearth.

"Well," began Grosnez. "As you doubtless know, it is Cou-Cou La Tanche's Flint..."

"How...how was your cr.. crossing?" asked Clouet suddenly.

"Not bad, thanks," said Piton.

Grosnez leaned forward and looked past Clouet to glare at Piton. "Yes, yes, it was all right. Now, as I was saying, it's La Tanche's Flint Jub'lee and there are various contests planned. I myself am in..."

"The fire," mumbled Clouet. He fumbled with one of the pouches, got it open and reached inside with his right hand. Then, with a surprisingly deft movement, he threw something at the hearth.

There was a sudden sizzling and pink flames leapt upwards. "That's better."

Grosnez tried not to show his irritation at being interrupted. "As I was saying, I am involved in the pr'ceedings and I've planned a display of magic which I hope will be worthy of the occasion."

Clouet looked at him, the bright eyes unblinking. Then he returned his gaze to the hearth.

"Occasion?" he queried after a few moments of silence.

Grosnez tutted in spite of himself. "Yes. Our High Elder's Flint Jub'lee."

"Ah... yes. Of course." Clouet was still staring into the fire. The pink flames had died down.

"I'm planning a magic display," continued Grosnez, "the climax of which should be the most exciting ever seen in Angur."

The hand reached inside the second leather pouch. Another deft movement. Sizzling. Blue flames.

"Ah! I'm so... so sorry. How rude of me! You must be, er, hungry and thirsty after your journey." Clouet turned to Piton: "Especially you. Let.. Let me get you both some, er, thing."

"That's an excellent idea, that!" said Piton with enthusiasm.

"Piton!" Grosnez glared at his servant, then turned to Clouet: "Thank you, but we're not that hungry. We had something before we left Lesur."

"No, I.. I insist," said Clouet. "You must have something. I usually eat at, er, this time in any case. And it's time to feed the, er, little.. the little ones."

So saying, he put both pouches down by the side of his chair, leaned forward to get his stick from where it reposed on the floor and then creaked slowly to his feet.

Grosnez followed the other's slowly receding back with a malevolent stare. After Clouet had left the chamber through an entrance that had suddenly appeared in one of the walls, an irate Chatel rounded on his servant: "From now on, you say nothing," he hissed. "It's going to be difficult enough getting the information we need out of that old fool without you encouraging him to go off at tangents."

Piton said nothing, just sat and stared disconsolately into the fire. He knew better than to voice his thoughts when his master was annoyed. After a while, he risked a sideways glance at Grosnez, who was sitting back in his chair, eyes closed, slowly massaging his goatee, clearly deep in contemplation.

Piton returned his gaze to the hearth. He sat back, letting the flames bathe him with their warmth. He yawned. His eyelids began to feel heavy. Slowly, but inexorably they moved downwards over his eyes while his chin tried to bury itself in the collar of his fur jacket as his head bent forward under the weight of drowsiness.

Suddenly, a cacophony of whooping and yelping, punctuated by staccato barks, erupted without warning, shattering the peace of the chamber and causing Piton to sit bolt upright in terror.

"Wh.. what's *th.. that*?" he stammered, eyes suddenly wide open, darting wildly about him.

Grosnez listened, head cocked to one side. The sound was slightly muffled and seemed to be coming from underneath them. It was evidently being made by some kind of animal, or, to be more precise, animals – he quickly concluded that more than one creature was responsible for the racket, but exactly what species he was at a loss to determine. It was somewhat reminiscent of a pack of dogs, and yet it was not dogs; of that he was certain.

"I know," he said, turning to Piton after a few moments' thought. "They must be Clouet's 'little ones'."

Piton shifted uncomfortably in his chair.

"I shouldn't ask too many questions," Grosnez went on. "Prob'bly best not to know."

Piton put his hands over his ears to cut out the noise and gazed mournfully into the fire. The yelping and whooping and barking continued for a while longer, but then subsided until it was no longer audible. Grosnez communicated this information to Piton, whose face registered relief on finding it to be true.

Not long after that, Verman Clouet reappeared, muttering to himself as he shuffled into the chamber with the aid of his stick. A large round wooden tray containing hunks of bread arranged around a steaming clay bowl was somehow supported by the index finger of his right hand. Three smaller bowls were stacked alongside the large one.

"Please.. please, er, hold this," he said when he reached his guests, indicating the tray with a nod of his head.

Grosnez motioned to Piton, who got up to take the tray from Clouet. As he relieved Verman of the article, he very nearly dropped it as it was unexpectedly heavy. Although he managed to hold on, some of the beefy broth inside the bowl slopped over its edge.

Clouet walked off into the shadows and then returned with a round, wooden table which he set down in front of the chairs.

"Help, er, help your, er, selves," he said as Piton put the tray down on the table. He proceeded to dip one of the small bowls into the broth, picked up a hunk of bread and walked unsteadily to his chair, his stick under his left arm.

Piton needed no encouragement and was soon ensconced in his chair, tucking into the food.

"So," said Clouet as Grosnez filled the remaining bowl, "you, er, need something for your, er, magic display."

"That's right!" said Piton excitedly, mouth full of meat. "A glowing liquid!"

Grosnez glared at him as he resumed his seat. "Yes, my loquacious servant is quite right. We saw T'loch in Lesur and he thought you'd be able to help us."

"Ah, T'loch!" said Clouet dreamily. "How is the, er, dear fellow?"

"Very well," said Grosnez hurriedly, not wishing to dwell on the matter of T'loch's health. "Now, about this liquid. We've been led to b'lieve that there's a container of it on Angur, but we don't know exactly where."

"You need to find someone called 'Stone-Ears'," began Clouet, chewing with evident difficulty on a piece of meat.

"*Stone-Ears?*" repeated Grosnez, queryingly.

"Yes," said Clouet, pulling a lump of gristle out of his mouth and throwing it in the fire, which signified its appreciation of the donation with a barely perceptible sizzle. "'Stone-Ears' Meade."

Clouet went on to explain that the individual concerned, whom he had known for many years, went by the name of Meade because of his fondness for a certain honey-based drink. If one plied him with liberal quantities of said beverage, it loosened his tongue to a remarkable degree and he could easily be persuaded to divulge everything he knew on the subject in question.

"I seem.. seem to recall that, er, old 'Stone-Ears' was a good, er, a good friend of the magician who orig.. who originally owned this particular cont.. container of, er, liquid." He picked up his jar of ale, put it shakily to his lips and took a few sips. A dribble escaped down his chin. "From.. from what he, er, told me once, the magician, knowing the liquid's, er, powers, poured it into a, er, special, er, vial which he hid in some, er, place, and confided its location in.. in him."

"And this Meade didn't by any chance tell you where it was?" prompted Grosnez, hopefully.

Verman shook his head, in the process spilling some of the contents of his jar, which he was still holding. "No, he, er, did not. He never would – at least not while, er, sober." He looked at Grosnez, reading the latter's thoughts: "And he was, er, sober when we spoke." He picked another piece of meat out of his bowl and popped it into his mouth. "But if you were to get him, er, sufficiently inebriated, then..."

"He would tell us?" Grosnez finished his sentence for him.

"I, er, believe he would."

"And where do we find this Meade?"

Clouet partook of another piece of meat, which he attempted to assist on its way with a mouthful of ale. Unfortunately, said chunk of beef was washed the wrong way, sending old Verman into paroxysms of spluttering and choking. Fearful that he would expire before divulging the information Grosnez needed, the latter went to his assistance and after much thumping and massaging of his back, he regained his composure.

"Th.. Thank you," spluttered Clouet.

"Have a drink," said Grosnez, holding the jar to the other's lips.

That worthy took a few sips. "That's better," he said wheezily. "Now, where, er, was I?... Ah, yes, the liquid." He peered at Grosnez: "Why do you, er, want it again?"

"The contest," replied Grosnez, trying not to show his exasperation.

"Ah yes, the, er, contest." He dipped his bread into his broth and shoved the broth-soaked piece into his mouth. A second later, he coughed and Grosnez feared the onset of another fit of choking, but the other recovered his composure and Grosnez relaxed.

"Yes, the liquid," said Clouet. "As you, er, said, the jar containing it is on Angur, but 'Stone-Ears' himself lives in Alb." He paused for effect. "In Piltdown."

Piltdown! Piton's heart sank when he heard this. It was bad enough that the land of Alb lay many days' journey to the north of the islands, but such was the reputation of the village of Piltdown that people living far beyond the shores of Alb knew of it. The idea of actually going there sent most people into terminal decline.

"I'm, er, afraid so," continued Clouet. "When you get to, er, Piltdown, ask for 'Stone-Ears' by name. Everyone knows him."

"From what I've heard," said Grosnez as he got up to help himself to more broth, "Piltdown isn't the safest place to visit."

"That, er, depends," said Clouet in an enigmatic tone, but did not elaborate. He yawned. "It's getting, er, late. You will, of course, be staying for the, er, night." This was said as a statement of fact rather than being posed as a question.

Piton was relieved to hear this and equally relieved when he realised that his master was not going to question the idea.

While they finished their food, Clouet gave them basic directions on how to get to Piltdown. Then, without further ado, he showed them to the two small, cave-like chambers where they would spend the night, and which he reserved for guests.

CHAPTER SEVEN

A NOCTURNAL VISIT

The Sun was barely above the horizon when Grosnez and Piton left Sersur. As the latter pulled steadily on the oars, he mentally cursed his master for insisting on setting off when most decent people were still in bed. He was feeling particularly tired, having not slept very well, despite the comfort of his surroundings. His slumbering had been disturbed by nightmares about being chased up and down stairways and along corridors by whooping and yelping creatures of indefinable form.

He wondered what on earth could be wrapped up in the skin bundle Grosnez had been carrying when he had awakened him, and which he was now cradling so carefully in his lap, but, as his tentative enquiry as to its identity had met with a curt "Never mind!", it was doubtless something his master should not have taken and thus the reason for their hurried departure from the island without even saying goodbye to their host.

Grosnez was staring past his servant at the slowly receding face of La Coupée, black against the gradually brightening sky beyond, and thinking about what Verman Clouet had told them. He was not sure that he believed Clouet's claim that he was ignorant of the whereabouts of the container with the mysterious glowing liquid, but there was nothing he could do about that. At least he now knew where to find someone who did know its exact location.

There was just one problem. Although, Clouet had given precise directions as regards finding the place, it would take quite a few days to get there; at least two by boat to Alb's southern coast and about the same by foot to the village itself. Time was of the essence as far as Grosnez was concerned, and the length of the intended journey did not please him in the slightest. But if he wanted to discover the location of that container, he would have to go - no matter how long it took - and that was all there was to it.

Then an idea suddenly struck him. Of course! It was so simple he wondered why he hadn't thought of it before. He was smiling as he turned to his servant:

"Piton, mon vier, I've just had an excellent idea. We have to get to this Piltdown place, and we have to get there as quickly as poss'ble. To go by boat would take far too long, so I pr'pose to fly."

"To fly? You mean, like through the air?"

"Yes, mon vier."

Piton looked somewhat bemused. "And how're you going to do that, Grosnez?"

"Simple. I'll get the dragon to fly us there; he's more than capable of carrying us. Don't just sit there gawking, fool; row as fast as you can. There are plans to be made and I want to see Mauger tonight."

* * *

T'loch was a little concerned. Although the meeting with Clouet had gone very well and those two would soon be on their way to Piltdown, Grosnez' theft of the sea-dragon egg was an unexpected and unwelcome development. He was very fond of old Verman, but for somebody with his powers and resources he ought to take better care of his possessions. In the case of sea-dragon eggs in particular, magicians had a special responsibility.

T'loch had spent the night in Lesur and had intended to return to Angur in the morning, but in the light of what had happened, he decided he had better make a detour via Little Sersur and drop in on the venerable Clouet in person.

* * *

While the lanky one and his spindly servant had been skulking around in Lesur and Sersur, Gastelois de Bois had been going over his proposed dolmen site with his assistant, Pierre de Lecq. The following morning, they returned to continue their survey. The idea today was to go over the area with hazel divining switches to check for blind springs and associated water courses[6], whose

---

[6] A blind spring, or water dome, is an up-flow of geothermal water rising through the earth under high temperature and pressure, which strikes an impermeable rock layer and then spreads out in all directions through any available spaces. Where these veins of underground water cross each other, a spiralling energy is created, which can be tapped into by placing a standing stone of a suitable rock type (quartz-rich granite being particularly effective) over the crossing point.

location played a very important role in the siting of a dolmen. If the presence of these was detected, the next stage would be the clearance of vegetation from the area so that they could be mapped out on the ground, in preparation for the staking out of the ground plan of the dolmen. The latter was done by referring to a previously-prepared plan made to scale by punching holes in a piece of animal hide to represent the positions of the upright stones that would form the walls of the dolmen, the plan being adjusted to take account of the subterranean water system.

In fact, there were a number of such plans 'doing the rounds', so to speak, and for those who wanted – or needed – to build a dolmen quickly, or who were just not particularly innovative, they were a godsend. The main problem with them, though, was that, as they were similar to a stencil, the final form of the dolmen was entirely dependant on how you viewed the plan and what you took to be the right side up. This explained why the *Rutual* passage-dolmen in Armor was a mirror image of the Arbreur Le Bois designed *Levitation House* upon which it was based.

Gastelois, however, fully intended to create a brand new design in honour of the High Elder's Flint Jubilee; not for him the cop out of using a pre-existing plan.

The location he had chosen was near the eastern edge of the Angurian plateau and commanded fine views of the sea and the coast of Armor beyond. The latter came very close to Angur on this side of the island, and only a relatively narrow channel, with tidal flats on either side, separated them. A strong swimmer could make the crossing with minimal difficulty, and in fact at the time of the extremely low equinoctial tides, it was even possible to wade across, although this could be quite a hazardous undertaking due to the existence of areas of quicksand.

On its landward side, the site bordered strips of fields that stretched westwards towards the brooding mass of the great central forest, while not very far away to its south-south-east, nestling lower down in the shadow of a grassy col, lay the little hamlet of Gor, named after the individual who had founded it. Although Gastelois had a regular team of specialists, he was confident that he could obtain the bulk of the additional workforce required for the new dolmen from there.

"I'm sure Gor will oblige," he said to Pierre as they walked over the site with their forked, y-shaped divining twigs (every descendant of the founder who became chieftain of the hamlet assumed his name upon taking office).

"I can't see there being a problem," agreed his assistant. He frowned. "This gorse will take some clearing; it's pretty thick. It's not making checking for springs partic'larly easy." He adjusted his grip on the hazel switch in his hands.

"We've coped with worse in the past," said Gastelois.

"That's true, that." Pierre scratched his tousled black hair. "Have you decided on the dolmen's design yet?"

"Not exactly," replied the other. "But I do have some ideas. Once we've got this area cleared, we'll get our stakes and try them out." At that moment, his twig suddenly jerked upwards, so forceably that it was very nearly wrenched from his grip. He glanced at Pierre and smiled: "That was a strong one! I think we've got something here." He walked slowly forwards, concentrating hard as he pushed his way through the gorse. "Definitely a spiral," he said after a few moments.

Pierre's hazel suddenly twitched in his hands. "Another one over here, Gastelois," he announced.

"Doesn't surprise me. I had a feeling about this place." He looked up at the Sun. "Well, time's getting on. We can double-check these two springs and look for others once we've cleared the site. Right now, I suggest we go and see Gor about workmen. If we're very lucky, we might even be able to make a start after lunch."

Pierre thought that that was being unduly optimistic, but kept his opinion to himself as he did not want to dampen Gastelois' enthusiasm.

* * *

By the end of that afternoon, Gastelois had assembled a team of workmen from Gor and he and Pierre had also notified the five specialists who regularly assisted them with the construction of dolmens. That evening he held a meeting in Gor's pub, *The Quernstone*, to discuss the project and to give the workforce a "goodwill" drink. This was traditional before the start of any building project and was done to encourage the loyalty of the workers. Before such projects were completed, further sessions invariably ensued to guarantee their continuing loyalty.

Later that evening, Sylvia d'Arass visited Gastelois at home to show him some rough charcoal sketches she had drawn of possible designs to decorate the interior faces of the orthostats of the new dolmen. She timed her arrival well, as he had only just arrived back from Gor. While she unrolled the animal skins and laid them on the floor of the main living area of his house, he went to get some refreshments.

"Those look excellent!" he said enthusiastically when he returned with two jars of cider, handing one to Sylvia. He stirred the cauldron of seafood stew simmering over the hearth in the centre of the room.

"Well, they're only some preliminary ideas," she said in a slightly dismissive tone. "They'll require quite a bit more work before I'm anywhere near satisfied with them."

Gastelois ladled some stew into a bowl and handed it to Sylvia.

"Thanks," she said. "How are your plans coming along?"

"Getting there," he said, taking a bowl himself. "I've had a few ideas, and I'd welcome your input."

He knelt on the floor next to Sylvia's hides. Picking one of them up, he scrutinised the spirals and general curvilinear patterns covering it. He put it back down and lifted another in its place. This had chevron patterns in horizontal rows with a series of parallel wavy lines above and below these near the top and bottom of the skin.

"I might do the chevrons in red ochre," said Sylvia, watching for Gastelois' reaction, "and the lines in charcoal."

"That should look pretty good," he commented, "especially set against a white background."

"That's what I thought," agreed Sylvia. She ate a few spoonfuls of seafood stew. "Mmm, this is delicious!" She washed the food down with some cider. "Talking of white backgrounds, I went to the quarry today to see about getting the clay I need."

"Ah yes. And how was the estimable Handois?" enquired Gastelois. Handois Argile-Blanc was the owner-manager of the island's only white clay quarry, which was sited near the northern end of one of the valleys that cleft the central area of the Angurian plateau and ran southwards towards the Bay of Aube.

"He was his usual cheery self," replied Sylvia. "But it actually turned out to be quite an entertaining visit."

"Oh? Why was that?"

"When I arrived, Handois was in the process of being inspected by Toubib…"

"Le Véroleux?" Gastelois interrupted her.

"The same," confirmed Sylvia. "He was there with one of his cronies from Health and Safety – François Le Modeste."

"I bet *that* had a lot to say for itself," observed Gastelois sarcastically.

"Oh yes!" Sylvia took a sip of cider. "When I arrived and saw them, I wasn't sure why they were there, but I got the impression that there had been some kind of incident which Toubib and François were investigating." She drank some more cider. "Handois told me later – after Toubib and the other one had left – that there'd been a minor accident the day before. Anyway, when I got to the quarry, François was standing on a wooden platform next to the lake attempting to show everyone how something or the other should be done when he slipped off the platform and took a dive straight into the water, head first."

"Excellent!" declared Gastelois between a couple of spoonfuls of seafood stew. He swallowed a mouthful. "What happened next?"

"Oh, François clambered out of the lake, completely white from head to foot – you know what those clay quarry ponds are like."

Gastelois nodded. He put his bowl down on the floor and picked up his cider jar. "He must've been a happy chap," he said as he put the vessel's rim to his lips.

"You could say that! He looked as though he'd just slipped into a chic little white number for a special occasion. He was far from amused when one of Handois' workers told him: "You look nice in that, mon vier!" I mean, if looks could've killed."

Gastelois laughed: "I wish I'd been there."

"You'd have enjoyed it," confirmed Sylvia. "You've had a few run-ins with that lot before, haven't you?"

"The Committee for Health and Safety? Yes, I've had occasion to regret their existence." He resumed the consumption of his seafood stew. "So you managed to sort out what you need?"

"Yes. After Toubib had gone, I eventually managed to steer Handois away from his moans and gripes about the world at large and life in general and tell him what I wanted, and he said that that would be no problem. He said just to let him know when I needed the clay and he would make sure it was delivered to the dolmen."

The DRAGON of ANGUR

"Good."

They finished their stew. Sylvia declined a second bowl, but accepted a top up of cider.

They then spent the rest of the evening talking about the new dolmen. Gastelois showed her the charcoal sketches he'd done of his current ideas for its design. She was, on the whole, complimentary, but thought he might have some problems with the *Pouquelaye and Earthworks Committee* over his proposals for the side chambers.

"We'll see," was his response to that. "Nothing ventured, nothing gained!"

Eventually, after much talk lubricated by quite a few ciders, Sylvia began to feel somewhat sleepy.

"Well," she said, yawning, "it's getting rather late. I'd best be going."

"You could always stay here for the night," said Gastelois, looking at her hopefully.

She shook her head. "Best not. I can't afford to let Marguérite or Pierre-Juste see me leaving here in the morning."

"I thought that didn't bother you."

"It does and it doesn't," said Sylvia enigmatically.

Gastelois decided not to push the point. "Let me walk you home then," he offered gallantly.

"That would be nice."

* * *

It was shortly after midnight when two figures crept furtively across the marsh to the south of the dragon's home. The night was clear and the Moon nearly full, so they were able to see where they were going without difficulty.

"Are you sure this is a good idea, Grosnez?" Piton asked his master. He was well aware of the opinion Old Mauger had of the two of them and so never liked to get too close to him.

"Of course it is, dolt!" replied Grosnez scornfully. "I never have bad ideas, me."

"But s.supposing he doesn't want to fly us to Piltdown. What then?" Piton was certain that the dragon would only take them under the strongest protest, and in fact he was fervently hoping that Mauger would refuse point blank - the idea of flying through the air clinging to the back of a dragon terrified him, to put it mildly.

Sinclair Forrest

"I'll persuade him," said Grosnez. "Now just keep quiet and follow me. I want to get into his cave without waking him before I'm ready. Is that clear?"

"Yes, Grosnez. Perfectly, Grosnez."

Grosnez led the way along the narrow, grassy paths that intersected the marsh's shallow pools of still, brackish water. The raucous chorus of myriad croaking frogs disturbed the nocturnal peace, and all but drowned the sound of the waves breaking on the shore not very far to the south. A moderate breeze was blowing from that direction, bringing with it the salty tang of the sea.

They eventually reached the base of the cliff in whose face the dragon's cave was located, stopping by the steep slope of scree that led up to its mouth.

"What now?" whispered Piton, his heart thumping apprehensively in his chest.

Grosnez was standing perfectly still, listening intently, his head cocked to one side and a hand cupping his right ear. "Shh!" he hissed. "I'm trying to hear if he's asleep."

"But Grosnez, if he's sleeping, you won't hear anything, you."

"Quiet, fool!" ordered the other. "Surely you're aware of the fact that Mauger snores - everyone is. I'm listening for that."

Piton nodded slowly, looking suitably chastened. "Of course," he whispered. "I'd forgotten about that." He began to listen too, his large ears pricked up in an attempt to catch the slightest sound.

Grosnez was straining hard to hear what he wanted to hear. *Curse those frogs!* It was virtually impossible to hear anything above their infernal croaking. If he'd had a suitable potion with him, he'd have tossed it into the marsh and silenced them for good.

At last, however, a faint but distinct noise reached his ears, and it was definitely the sound of snoring. *Good old Mauger*, thought Grosnez. *As predictable as ever.* He turned to his servant:

"Come on," he whispered. "He's asleep. We're going up. Now not a sound. Don't speak or do anything unless I specific'lly tell you to. Got that?"

Piton nodded. Then an idea occurred to him. "Gr.Grosnez," he said softly. "Grosnez, per'aps I could stay down here and keep a lookout... in case anyone comes."

The DRAGON of ANGUR

The other shot him a disdainful look. He knew very well why Piton wanted to remain where he was. "Certainly not! I want you in the cave with me. Nobody's going to come - not at this time of the night." With that, he began to climb the scree slope, treading carefully so as to make as little noise as possible.

Piton followed him reluctantly, glaring daggers at his back. He was feeling absolutely wrecked after his long row back from Sersur and wished he were in bed asleep, where all decent people should be at this hour, not out here in this marsh paying nocturnal visits on dragons. Mauger was not going to be happy when he saw them, and Piton did not relish the prospect of being in the cave with him when they woke him.

They reached the entrance to the dragon's home without incident, and Grosnez peered into the darkness beyond. They could both hear Mauger's snoring very distinctly now, and, after a few moments Grosnez fancied he could make out a large mass lying on the floor a little way in from the entrance.

"Come on!" he whispered to his companion. "Let's get on with it."

Piton followed him into the cave, both of them stepping very carefully so as to avoid waking the dragon prematurely. As their eyes grew accustomed to the gloom, they could see Mauger's sleeping form with increasing clarity. Lying there peacefully, his scaly chest rising and falling rhythmically with his noisy breathing and smoke drifting lazily from his broad nostrils, he did not look particularly terrifying - despite his bulk and the fact that he was a dragon - and after a short while, Piton found himself feeling a little more relaxed about their enterprise, although it would be untrue to say that some misgivings did not remain.

Grosnez studied the creature for a few minutes, stroking his chin pensively. At length he walked slowly over to Mauger's large head and knelt by his right ear.

"Mauger," he said softly but firmly. "Mauger, wake up. I want a word with you."

The dragon did not stir, but continued to snore peacefully.

Grosnez tried again, speaking more loudly. This time the dragon stirred slightly and emitted a sort of groan. Piton involuntarily took a step backwards. Grosnez had another go:

"Mauger, wake up! I need to talk to you. Come on, wake up!"

The creature groaned again, a little louder than before. He moved his head slightly and then let out a long sigh. His right eye opened slowly, blinked, and then regarded Grosnez fixedly.

"That's right, worm, wake up. I want to talk to you."

Old Mauger yawned and emitted another sigh. "Grosnez Chatel! What do you want?" he asked in a languid voice, still half-asleep.

"I need a favour of you."

"What? Now?" He moved his head slightly and peered myopically through the entrance of his home. "It's still dark!"

"Yes, Mauger, it's still dark. I'm sorry about the time, but I had to see you urgently."

"Is that why you've disturbed me in the middle of the night?"

"Yes."

The dragon grunted, turned his head slightly and noticed Piton who was trying to hide out of his sight in a recess in the cave's wall. "And I see you've kept poor little Piton up way past his bedtime," he said sarcastically. "Couldn't it have waited until morning?"

"No," said Grosnez. "Time is of the essence."

Another grunt. "I see: in a hurry as usual, Grosnez."

"Some matters can't wait, Mauger."

"Evidently." He sighed. "All right. Let's get this over with so I can get back to sleep. What do you want?"

Grosnez took a deep breath. "I want you to fly me and my servant somewhere."

"*Fly* you?" The dragon made no attempt to disguise his surprise.

"Yes, Mauger, fly. You do remember how to fly?"

"Of course I do," retorted the other scornfully. "But where to, for goodness sake?"

"A small village called Piltdown, in the land of Alb."

"But that's a long way away! Why do you want to go there?"

"That's my business, but I've got to get there as quickly as poss'ble."

Mauger snorted, then accidentally inhaled some smoke which precipitated a noisy fit of coughing which had Piton cringing in his recess. When he had recovered, he said: "Well, if you're going to take that attitude, I won't bother helping you. Now go away and leave me in peace."

The DRAGON of ANGUR

Grosnez sighed. "Oh all right, I'll tell you - but only if you promise to keep it to yourself."

"Very well."

"It's to do with something I'm planning for La Tanche's Jub'lee."

"Oh yes?" Mauger nearly said something else, but thought better of it.

"Yes. I'm trying to find something that'll help me with the display of magic I'm going to put on, and the only person who knows where this thing is lives in Piltdown."

"Which is why you want to go there."

"Yes."

"Well, I don't know how to get there," said Mauger emphatically.

"I can direct you," said Grosnez reassuringly.

The dragon was silent for a few moments. Then he said: "I don't know if I could fly that far now. A few years ago perhaps, but..."

"You can do it, Mauger. I know you can."

"Do you? I think I'd be lucky to get as far as Lesur." He yawned. "Why don't you go by boat?"

"Take too long. I haven't the time."

"But it would be much safer. I might crash into the sea or something."

"I'm prepared to take that risk."

"Well I'm not. Go by boat."

"Gr.Grosnez," piped up Piton timidly. "I think Mauger's right. Let's go by boat."

Grosnez rounded on him: "Shut up, fool!" Then he added in a softer voice: "Old Mauger doesn't know his own cap'bil'ties, that's all."

"Perhaps he doesn't," said the dragon. "But then again perhaps he does."

"Look," said Grosnez, turning back to him, "it's not as far as you think. You used to fly much further."

Mauger snorted. "No doubt I did, Grosnez. But that was a good many years ago."

"I know that!" Grosnez was growing impatient. "But you're still perfectly healthy. I think you can make it to Alb without any diff'culty."

"You do, do you? Well, I could say it'll be your funeral if anything happens but the trouble is it could also be mine. It just seems too risky to me." He lapsed into silence for a few moments, and then asked: "Besides, what do I get out of this other than possibly killing myself?"

Grosnez frowned. It had not occurred to him that Old Mauger might ask him that. His brow furrowed as he tried to think of a suitable offer. Eventually, he thought of something. "I know," he said smiling. "I'll concoct a special potion that'll make you years younger."

"Pah!" spat the dragon contemptuously. "You couldn't even make *yourself* younger."

Grosnez glared at him. "But this is important Mauger. I want to get my display ready in plenty of time for La Tanche's Jub'lee. And I'll want to do some trial runs beforehand, to iron out any snags, so I must get to Piltdown as quickly as poss'ble."

"Even at the risk of your own life?"

"Yes."

"You're madder than I thought!"

"Per'aps," said Grosnez. "But I don't think it'll be as dang'rous as you're making out." He let out an exasperated sigh. "So, are you pr'pared to take us or not?"

The dragon yawned. "Apart from the risk involved, I don't see why I should - you've yet to make me an offer I, er, can't refuse, as they say. Basically, it doesn't matter to me whether you get to Piltdown tomorrow, next month, or next year. In fact, it wouldn't bother me if you never got there at all, so why should I put myself out for you?"

Grosnez let out a sigh of even greater exasperation than the previous one. This was becoming impossible! He scratched his head and stared pensively at the creature. How could he persuade him to take them to Piltdown? What weaknesses did Mauger have that he could play on? Could he bribe him somehow - with something other than potions? He did not like the idea of delaying matters, but maybe if he left him to think about it for a while...

"Look, Mauger," he said, "it was prob'bly silly of us to disturb you with something like this in the middle of the night. After all, it's evidently a big decision, so why don't you sleep on it? We'll come back tomorrow afternoon and we can discuss it again then."

The dragon thought about this, and then said resignedly: "All right, I'll think about it. Come back tomorrow. But don't get your hopes up - it's extremely unlikely that I'll agree to take you. Now go away and let me sleep."

"Fair enough," said Grosnez. "Come on, Piton, let's leave this tired old worm alone."

With that, they bade Mauger good night and left his cave, carefully making their way down the scree slope outside and then retracing their steps across the marsh en route for Grosnez' home.

* * *

The dragon stayed awake for a little while after they had gone and ruminated on the meeting. Should he take them or shouldn't he? Maybe T'loch would want him to. In fact, perhaps it was T'loch who had put the idea into Grosnez' head in the first place.

He probably could make the flight all right, if he prepared himself properly beforehand and had some stops on the way. He could land on Lesur and on that other island to the north of Lesur: Ortac. Then a third rest as soon as they reached Alb, before going on to Piltdown. Yes, he could probably do it all right.

But should he? He did not care for Grosnez, or for that whining servant of his. Of course, he could always drop them in the sea on the way over - that would be doing Angur a great service - but no, that was totally against his nature, although the idea was tempting.

He had to admit that the journey could well be an exciting one - it would certainly make a change. He should consult T'loch - yes, that would be the best thing to do. Now, all he had to do was drift into a peaceful slumber and make dream-contact with him.

He yawned, stretched, and shut his eyes...

CHAPTER EIGHT

THE FLIGHT TO PILTDOWN

The following morning, the task of clearing the site of the new dolmen began in earnest. It was now a couple of days before the spring equinox and Gastelois wanted to get as much done as possible before everyone downed tools for the festivities.

He helped with the clearance. In his father's day, the job had been made easier by the involvement of Old Mauger, who had used his fiery breath to burn down the vegetation to be cleared. This had saved a lot of time, particularly where trees were concerned, and had made the removal of gorse and bramble thickets an altogether less arduous and painful task than was often the case when more conventional methods were employed.

Unfortunately, on one particular project, in the north-west of the island, Arbreur Le Bois' last as it turned out, the dragon had been rather too enthusiastic, and the resulting conflagration had come close to incinerating the nearby settlement of Grantez-sur-Montais, whose good people had commissioned the dolmen in question. It was only due to the prompt action of Arbreur and his workforce and the people of the settlement that disaster had been averted, and from that day on only conventional methods of clearance had been employed.

Gastelois and his team of twenty men had been wielding their flint sickles and polished stone axes for about two hours when the man from the *Dolmen and Granite Workers' Union* arrived on the scene. Everyone was so engrossed in their work that they did not notice him turn up.

"Ex.. excuse me."

Nobody reacted.

The small, officious looking man cleared his throat. "Excuse me," he said again, louder.

This time, one of the workmen heard something and looked around. Recognising the individual immediately, he turned to

Gastelois who was standing a few feet away in discussion with two of the other workers: "Oi, Gastelois! Trouble's here."

The D.G.W.U. man glared at him and then walked up to Gastelois, who had turned around to ascertain the definition of trouble in this particular instance. When he saw who it was, he greeted the new arrival affably enough, despite feeling anything but:

"Ah, René! Good to see you. How are you these days, mon vier?"

"I'm fine, thank you, Gast'lois," replied René Pipon with feigned courtesy.

"What can we do for you on this fine morning?" asked Gastelois, who knew perfectly well why the other was there.

"I'm checking union memberships," replied Pipon. "As you are well aware, all dolmen workers have to belong to a union otherwise they cannot be employed on a site. So I want to check that your men are all members of a recognised union, them."

Gastelois nodded. "Of course." He turned to his team: "Men, can I have your attention please. Our friend here from the D.G.W.U. wants to check union membership. Hands up who belongs to the Dolmen and Granite."

Twelve people raised their hands. Gastelois looked slightly puzzled, while Pipon frowned. This was fewer than one normally would have expected out of a group of twenty. The majority of the remainder should have belonged to the next biggest union, the *Amalgamated Stone Leverers and Earthworkers' Federation*.

"A.S.L.E.F.?" asked Gastelois.

Five hands went up.

That left three men.

"You three," said Pipon. "You must belong to N.U.M.B., then." This was a reasonable enough assumption on his part considering that the *National Union of Mound Builders* had a fair membership in the island.

The three stout fellows, looking very similar which was not all that remarkable once you realised that they were brothers, shook their heads slowly in unison.

While Gastelois looked quizzically at the three, Pipon tutted irritably. "You must be members of *some* union," he said.

Again three heads were shaken slowly.

"I'm not," said Gaston Tourvel, a stalwart fellow slow of speech, but not of wit.

"Nor me," added his twin brother, Gaetan.

"Me neither," said their younger brother, Gerard.

René Pipon glared at them through narrowed eyes. "Well, you'll have to join one or you can't work here. May I suggest the *Dolmen and Gran...*"

"We do not want to join a union," said Gaetan Tourvel emphatically. His brothers shook their heads slowly.

"Well, you have to!" repeated Pipon vehemently.

"Look," said Gastelois with a sigh, "this is getting us nowhere. I've a deadline to meet and we've a lot of work to do. The Tourvels can always sort out their union membership with you later."

"They can't do any more work here until they're members of a union," stated Pipon as if that were the last word on the subject. "You of all people, Gast'lois, should know the rules."

"Rules can be bent from time to time, René."

"Not union rules."

"Oh come on! Where's the harm? They can work for today and tomorrow, and then something can be sorted out when we resume work after the equinox festivities."

There were grunts and nods of approval from the workforce, all of whom had been following the foregoing conversation with increasing interest, wondering where it was going to lead.

"It would set an undesirable prec'dent," said Pipon. He looked Gastelois' team up and down for a few moments before continuing: "And I don't know how many of the brothers here would be keen on carrying on working alongside non-union men, them. They know the rules, and the penalties for breaking them."

Much muttering broke out amongst the workers, particularly the *D.G.W.U.* members.

René Pipon nodded in satisfaction. He turned to Gastelois: "And if you persist in defying union rules, mon vier, I shall have no altern'tive but to call for industrial action."

"Oh for goodness sake!" exclaimed Gastelois. He sighed in exasperation. "You leave me no alternative," he said to Pipon. He turned to the Tourvel brothers, who regarded him impassively, arms folded across their broad chests: "You three had better go home for now. I'll try to sort something out for you."

"We're not joining a union," said Gaston Tourvel adamantly. "Especially not *his*!" he added, glaring at René Pipon.

"Well," sighed Gastelois, "it seems I won't be able to employ you then."

"That's up to you. Gaetan, Gerard, let's go."

With that, the three brothers picked up their flint sickles and, without a single glance backwards, strode away from the site.

Gastelois watched them for a few moments and then turned to Pipon: "Perhaps, René, you'd like to find some replacements for those three – some that would meet with union approval," he added sarcastically.

"I'm not in the employment bus'ness, Gast'lois," returned the other. "Good day to you." With that, he nodded to Gastelois and his team, turned on his heels and walked smartly away from them.

"I'm going to see La Cloche about this," Gastelois called after him.

"You do that," said Pipon without looking back.

Gastelois glared at him. "Okay men," he said. "Let's get on with it. We've wasted enough time."

* * *

Grosnez and Piton returned to the dragon's cave early that afternoon. The wisps of smoke drifting lazily upwards from the entrance confirmed that Mauger was at home. They reached the scree slope leading to the cave and Piton reluctantly followed his master up it. He was fervently hoping that the dragon had decided not to fly them to Piltdown, but somehow he sensed that this would prove not to be the case.

Mauger, who was lying stretched out on his back on the cavern floor, yawned as his visitors entered and then rolled over on to his stomach.

"Well, have you made up your mind yet?" demanded Grosnez.

"Yes, I have," replied the dragon in a bored voice.

"Well?"

"My, we do sound impatient."

"I haven't time to muck about, Mauger. Are you going to take us to Piltdown or aren't you?"

The dragon stretched out his long snout, grabbed a small piece of limestone from a nearby pile and began to chew it noisily. He watched them for a few minutes, amused by the increasingly impatient expression on Grosnez' face. At last he said: "I'll take you. When d'you want to go?"

Piton made no effort to conceal how he felt and stared miserably at the dragon, but Grosnez breathed a sigh of relief.

"Thank goodness for that!" he exclaimed. "I want to go tonight. Come up to my place as soon as the Sun's set. We'll leave from there."

"If you say so. Now leave me alone so I can get some sleep. I want to be refreshed and alert for the trip."

"Fair enough. Come on, Piton, we have things to do before the flight."

With that, Grosnez left the cave, Piton trailing along behind him. Mauger waited for a few moments, and then crawled to his entrance and peered out into the warm, sunny afternoon. He watched the two figures heading away across the marsh. What an incongruous pair they made: the tall, lanky magician and his small, timid servant. He felt sorry for poor little Piton sometimes, although the latter would never have believed that, and occasionally wondered how he had ever come to be involved with such a rotten piece of work as Grosnez.

Mauger let out a deep sigh and then slowly retreated to the depths of his cave. A good sleep was called for, and then he would probably feel more ready for this absurd flight. T'loch had promised him something to give him more energy, so he would go to see him on his way to Grosnez' place. He settled himself more comfortably, yawned, and shut his eyes. Sleep, refreshing sleep...

* * *

Vraicer T'loch was hanging upside down over his seaweed fire, letting its pungent smoke bathe his body from head to toe. He was most satisfied with the way things were progressing. At first, it had not been easy persuading the dragon to take those two fools to Piltdown, but eventually Mauger had realised the importance of the trip for the success of his plans.

Of course, the promise of a special potion to give him more energy for the journey had helped to overcome Mauger's reluctance, and T'loch had told him of a place in Alb not far from Piltdown where he would be able to find a sufficient quantity of 'dragon-food' to enable him to make the return flight to Angur without any problems.

As soon as he had finished sleep-talking with the dragon, T'loch had made contact with his old friend 'Stone-Ears' Meade to ask for his assistance. He had filled him in on what was going on with regard to Grosnez, and had told him of the latter's forthcoming visit to Piltdown to see him about the glowing liquid. Now old 'Stone-Ears' might have been rather deaf and have a fondness for the booze that was decidedly detrimental to the liver, but despite these handicaps and his advanced years, his mind was still alert and he quickly grasped what T'loch required of him. He agreed to help.

T'loch then turned his mind to other matters. Time was getting on, and before long he would have to start preparing the energy potion for Old Mauger. There was no problem with the ingredients - he had everything he needed in his basement store - but the actual preparation and cooking would take a fair amount of time, and the mixture would have to stand and cool before the dragon could drink it.

But he would hang here and enjoy this soothing smoke for just a little while longer. It was *so* relaxing.

* * *

The day wore on, and evening eventually arrived. The Sun slowly sank in the west, suffusing the sky there with a bright orange glow which became progressively redder as time passed. Gradually, a few stars began to appear faintly in the deepening blue of the heavens, almost as if some celestial lamplighter were doing his rounds.

Refreshed by a good sleep, Old Mauger busied himself getting ready for the flight. He was actually now feeling quite excited about the venture, possibly because he had just dreamt about some of the more spectacular aerial exploits of his youth, and it was clear that flying still appealed to him, perhaps more than he had realised. He rooted out an old safety harness that he used to wear on his back in his younger days when he flew people between Angur and the other islands. He had thought it lost, but he found it amidst a pile of junk in one of the many dark recesses of his cave. He would not be able to put it on himself; T'loch could do that for him.

He had a supper of special 'dragon-food', without which he would not have been able to fly - it was indeed fortunate that he still had some in his home. He chewed the white, rocky chunks very carefully and thoroughly so he would not end up with indigestion.

After that, he lay still for a while to give his stomach juices time to react properly with the food.

This special meal was a very important prelude to any dragon flight; its digestion resulted in the production of large quantities of a light gas that played a vital part in overcoming the heaviness of the creature's not inconsiderable bulk. Without the buoyancy that this gas provided a dragon simply could not fly.

He waited until the Sun had set and a deep twilight had descended on the island; then he left his cave, spread his wings, and gave them a few trial flaps. They did not feel very strong. He tried again, running down the scree slope in front of his home as he did so. He stopped at the bottom, panting. He gave a belch, and a jet of flame shot from his mouth, scaring a few birds which rose from a nearby bush squawking their indignation. Well, at least *that* was working all right. He flapped again, and continued to beat his wings, feeling progressively stronger, until, at last, he began to rise. Then he made one circuit of his home before heading north towards the old forest and Vraicer T'loch.

T'loch was waiting for him in the clearing outside his house when Mauger arrived. He had lit a fire to help the dragon find the clearing. Near this fire stood a large, black cauldron.

"How did it go?" he anxiously asked the dragon once the latter had landed.

Mauger stood before him, panting heavily. "Not... bad... not bad," he gasped. "Pretty... pretty tiring, though." He fought to control his panting. "I'm... I'm not sure... I can... make it... all the way to... Alb."

"You're probably just out of practice, that's all. My potion will help." He indicated the cauldron. "Drink as much as you can."

Mauger suddenly remembered something: "Vraicer, I've forgotten the harness!"

"What harness?"

"It's one I used to use when I took people on my back, time past. I found it earlier and put it aside to take with me. But I've left it behind in my cave."

T'loch shrugged his shoulders. "That's just unfortunate," he said.

"But how will Grosnez and Piton manage?"

The DRAGON of ANGUR

T'loch permitted himself an evil chuckle. "They'll just have to hang on as best they can. Now, you'd better start drinking my brew."

The dragon dipped his snout into the large cauldron and began to noisily slurp down the purple liquid it contained.

T'loch went on: "Remember, don't let Grosnez hassle you into flying faster than you want to. Go at the speed at which you feel most comfortable. And if you want to, land on Ortac for a rest. In fact, I think you should. You shouldn't need to make a stop in Lesur, but if you feel you have to, by all means do." He paused for a moment before continuing: "Verman has explained to Grosnez how to get to Piltdown, so ask Grosnez if at any stage you have trouble recalling the directions I gave you earlier." He paused for a brief moment before asking: "Now, you remember where to get the dragon-food when you get to Alb?"

Mauger lifted his dripping snout from the vessel and nodded, immediately plunging it back in again.

"Good," said T'loch. He smiled as he watched the dragon finish off the potion - evidently he could still make a tasty brew! "Right, any questions?"

Mauger shook his head.

"Okay, off you go, and good luck! And don't worry; I'll be keeping an eye on proceedings from here."

The dragon belched. He could feel the potion giving him strength already. He flapped his wings noisily, and then slowly began to rise. Yes, he felt much better now. Soon he was above the surrounding tree-tops, and after circling the clearing once, he flew off in a west-north-westerly direction, heading towards Grosnez' cliff-top home.

T'loch watched him until he was out of sight, and then went indoors. He fervently hoped that the dragon would be all right and that everything would go according to plan.

* * *

They had not been flying for very long, and were about halfway between Angur and Lesur, when Piton very nearly fell off. Mauger had been heading vaguely in the direction of the latter island, just in case he needed to stop there for a rest, but he then decided that this would not be necessary and so made an abrupt course change to put him on a more direct route to Ortac. It was the suddenness of this change that nearly dislodged the unfortunate Le Malin from his precarious position on the dragon's back.

As he felt himself going, Piton let out a tremendous high-pitched shriek, which nearly caused Grosnez to leap from Mauger's back in shock.

His master wheeled around rapidly and grabbed him in the nick of time. As he steadied him, he said: "Now calm down, you. You're all right. Just pay more attention so you're alert when Mauger makes any course changes."

Piton was trembling violently, having been scared out of his wits. "I'll... I'll try, Grosnez. I'll try." He pressed his bony legs closer to the dragon's scaly flanks and put his arms around Grosnez' waist for extra safety. He would be *very* glad when this nightmare was over.

He had never flown on a dragon before, and the reality was proving just as terrifying as his imagination had told him it would. It would have been bad enough without that near disaster just now, but that had made it worse - much worse! Not only that, but the wind, exaggerated by Old Mauger's speed, was whipping and tearing at him, seemingly trying its best to snatch him from his perch. It was also cold, and was chilling him to the marrow, despite the extra warm clothes he had put on for the trip. And to compound his misery even further, the dragon's motion was making him feel quite sick.

To this catalogue of woes could be added Piton's fear that Mauger might fly into something - another dragon, for instance. This was not as ridiculous as it might seem. Mid-air collisions between dragons had been known to occur, and with more frequency than you might suppose. And as Old Mauger's eyesight was no longer of the best... Fortunately, though, they seemed to have the sky to themselves on this particular night, and there was a bright moon to aid visibility.

Of course, the dragon might suddenly die on them in mid-flight and plunge into the sea, taking them with him. That had been known to happen too, and, after all, he *was* old.

Yes, Piton would indeed be glad when this nightmare was over - very glad indeed!

* * *

They eventually reached Ortac, the most northerly of the islands in the group and lying just a few miles to the west of the northernmost tip of Armor. Mauger decided to take Tloch's advice and land there for a rest. Consequently, he descended towards the island, venting off gas in short, fiery bursts to lose buoyancy, and came down in an open, grassy expanse near the west coast, a safe distance from the nearest habitation.

"I hope you don't need to stay here for long, you," Grosnez remarked to the dragon, as he and Piton dismounted.

"Typical, Grosnez, quite typical!" said the dragon in a bored voice. "As impatient as ever. But don't worry; we'll be on our way shortly."

"Good!"

As far as Piton was concerned, the longer they remained on Ortac the better. He was greatly relieved to be on solid ground again, and would quite happily have stayed where he was, especially as he was not looking forward in the slightest to visiting Piltdown. He even considered asking his master if he could wait for him in Ortac - he could be collected on the way back - but he thought better of it.

Soon - too soon, in Piton's opinion - they were on their way again, and it was not long before the most northerly of the islands in the Angurian archipelago had become but a small, black blob on the moonlit sea, eventually disappearing completely into the night.

* * *

The next stage of the flight passed without drama, and Piton breathed a huge sigh of relief when the chalk cliffs forming part of the southern coast of Alb came into sight, a ribbon of white gleaming in the moonlight. When he was almost directly above them, the dragon turned east, following the coast line for a few miles until he spotted a particular crescent-shaped bay with a small settlement overlooking it that T'loch had described to him when giving him directions for the journey. Then he banked steeply to his left and headed inland in a north-easterly direction.

He vented off a little gas in a fiery jet to enable him to lose a little height and kept his eyes peeled for any signs of Piltdown, which should have been lying somewhere directly ahead. Although the Moon was low in the west by this time, and there were a few clouds around, visibility was still reasonable.

The dragon was presently flying over a large forest, a dark mass brooding silently beneath him and stretching as far as the eye could see in all directions. It was much larger than the old forest on Angur, and it was anybody's guess what might lie concealed within its depths.

It gave Piton the willies, to put it mildly, and as he looked apprehensively down at it, he began to imagine all manner of horrors lurking in the trees and waiting for the opportunity to leap up and pluck him from the sky. He then pictured himself strapped to a spit and being roasted slowly by a leering ogre who dribbled hungrily as he contemplated his meal.

It was just at the moment that he visualised the ogre's face close up that the dragon hit an air pocket and dropped by at least a couple of hundred feet before recovering. The shriek that rent the night air would probably have terrified anything in the shadowy vegetation below and put paid to any plans of plucking hapless travellers from the sky and roasting them for dinner.

Fortunately nobody fell off, although Grosnez came pretty close, what with the shock of the sudden drop combined with that of the scream from behind him, which had been even more ear-splitting than the one Piton had emitted when he had nearly fallen off earlier in the flight.

"Get a grip on yourself, mon vier," growled Grosnez when he had recovered. "These things happen on flights and you just have to get used to them."

Get used to them! thought Piton. That was most unlikely as he had absolutely no intention of ever making another dragon-flight once he was safely back home in Angur, and so he would not be availing himself of any opportunity to become accustomed to such nasty experiences. *Get used to them indeed!*

* * *

Mauger was becoming a little worried. He should have been able to see signs of Piltdown by now. They had crossed the eastern edge of the forest a short time earlier and were now flying over a gently undulating landscape of what seemed to be fields and meadows and patches of woodland. The dragon cast his mind back to the directions T'loch had given him and what landmarks he should look out for. A river should have been visible running north south through a shallow valley a little way to the east of' the forest, but the one feature that would have told him that he was very near Piltdown was a large white mound on the summit of a ridge a mile or so to the south of the settlement. So far, there had been no sign of the river, let alone the mound, and the dragon was beginning to tire. Before long, he might well have to make an emergency landing.

With this in mind, he decided to lose more height, peering from left to right as he did so for any sign of the recalcitrant village or the aforementioned landmarks.

Grosnez had realised that something was wrong. "What's up, Mauger?" He asked anxiously.

"I... I can't seem to... find the... wretched place," panted the dragon.

"But surely we should be almost there by now?" Grosnez said, staring around him. "We should be able to see it from up here." He glared at the back of Mauger's head. "You haven't gone the wrong way, you?"

"I don't think so - not unless *you* gave me the wrong directions."

"That I did not!" said the other in aggrieved tones. "Have we reached the river yet?"

"Not that I've seen."

"Well then, stop panicking. I'm sure we'll be there soon."

"But Grosnez, surely we should have... seen the... river by now," panted Mauger. "I... thought it was... just beyond the forest."

"So I'm led to b'lieve," said Grosnez.

"Supposing... we've... missed it?"

"We haven't missed it!"

"Well, we'd... better... find... it... soon. I'm getting... very... tired."

"What's he mean he's getting tired?" squeaked Piton. "He can't get tired - it's still a long way down. I don't want..."

"Oh be quiet!" snapped Grosnez irritably. He then patted the dragon on his scaly back. "Don't worry, Mauger, we'll soon be there."

The dragon snorted. Few things irritated him more than being patted on the back like some domesticated dog. He flew on.

* * *

Eventually, Old Mauger spotted a silver streak glinting in the moonlight over to the north-east. That had to be the river, although it seemed rather far away; they were obviously further south than they should have been. But it was a relief to see it at last, and he banked left to head in its direction.

Grosnez, who had noticed the river at about the same time, came to the same conclusion about their position. Annoying though that was, he was just as relieved as the dragon that the waterway was within sight.

None of them, however, was more relieved than Piton. "There it is! There it is!" he shrieked upon seeing it. But he would be happiest once they were actually down on terra firma.

As he approached the river, the dragon vented off gas to lose buoyancy and thus height, taking care not to release too much. The last thing he wanted to do was to vent off too much too soon, so that he ended up having to land prematurely a considerable distance from their destination. When they reached the water, Grosnez told him to follow it northwards – which he was going to do anyway, as per Vraicer T'loch's instructions.

They headed upstream, all the time keeping their eyes peeled for any sign of the white mound or indeed the village of Piltdown itself. Then Piton suddenly spotted a huddle of houses over to his left and excitedly drew Grosnez' attention to it.

"Wrong side of the river, mon vier," was his master's matter-of-fact response.

A crestfallen Le Malin looked to his other side, and immediately brightened. "Look, Grosnez. Over there!" He pointed at another collection of buildings, crowded together on a low hilltop to the east of the river.

Grosnez looked. "Have we seen the mound yet?" he asked.

Piton shook his head.

"Well, that's not it either then, is it?"

More shaking of the head. "No, Grosnez."

"Keep looking for the mound. Don't forget what old Verman told us: its whiteness should make it unmistakable. If our information is correct, Piltdown should lie just to the north of it."

"Why shouldn't our information be correct, Grosnez?" Piton was suddenly alarmed.

Grosnez shrugged his shoulders, but did not say anything. Instead he permitted himself a faint smile; he enjoyed winding his servant up.

They flew on, Mauger continuing to follow the river northwards. To either side lay moonlight bathed, gently undulating countryside patch-worked with fields, meadows, copses of trees, and the occasional slumbering hamlet. Another river appeared ahead, snaking away eastwards from the one they were following, and as the dragon approached the confluence of the two, he seemed to hesitate, as though he were uncertain which direction to take. But the hesitation was only momentary, and he maintained his current course.

At first, Grosnez had wondered whether they should have followed the second river, particularly as it seemed to be heading in the general direction of what appeared to be a substantial settlement lying to their north-east. But he quickly realised that that would have been a mistake – going by what Clouet had told them, the settlement was too large to be Piltdown. Besides, they had yet to see the mound, and it would be folly to make any course changes before that was in sight.

* * *

It came within sight not very long afterwards: a large hillock or mound shining white in the moonlight near the summit of a grassy ridge to the north-north-east of them.

Phew! thought Mauger. *That must be the white mound Vraicer told me about.* With this in sight, the dragon felt renewed strength, knowing that they were now very close to their destination.

"Excellent!" exclaimed Grosnez. "That's the white mound we're looking for. The village should lie a mile or so to its north."

"It's very bright," observed Piton of the mound. "Why's it so bright, Grosnez?"

"It's all the spooks and goblins that live inside it, mon vier. They light up the mound to lure unwary travellers into their clutches. In fact, they may even have spotted us coming and be trying to lure us even as we speak. But we're too clever for them, aren't we Mauger."

"If you say so, Grosnez," said the dragon in a bored voice. "Don't worry, Piton," he added as that worthy began to bleat in panic, "your master is having you on."

"Pah!" spat Grosnez in disgust. "Trust you to spoil it."

Mauger laughed. "My pleasure, Grosnez, my pleasure."

Grosnez muttered something rude in a low voice at the dragon's expense, which if the latter heard, he chose to ignore, instead banking slightly to his right to put him on what he hoped would be a direct course for Piltdown.

A little while later, as they passed to the west of the mound, the moonlight bright enough to cast their shadow on to it as they went by, they perceived their goal - an ill-assorted collection of ramshackle buildings huddled together on the broad floor of a shallow valley lying on the far side of another grassy ridge.

"There it is!" cried Grosnez in excitement. "Quick, Mauger, we must find a landing spot a little way away. We don't want any of the inhabitants to see how we arrived."

"Where would you suggest I land, then?" asked the dragon.

"Not too close, not too close!" squeaked Piton, who had been regarding the village with increasing dread from the moment they had set eyes on it.

"Oh, shut up!" snapped his master. "Somewhere this side of that ridge I think would be fine."

"Right."

Just then, disaster struck. Mauger was about to commence venting off some gas in a series of controlled exhalations that would permit him to make a gradual, spiralling descent, when something ticklish lodged itself in one of his nostrils. He sneezed violently, not once, but three times, nearly throwing Grosnez and Piton in the process.

The sneezing was accompanied by much fiery emitting of gas, resulting in the dragon losing too much buoyancy too quickly, and he began to plummet earthwards.

"Hold on!" he managed to instruct his hapless passengers.

This they did not need to be told, clinging for dear life to the dragon's back as they were, with the ground rushing up to meet them. Mauger frantically flapped his wings in an effort to brake his descent and succeeded in changing the attitude of his plunge from a vertical drop to a steep angle. But all this activity had thrown him off course and he was now actually heading away from Piltdown. Shooting over the edge of a ridge, he plummeted down the side of the valley beyond, scraping the tops of some trees, managed to level off some more before reaching the bottom, and then narrowly missed a lone oak tree before plunging belly-first into a malodorous marsh that lurked by a bend in a river – the same river, in fact, which he had been following earlier.

The DRAGON of ANGUR

"Hold on!" he managed to instruct his hapless passengers

Grosnez and Piton were thrown from the dragon's back into the muddy soup of the swamp, which gurgled rapaciously as it swallowed them.

Grosnez came spluttering to the surface first and just stood where he was, waist deep in the stinking mire and covered in weed. He glared around him and came face to face with – would you believe - another dragon, who was contemplating him through a smoky haze from in front of a small copse of trees near the northern edge of the marsh.

"Hey man, dig the costume!" observed this creature, referring to the vegetation adorning Grosnez' person. It was chewing on some species of weed, strands of which were hanging from its lower jaw.

Grosnez opened his mouth to say something, but no words came forth.

"Neat landing!" was the other's next observation, this time directed at Old Mauger who was lying prone in the marsh, panting and wheezing, and generally feeling that the stuffing had been well and truly knocked out of him.

A sudden fit of coughing and gasping emanating from a clump of reeds heralded Piton's emergence from his marshy ducking.

"Wh. What's going on?" he spluttered. "Wh.. Where am I?"

"My, my! Another one!" exclaimed the dragon by the trees. "Oi wonders if there be any more characters in this nocturnal entertainment." He exhaled a cloud of smoke and then chuckled merrily.

"You seem very happy," observed Old Mauger, who had recovered sufficiently to begin to take stock of his surroundings and had noticed that he was not the only dragon in the neighbourhood.

"You don't know what I'm smoking, man!"

The other was not certain exactly what this response meant. "I'm Mauger," he said, by way of introduction.

"Otis the name; cool the game!"

"Indeed!" remarked Grosnez acidly. He had decided that he had had enough of standing around in the marsh and was now wading through it towards the firmer land on which the dragon called Otis was sitting.

Old Mauger and Piton were doing likewise, the latter still trying to come to terms with what had happened and complaining endlessly about his predicament as he gingerly made his way through the swamp. Otis regarded them in amusement, silently smoking and chewing on his weed.

"What brings you dudes to these parts?" he eventually asked once the others were all on terra firma.

"We were trying to get to Piltdown," said Grosnez.

"Oh yes?" The dragon looked at him with interest. "Not many people want to go *there*."

"So I believe," said Grosnez. He massaged his chin slowly. "Actually," he said, "you might know the individual we've come to see."

"Oh?"

"One 'Stone-Ears' Meade."

Otis nodded. "Yes, I know him well. Cool guy!" He blew a smoke ring into the night air. "None of my business, but why d'you want to see him?"

"I need to ask him something."

The other laughed. "That should be fun," he said.

"Why?"

"He's as deaf as a post! Great guy and all that, but when it comes to holding a conversation with him, well, that's not so cool, man."

Grosnez glared at the dragon. Clouet had not said anything about this Meade individual being deaf. Thinking about it, though, he could kick himself. With a name like 'Stone-Ears', he should have realised that the man would be afflicted with impairment of the hearing.

"However," continued Otis, "all is not lost. He has a friend, one 'Hand-Tongue' Eddie, who endeavours to act as an interpreter. The problem is, though, he's not always successful."

"Great!" said Grosnez. "Just great! I come all this way to see someone on a matter of some importance and I find I'm faced with a commun'cation problem."

"Does this mean we can go home?" asked Piton hopefully as he stood shivering in his wet clothes.

"No it does not!" retorted Grosnez with vehemence. "I'll get the information I need even if I have to..." He broke off in mid-sentence and smiled at Otis. "Patience and persev'rance will get me what I require."

"I'm glad to hear it, my man," said Otis. He glanced up at the eastern sky where a slight lightening heralded the onset of daybreak. "It'll be daylight before too long, but I rather fancy it's a bit too early to be gadding into Piltdown just yet. You should get some rest - you all look exhausted."

"That's probably a good idea," said Grosnez. He shivered. Like Piton, he was feeling the effects of his damp clothes and the cool night air.

Otis looked the two of them up and down, still chewing on his weed. "May I suggest that you remove your clothes before you catch your death of cold. I'll dry them for you while you sleep."

Piton needed no further encouragement, and immediately began stripping off, with Grosnez doing likewise, the two of them spreading their clothes over a couple of nearby bushes. Otis then blew some hot air over the two Angurians to dry and warm them, and then showed them a snug spot amongst the trees behind him where they could bed down.

"Be sure you don't let us sleep for too long," said Grosnez as he settled down in the cosy hollow Otis had indicated.

The dragon assured him that he would not and then turned to Old Mauger, who had been lying quietly on the ground gradually regaining his strength. "While those two dudes are gallivanting around in that village, what say you that we go hang loose at my place? It's over there." He nodded to his left, to where a cave was just discernible in the base of the ridge to the east of the marsh, its night-blackened mouth framed by the trees growing on either side of it.

Mauger was not sure what 'hang loose' meant, but as it sounded like a suitably relaxing occupation, he nodded in agreement.

"I'll shortly rustle up some breakfast, and then we can have a chat and a smoke," Otis went on. "But in the meantime, I suggest that you, too, get some rest." Adding: "Unless the weather's really cold or wet, I prefer to sleep outside – if that's all right with you?"

Mauger nodded slowly, too tired to move from where he was lying. He drifted off to sleep, glad that fate had caused him to come down right next to a friendly member of his own species. Maybe this little expedition was not going to turn out so badly after all.

Otis watched him snoring peacefully, wisps of smoke puffing rhythmically from his nostrils in time with his breathing. He was very much looking forward to talking with Mauger, as it was ages since he had last been in the company of another dragon. He yawned and then rolled on to his back, where he lay watching the gradual fading of the stars as they were consumed by the inexorable march of daylight from the east.

CHAPTER NINE

PILTDOWN - 'STONE-EARS' MEADE

The village of Piltdown was, by the common consent of those who did not live there, the sleaziest, most run-down collection of malodorous, worm-eaten hovels in the civilised world. It housed an equally-squalid collection of humanity who practised virtually every species of criminal activity imaginable and some that most decent people would have deemed unimaginable. They would not think twice about doing in their nearest and dearest if it served their purpose, and frequently did! Strangers who had the misfortune to arrive in the place unaware of its particular charms were lucky to leave it in one piece - if indeed they actually left it at all.

Piltdown, therefore, was a place to be avoided at all costs. People who went there intentionally invariably did so for nefarious purposes, which of course was exactly why Grosnez and Piton were going. Otis had woken them soon after the Sun had shown itself above the horizon and, after the dragon had given them directions, they set off southwards along a narrow track bordering the eastern edge of the marshy area where they had landed. They duly reached the northern bank of a small river, a tributary of the larger one they had followed earlier during their aborted nocturnal approach to Piltdown, and which joined its parent after flowing in past the southern end of the ridge overlooking the marsh. According to Otis, if they headed north-east along this bank, they would come to a spot where the river was crossed by a bridge of stone slabs. All they then had to do was follow the path that led away from the bridge and it would take them straight to the village.

After rounding the end of the ridge, they found themselves in a shallow valley whose tree-cloaked sides sloped gently down towards the river. They had a good forty minutes walk to their destination and Piton whined endlessly for most of the way. Not only was he feeling a bit bruised and battered from the crash (despite the relatively soft landing in the marsh), but he was as terrified as ever at the prospect of going into Piltdown. He was quite convinced that he was going to get his throat cut before the day was through and stroked that part of his anatomy gingerly as he walked. Grosnez became so fed up with his minion's moaning that he threatened to leave him in Piltdown when he left, the idea of which was so horrifying to the hapless Le Malin that he shut up on the spot.

The walk along the riverbank was not of the easiest. Although there appeared to be some species of path, it was obviously so little used that it had become well and truly overgrown, and the long, weed-choked grass growing along most of its length combined with the uneven nature of the ground underfoot hampered their progress quite considerably. Both men stumbled a number of times, which of course made Piton feel even more miserable than ever. But it could have been worse. The far bank looked as though it would present even more of a challenge to progress, with much thicker undergrowth and trees crowding virtually as far as the water's edge.

They eventually reached the aforementioned bridge, a simple affair consisting of a row of flagstones supported by piles of rocks, which you found yourself hoping were more stable than they looked. As Piton turned left to follow his master along the track that led from the river to Piltdown, he glanced back at the bridge, very glad that they did not have to cross it.

The path climbed up the side of the valley, snaking through the wood of oak and alder. Evidently this route was used more frequently than that along the riverbank, for it was as free of progress-hindering vegetation as the other was thick with it. The track duly levelled out as it crossed the crest of the slope, and Grosnez and his servant emerged from the trees to see a panorama of fields, hedgerows and copses spread out before them. They walked on, the way now lying between hedge-topped banks that separated it from the fields on either side.

The early morning air was stirred by a stiff breeze that wafted the village's odious smell to the two men some time before they came within sight of any of its buildings. The odour was not easy to describe - suffice it to say that it was not in the least wholesome - and as soon as it reached Piton's nostrils he started whining again with renewed vigour. Grosnez promptly rounded on him, repeating his threat, and once more the other lapsed into silence. They followed the path up the side of a grassy hillock, entered the copse of oak trees growing on its summit, and then emerged from this to behold their destination lurking a few hundred yards ahead of them.

The sight of the village set Piton's nerves off afresh and he begged his master to let him stay where he was. Grosnez could go ahead on his own, complete his business and then come back for him afterwards; he would wait here in the safe shelter of this copse. But Grosnez would not hear of it, simply reminding Piton yet again of what would happen to him if he did not shut up and stop his infernal whining once and for all.

Grosnez knew exactly where in the village to aim for - the pub. Despite the earliness of the hour, he knew that it would be open. In fact, *Dawson's* frequently stayed open all day and all night, not shutting as long as there were customers, although very often the landlord would retire to his bed in the attic and leave his customers to fend for themselves. A dicy state of affairs in a place like Piltdown, you would have thought, but the landlord reasoned that if people smashed the place up, they would have nowhere to drink (his pub being the only such establishment in the village), and knowing the average Piltdown man's fondness for the ale, he was pretty certain that they would treat his property with a fair degree of respect. This, of course, did not mean that fights never took place. Indeed, there was some form of skirmish every night, but the participants invariably damaged themselves more than they did the pub.

Dawson's stood on one side of the village square - a misnomer, since the area in question was actually circular. Its grassy expanse would undoubtedly have developed into an impenetrable mass of weeds and brambles had it not been grazed by the sheep, goats and cattle that were allowed to roam freely throughout the village - their human owners would certainly not have bothered about keeping it presentable. However, a rectangular patch occupying the central part of the square evidently did have some care lavished on it, for it had a distinctly manicured appearance that was at odds with the remainder. But although it was its neatness that first attracted Grosnez and Piton's attention, their eyes were quickly drawn to a singular arrangement of three upright pieces of wood, each no more than a yard or so in height, standing close together in a row near one end of the rectangle. Quite what this set up signified, they could only guess, but they had little doubt that some eldritch ritual was involved.

The pub itself was an exceedingly dingy hole of thoroughly dilapidated aspect, built of a mixture of wattle and daub and stone, and roofed with roughly-hewn logs and thatch. In shape, it approximated to a longhouse, but the rectangular base-plan of a normal Albian member of this species had here given way to something approximating to a drunken, lop-sided trapezium - no doubt due to the fact that the builders had been boozed to the gills at the time of its construction.

Notwithstanding this early handicap in life, it had managed to remain standing for a good many years, although it was now in a sorry state of repair. Much of the wattle needed redaubing, and some of the stonework was crumbling badly. The roof sagged in a number of places, although it was remarkably free of holes. Inside, the place was chiefly notable for its smell: an unwholesome mixture of stale ale, sweaty bodies, products best described as of biological origin, and odours that could not easily be identified as to their source. The fact that the landlord kept a small number of swine in one corner did absolutely nothing for the freshness of the air either. The interior was also quite remarkably dark, even by the standards of the time, and the few animal-grease lamps that were kept burning almost constantly had very little effect on the pervading murk. It was only when there was a good fire going in the central hearth that you could say that the place was decently lit, but this only happened during the winter months and was hardly a regular occurrence even then.

It was into this reeking den of iniquity that Grosnez and Piton presently walked. The latter cast anxious glances about him, expecting at any moment to be assailed by some knife-brandishing maniac intent on slitting his throat or disembowelling him. Contrary to his expectations, however, none of the pub's customers - and there were quite a few of them considering how early in the morning it was - gave either him or his master more than a cursory look. Piton was surprised to see so many people there at this time of the day, although by the stupefied appearance of a good fifty percent of them, it was quite clear that these had been at the ale for most, if not all, of the preceding night. Some customers had already succumbed to the effects of their imbibing and were lying crashed out on the floor. One particularly obese specimen was sleeping with his head resting against the side of one of the pigs, which was itself stretched out full length on its other side. The man was snoring and the pig was grunting, and you would have been hard put to decide which of the two was making the greater racket.

Grosnez scanned the pub's dingy interior, noting the round tables, formed from sections of tree trunk, arranged haphazardly throughout the room, some with customers, some without. His eyes eventually fell on one particular table near the right-hand end of the bar counter, which ran the length of the end wall to his left. Two men were sitting opposite each other, engaged in a conversation that was being conducted with the aid of some form of sign language. The one for whose benefit the other was engaged in the signing was an elderly individual with thinning, grey hair who sat hunched over the table, attentively following the air-stirring gesticulations of his companion.

Grosnez nudged Piton and nodded in the direction of the two men. They approached the table, drew up a couple of free stools, and sat down without waiting to be invited. The others' obvious annoyance at this unwarranted intrusion was quickly assuaged when Grosnez enquired what they were drinking and then ordered a full jar of mead for the elderly individual and one of beer for his companion. The latter, a rotund, middle-aged man with a ruddy face who, it seemed, dribbled more drink from the corners of his mouth than he actually swallowed, asked the two visitors what they wanted.

"My friend and I are collectors of the unusual," replied Grosnez, doing his best to disguise his Angurian accent by trying to assume a more or less neutral one, "and we are looking for a special container. We are seeking one 'Stone-Ears' Meade who we have been led to believe might be able to help us and point us in the right direction."

"Then you need look no further," said the rotund one. "My friend here is the one you seek."

He nodded towards his companion, who grinned jovially, displaying a wonderful set of gums sparsely populated with crooked teeth that looked as though they were going to fall out at any moment. "And I am Eddie. My friends call me 'Hand-Tongue' because of my ability to 'speak' with my hands."

"Excellent!" said Grosnez. "As I just said, we are looking for a particular container and we were hoping that 'Stone-Ears' would be able to point us in the right direction."

'Hand-Tongue' Eddie repeated what Grosnez had said, enunciating the words clearly to help 'Stone-Ears' read his lips, and making suitable gestures with his hands as well.

However, what 'Stone-Ears' then said speedily brought Otis's earlier remarks back to Grosnez: "No, I have no horses for sale."

"Horses?" queried Grosnez. "I don't want any horses!"

"What's a horse, Grosnez?" piped in Piton.

"Shut up and keep quiet!" hissed Grosnez in an aside to his servant. The other looked suitably chastened and spent the next few minutes trying to work out what this thing called a horse could be.

"I'll try again, mate," offered Eddie helpfully. He repeated what Grosnez had originally said, and this time it was clear that 'Stone-Ears' had at least grasped the essence, for he said:

"You are unusual collectors who need pointing, and you are looking for containers." He downed a quantity of mead and smacked his lips noisily. "And you have come to me for help?"

Grosnez nodded, relieved that he appeared to be getting somewhere.

"How, er, may I be of assistance?" asked 'Stone-Ears', leaning forward across the table.

Grosnez winced involuntarily as the Meade's breath, replete with halitosis, hit him full in the face. "I'm looking for a container of a very special liquid, and it's vital that I find it as quickly as poss'ble."

'Hand-Tongue' Eddie communicated this to his companion, who nodded, indicating that he had understood. Then, before Grosnez could say anything else, Eddie made a comment that came as something of a shock:

"You sound as if you're from Angur. 'Stone-Ears' has a friend from there, and there's something about your voice that reminds me of his."

Grosnez swallowed hard. He had thought he had been doing a good job of disguising his Angurian accent. Evidently not! Piton started violently and knocked his jar over. Grosnez promptly kicked his ankle and Piton, equally promptly, fell off his seat.

"Please excuse my friend," apologised Grosnez. "He's a little careless." He cleared his throat. "I'm not from Angur, but I spent quite a few years there some time ago - maybe I picked up the accent to some extent."

This information was conveyed to the Meade, who nodded slowly, never once taking his eyes off Grosnez. Piton had meanwhile picked himself up off the floor and was brushing himself down. He looked somewhat peeved and was quite clearly longing to be away from the place. He resumed his seat beside his master, who then, in a surprising show of generosity, ordered him another drink.

"What is this liquid you seek?" asked 'Stone-Ears'. "And what is so special about it?"

Grosnez told himself to play this one very carefully. He had prepared what he thought to be a reasonable story en route from Angur, and he wanted it to sound as convincing as possible. He was aware that 'Stone-Ears' probably knew more about the liquid than he was likely to let on, so he would have to tread cautiously. After taking a sip of mead - Grosnez, too, was quite partial to the stuff and had ordered a jar for himself - he began:

"I am an Elder from the island of Glorn, which lies many days' travel from here across the Sunwise Sea. Myself and some of my fellow Elders are travelling the world looking for ways to rid our island of the horror that has been visited upon it.

"You see, our homeland is being terrorised by the Mirrum, a fearsome monster from the sea. Its breath has brought a great plague upon my people, and we are searching for a cure for this and for a way to destroy this beast. I have already visited the people of the Boinne, who are held in great esteem by those interested in magic and ancient lore, and although they couldn't help me themselves, they spoke of a liquid which glows with a magical light. If I could find some of this liquid and bring it to my people, I might well be able to rid them of this dreadful pestilence that afflicts them.

"The wise men of the Boinne were unable to tell me exactly where I could obtain some of this liquid, although they thought that a container of it lay hidden somewhere to the south of Alb. However, they did tell me that they knew of someone who might know where that particular container could be found."

Eddie finished communicating all of this to 'Stone-Ears', who then said: "And that someone happens to be me, hmm?"

"Yes," said Grosnez. He looked intently at the Meade. *Well, my friend, you didn't seem to have much trouble understanding all of that.* He drained his jar and then stared into the other's grey eyes. "Can you help me? It's imperative that I find that container and get the liquid back to my people as soon as possible."

'Stone-Ears' looked at Eddie, who repeated Grosnez' words in his usual way.

"I think I can help you," said the Meade. "But your vessels are empty. Eddie?" He turned to his companion.

"I'll get them," said that worthy. "Would you like the same again, or something different?" Before waiting for a reply, he added, looking at Piton: "Us beer drinkers were drinking *Dawson's Antiquity,* a local brew made here in Piltdown – in this very pub, in fact. However, as it's the time of the spring equinox, we can now partake of a very special ale, brewed locally, although not in the village. You should take the opportunity of trying it while you're here - *Hooke's Old Extendable* is only available at this time of year."

"I... I'd certainly like to try it," said Piton, glancing nervously at Grosnez as if seeking his master's approval.

Grosnez nodded. "I'll have some too, if I may. I'm very fond of mead, but if this beer's as good as you suggest..."

"Fine," said Eddie. "And I'll get us some food - 'Stone-Ears' and I usually have breakfast in here around this time. I take it you'll join us?"

"Yes," said Grosnez, who was feeling a trifle peckish.

"Yes please. Thank you very much," said Piton, who was feeling ravenous.

Eddie collected the empty drinking-vessels from the table and proceeded to the bar.

'Stone-Ears' was slowly massaging his chin and looking at Grosnez. "As I said, I think I can help you. The container you are seeking is fairly small, about this much in height," he indicated the size by holding one hand flat above the other about six inches or so apart, "and shaped like a tall jar with a narrow neck. It's made of a strange material you can see through. The liquid it holds does indeed glow, with a yellowy-green light. But as it is possessed of magical attributes, it must be handled with respect, and I strongly recommend that, if you do find it, you take it to the people of the Boinne, who will be able to instruct you in its proper use."

Sinclair Forrest

At that point, 'Hand-Tongue' Eddie returned with two jars brimming with ale and set them down in front of Grosnez and Piton.

"There," he said. "I bet this is the best beer you've ever tasted." He returned to the bar to collect the other two jars.

Grosnez took a mouthful of beer, swilled it around his mouth to savour the taste, and then swallowed. He repeated the exercise, then nodded slowly.

"Most palatable," he said. "An excellent brew."

Piton was equally enthusiastic: "Very pleasant. Yes, very pleasant indeed!"

Eddie returned with the other two jars and handed one to 'Stone-Ears'. "The food should arrive shortly," he said as he resumed his seat. He took a gulp of ale and then asked the two Angurians what they thought of *Hooke's Old Extendable*.

"Very good indeed," said Grosnez. "Now, 'Stone-Ears' was telling me about this container of liquid we're after." He drank some beer, smacked his lips in satisfaction, and then asked the Meade: "Do you know exactly where it can be found?"

Eddie was in the process of communicating this to his companion when he was suddenly interrupted by a violent commotion in another part of the pub. Two men had suddenly leapt to their feet and were now shouting at each other at the top of their voices. Even then, it was difficult to tell what their problem was, for such was their state of drunkenness that their speech was slurred to an extent that rendered it all but incomprehensible.

As this was a common occurrence in the pub, it was ignored by the majority of the other clientele, and Eddie, after watching the altercation for a few moments, then did likewise and repeated Grosnez' question about the location of the container to 'Stone-Ears'.

"It's on an island," said 'Stone-Ears'. "To the south of Alb."

This is very interesting, thought Grosnez. "Which island?" he asked.

Once again, Eddie communicated to 'Stone-Ears' what Grosnez had said.

"Angur," stated the Meade matter-of-factly.

"Angur!" exclaimed Grosnez in mock surprise and astonishment. So, that fellow Le Crochon Piton spoke to had been right - it *was* on the island. But he needed to know the precise spot where to look.

"Angur," repeated 'Stone-Ears'. "Yes, that is where you need to look."

"But exactly where on Angur?" asked Grosnez.

Eddie was just about to repeat this for the Meade's benefit when the verbal altercation still going on escalated into a physical one and the fists started to fly. Then the two participants became locked in a tight embrace, rolling around on the floor, and repeatedly trying to get a good punch or kick in, depending on which limb they could get free for long enough to deliver a good blow.

They rolled straight towards a stool, and managed to crash into this with sufficient force to dislodge its occupant who landed squarely on the side of the pig reposing full-length on the floor nearby. Said animal let out an anguished squeal, staggered to its feet, and promptly bit the backside of the unfortunate individual who had been sleeping on its flank, but who had been catapulted into a kneeling position by the pig standing up. Said man emitted a shriek of pain, seized the one from the stool and delivered a respectable punch to his jaw. When he had recovered from this, the latter grabbed the stool and, hurling invective, charged at his assailant with it. Meanwhile, the other two had got to their feet, and were trying to knock the living daylights out of each other with blows to anywhere they could reach, at the same time uttering oaths and obscenities at the expense of each other and their relatives.

The majority of the pub's clientele seemed to be either blissfully unaware of the proceedings or were ignoring them completely, although there were a few following them with avid interest. Grosnez, Piton, Eddie and 'Stone-Ears' were all watching, the latter two with amusement, Piton with apprehension, and Grosnez with downright annoyance at having been interrupted and thus at having to wait for the information he required.

Grosnez leant over and said in Eddie's ear: "Can we go somewhere else? We can't really hold a sensible conversation here."

"But it's fun, this," said Eddie.

"I haven't got time for fun," grumbled the other.

"And we haven't had our breakfast yet."

"That can wait."

Piton's face assumed a downcast expression at his master's remark; his stomach was feeling emptier by the minute, despite the beer.

"Oh, all right," said Eddie reluctantly. He tapped 'Stone-Ears' on the shoulder to attract his attention, and when the latter turned around, his companion, gesticulating in the usual manner, told him what Grosnez wanted.

The Meade's face assumed a look of considerable disappointment. The fight was showing every sign of becoming a good one, perhaps even of escalating into a full-blown tavern brawl as another person had become embroiled in the conflict and one or two others were seriously considering joining in.

"Well?" demanded Grosnez, a trifle rudely.

'Stone-Ears' did not need Eddie to interpret that for him - the expression on Grosnez' face and his general manner were sufficient.

"Okay," he said resignedly. "We'll go to my place. My stick please, Eddie."

Eddie reached down beside him and picked up a stout cane of oak that had been reposing on the floor next to their table. He handed it to 'Stone-Ears' who leant on it as he stood up.

They made their way out of the pub, keeping an eye on the fight as they did so. Piton cowered close to his master, terrified that he would get dragged into the battle before he had a chance to reach the relative safety of the outside world. But reach it he did, breathing a sigh of relief as the pub door closed behind him on the flying fists, flailing limbs and obscene oaths.

The Meade residence lay on the eastern edge of Piltdown, in one of the short streets that radiated from the village square. As Grosnez and Piton accompanied the others along the uneven, pot-holed, litter-strewn excuse for a path that circumscribed the circular square, the alcohol they had drunk combined with the fresh morning air made them feel decidedly light-headed. That *Hooke's Old Extendable* was certainly a potent brew, and, unless one was used to it, not the most advisable concoction to imbibe before breakfast as the two Angurians had done.

While they had been in the pub, a couple of goats and half-a-dozen cows had wandered on to the square, and were now contentedly feeding there, swishing their tails and occasionally shaking their heads to rid themselves of troublesome flies. One cow was standing with its rear half over the path a little way ahead of the four men and, as they approached it, said animal raised its head, turned it slowly in their direction, lifted its tail, and, still chewing the grass in its mouth, proceeded to relieve itself on the path. While the cow regarded them with a look that had more than a hint of mischief, they skirted the steaming legacy of this performance, which was already attracting its fair share of flies that buzzed excitedly as they homed in on it.

As the four of them walked past the square, the attention of the two Angurians was once again drawn to the row of three wooden posts sited near one end of the rectangular area occupying its centre. Grosnez was about to ask what these were for, when suddenly a babble of voices emanating from one of the streets on his left distracted him. A few moments later, a group of eleven men ran into the square and headed straight for the enigmatic rectangle. One of these was carrying another post, while another was the bearer of a piece of flat wood, one end of which had been fashioned into a hand grip.

Grosnez found his voice: "What's going on here, mon vier?" he asked Eddie as he and the others stopped to watch.

"They're practising for a cricket tournament," said Eddie matter-of-factly, as if it were the most natural thing in the world to be doing at this time of the morning.

"A *cricket* tournament?" repeated Grosnez.

"Isn't that some kind of grasshopper?" squeaked Piton.

"Shut up!" said Grosnez curtly.

"It's a local game," went on Eddie, "invented here in Piltdown."

"Ah!" said Grosnez. "How's it played?"

By now the eleven men, or *cricketers* as they were known, were arranging themselves on and around the rectangle. The one with the extra post appeared to be pacing out a distance from the row of three already in position. When he had reached what was evidently the right spot, he proceeded to drive the post into the ground using a hammerstone, taking care to ensure that it remained upright.

"There are two teams," began Eddie, by way of explanation. "Each has eleven men. One team bats, one player at a time, while the other fields."

"Bats?" queried Grosnez.

Piton shuddered. Not only did this game appear to involve grasshoppers, but it now seemed that those horrible flying mice had something to do with it as well.

"Yes," said Eddie. "The bat is that flat piece of wood that chap standing in front of the wicket is holding."

"The wicket?"

"Yes, those three pieces of wood. They're also known as the stumps."

"I see," said Grosnez.

"That chap squatting behind the stumps is the wicket keeper."

"So he looks after the, er, wicket?" asked Grosnez.

Before Eddie could answer, Piton interjected: "Does he keep a lot of wickets?"

Grosnez glared at him. Eddie looked puzzled.

"I.. I mean," said Piton, "does he have many at home?"

"No, no," replied Eddie, shaking his head. "It's just a term to describe what he does." He paused, then said: "Look! They're about to start playing. The batsman is ready and the fielders – those are the players standing around – are in position." Another pause. "Here comes the bowler."

He pointed towards one of the men who was in the process of running towards the solitary stump. As he approached it, he brought his right arm over his head and launched something – Grosnez and Piton could not see exactly what it was – at the man with the bat standing in front of the other three stumps. This worthy duly raised his bat and, taking a swipe at the missile as it arrived in his vicinity, struck it with a resounding *thwack* and sent it hurtling towards the far side of the square, a fielder promptly setting off in hot pursuit. Then, keeping an eye on the fielder, the batsman ran as fast as possible towards the far stump, touched the ground by this when he reached it, and then ran back to the wicket, getting there just as the missile, thrown by the fielder who had retrieved it, sailed past the three stumps, missing them by the narrowest of margins.

"You see," said Eddie, "the object of the game is for the batting team to score as many runs as possible."

"Runs?" queried Piton.

The DRAGON of ANGUR

"Yes," said Eddie. "One run is the distance between the wicket and the other stump."

"Obviously, dolt!" said Grosnez sharply, glaring at his servant.

"The fielding team has to try to get all the batsmen on the opposing team out for as few runs as possible," continued Eddie. "Then it's their turn to bat. The winning team is the one that scores the most runs."

"I see," said Grosnez. "And how do you get a batsman, er, out?"

"Three ways: if the bowler hits the wicket with the cricket ball; if one of the fielders throws the ball at the wicket and hits it while the batsman is running between the stumps; or if the batsman hits the ball and a fielder catches it before it hits the ground."

Grosnez nodded. Just then, the cricket ball landed not very far away and rolled towards his feet. Stopping it, he bent down and picked it up, turning it over in his hand with his thumb as he examined it. Its surface had a hard, leathery texture that yielded very slightly to pressure.

"Here, mate!" someone called. "Toss it back!"

Grosnez looked up. The cricketers were all looking at him. He threw it back in what he hoped was the right direction, and the playing continued.

"So that was a cricket ball?" he queried.

Eddie nodded.

"What's it made off?"

"Skin of an aurochs' bollocks filled with clay," replied the other matter-of-factly.

Grosnez made a face and involuntarily wiped his hand on his tunic. "Who do you play against?" he then asked.

"The neighbouring villages – they all have teams. There's a tournament that's held annually just after the spring equinox. I believe we'll be playing against Greater Scufflings first." He looked pensive, then said, half to himself: "Or is it Lesser Scufflings? I can't recall."

"What's the winner get?" asked Piton; an innocent enough question, although from the look Grosnez gave him, you'd have thought it was anything but.

"The ashes," was the strange reply.

Grosnez' face assumed a rather bemused expression. "The ashes?"

"Yes. The ashes of William the Graceful, a local medicine man who was the founding father of cricket. They're held in a special urn that the winner of the tournament gets to keep until the next one the following year."

"Who's got it at the moment? Piltdown?"

"Unfortunately not. Clapwater's won it for the past two years in succession, but we're confident we'll get it back this year."

No sooner had he finished speaking than the cricket ball flew past them, narrowly missing 'Stone-Ears' Meade's left ear and entered the window aperture of a hovel behind them. There was a howl of pain mingled with surprise as the missile found a target. Next moment, the building's front door was thrown open and a bucketful of things unmentionable flung in their direction. The foul stream hit the path immediately behind 'Stone-Ears', splashing his feet. He wheeled around and glared at the perpetrator of the deed, a buxom, elderly wench whose rotund face was livid with rage.

"Watch where you're throwing that muck, woman!" shouted the Meade. "You could have covered me with it."

"Watch where you're throwing your bollocks!" came the curt reply. "Next time I'll make sure I *will* cover you – from head to foot!"

This was repeated by Eddie for 'Stone-Ears" benefit in the usual fashion, causing the latter to shake a fist at the woman. Not that she noticed, as she was already on her way back inside by this stage, so it was her stooped back and exceedingly ample posterior that received the benefit of the Meade's response.

Leaving the players to negotiate with the buxom one for the return of their ball (which was probably not going to be all that easy), Eddie and his companions continued on their way, 'Stone-Ears' muttering things at the woman's expense. Four nearly naked children, playing a game of tag, then came running out of the next street and charged about the place in boisterous high spirits with much laughing and shouting. One of them shot past 'Stone-Ears' without looking where he was going, very nearly knocking him over and temporarily upsetting his balance.

The Meade tottered unsteadily for a few moments before regaining his equilibrium, only to have it upset again by another of the urchins haring past hard on the heels of the first. The old man steadied himself, and then waved his stick menacingly at the two boys as they ran away across the square.

"Look where you're going, you little wretches!" he called after them, but they paid no attention.

Gaining the entrance to the Meade's street without further incident, they turned into this and walked along it, passing a couple of singularly dilapidated thatch-roofed shacks on their left and two in not much better condition on their right. At the third door on the left, 'Stone-Ears' stopped.

"Here we are!" he said, a hint of pride in his voice.

In the context of this particular street, the pride was justified, for the Meade residence was an altogether better-looking establishment than any of the other properties. Constructed using the ubiquitous wattle-and-daub technique, its walls were more perpendicular and less bowed than those of any of its fellows, while the thatch covering of its pitched roof was similarly in better condition. Two small windows, one on either side of the door and each provided with shutters to exclude the weather and prying neighbours if necessary, permitted light to enter the interior.

Why this particular building should be in such good condition when the others in the street were all in varying states of disintegration was at first difficult to comprehend. However, the persistently curious would have discovered that the place was regularly and religiously maintained completely free of charge by a local family of artisans in exchange for the Meade's continued silence on a certain very delicate and dark matter pertaining to said family's ancestry.

'Stone-Ears' pushed open the door, which swung inwards easily on its wooden hinges, and led the way inside. The interior primarily consisted of one rectangular room with a central, stone-lined hearth near which cooking pots and equipment lay in neat arrangement. Four wooden stools were positioned around a rectangular table between this hearth and the left-hand end of the room, while a straw bed lay against the wall at the opposite end.

"Have a seat," said 'Stone-Ears', indicating the stools. "I'll get us some breakfast."

Grosnez would rather the other had just given him the information he was after, but managed to curb his impatience. It was obvious that 'Stone-Ears' was not one to be hurried, and breakfast was, in any case, probably a good idea.

'Stone-Ears' walked unsteadily over to a ladder leaning against the wall opposite the entrance and proceeded to climb this. It led up to a wooden platform that extended out over the room level with the base of the pitched roof, forming a sort of half-attic. Arranged on top of this in neat rows were clay vessels of various shapes and sizes, as well as a considerable number of sacks.

Grosnez watched the Meade's progress up the ladder with much apprehension, convinced that at any moment the old man would lose his balance and fall off, and he was greatly relieved when the latter made it safely on to the platform where he proceeded to rummage around amongst the sacks.

"I'll toss the bread down to you, Eddie," he called out a few moments later.

"Right, mate," replied Eddie, walking over to the base of the ladder and looking up.

'Stone-Ears' reappeared with a couple of large round loaves tucked under his left arm, while in his right hand he held a small clay jar. He carefully put the latter down on the platform and then chucked the loaves one at a time to Eddie, who caught them and took them over to the table. 'Stone-Ears' picked up the jar and manoeuvred himself on to the ladder, which he proceeded to descend rather unsteadily.

Grosnez watched him with renewed apprehension, but his fears proved unjustified and before long the Meade was sitting with them at the table, the small clay jar safely in the middle between the two loaves. There was also some butter, as well as both cow's cheese and goat's cheese, and, of course, a large flagon of ale, all of which Eddie had obtained from a shelf attached to the end wall nearest the table.

'Stone-Ears' picked up a flint knife from the table and cut each loaf in half, passing three of the halves to his companions and saving one for himself.

"Help yourselves," he said, pointing at the food on the table. "The cheese on the left is from cow's milk, the one on the right from goat's; there's honey in the small jar. I can get more bread if you want it."

Grosnez and Piton thanked him, the latter more profusely than the former, and proceeded to eat, breaking the bread with their hands and using the flint knife each had in front of him to spread the butter and honey and cut the cheese. Eddie poured handsome

The DRAGON of ANGUR

measures of the ale, which turned out to be nothing less than the fearsomely potent *Hooke's Old Extendable*.

"I have my own private supply specially delivered every year," explained 'Stone-Ears'. "It's the only beer I actually like. The rest of the year, I stick to mead."

"Well, it's certainly one of the nicest brews I've ever tasted," said Grosnez, after swallowing a couple of mouthfuls to wash down some bread and cheese he had just eaten. "But tell me, the location of this container - exactly where on Angur is it to be found?"

Eddie repeated the question for 'Stone-Ears" benefit, using his hands in the usual way.

The latter looked furtively around him, as if he suspected the presence of eavesdroppers, and then leaned forward across the table. "It's buried somewhere in the east of the island," he whispered, "in a spot that's not easy to identify precisely."

Great! thought Grosnez. "Well, can you be as precise as possible?" he asked.

"I'll try," replied the other, after Eddie had repeated the question for him. He swigged some ale, gulping it down noisily. "Are you familiar with the settlement of Gor?"

"I don't know it that well," lied Grosnez, "but I do remember it."

"There's a track that leads up through the woods to the headland above it. You follow this. When you get to the top, continue along the path for a hundred paces or so until you reach a second track leading away from it. Take this one. You will see a copse of five or six Elm trees ahead of you, a little way over to your left, overlooking an area of gorse and bracken. Make for the copse, and when you reach it, stand with your back to it so that you are facing directly out to sea. Then walk forward twenty paces." He paused, looking pensive. "Or was it twenty-five? I, er, can't quite recall. Anyway, somewhere around there you'll find the vial buried."

"I see," said Grosnez. "How deep is it?"

Once again, Eddie repeated Grosnez' question, holding his left hand above the table to indicate the level of the ground and moving his right vertically below it to indicate depth.

"I'm not sure exactly," said the Meade. "But I don't think it's all that far beneath the surface."

"Fine," said Grosnez. "Let me just repeat what you've told me to see if I've got it right."

This he successfully did without forgetting a single detail, Eddie conveying his words to 'Stone-Ears' in the usual fashion. Then Grosnez turned to Piton: "I hope you've been paying close attention, because later I'm going to test you on these directions to see whether you remember them."

"Yes, Grosnez, I have, Grosnez," said Piton quickly, after hastily swallowing the mouthful of beer he had just imbibed. He had fortunately foreseen just such a possibility and had made a point of paying *very* close attention to the Meade's directions.

"Good," said Grosnez. "You know what'll happen if you forget them."

"Yes, Grosnez, I do, Grosnez," said the other.

"Right," said his master, turning to 'Stone-Ears'. "You have been very helpful and kind - this breakfast's been most welcome. But I fear we must be on our way - the sooner we find that jar and its liquid, the sooner we'll be able to return home and help our people."

"I understand," said 'Stone-Ears' after Eddie had repeated Grosnez' words. "But we were hoping that you might stay for just one more day, especially as it's the spring equinox tomorrow and you would both be welcome to join in the festivities."

"That's very kind of you," said Grosnez. "But we really must be going. We've a fair walk back to our boat, and time is of the essence."

"Well if you won't stay," said Eddie, "at the very least let us give you some food and drink to take with you for the journey."

"That would be much appreciated," said Grosnez. *Excellent!* he thought. *Soon I'll be back on Angur and the liquid will be mine. Then once Old Mauger is out of the way playing his part in the festiv'ties for that fool La Tanche's Jubilee, I'll remove the turtle shell from his cave.* He gleefully rubbed his hands together under the table. With both the shell and the glowing liquid in his possession, he was going to be very powerful. Yes, very powerful indeed!

CHAPTER TEN

MANNEQUIN DE PERRELLE

The lone, cloaked figure making his way along a path in the north-west of Angur was confident that he was doing so completely unobserved. A white dew, glistening in the early morning sunlight, carpeted the open common over which the path led. A concert of twittering and chirruping filled the air as many avian voices greeted the new day. There was a freshness and vibrancy in the atmosphere and even the great, dark forest lying behind the walker seemed less brooding than usual.

A grassy mound stood some distance ahead, a little way to the right of the path's current direction. Normally such a mound was a homely, welcoming thing, but to the cloaked figure approaching it, this particular example was a pustule erupting from the skin of the land.

Vraicer T'loch glowered at the mound. He was relieved to note that no smoke was issuing from its summit as this meant that its owner was not at home. Of course this was something that he knew already, but the lack of smoke was reassuring. Time, however, was getting on and Grosnez was possibly on his way back from Piltdown at that very moment. T'loch quickened his pace.

He took a fork in the path that led through a gorse thicket to the entrance in the eastern perimeter of the mound. He stopped briefly by the megalith-framed heavy wooden door, tempted to break in to see what 'treasures' lay within. The temptation was only momentary; apart from any other considerations, there was no time.

He noticed that a narrow track had been trampled through the heather lying between the mound and the nearby cliff top. He followed this as far as he could and then stood at the edge of the cliff, getting his bearings.

The cave he was trying to reach lay somewhere below. But was it to the left or right? He could not recall. The problem was that there were two paths snaking down the cliff face, each heading in the opposite direction. He looked one way and then the other, massaging his bearded chin pensively.

After a few moments' deliberation, he came to a decision and took the left-hand route, climbing down as quickly as the narrow, tortuous path and his nerves would allow. He slipped once or twice on loose stones, but managed to keep his balance, making use of the odd root projecting from the cliff face. As he descended, he occasionally glanced at the sea, foaming and boiling as the waves crashed against the rocks uncomfortably far below. Sometimes it was on his right, sometimes his left, depending on the direction of the path as it snaked down the cliff face. Although he was a good swimmer, he did not fancy his chances if he should end up in the frothing, turbulent mass below. Further out, a bank of whitish-grey was building up as a sea fog developed with the approach of high tide, increasing the chill of the offshore breeze.

T'loch eventually reached the relative safety of some flat rocks at the base of the cliff and proceeded cautiously over these, keeping the cliff face close by on his left. After a short while, he reached a chasm leading in from the open sea and continuing into the cliff in the form of a sea cave. He smiled, confident that this was the cave he wanted.

He climbed down towards its entrance, keeping a wary eye on the changing sea level as the waves surged in and out of the chasm. Once at the cave mouth, he noticed that a narrow rocky ledge, barely a foot wide and only just above the high tide mark, ran inwards along the wall nearest to him and disappeared into the damp darkness of the cave's interior.

Clambering on to the ledge, he made his way inwards for a few feet and then stopped. As the sound of the waves flooding into and ebbing out of the cavern echoed around him, he reached inside the folds of his cloak and pulled out a small, reddish ball. Muttering a few words, he tossed this up and ahead of him with a deft movement of his right arm. There was a loud crack, audible even above the booming and sucking of the sea, and the whole cave was suffused with light; not a blinding, overpowering light, but sufficient for T'loch to see his surroundings with reasonable clarity.

The yellowy-orange glow from the ball, which was hovering a little way further in near the cave roof, revealed that the cavern narrowed as it went deeper. A small shelf of shingle sloped gently out of the sea at the far end and three small, leather-hulled boats were tied to a stout post sticking out of this subterranean beach.

Excellent! thought T'loch as he walked along the ledge as quickly as its narrowness and slippery, uneven surface would permit. This was without doubt Grosnez' cave. *Now, where would he have hidden that sea-dragon egg?*

Then, just as he reached the beach, his eyes fell on a small cleft in the rock wall on the far side. He walked smartly over to this, the shingle clattering beneath him as his boots dislodged pebbles of varying sizes. Reaching the hole in the rock, he muttered something and the red ball swooped down from above to hover just behind and slightly above his head, its light clearly illuminating the recess ahead of him.

The cleft in the rock widened to reveal a small, almost ovoid chamber beyond. Nestling on a bed of kelp covering the chamber floor was a large, bluish-green egg with a smooth, leathery surface. Reaching in with both hands, T'loch gently lifted it and drew it out. Then, carefully enveloping it in the folds of his cloak, he turned to leave the cave, the ball of light now helping to illuminate his way out. Once he was close enough to the exit for its assistance to be no longer required, he intoned a few words, the ball returned to his hand and was once again safely inside his cloak.

* * *

Gastelois de Bois was not in the best of humours. After that unexpected run-in with that pompous idiot from the *Dolmen and Granite Workers' Union* the day before (in the end he had decided not to see La Cloche about the matter), he was not in the right frame of mind to deal with the individual from the Pouquelaye and Earthworks Department whose arrival at the site was now imminent.

Over the past few years, the P. & E. Committee had become increasingly obsessed with petty detail, with the result that applications to build dolmens and related structures were invariably delayed while they debated matters such as the colour of a particular stone in a new dolmen's chamber or the shape of one that was to be used at some point in its passage. Their latest obsession was with a particular type of fine-grained granite from Mont Mado, an area in the north of the island. They were adamant that every new dolmen should include at least one stone of Mont Mado granite, which was fine if your site was in that particular neighbourhood, but decidedly inconvenient if it happened to be located a considerable distance away, such as overlooking the east coast as Gastelois' new one was.

He looked around at his men labouring on his new creation and dreaded to think what stupidity would be imposed on it. He consoled himself with the thought that he was not alone in this regard. In Lesur, his friend Thière's position was no better. In fact, not long before the recent Carnac conference, the unfortunate de Guérin had fallen foul of the Lesurian Pouquelaye and Earthworks Committee for adding side chambers to a dolmen so that they were accessed from the passage as opposed to the more usual arrangement whereby they opened off the main chamber. In the end, he had only got away with it because the dolmen in question belonged to the redoubtable Philoche du Tus, and that worthy had created merry hell when the P. & E. had suggested to Thière that he might like to reposition the new chambers elsewhere, stating vociferously that the members of said committee might find themselves repositioned if they were not careful.

By the previous evening, the site had been cleared of vegetation and deturfed, and all the blind springs and associated veins of water located and mapped out. Now, armed with a number of charcoal sketch-plans, Gastelois was trying out the first of his ideas for the design of the new dolmen. Under his direction, his men were laying out the plan on the ground with the aid of stakes linked by ropes pulled taut to maintain accuracy. Each length of rope was knotted at intervals of approximately two and three-quarter feet, this being the basic unit of measurement for dolmens, stone circles and other related constructions that had been standardised a good many years before. Once he was satisfied, Gastelois would prepare an accurate plan stencilled out on a large piece of animal hide in the usual way.

As was normal practice, they had started at the western end with what would become the main chamber (although when it came to actually building the dolmen, construction would start with the passage). Gastelois had opted for a simple half-moon shape for the ground plan of this part of the dolmen, but he intended to go for a fairly elaborate arrangement where the side chambers were concerned. These would open off the main chamber in the traditional fashion, but would be more numerous than usual, so that the prize dolmen would be useable not just by the winner and his immediate family but by his extended one as well, as was becoming the fashion. The passage would be normal, with a conventional splayed entrance.

Doubtless Gastelois' plans would be frustrated in some way or the other by the *Pouquelaye and Earthworks Committee,* but he fervently hoped that he would be allowed to do what he wanted, particularly as his new creation had been born from a special occasion and should therefore be worthy of it.

Mannequin de Perrelle arrived towards the end of the morning. The P. & E. man was a tall, skinny individual whose thinness bordered on emaciation, the sallow complexion of his equally gaunt face thrown into relief by the blackness of the rather straggly hair that framed it. His dark, sunken eyes quickly spotted the worthy de Bois, who was engrossed in checking a measurement and had not noticed his arrival.

Mannequin de Perrelle

"Good morning, Gastelois!" The voice was nasal, slightly constricted, as its owner had a cold.

The other looked up. "Ah, good morning, Mannequin. How are you today?" he added civilly.

"As well as can be expected," was the response. "Now, show me what you pr'pose to do here. I can't spend too long here as I've got some pr'blem to attend to next."

"Nothing too bad, I hope," said Gastelois, secretly hoping otherwise.

"Some bright spark has seen fit to use seaweed curtains in the windows of his house when we specific'lly told him he had to use leather ones!"

"That's tragic," said Gastelois, trying not to smile. "I hope you'll find our plans satisfactory."

"That depends," said the other in a tone of nasal non-committedness.

Armed with his plans, which he would refer to when necessary, Gastelois proceeded to take the Planning worthy around his site, starting with the main chamber. He had not got very far before his visitor interrupted him:

"Where are you going to put the Mont Mado granite?"

"Ah!" Gastelois looked at him blankly for a few moments.

"The Mont Mado granite stone. There has to be at least one. Where's it going, it?"

Gastelois recovered his composure. "Not quite sure yet," he said. "Probably somewhere in the main chamber."

Mannequin de Perrelle nodded slowly. The answer seemed to satisfy him. The tour continued.

"Where are you putting the gap?" was the next question, a few moments later.

"Usual place," said Gastelois. "One side of the main chamber or the other; not sure which yet."

More slow nodding. "Make sure it's of the required dimensions."

Gastelois felt irritation welling up inside him. He of all people did not need to be reminded of such things.

Some years previously, a dolmen had collapsed while under construction in Armor, crushing a group of workers and trapping several more: the victims had been unable to get clear as one of the capstones of the main chamber came down on top of them. Others inside the dolmen escaped that particular fate, but had been caught on the wrong side of the fallen capstone and had thus been unable to get out via the passage; they had to wait for some considerable time while their colleagues on the outside dug through the partially-completed mound surrounding it to reach them and so release them.

After this tragedy, an edict had gone out to the effect that there had to be some means whereby workers could escape quickly from a dolmen if a collapse threatened. After much head-scratching by builders of dolmens far and wide, one member of the breed had come up with the suggestion of leaving a gap in the wall of the main chamber, which could be closed by either a megalith or dry-stone walling once the rest of the structure had been safely completed. The idea was so beautifully simple that it was surprising that it took as long as it did for someone to come up with it.

"Right," said Mannequin, seemingly satisfied with what he took to be Gastelois' proposals for the main chamber. "I pr'sume that the chamber will narrow into the passage in the usual way." This was said as a statement of fact, rather than a question.

Gastelois, however, had a surprise in store for him. His men had not got around to laying out the plan of the proposed arrangement of side chambers before the P. & E. man's arrival, and so he showed him the relevant sketch plan of what was intended.

As he studied this, Mannequin de Perrelle's face assumed the appearance of one about to succumb to an apoplectic fit. The plan showed three small, rectangular chambers on each side, arranged in an arc curving out from what the worthy from Planning had assumed to be the passage end of the main chamber and then curving in again as it approached what would be the start of the passage itself.

"This shows six side chambers," he spluttered eventually.

"Yes," said Gastelois matter-of-factly.

"Six!" exclaimed the other.

"Yes, six," repeated Gastelois. "Is that a problem?"

"Six!" echoed Mannequin. He sniffed. "Why so many?"

Gastelois looked at him and frowned. De Perrelle was clearly going to give him a hard time over the side chambers.

"Well," he began by way of explanation, "as this new dolmen is intended for the prize winner of the dragon contest, who won't be from these shores, it should be able to accommodate the needs of his family too."

The Planning man sniffed loudly. "So?" he said in a tone that showed that he did not go along with the dolmen builder's reasoning. "I don't see why you need so many side chambers." More sniffing. "I know of other fam'ly dolmens – a regrett'ble trend and I'm not the only one to think so – and none of 'em has so many chambers."

"Then this one will seem bold and adventurous," said Gastelois, adding: "as befits one being created for the winner of a contest in honour of our High Elder's Jubilee."

"And what about the ritual area?" demanded Mannequin, looking around him. "As you well know, the bigger and more elab'rate the dolmen, the bigger we require the ritual area in front of the entrance to be."

"And the number of side chambers is one of the factors," said Gastelois, nodding. "I'm well aware of that."

De Perrelle looked towards what he assumed was going to be the entrance area, or forecourt, of the new dolmen. This was where a large number of the rites and rituals associated with a passage-dolmen's many functions took place and it was thus a very important part of the site.

"Your ritual area doesn't seem very big," he observed.

"We can always enlarge it if necessary," retorted Gastelois, not really bothering to hide the irritation he felt from his voice.

The other grunted. He extracted a grotty-looking rag from the sleeve of his leather tunic and blew his nose loudly. "I'm not happy with this, but I don't intend to waste any more time here t'day. I've got other matters to attend to. I suggest you think about r'ducing the number of chambers and," he raised the hand holding the now rather damp rag as Gastelois opened his mouth to say something, "I'll be back the day after t'morrow to inspect your r'vised plans. Good day!"

With that, Mannequin de Perrelle turned on his heels and walked smartly off the site, sniffing noisily. Gastelois and his assistant, Pierre de Lecq, who had been shadowing Gastelois and de Perrelle during the whole of the latter's visit, stared after him, expressions of consternation on their faces.

"Well, I s'ppose that was to be expected," remarked Pierre after a few moments as he gazed at the diminishing back of the Planning man.

Gastelois nodded slowly, but did not comment.

The DRAGON of ANGUR

"You could always complain to the Elders," suggested the other. "After all, it is their project."

Gastelois nodded again. "That I could, Pierre, that I could." He sighed. "Doubt it'd do much good, though. You know how easily they cave in on planning issues." He stopped staring at the receding form of Mannequin de Perrelle and turned around. "Although if that idiot causes us any more trouble, I might just say something."

He then looked at his men, who had been standing idly around during the meeting with de Perrelle. "Come on, back to work," he said to them. "Let's see what we can do about these side chambers."

* * *

Some time later, T'loch was hanging upside down, eyes shut, meditating over his seaweed fire, its pungent smoke bathing his body.

Verman! Verman!

Yes, my friend? The voice drifted into T'loch's thoughts.

I have your egg.

Ex.. excellent! Was it... was it, er, difficult?

No. Not at all.

That is pleasing to, er, hear. Verman Clouet's relieved face floated before T'loch's. *What, er, now?*

We'll stick to my plan. It's some way off hatching, so there's enough time.

Good. You'll, er, keep me in.. informed of, er, progress?

That I will, Verman. That I will.

With that, Clouet's face began to fade from T'loch's sight. The latter continued with his meditation, the smoke from the fire curling around his motionless body.

CHAPTER ELEVEN

AN UNEXPECTEDLY USEFUL ENCOUNTER

Old Mauger was relieved when Ortac came into view on the southern horizon. He had been flying non-stop since leaving Piltdown and was feeling rather tired. He would land on the island for a break, just as he had done on the way over to Alb. When he told his passengers what he proposed to do, Grosnez did little to hide his irritation and Piton did even less to hide his elation – it would be great to stand on solid ground again, even if it were only for a short while.

Resigned to this interruption in the flight, Grosnez suggested that, rather than landing on Ortac itself, they should land on the neighbouring islet of Bur, lying off Ortac's north-western coast. Nobody lived on Bur, so Grosnez reckoned that it would be safer to head for here as opposed to the main island. They came in low from the west, using the Sun's glare behind them to minimise the chance of being seen.

The dragon landed in a small cove on the northern coast of Bur. Sand dunes topped with marram grass bounded it above the high tide level and beyond these a stand of trees, bent under the constant battering of offshore winds, dominated the skyline.

Grosnez and Piton dismounted. All seemed quiet and peaceful. While Old Mauger went for a snooze in the shelter of a dune, Grosnez decided to reconnoitre the area. Piton reluctantly followed his master as the latter, keeping low, climbed up towards the trees. Peering out from the cover of these, they surveyed their surroundings.

Ahead of them lay a sandy plain, with marram grass again the dominant vegetation, its sharp-edged blades waving in the breeze. Here and there, small outcrops of grey, lichen covered rock jutted from the ground, clumps of yellow-flowered gorse growing out of cracks in them and adding some brighter colour to the scene.

Away to their left, the land rose up steeply to a rocky plateau whose summit was encircled by a ring of standing stones, spaced

The DRAGON of ANGUR

at even intervals. Within the area so enclosed, stood a number of wooden platforms, upon some of which lay bundles in varying states of unwrappedness. Gulls and other seabirds clustered around these, squawking and screeching incessantly as they tore at them with their sharp, pointed beaks. To the uninitiated, these structures with their mysterious 'packages' might have been something of an enigma, but to Grosnez and Piton, they were all too familiar. The stench wafted to their nostrils by the north-easterly breeze only confirmed what they already knew.

"No wonder this place is uninhabited," said Grosnez grimly. "I knew nobody lived here, but it never occurred to me why."

Piton did not say anything, but stared at the plateau, eyes wide with terror at the sight of the decomposing corpses on the platforms and their attendant carrion-feeding birds.

Something then distracted Grosnez' attention from the macabre sight on his left; something that he suddenly noticed out of the corner of his eye. Looking ahead, he turned very pale. There, sailing towards them across the channel that separated Bur from Ortac, was a flotilla of boats.

"Come on!" he said to Piton through gritted teeth. "We've got to get out of here!"

Piton stared at him blankly. He, too, had noticed the boats, but their significance had escaped him.

"Hurry fool! There's a funeral party coming!"

Realisation dawned, but if Piton had needed any further encouragement to depart the scene, it was suddenly provided by a gull dropping a partially-defleshed bone on the ground immediately in front of him, narrowly missing his head. Letting out a strangulated shriek, he turned on his heels and fled after his master, who was running back towards the dune where Old Mauger was snoring peacefully, blissfully unaware of what was going on.

Soon a rudely awakened dragon was winging his way southwards with two relieved passengers clinging to his back.

* * *

"What's the matter, Mauger?" asked Grosnez, sensing the dragon's hesitancy.

"It looks very cloudy, Grosnez," said Mauger.

"So?"

151

Sinclair Forrest

"Lot of low cloud ahead – sea fog. I don't think I'll be able to land."

"What d'you mean?" Grosnez was becoming anxious, fearful of yet another delay.

"There's too much fog around Angur; it won't be safe to land there."

"Don't be ridic'lous!" said Grosnez sharply. "You can get down alright. You must've landed in fog before, surely."

"Yes – when I was younger and my senses were sharper."

Grosnez wished he had his dowsing sticks with him; with their assistance in determining where the land lay in the fog, the dragon could have made an 'instrument' landing if, as he claimed, his senses were not up to it on their own.

"Gr.. Grosnez," piped up Piton. "If M. Mauger..."

"Shut up!" snapped his master, cutting him short. "As I've said more than once before, Mauger doesn't know his own cap'bilities."

"I think I do," said the dragon quietly as he eyed the greyish white bank of fog ahead completely shrouding Angur.

He looked over his shoulder to his right, back towards the gradually receding shapes of Lesur and Sersur, both islands still relatively fog-free, especially the latter. He glanced ahead and then back again. Then, without a word, he banked steeply and did a one-hundred-and-eighty-degree turn, his long snout finally pointing towards Sersur.

"What're you doing?" demanded Grosnez as he and Piton clung on for dear life.

"Diverting to Sersur," explained the dragon, venting off gas in a couple of fiery bursts to lose buoyancy and thus altitude.

"Not on Little Sersur!" cried Grosnez as Old Mauger lost height.

"Upset somebody there, have we?" asked the dragon sarcastically.

"Never you mind," retorted the other.

"Thought so."

They eventually landed in a small field not far north of La Coupée. Grosnez was certain that the dragon had deliberately chosen a spot as close to Little Sersur as possible, but decided not to waste his breath saying anything. At least from where they were they had a good view towards Angur and could therefore see when the fog began to lift.

Piton was not happy about being on any part of Sersur and, as Grosnez debated what to do for the duration of this latest delay, whined and moaned incessantly about his predicament. His master eventually told him to shut up in no uncertain terms, whereupon he lapsed into a sullen silence, fearfully looking around for signs of belligerent Sersurians popping out of the hedgerows to take him apart for daring to be on their island.

A few moments later, he thought his worst fears *were* going to be realised, for a couple of the natives did indeed appear on the scene. These two came ambling along the lane to the west of the field, heading in the direction of La Coupée. When they spotted the dragon and the two strangers, they started gesticulating wildly and nearly fell over each other in their excitement.

Once they had recovered from their surprise at seeing Old Mauger, they clambered on to the top of the bank bordering the field and hailed the new arrivals:

"Good morning!" they said in unison.

"Er, good morning," returned Grosnez.

"G.g.good m.m.morning," stammered Piton.

The Sersurians started to walk across the field towards them. Piton watched them apprehensively.

Grosnez was interested to notice that they both looked very much alike, virtually identical in fact. They were the same height, stocky with round, jovial faces topped by untidy mops of brown hair. They were wearing exactly the same attire – tunics, breeches and boots of reddish-brown leather.

"Welcome!" they said, again in unison, when they reached the two Angurians and simultaneously extended their right arms to shake hands with them.

This surprisingly cordial greeting was not at all what they had expected. Piton, who had virtually no first-hand experience of Sersurians and whose impressions of them were almost entirely based on hearsay and rumour, was especially taken aback by the warmth and friendliness of these two.

"What brings you to Sersur?" asked the one to Grosnez' left.

"We weren't intending to stop here," replied Grosnez, shaking the offered hand while Piton nervously shook hands with his companion. "But the dragon decided he couldn't land on Angur due to the fog."

"That's Old Mauger, isn't it?" said the other Sersurian, nodding in the dragon's direction.

"I am indeed he," confirmed Mauger in a tired voice.

"I'm Philoche d'Ane," said the Sersurian.

"And I'm Philippe," said his companion.

"Pleased to meet you," said Mauger in an it-wouldn't-particularly-bother-me-if-I-met-you-or-not tone of voice.

"As you may be here for a little while, would you like some refreshments?" enquired Philippe.

"That's an excellent idea!" said Piton enthusiastically, now more or less over his nervousness.

Grosnez glared at him and then beamed at the two Sersurians: "That's very kind of you." Then, realising that he had not introduced himself, added: "Oh, I'm Grosnez Chatel and this is my, er, friend, Piton."

Piton was most surprised at the way his master had introduced him and gave him a puzzled look, but another glare from the latter stopped him from going further and actually commenting on it.

After reassuring them that the dragon would be perfectly safe dozing in the field, the two Sersurians invited them back to their home for the proferred refreshments.

Philoche d'Ane and his twin brother Philippe lived not very far away at the end of a narrow track that descended gently through a small, shallow valley. The house itself stood near the head of this, overlooking the sea. It consisted of a cosy collection of wooden sheds of somewhat ramshackle appearance sprouting haphazardly from the circumference of a steep-sided grassy tumulus. This covered a corbel-vaulted circular stone chamber approached by a short passage leading in from the entrance in its eastern, landward side. A horseshoe of evenly spaced, tall elm trees framed the house on three sides, the open end facing inland.

Philippe pushed open the oak door closing the entrance and led the way inside. The smell of lamps of burning animal grease greeted Grosnez and Piton as they followed him into the stone passage. Grosnez had to bend quite low to negotiate it due to the usual lack of headroom. Piton, on the other hand, being somewhat

The DRAGON of ANGUR

lacking in stature especially compared with his master, did not find it so awkward.

The chamber at the centre of the mound was a particularly cosy affair, furnished with all the impedimenta of domesticity you would expect. It was notable for the number of animal-skin paintings adorning its curved wall, just about visible in the illumination provided by the shaft of sunlight that filtered down through the hole in the roof directly above the ubiquitous central hearth. These mainly depicted fishing and hunting scenes, but a few were abstract. It turned out that they had been painted by the twins' father and grandfather, both artists of considerable local standing.

Before long, Grosnez and Piton were sitting at a round, wooden table, each tucking into a large platter of smoked fish, oysters and bread, washed down by generous measures of cider. The meal was very welcome, as the flight from Alb had given them considerable appetites. Philippe sat down with them, joining them in a jar of cider. He and his brother had already partaken of a good breakfast so food was not a priority. While they were eating, Philoche disappeared to take a large bucket of some pungent herbal drink to Old Mauger, rightly assuming that it was not just the two Angurians who were in need of refreshments.

"So," said Philippe after his brother had left, "you've been away somewhere, then?"

"That we have, mon vier. We've been..." Piton stopped in mid-sentence as Grosnez shot him a don't-you-dare-say-another-word-I'll-do-all-the-talking sort of a look.

"Indeed," said Grosnez. "We had to visit an old relative of mine who lives in the south of Alb. Word reached me that she'd been taken very ill, her. That's why we enlisted the serv'ces of Old Mauger - so we could get over there as quickly as poss'ble."

"I'm sorry to hear that," said Philippe with genuine sympathy. "I hope all is okay."

"Yes, thanks. But it was touch 'n' go for a while, touch 'n' go." He took a large swig of cider and smacked his lips noisily in appreciation. "Good stuff this, mon vier."

"Glad you like it. Some more?"

Grosnez accepted and slid his jar across the table in the other's direction.

Philippe turned to Piton: "Some more for you, too?"

"Er, yes, yes please." He gulped down the remainder of the cider in his jar, dribbling copious amounts down his chin in the process, before handing the empty vessel to their host.

While the latter was replenishing their jars, Grosnez got up and walked over to the paintings to look at them more closely. They had certainly been executed with great skill and a fine eye for detail. One scene in particular caught his attention. It showed a long-necked marine animal being pursued by two boatloads of what he took to be fishermen, although they did not appear to be armed with the expected spears. Especially interesting was the line of yellowy-green dots along the lower part of the animal's slightly bulbous body, just below the level of the top of the two flippers, the upper part of which could be seen protruding from the series of wavy lines that clearly represented the sea. A smile briefly flickered across Grosnez' face. He knew what he was looking at: a depiction of that rarely seen, almost mythical creature, a sea-dragon. It was amazingly realistic, almost as though the artist had painted it from life.

He peered at the dots. He was intrigued to observe that when they fell into the shadow of his body, they seemed to glow with a light of their own, as if the paint possessed a phosphorescent quality.

"I see you're admiring our sea-dragon," said Philippe, who had just returned with the jars, brimmed with more cider.

"Yes," said Grosnez, turning around. "It's very good."

Philippe nodded, putting the drinks on the table. "Yes." He sat down. "Our grandfather painted it after seeing one on an expedition he'd gone on."

That explains why it's so lifelike, thought Grosnez. Out loud, he remarked: "He's used a very interesting paint for those spots."

"I believe he got it from Verman Clouet, our local magician."

Piton shifted uncomfortably at the mention of Clouet's name.

"Is that so?" Grosnez raised his eyebrows. *Fascinating,* he thought.

"Yes." Philippe pushed a jar in Grosnez' direction as the latter returned to the table and resumed his seat. "Apparently it's not paint at all, but some liquid from an actual sea-dragon. Goodness knows how old Verman got hold of it, but these magicians seem to be able to get all sorts of weird and wonderful things, them. But Philoche knows more about it than I do."

If up to this point Grosnez had been only mildly interested in what he was hearing, he was acutely interested now. *A liquid that glows in the dark*, he mused. *Was it just possible that the glowing liquid they needed was the same substance as had been used in this painting?*

At that moment, Philippe's brother came back into the chamber, returning with the now empty bucket. "What do I know more about, me?"

"Sea-dragon liquid. Friend Grosnez here was admiring grandfather's painting."

Philoche pulled up a seat and joined them at the table. "Ah yes. A fine piece of work."

"Philippe was just telling me that those spots on the dragon's body were made with the liquid from a real one," said Grosnez, anxious to learn more. "Why would he go to the trouble of using actual dragon liquid instead of some other, more easily obtainable substance?"

"Realism," said the other. "Grandfather was a stickler for realism; the more lifelike his paintings, the happier he was. He told us that the sight of the spots glowing at night on the sea-dragon he once saw made a lasting impression on him. He did try to reproduce it with paint, but he could never get it right, so he decided that only the real stuff would do."

"I understand he got it from old Clouet," said Grosnez.

"Yes, that's right, but if he knew how Verman got it, he wasn't telling. Rumour has it, though, that Verman either has or certainly had a sea-dragon of his own. In fact, it's common knowledge in these parts that he keeps a number of, er, interesting creatures, although I don't believe anyone has actually seen any of them."

"*Really?*" Grosnez pretended to be amazed. *Interesting creatures, eh! Probably the 'little ones' old Verman had mentioned.*

"Yes," continued Philoche. "According to a legend grandfather heard, there was a select group of magicians who were able to tame and control the sea-dragons. They lived on an island far away across the *Sunwise Sea*. They..."

"I've heard that story," said Piton excitedly, interrupting him.

Grosnez glared at his servant, displeasure clouding his features. "It's quite a well-known story, I b'lieve," he said to Philoche. "But do go on."

"Well, these magicians apparently raised young dragons from hatchlings and milked them for various substances that they used in their spells and potions; by all accounts, the younger the dragon, the better the quality of what they produced. It's also believed that the magicians were somehow able to keep the dragons young – just as they were apparently able to stop themselves from growing old in the normal way."

"Yes, I'd heard that too," said Grosnez, nodding.

"The dragons guarded the island against unwelcome intruders, but they couldn't guard it against powers beyond their own. One day, a great glowing fireball, brighter than the full Moon, came out of the heavens and struck the sea close to the island, causing huge waves to engulf it."

"And it's b'lieved that some, if not all, of the magicians escaped from the island along with their dragons," said Grosnez.

"Exactly. The legend suggests that they knew what was going to happen."

"And that old Verman Clouet might be one of them." He eyed the other closely to see what reaction this remark produced.

"Indeed so," agreed Philoche without hesitation, nodding. "And your own Vraicer T'loch."

"Well, that's the rumour anyway." Grosnez gulped down some cider and smacked his lips noisily. "But to go back to this glowing liquid. Does it have any other, er, qualities?" He stared intently at Philoche.

The other studied him equally intently. He was not sure exactly why, but he decided that a degree of discretion was called for. "I don't know," he said, shaking his head. "Grandfather wasn't specific – just that the magicians used the various substances they got from the sea-dragons in their potions and spells, as I said." He paused for a moment. "Why?"

"Oh, no partic'lar reason. Just int'rested," said Grosnez with forced nonchalance. Then quickly changing the subject: "I wonder if the fog's cleared yet."

"Let's go and have a look," suggested Philippe. "I'd have thought it should be starting to lift by now."

With that, the four of them left the twins' home and made their way back up the track to the lane at the top of the small valley. From there they would be able to see whether Angur was still shrouded in fog.

The DRAGON of ANGUR

To Grosnez' relief, the fog was considerably less dense than it had been, and parts of the Angurian coastline were now visible between patches of white where the sea mist was stubbornly resisting the dispersing effect of the Sun's warming rays. He was certain that he would be able to persuade the dragon to take off, despite areas of Angur's north coast still being fog bound, as by the time they reached their destination, visibility should have improved sufficiently for a safe landing.

Thanking the two brothers for their hospitality, he and Piton bade them farewell, and then made their way along the lane to the field where Old Mauger was lying snoring peacefully in the morning sunlight.

Philoche and Philippe watched them go, waving and smiling politely.

As soon as he was sure that the two Angurians were out of earshot, Philoche turned to his brother: "A couple of queer fish, aih?"

The other nodded: "Yes, the tall one seemed rather too interested in the uses of the milk that glows. You were probably wise not to give too much away."

"Mmm," agreed Philoche. "I just hope I didn't say more than I should've done."

* * *

The north coast of Angur was drawing closer with each passing moment, but with each passing moment Mauger was growing increasingly tired. Almost on the point of exhaustion, he was finding it increasingly difficult to remain airborne. He was beginning to doubt whether he would make it as far as dry land and was seriously contemplating ditching in the sea. He was certain that, if it had not been for Philoche's herbal drink, he would have been in the sea already.

Sensing that all was not well with the dragon, Grosnez actually tried to reassure him: "Won't be long now, Mauger," he said softly. "Soon be there."

Of course his reasons for such encouragement were far from altruistic, his motives having rather more to do with self-preservation than with anything else.

During the flight from Sersur, his mind had dwelt on nothing except sea-dragons and glowing liquids. He was anxious to find the container and study its contents. If these turned out to be the same as the substance used for the spots on that painting, as he strongly suspected would be the case, then this would be conclusive proof that they had come from a sea-dragon. It would make sense, too; after all, those magicians had used the dragon liquids for sundry spells and potions, so it stood to reason that the substance required to make the turtle shell work would come from such a creature.

There was something else, too. Something that filled him with great excitement. The egg he had taken from Clouet's place. It was almost certainly a sea-dragon egg. If he could hatch it, he would have his very own sea-dragon to supply him with substances for his own spells and potions. What could he *not* achieve? The possibilities were endless.

Suddenly, his reverie was broken. Piton had spotted something in the water. "What's that?" he squeaked in nervous excitement, pointing to the right of Old Mauger's head.

"What's what?" demanded Grosnez, an irritated tone to his voice.

"*That!*" repeated Piton, jabbing his finger into the air.

Grosnez peered in the indicated direction. The dragon turned to glance at Piton and then he, too, followed the others' gaze.

To be frank, they did not have the slightest notion of what they were looking at. Some species of floating contraption (for want of a better description) appeared to be wallowing in the water a little way to the west of them some distance off Angur's northern cliffs. As far as they could make out, it consisted of two long, rather bulbous hulls joined together amidships by a series of horizontal planks. Each hull sported a team of oarsmen, who seemed to be trying to outdo each other as to who could row the faster. That this battle royal was proving to have no clear victor was evidenced by the corkscrew path the contraption was ploughing through the waves.

But oddest of all was what appeared to a long tree-trunk running from stem to stern along the thing's centre line, terminating at one end in what could best be described as a large bucket, and at the other in what looked like a basket full of stones. It was evidently supported in the middle by a tall, trestle-like, wooden frame that stood on the platform of transverse planks connecting the twin hulls and around which frame clustered a small group of people, all evidently trying to hang on for dear life as the vessel steered its erratic course westwards.

The DRAGON of ANGUR

"What's that?" squeaked Piton in nervous excitement

Then, as the dragon and his passengers watched transfixed, the bucket end of the arm suddenly, for no apparent reason, shot skywards and then forwards. The rapidity of this movement combined with the craft's forward momentum caused the latter's bows to dive under the waves, driving ever deeper until both hulls stood straight out of the water like a couple of ducks going after food. The resemblance, however, endured but briefly, for, unlike the feathered variety, these two 'ducks' continued to rotate until the entire contraption was upside down in the water.

The unfortunates crewing this vessel, who had been flung clear during its maritime cartwheel, were now climbing on to its upturned hulls one by one, spluttering and coughing after their unexpected immersion. One individual, who had hauled himself out of the water, was now standing atop one of the hulls, doing his best to keep his balance while gesticulating with his arms and apparently shouting commands, for evidently he was in charge.

So intent had Mauger and his companions been on watching the performance below them that none of them had been keeping an eye on where they were going.

Then Piton looked up and let out a shriek of alarm. Grosnez turned and managed to shout a warning: "Mauger! Look out! The cliff!"

The dragon, suddenly alerted to the proximity of the cliff face, flapped his wings vigorously in an attempt to gain height. By some miracle, he managed to clear the face and fly over the summit, but the effort had been too much for his failing strength and he did an unceremonious belly flop on to the heather-covered common just inland from the cliff edge, then slid for a few yards before coming to a halt.

Somehow, Grosnez and Piton both managed to hold on.

"We're home," announced Mauger panting, smoke rising from his flaring nostrils.

"So I gather," said Grosnez as he dismounted. "Thanks for the ride."

"You're welcome," said the dragon without meaning it.

"Come on, Piton," said Grosnez as his servant dismounted. "As we've landed some way away from home, we've got a bit of a walk."

"Yes, Grosnez."

Old Mauger watched them head off westwards. He had not landed *that* far from Grosnez' home. Anyway, a walk would do them both good. He would lie here a little while longer and then he would make his way home too.

* * *

T'loch was ensconced across the entrance to Old Mauger's cave, sitting half in and half out of it, staring out over the paludal area beyond. Other than the mutterings, croakings and rustlings of the denizens of the marsh, animal and vegetable, the day was still. The dragon was snoozing peacefully at the rear of his home, the gently rising and falling mass of his body only just discernible in the gloom, a haze of smoke around his nostrils.

"You did very well," said T'loch gently. "Much has been accomplished during the course of that trip. I am well pleased."

Old Mauger stirred and grunted. His snout widened slightly as he smiled a dragonly smile. Although spoken softly, he had heard the magician's words as clearly as if they had been uttered at a normal conversational level. "Thank you," he said dreamily.

"Is the potion beginning to take effect yet?"

The dragon grunted again. He was regarding T'loch's figure, silhouetted against the daylight outside the cave, through half-open eyes. When T'loch had arrived at his home, he had given Mauger a special drink that would initially act as a stimulant for long enough for the two of them to discuss the Piltdown trip and Grosnez' quest for the vial of liquid, but would then send the dragon into a deep, dream-free slumber that would rejuvenate him and fully restore his strength after his long journey.

"It was kind of Philoche to give you that drink on Sersur," said T'loch.

"Yes," mumbled the other. "I don't think I'd have made it back without it, despite the decent breakfast Otis gave me before I left Alb." He stretched his long body and yawned noisily. "In fact, it was touch and go as it was."

"I know," said T'loch, a trifle grimly. "But at least you got back safely." He watched a kestrel hovering silently over the marsh, occasionally adjusting its position slightly by slipping a little to its left or to its right. Suddenly, it dropped like a stone, abruptly arresting its descent a few feet above a grassy clump in one of the marsh pools. After staying in this position for a few moments, it rose up to resume its original higher position.

T'loch continued: "Old 'Stone-Ears' gave Grosnez exactly the directions for locating the vial I told him to – very reliable is my old friend Meade – and that fool and his whingeing servant will doubtless soon be off looking for it." He smiled wryly: "They're in for quite a shock."

Old Mauger yawned. T'loch's potion had initially revived him as it was meant to do, but now its secondary effects were showing signs of kicking in. "I'm feeling sleepy," he said.

"Right," said the other, getting to his feet and coming into the cave. "I've got something for you."

"Oh yes?" Mauger stifled another yawn. "A present for me?"

"Not exactly," replied T'loch. "Something I want you to look after for the time being."

So saying, he walked up to the dragon and knelt beside his head. Reaching inside the folds of his cloak, he pulled out a bluish-green, leathery ovoid and carefully laid it on the ground.

Mauger recognised what it was at once. "A *sea-dragon* egg!" he exclaimed. "What are you doing with *that*?"

T'loch quickly explained how it had come into his possession - how Grosnez had stolen it from Verman Clouet and how he, T'loch, had retrieved it from Grosnez' cave.

"I take it Grosnez doesn't know you've got it," said the dragon when the other had finished.

"No, not yet. It will be interesting to see what he does about it when he finds out it's gone."

"And you want me to look after it?"

"Yes please. Just put it somewhere safe. Oh, and don't worry, it's some way off hatching."

"I know that," said Old Mauger, a slightly irritated tone to his voice. "I can sense such things."

"Of course," said T'loch apologetically. "Right, you get some rest. I'll come back in a few days' time and we'll discuss things further. There will doubtless have been some developments by then."

The dragon bade him a sleepy farewell. Through drooping eyelids, he regarded the egg reposing nearby. He would deal with it when he woke up.

CHAPTER TWELVE

EQUINOX

Fortunately for the ceremonies on Angur, the day of the spring equinox dawned bright and clear, although there was a hint of sea fog in the air. Long before the first rays of the awakening Sun began to brighten the eastern sky, however, the people of that island were making their way from their homes to its most south-easterly point where its priests had one of their two ritual centres and observatories. Situated on a low, flat promontory jutting into the sea, it consisted of circles and alignments of wooden stakes and standing stones, and was mainly used to plot the position of the rising Sun and observe the Moon and the stars.

The other centre was to be found on Angur's western coast and was in fact the larger and more impressive of the two, with the priests' principal settlement situated nearby. While it, too, had a vital astronomical role to play and would be the focus of the equinox sunset ceremonies at the end of the day, it served another, equally important function. For it was here that the recently departed were brought for the commencement of the rituals that would ensure their safe journey to the spirit world and the abode of the ancestors.

No such thoughts of departure, however, were in the minds of the people as they walked towards the south-east of the island. Although the clear night and full Moon made for easy progress, some of them carried flaming torches as a further aid to visibility. A carnival atmosphere dominated the proceedings, with much chatting and laughing and singing and dancing along the way, despite the earliness of the hour.

The celebrations went without a hitch. When the people arrived, young and old alike were invited to partake of a warm broth of seafood simmering in large vessels standing over open fires at the megalithic trilithon marking the entrance to the ceremonial area. They were also given a drink of a suitably mind altering beverage to help them get into the right spirit for the proceedings.

The Sun duly appeared above the eastern horizon, its arrival welcomed with the blast of horns and much chanting by priests and populace. Semi-naked maidens of more than passing comeliness and youths of reasonably impressive physique cavorted in front of the circles and alignments of wooden posts and standing stones to the accompaniment of flute-like instruments enthusiastically played by musicians seated nearby.

Gastelois attended with Sylvia d'Arass and Marie-Hélène. Although he appeared to be joining in with as much enthusiasm as his fellow Angurians, in reality his mind was elsewhere. Tomorrow, when the island was back to normal, he would have to start looking for suitable megaliths for the new dolmen - the east coast foreshore would be a good place to begin - and later this evening, once the sunset festivities had been concluded, he would visit the High Priest to discuss their transportation to the site.

A group of specially-trained priests would use levitation[7] to assist with the moving of the larger stones from source to destination, and Gastelois hoped that this would be accomplished without untoward incident or drama of any kind. Somehow, though, he doubted it; the priests' track record in this respect was not particularly encouraging.

Once the megaliths had been selected, any trees and vegetation along the routes to their new abode would have to be cleared to facilitate their transportation. If the majority of the stones could be obtained from the eastern foreshore as he hoped, this clearance should not prove too strenuous a task as it was a fairly short distance from there to the site. Of course he had to include at least one block of Mont Mado granite to keep the Planning Department happy, which was a total pain in the proverbial as moving that from the quarry in the north of the island could quite easily cause more hassle than all the other stones put together. He would select the smallest block he could get away with.

The celebrations continued with unabated enthusiasm, with much rejoicing at the safe arrival of spring. Although it was not

---

[7] The traditional method of levitation employed a number of specially-trained priests (the standard number was seven, although multiples of that were sometimes used for especially large items) who, arranging themselves in an arc behind the object to be moved, used a combination of drums, bone trumpets and chanting to produce sound waves of such a frequency and intensity that the object, somehow defying gravity, lifted off the ground. It could then be moved with relative ease in the required direction.

something that many other people would have been thinking about at this time, if indeed any at all were, Gastelois found himself musing on the sometimes questionable coordination of the efforts of the priests who ran Angur's two ritual centres. Both groups were supposed to work in association with each other and compare the results of their observations.

This, however, was not always the case and there had been not a few times in the past when one group had suddenly announced the imminent materialisation of some astronomical phenomenon, to the total surprise and considerable consternation of the other lot who had not been expecting it to occur at that particular time. Depending on the outcome of the prediction, one set of priestly faces had smirked, while the other had exhibited embarrassment.

On one especially memorable occasion, the eastern group had predicted a particularly splendid lunar eclipse, which was due to take place in the small hours of the morning. A large percentage of the population had stayed up late to view the phenomenon and the clouds that earlier in the day had threatened to obscure the proceedings obliged by staying away. But the full Moon had remained resolutely bright throughout, its brilliant white face neither dimmed nor reddened by the passing of the Earth between it and the Sun.

Gastelois had been one of those watching. His initial annoyance at the non-occurrence of the eclipse had given way to wry amusement as realisation dawned that there had been yet another cock-up by the priests. They had not got it entirely wrong, however. There *had* been a lunar eclipse – two days later.

Gastelois smiled at the recollection. Hopefully all would go smoothly today and the priests at the western centre would be adequately prepared for the sunset ceremonies. To be fair, though, previous disruptions of the equinoctial rituals and festivities had been down to the weather misbehaving and not due to miscalculations or mistakes on the part of the priests. The presence of the High Priest and senior members of the priesthood at the eastern centre in the morning and at the western one in the evening at the times of both equinoxes (and the two solstices as well) tended to ensure that everything ran smoothly.

One could never be certain, however; there was always a first time for everything...

* * *

The two figures creeping stealthily along the path winding its way between the hedgerows looked as incongruous as ever: the tall, lanky one with the pointed chin followed reluctantly by the short, spindly one with the pointed ears. There was no one around to question their intentions as the island's population had transferred its equinoctial celebrating to every pub on Angur, which were consequently bursting at their seams.

In fact, on one such occasion several years previously, so many had crowded into *The Croaking Crapaud* that it had indeed burst at its seams, sending its hapless clientele sprawling over collapsing wattle-and-daub walls while its thatched roof, deprived of support, descended unceremoniously on top of them. Fortunately there were no serious injuries, doubtless due to the alcoholically-relaxed state of the drinkers.

Later on, the people would make their way to the west of the island for the sunset festivities. That, however, was still some time off and Grosnez knew that they were unlikely to be disturbed, although Piton was as nervous as ever.

"Gr.. Grosnez," he squeaked at one point. "Suppose we're seen?"

"So?" demanded the other without turning around.

"Well, what're we going to say to..."

"Oh shut up!" snapped Grosnez, not waiting for Piton to finish. "No one's going to bother us – they're too busy getting pissed, them."

"Yes, Grosnez. Sorry, Grosnez."

The path led on between the hedgerows, on either side of which fields spread out almost as far as the eye could see. Wheat was growing in some of these, whilst in others aurochs grazed contentedly, their tails occasionally swishing to ward off irritating flies. Here and there stood copses of trees, like advance guards of the great dark forest that brooded on the western horizon.

Eventually, Grosnez and Piton reached the headland overlooking the settlement of Gor. Due to the trees cloaking its slopes, the village was hidden from their view, but the din emanating from the *The Quernstone* told them that the place was far from deserted.

Grosnez scanned his surroundings through narrowed eyes. "There," he said after a short while, pointing with a long, bony finger to where a path emerged from the trees. "That's our starting point. Come on!" He began to walk briskly towards the spot in question.

"Now, what did that deaf old fool say?" he said when he reached it. "Head along this track for a hundred paces until we get to a second one."

"Yes, Grosnez. That's right, Grosnez," agreed Piton, too nervous at this juncture to be able to recall exactly what 'Stone-Ears' Meade had told them.

They duly reached a fork in the path. "Right, here we are," said Grosnez, who had been counting his paces. "We take this one." He then pointed towards a stand of trees ahead of them and a little way over to their left. "That must be the copse. C'mon, mon vier!" With that, he strode off along the narrow track.

Piton hurried to keep up with him, ears anxiously pricked up for any indication that the populace of Gor had ceased boozing itself to the gills and was coming after them. Quite why the good people of the village should come after them was another matter, as most certainly they were unaware of the presence of two miscreants in the neighbourhood, let alone what they were up to.

As they approached the copse, Grosnez frowned. According to the Meade's instructions, there should have been five or six Elm trees overlooking a mass of gorse and bracken under which, twenty to twenty-five paces in from one of the trees ('Stone-Ears' had been unable to recall the exact distance and had not specified the precise tree), was buried the vial of liquid they desired to find.

However, it was becoming apparent to Grosnez that all was not quite as the Meade had described. For one thing, there appeared to be only three trees; for another, most of the gorse and bracken was gone, apparently cleared away and recently at that. But what struck them more forcibly than anything else, once they were close enough to see it, was the series of stakes that had been stuck into the ground to mark out the plan of something.

It did not take Grosnez long to figure out what that something was. As they stood staring at the area, Piton watched his master's face turn increasingly puce with rage.

"Wh.. What's the matter, Grosnez?" he ventured after a few moments.

"You... You know what *this* is?" hissed Grosnez between clenched teeth.

"No, Grosnez, I don't, Grosnez."

"This is the site of the new dolmen – the prize dolmen for the dragon contest!" He made clicking noises with his tongue. "They've got the plan marked out; that's what those are for." He nodded towards the stakes.

"What're we going to do, Grosnez?" asked Piton.

"I'm not sure yet, fool," was the gruff response. He massaged the point of his chin pensively. Then, without a word, he began to walk past the stakes, heading for the far end of the clearing.

Piton followed him, keeping his mouth shut. He was sure his master would reveal all in due course.

He was right. When Grosnez reached the three surviving Elm trees, he turned to his servant: "Right, as that idiot 'Stone-Ears' couldn't be specific, we'll walk twenty to twenty-five paces in from each tree in turn, including the two that have been cut down." He nodded towards a couple of stumps standing forlornly to the left of the Elms. "Then we'll see what we've got."

A little while later, at the end of this exercise, Grosnez' mood was no better. In fact, if anything it was worse. Not only was there no sign of any disturbance of the ground to indicate where something might have been buried, but each time they had paced the distance from one of the trees, they had ended up within the area marked out by the stakes; in other words within what would become the interior of the new dolmen. As work on the new structure progressed, it would become increasingly difficult to carry out clandestine investigations of the search area. They would therefore need to find the exact location of the vial and excavate it as quickly as possible.

Grosnez made a decision. "Come on," he said. "There's no time to lose."

"Where're we going, Grosnez?"

"To see La Cloche."

* * *

After the last segment of the setting Sun had slipped beneath the western horizon, the assembled multitude began to wend its way homewards. Having said goodbye to Sylvia and Marie-Hélène, who had been with him throughout the day, Gastelois stayed behind to see the High Priest to arrange for the levitation of the megaliths for the new dolmen.

He gazed into the western sky, a freshening sea breeze ruffling his fair hair. Clouds were building above the horizon, their undersides warmed red by the rays from the now vanished sun. Away in front of him, at the edge of the heathland that was the predominant feature of the southern half of the western coastal plain and overlooking the seashore, rose the wooden stakes and standing stones of the circles and alignments used by the priests to plot the movements of the Sun, Moon and stars. Enshrouded in silence now that the equinox festivities were over, they stood silhouetted against the gradually darkening sky.

Gastelois glanced at the clouds massing over the horizon. *Looks like rain,* he mused. *Hope not – I've got enough problems without the weather turning against me.*

He gave an involuntary shiver as he turned to walk inland, the dark mass of the low cliffs bounding the western edge of the central plateau ahead of him assuming a slightly menacing appearance in the gathering twilight. This rocky rampart was breached by a number of wooded valleys leading eastwards up to the higher ground, and at the mouth of one of these lay the principal settlement of the Angurian priesthood, the homely glow emanating from the lamps and hearths of its buildings going some way towards relieving the gloomy aspect of the nearby rock wall.

This settlement covered quite an extensive area, spreading out from both banks of the small river that ran through the valley and across the heath on its way to the sea. When Gastelois reached the river, he followed it inland towards the low, grass-covered earth bank that encircled the settlement, a ring of standing stones surmounting it like ever-watchful sentinels. Two larger menhirs flanked a gap in the bank through which the river flowed, this being the main entrance.

As he made his way inside, following the path that ran close by the river's northern bank, Gastelois eyes were drawn to where the river bisected a circular area at the centre of the settlement. Two rings of standing stones, one on either side of the river, subdivided this central area into two distinct zones.

The space encircled by the northern ring was dominated by a large wooden round house whose circular timber wall was not quite perpendicular, while its sagging, conical roof of logs and thatch was in almost as precarious a state as that crowning the similar, even larger edifice that graced the Town Mount.

Within the southern ring of standing stones stood a large gallery-dolmen, similar to *The Old Vraic and Coracle.* It looked somewhat neater than the latter as it did not have wooden lean-tos tacked on to its sides. Like the pub, it had no enveloping mound, but it differed from it by having a short, but pronounced entrance passage with, uncommonly, the entrance at its western end. In addition, this dolmen possessed one other rather unusual feature – towards its eastern end, the main chamber made a right-hand turn to form what was in effect a large side chamber sprouting from its southern side.

In the distance, beyond the central area, what seemed to be a particularly ramshackle wooden edifice straddling the river was just visible. It was difficult for Gastelois to make out its form clearly in the gathering gloom, but it looked like a cross between a trapezoidal long house and an egg, as though it could not make up its mind which shape it preferred.

The path Gastelois was following curved around the outside of the northern circle of standing stones, and from equidistant points along this section, serpentine paths bordered by yet more standing stones, alternately squat and thin, snaked outwards, each one leading to a group of three circular, stone dwellings. There was an identical arrangement on the other side of the river: exactly the same number of serpentine paths leading from the southern stone circle to more houses.

Of moderate size, these priestly habitations stood near the perimeter of the settlement, close to the ditch that bounded the inside of the encircling bank. Each house consisted of a short entrance passage of megalithic uprights roofed by capstones, which led into a drystone-walled circular living area surmounted by a corbel-vaulted roof that was somewhere between a small pyramid and a dome in appearance. A hole in the summit of this allowed the escape of smoke from the hearth directly below, flickering firelight from which was visible through the window apertures.

As he approached the centre of the settlement, Gastelois glanced up at the yellow orb of the full Moon, recently risen in the eastern sky. As it climbed, it would grow whiter and brighter, its reflected light strong enough to cause distinct shadows. Coming to a bridge of wooden planks spanning the river, he crossed to the path on the other side and headed for the southern circle.

Leaving the path, which curved around the circle in the same way as the one on the northern side, he entered the ring, its stones almost as tall as he was, and made his way towards the western end of the gallery-dolmen, almost directly in front of him.

The DRAGON of ANGUR

Twilight was giving way to night as Gastelois knocked three times on the heavy wooden door of the entrance. There was some species of muffled response from the other side and then the door creaked open, seemingly unaided. As Gastelois entered, the thick, rather soupy odour of mind-altering substances assailed his nostrils. He made his way along the torch-lit passage, stooping to avoid cracking his head on the undersides of the low-set capstones that roofed it.

He reached the main chamber, relieved to be able to stand up straight. At least this particular edifice's passage was quite short in comparison with that of true passage-dolmens, not to mention slightly higher. Although a low passage was a common feature of the latter type of dolmen, because of its acoustical properties (and Gastelois of course as a builder was obliged to take this into account), it was one that he came to appreciate less and less the older he got.

Haut-Maître Hacquebuttier Le Grandin, High Priest of Angur and all its dominions (that is to say the sundry reefs and islets that were scattered offshore) was sitting on the low sill-stone across the entrance to the side chamber at the eastern end of the main chamber, relaxing in his home after a hard day as Master of Equinoctial Ceremonies. A large, rotund man with a shining, bald head, the High Priest was leaning forward, warming his hands on the heat from the logs burning in the hearth on the floor of the main chamber, their fiery glow making his cherubic face seem even redder than usual.

"Ah, Gastelois!" he greeted his visitor with a smile. "You've come to discuss the transportation of stones for your new dolmen."

"That I have," the other replied, adding: "It's good of you to see me at this time of day."

"Don't mention it," replied Le Grandin, motioning the dolmen builder to sit down on a large upturned log near the hearth. "I'm just taking it easy."

"I thought the ceremonies went very well," commented Gastelois, somewhat obsequiously.

"Thank you. I didn't think they went too badly myself." He gave the other another smile. "So tell me, when do you need us? No, wait! Let me get you some refreshment. I take it you'd care for a drink?"

"Er, yes. Thank you very much." Gastelois had to admit that he was feeling quite thirsty and therefore a jar of the priests' own special reserve ale, brewed in the ramshackle building up river, would be most welcome.

"Something to smoke as well?" asked Le Grandin as he made his way over to a stone dresser standing against the far wall of the main chamber. Next to this there reposed a large vat with a long-handled wooden ladle leaning against it.

His visitor declined. Occasionally he would partake of the mind-altering weed derived from the hemp plant, large numbers of which were cultivated on the plateau immediately above the settlement, but right now he wanted to keep his mind clear. A jar of ale would be more than sufficient to satisfy him for the time being.

The High Priest returned with a couple of large drinking jars, considerably more commodious than the biggest Boileau Le Gobel produced in *The Old Vraic and Coracle*, even on special occasions (and his were larger than those to be found in any other Angurian ale-house).

"So," Hacquebuttier began, handing his visitor one of the vessels and then resuming his seat on the sill-stone, "you require our assistance."

"Yes please," said Gastelois. He took a drink of ale and then contemplated the contents of his jar. The priests' brew always had a unique taste, and this particular one was no exception. He suspected that it contained mind-altering ingredients over and above the alcoholic variety, ingredients that never found their way into the brews sold over the bars of the local pubs. "We hopefully have the design of the dolmen finalised..."

"P & E approved it?" asked the High Priest, interrupting him. He reached down and retrieved the pipe that he had left resting against the front face of the sill-stone.

"Er, not yet."

"A few problems then?" Le Grandin tapped the bowl of the pipe on the stone to remove the remnants of the previous smoke.

"You could say so."

The High Priest studied the other, while at the same time refilling his pipe with some of the contents of the small leather pouch that had been reposing beside him atop the sill-stone. He could see that Gastelois did not want to dwell on this point, so he did not press it any further. Moving on, he said: "Can you give me some idea of what the finished dolmen is going to be like, so I can work out how many priests you'll need for the levitation."

As Hacquebuttier embarked on the somewhat lengthy ritual of lighting his pipe with a taper from the hearth, Gastelois proceeded to describe his new dolmen, trying to give as accurate a picture as he could of what the completed structure should look like. It would doubtless have been easier had he had his plans with him, but he had not wanted to carry these around with him during the equinox festivities. As the High Priest enveloped himself and his immediate surroundings in clouds of sweet smelling, blue smoke, Gastelois tried hard not to cough, as to have done so would have been most impolite, particularly in the present company.

"Do you want our help for all the stones, or just the big ones?" asked Le Grandin when the other had finished.

Gastelois thought for a few moments. Without question the priests' levitational skills, if you could call them that, would be required for the transportation of the larger megaliths, with all the risks that this process would entail, but a group of stalwart workmen like those of his own team could easily manage the smaller rocks using log trackways, ropes and levers. The only problem was that while this traditional method of moving stones was safer and more reliable, it was considerably slower, and, thanks to Mannequin de Perrelle, time was not on his side. Levitation could be employed to make the smaller stuff lighter and thus easier and quicker to move. Dare he take the risk of involving the priests right down the line?

He looked at Hacquebuttier, who was regarding him impassively through the haze of smoke produced by his pipe. Memories of past disasters materialised in his mind.

"We'll certainly need you for the larger ones, especially the chamber uprights and capstones," he said eventually, hedging his bets. "We'll see how we get on with the smaller rocks; we can always call on you if necessary." He paused, then added: "If that's all right with you, of course."

"Of course it is," confirmed Le Grandin, removing the pipe from his mouth and favouring him with another smile. "As long as you give us enough notice."

"I'll do my best, but you know what it's like."

"Indeed I do." He drew on his pipe. "Right, as it seems you'll be using quite a few large stones, I think you'll need the standard team of seven. Now, there's a slight problem at the moment, especially if you need us soon."

"Oh?"

"Yes, two of my levitation priests have stinking colds."

"Ah!" said Gastelois, nodding slowly. "I can see why that would be a problem."

A bad cold would seriously hinder one's ability to produce the right notes when taking part in the levitation chant. A wrong note at a crucial moment could be very dangerous, not to mention the potentially even more disastrous effect of a cough or a sneeze. In fact, he knew of one particular occasion when a priest had sneezed violently while assisting with the erection of a menhir on the outskirts of the village of Bagot de Lecq on the north coast. He had not been there to witness it in person, but by all accounts the results had been spectacular. The stone, some twenty tons of best Mont Mado granite, had reacted to the sudden nasal eruption by launching itself like some megalithic missile at the nearest house, whose wattle and daub walls had failed to arrest its progress, after which it had removed the thatched roof of the next before embedding itself in a third. Needless to say, the villagers had been far from amused, especially the ones whose dwellings the menhir had 'visited'.

"I don't think we'll need you for a few days yet," continued Gastelois after some reflection. "Mannequin de Perrelle is due at the site some time tomorrow and I just hope he approves my plan. If not..."

"More delays."

"Exactly." Gastelois drank some more ale. He looked at the High Priest: "How long before the two are fit?"

Le Grandin shook his head: "That I don't know; poss'bly only a day or two, but it could be longer."

Gastelois did his best to hide his irritation. What with Planning causing problems and now this, it seemed he was destined to suffer delay after delay. Did his new dolmen have any chance of being finished on time?

Then an idea struck him: "Would it be possible for me to borrow a couple of your priests now - or even just one if you can't spare two? That way they could be with us when we select the stones, so they would have an idea in advance of what needs to be moved." He peered hard at Le Grandin.

The DRAGON of ANGUR

That worthy puffed long and hard on his pipe, sending out more clouds of sweet-smelling smoke. Again Gastelois tried hard not to cough. He waited patiently for the High Priest to say something.

Eventually, Hacquebuttier pulled the pipe from his mouth, briefly examined its bowl and then looked at Gastelois.

"Yes, I think that would be poss'ble. I can see the point." He pondered for a few moments and then said: "I think I know the two to send. I'll have a word with them in the morning before I go to the Assembly and they can then go over to your site. Where is it again?"

Gastelois reminded him.

"Ah, of course," said Le Grandin. "They can presumably stay near there while they're with you?"

Gastelois nodded. "Yes indeed," he confirmed. "I'm sure *The Quernstone* in Gor will have room. Some of my men are staying there already."

"Excellent!"

After that, they talked for a little while longer, not only about the dolmen, but about other things as well.

Eventually, Gastelois decided it was time to leave. He could see that Hacquebuttier was tired after the exertions of the day and he knew that the High Priest had a busy schedule ahead of him, as the Elders reconvened to continue with the current Major Session after breaking off for the equinox. Besides, he, too, was feeling rather tired and there was a nocturnal walk home to face before he could retire to his bed. At least there was a bright Moon to illuminate his way.

So, draining his jar of ale, he thanked Le Grandin for his time and hospitality. The latter bade him good night, adding that he would contact him as soon as the two cold-stricken priests had recovered, which, on reflection, he was sure would not be too long.

CHAPTER THIRTEEN

DIGGINGS IN THE DARKNESS

The following morning, Angur awoke to a leaden, overcast sky from which rain had been falling steadily since before dawn. It was showing no signs of easing when Grosnez and Piton set off first thing to see Clychard La Cloche. Despite Piton's protestations that they should wait until the rain stopped, his master was adamant that they leave without delay.

They had thought about calling in at union headquarters the previous afternoon to see him, but Grosnez had decided against it, correctly surmising that the head of the *Dolmen and Granite Workers' Union* was mostly likely participating in the equinox festivities and would therefore not be at home.

They arrived, soaked through, at the entrance to *Levitation House* and Grosnez knocked on the heavy wooden door. There was no response. He knocked again. Still no reply. Grosnez tutted impatiently. He rapped repeatedly on the door. Nothing. No indication whatsoever of any life inside.

Grosnez let out a long sigh of exasperation. He turned and glared at Piton as if it were the latter's fault that his knocking had failed to rouse anyone.

He decided to give it one more try, but just as he was about to strike the door with his raised fist, it creaked slowly open. The stale odour of last night's alcohol wafted out from within.

A bleary-eyed La Cloche blinked as he peered out into the grey light of the wet morning.

"Ah, Clychard!" said Grosnez. "You're in, you."

"What d'you want?" grumbled the other, shivering in the damp, chill air.

"To have a word with you, mon vier."

"Can't it wait?" Like the majority of Angurians who were either already awake or who would wake up in the course of the morning, the union chief had one humdinger of a hangover. The last thing he wanted at this precise moment was a couple of visitors. "I don't want to see anyone," he growled irritably.

Grosnez was having none of it. "Well, you'll see me!" he said emphatically, pushing past the hapless La Cloche and starting to make his way along the dark passage to the main chamber of *Levitation House*.

La Cloche looked helplessly at Piton, who shrugged his shoulders, too wet to give a toss about his master's behaviour.

"Well, you'd better come in too, I s'ppose."

"Th.. thank you," mumbled Piton, glad of a chance to shelter from the weather.

He did not stay inside for long, however. No sooner had he followed Clychard into the main chamber than Grosnez, who was standing by the hearth in the centre of the chamber floor attempting to warm his hands over the remains of last night's fire, frowned at him and said: "Piton, you can go to the new dolmen and keep an eye on things. I'll want a full report later on how it's pr'gressing."

"But Grosnez, I..." Piton started to protest.

His master did not have to say anything; the expression on his face was sufficient.

"Right, Grosnez. I'm going, Grosnez."

When Piton had left, Grosnez turned to La Cloche, who was on his hands and knees fumbling around by the hearth: "I'm sorry to disturb you, mon vier, but it couldn't wait. We got back from Piltdown the day before yesterday."

"Ah yes. How was your trip?" The union chief was sticking a firebrand in those embers still glowing in the hearth, trying to persuade it to ignite.

"Interesting," replied Grosnez, watching the other. "Why don't you put a log on that?"

La Cloche nodded and, with his spare hand, picked up a small log from a nearby pile and dropped it on to the fire, sending sparks into the air. "Did you find out where the container is?" he asked.

"Yes."

"Excellent!" La Cloche pulled the brand out of the fire, which was showing more signs of life, thanks to the log. The oil-soaked rag wrapped around the stick's end was alight. "Good!" he muttered, standing up and carrying the flaming brand over to the torches wedged between some of the megaliths forming the walls of the chamber. He started to light each of them in turn.

"Ah, that's better!" he exclaimed in satisfaction as the interior of the chamber gradually brightened.

Grosnez went over to a stool he had noticed and took it over to a spot near the hearth. He sat down.

"So, I take it you've now got the container and that's what you've come to tell me," said La Cloche as he finished lighting the torches.

Grosnez shook his head. "No, there's a problem."

The other extinguished the firebrand by immersing the flaming tip in a bucket of sand. He then walked over to a wooden table near one of the chamber walls and, as he poured himself a jar of beer from a jug reposing on this, he asked: "What problem? You said you found out where it was."

"Yes, and that's the problem."

La Cloche was puzzled. He lifted the jar to his lips and took a large swig. Noticing Grosnez watching him, he remarked: "Hair of the dog. I drank far too much yesterday, as usual. This'll help numb the hangover." Then, remembering his manners: "Sorry, mon vier, would you like some?"

"No. No thank you. I want to keep my head clear."

"So, what's this problem?" asked La Cloche, pulling up a stool by the hearth alongside Grosnez.

"It's buried on the site of that fool de Bois' new dolmen."

The union chief's piggy little eyes tried to change places. "You certain of that?"

His companion nodded. "We went to look for it yesterday while everyone was busy with the equinox. I followed the directions precisely and there can be no doubt."

Clychard La Cloche massaged his eyes. "So, what can we do?"

"That's why I'm here. I thought you might have some ideas, you."

The other looked pensively into the fire. The log shifted. He reached down and put another one on, propping it up against the first.

"I know we're going to have to dig for it," went on Grosnez. "But that's not without its risks. And the longer it takes to find it, the more diff'cult it'll get as work on the dolmen progresses"

La Cloche nodded. "But digging's the best option for now. We don't want to do anything more drastic, at least not immediately."

Grosnez stared at him quizzically, his brow furrowing.

"I mean," continued the union chief, "I could use my position and get a strike called or something like that, so you could dig in peace." He took a large gulp of beer and smacked his lips noisily. "You should start tonight. The Moon's still full so you'll have plenty of light."

"Yes – if the weather clears. I just hope we find it quickly. The longer it takes, the greater the risk of being discovered."

"That's true, that!" La Cloche swigged some more ale. "I suggest, though, that you dig for a couple of nights and then if nothing turns up, we'll review the situation." He stood up, somewhat unsteadily. "As I said, I can always call a strike, although I'll need to find a good reason."

Grosnez likewise got to his feet. "Well," he said, "let's hope it doesn't come to that."

"Indeed," agreed La Cloche. "By the way, if you need to see me tomorrow, I'll be at Mont Mado in the morning."

"Fine."

"Right, if you'll excuse me, I think I'll go back to bed," said La Cloche, yawning. "I need more rest."

"Thank you for your time," said Grosnez with mock graciousness.

"Oh, one other thing," added the union chief as his visitor made to leave. "If necess'ry, I know someone at Planning. Contacts can be very useful..."

* * *

Contrary to expectations, the weather did in fact improve as the day progressed. Although the skies remained heavy with the threat of more showers, the rain gradually eased, became intermittent and finally ceased altogether by early afternoon. Despite the less than ideal conditions, Gastelois and his team had the ground plan of the new dolmen laid out by midday, work having resumed at the site first thing in the morning. They had also cleared more vegetation to increase the size of the ritual forecourt area, where Gastelois was now standing with his assistant, Pierre de Lecq, looking along the roughly parallel line of stakes and knotted ropes that delineated the passage.

"Well, that should do for now," said Gastelois. "Let's hope Mannequin doesn't give us any grief."

"He shouldn't, him," said Pierre. "We've included the safety gap in the main chamber and the position of the Mont Mado stone is clearly marked." He looked at his companion: "You're worrying about the number of side chambers."

Gastelois nodded. "Yes." He stroked his chin pensively. "Perhaps three each side *is* a trifle excessive."

Pierre shrugged his broad shoulders. "Perhaps. We've enlarged the ritual area more than sufficiently, in my opinion, so he shouldn't complain about that."

"He probably will," said the other, a trifle morosely.

"Well maybe we'll be able to reach some sort of compromise."

Gastelois favoured Pierre with a rueful smile. "Compromise? Not in their vocabulary, mon vier."

His assistant had to agree with him.

"When's he supposed to arrive?" Gastelois asked after the two men had contemplated the site in silence for a few moments.

"Early afternoon, I b'lieve," replied Pierre.

"Good. Let's go down to Gor and get some lunch. I feel quite peckish and a good jar of cider wouldn't go amiss."

"Good idea. Martin and the others might be there. I'd imagine they'll be thinking about taking a break from searching for megaliths, them."

"That's true," said Gastelois. "I wonder whether they've found anything suitable."

With that, he told the remainder of the workforce still on site to head for Gor for lunch. They needed no encouragement and immediately downed tools and set off for the settlement.

* * *

Piton breathed a sigh of relief. He was stiff and cramped, not to mention soaked through, after having spent the morning hiding in the branches of a lone oak tree a short distance away from Gastelois' site. From here he had an excellent view of how work on the new dolmen was progressing and his keen sense of hearing could even make out a fair amount of what was being said by those involved

The DRAGON of ANGUR

in its construction. Thus he had learned of the imminent arrival of Mannequin de Perrelle, an event he was eagerly anticipating as he was sure there would be problems.

For the time being, though, he could climb down out of the tree, stretch his legs and get a bite to eat. He would have to go to *The Quernstone* – there was nowhere else in the neighbourhood - but he would sneak in, buy his lunch and quickly sneak out again with it rather than consume it in the pub and increase the risk of being seen by the dolmen builders.

He descended from the tree, hung around for a little while to give Gastelois and his workers enough time for a decent head start, and then set off for Gor himself.

* * *

The Quernstone stood in the middle of a row of houses nestling at the foot of a grass and gorse-covered col overlooking a small, sandy cove that served as Gor's harbour. On its the south-eastern side, the col was overlooked by a steep-sided rocky promontory, while to the north-west, it rose up to meet the edge of the Angurian plateau. Sitting in the middle of the col was the settlement's gallery-dolmen, as fine an example as could be found anywhere on Angur.

Soon Gastelois and his men were ensconced in the pub, sitting at a couple of large oaken tables. Once he had ascertained what everyone wanted to eat and drink, he and his assistant went up to the bar to order the desired comestibles.

"Let me buy these," said Pierre de Lecq once the order had been placed. He produced a large ormer shell from his pouch and handed it to the landlord.

Hacquoil Le Buvet examined the proferred shell closely, running his fingers slowly over its smooth interior surface and then its rougher outer one.

"Excuse me a moment," he said. He came out from behind the bar and walked over to the pub's main entrance where he briefly held the shell up to the daylight before coming back inside.

Gastelois and Pierre had followed these antics with increasingly puzzled expressions on their faces.

"What's up?" asked Gastelois as Le Buvet returned behind the bar.

"It's fine," pronounced Le Buvet as if that were sufficient to answer the question.

"What d'you mean it's fine?" queried Pierre.

"It's not a forgery."

The two dolmen builders looked blankly at Le Buvet, clearly at a loss as to what the latter was going on about.

Hacquoil then explained that it had recently transpired that someone, or perhaps more than just one person, was trying to inflate the value of ormer shells by deliberately boring extra holes in them, the number of holes in a shell dictating its value. By carefully examining a shell, you could tell whether a hole had been produced naturally or with the aid of a flint point guided by criminal intent. As the guilty party had yet to be caught, all ormer shells were to be treated with suspicion in the first instance.

"I would never pass over a dodgy shell," stated Pierre emphatically when the other had finished, looking totally mortified.

"Not knowingly perhaps," said the landlord as he started to pour jars of cider or beer.

"Unbelievable!" stated Pierre with feeling as he and Gastelois took the first of the drinks over to their men. "Whatever next?"

"Someone might try to forge a block of Mont Mado granite," said Gastelois matter-of-factly, his eyes twinkling mischievously. "Ah! Here's Martin and the others."

Martin Le Blancq, a tall, lanky individual whose name aptly described his particularly pale complexion and white hair, had just strode into the pub accompanied by three other members of Gastelois' team. They had spent the morning searching for suitable megaliths on the foreshore to the east of the dolmen site.

"How'd it go?" asked Gastelois, depositing the jars he was carrying on the nearby table.

"Pretty successful," replied Martin, eyeing the jars. "We found a number of boulders that I'm sure will be suitable."

He went on to say that some of these were lying free and would not even have to be quarried, while most of the remainder could, in his opinion, be persuaded to part company with the rock to which they were attached without too much difficulty.

"Excellent!" exclaimed Gastelois when Martin had finished. "Right, beer or cider?"

"Beer, please," said Martin in a sort of I-thought-you'd-never-ask tone.

In due course, Gastelois, Pierre and the seventeen other members of the workforce were tucking into bowls of shellfish broth accompanied by hunks of bread and washed down by liberal quantities of ale or cider. The morning's toil had combined with the weather to give them all hearty appetites, and the meal was consumed with much enthusiasm, with little time between mouthfuls for conversation.

Once hunger and thirst had been sated, voices were rediscovered:

"As I mentioned first thing, Le Grandin is sending over a couple of levitation priests to see which stones we are intending to use."

"Any idea who?" asked Fortin La Berfote, a particularly cynical individual who viewed the priests' involvement as a necessary evil. He was convinced that each attempt at levitation was doomed to end in disaster and pronounced it a fluke whenever one did not.

Gastelois shook his head. "No. Hacquebuttier didn't tell me." He glanced towards the main entrance. "I'm surprised they haven't shown up yet."

As if on cue, the door creaked open.

"Talk of the *Teus!*" exclaimed Eustin Le Mince, a thin, but wiry individual sitting on Gastelois' right whose somewhat slender frame belied his not inconsiderable strength and stamina.

The two characters who walked into *The Quernstone* could hardly have presented a more contrasting pair. If it had not been for their ochre-coloured robes and belts of braided leather, you would have sworn that they could not possibly have had any connection with each other.

The first was so undersized he looked as though he had missed out on his mother's milk, and then most other meals throughout his childhood. His 'habit' was several sizes too big, dragging on the ground around his feet and threatening to trip him up at any moment. A particularly gaunt face, the sallow skin stretched over the skull like dried seaweed, was framed by strands of grey, straggly hair which fell listlessly on to his narrow, bony shoulders.

At least four, if not five, of Esclenquier Le Digot could have fitted into the huge frame of his companion, Asceline Le Doublier. Whereas there were masses of room to spare within the clothes of the former, those of the latter were literally bursting at the seams. A face as rotund as the body it surmounted was chiefly notable for its expansive, scarlet-hued cheeks, its bright, sparkling eyes and the quantity of its chins.

Gastelois stood up to greet the two priests: "Ah, Maître Esclenquier, Maître Asceline! Welcome! I trust the day finds you well?"

"It does," replied the diminutive Le Digot in a tone of voice that suggested that it was something of a miracle that it did.

"We have come on the instructions of Haut-Maître Le Grandin to see the stones you are intending to use in your dolmen," said his large companion in measured tones, his chins wobbling rhythmically with his words.

"Of course," said Gastelois. "Please be seated. We are honoured that you've come and we are all very pleased to see you." His obsequiousness was intentional; the priests expected and received a great deal of deference from the populace, despite what the latter thought and frequently said of them behind their backs.

At that point the landlord, recognising two members of the priesthood, rushed over and bowed, almost doubling himself in two in the process.

"Honoured sirs," he fawned, "it is with great pleasure that I welcome you to this humble place." His manner was even more servile than Gastelois'.

"We will require accommodation," said Le Digot. He looked up at Le Buvet sternly: "I trust you have something suitable."

"My... my best accomm'dation is at your disposal, sirs," said Hacquoil. He indicated the half-attic that ran from the far end of the pub, its floor extending over the main room of the pub at the level of the base of the building's pitched roof. Access to this was gained by means of a ladder from the pub floor. "How long will you be staying?" he asked.

"That depends," said Le Digot. "As long as is necessary."

"I'll have to do some re-arranging," said the landlord, suddenly remembering that the majority of Gastelois' workforce was sleeping upstairs. He looked at the dolmen builder, as if expecting him to read his mind, which the latter duly did.

"How many?" Gastelois asked resignedly.

"Three,"said Le Buvet. Then, glancing at the expansive form of Asceline Le Doublier: "No, four."

Gastelois nodded slowly. He knew what was required. There may have been only two priests, but they needed more personal space than the ordinary mortal and therefore four of his men would have to give up their sleeping areas to accommodate Messrs. Le Digot and Le Doublier.

"Right," he said. "I'll sort it out later."

The two priests then handed the bag each of them had been carrying over his shoulder to Le Buvet who, after enquiring what they required by way of sustenance, hurried off to attend to their needs.

"Martin here is in charge of finding suitable boulders," said Gastelois once Esclenquier and Asceline had settled themselves opposite the dolmen builder at the table.

"That's right," said the worthy Le Blancq, hastily finishing a mouthful of bread. "We spent some time looking this morning and we found some def'nite poss'bil'ties."

"And you will be continuing after lunch?" prompted Gastelois.

"That's right," confirmed Martin. "We look forward to your advice and assistance." He inclined his head deferentially towards the two priests.

"We will, of course, have to see the dolmen site first," said Le Doublier.

"Of course," said Gastelois. This was quite normal, although he had never been able to fathom why they should need to.

The priests' food and drink arrived shortly after that. Esclenquier consumed his as if it might be taken away from him at any moment, while Asceline treated his as if every mouthful were his last, chewing the food very slowly and taking an age before he swallowed it.

Eventually, they had all finished eating, and, after being reassured by an excessively servile Hacquoil Le Buvet that their accommodation would be sorted out by the time they returned that evening, the two priests accompanied Gastelois and his men back to the dolmen site.

* * *

Gastelois was furious. They had waited all afternoon for Mannequin de Perrelle to turn up, and now that he had condescended to put in an appearance, it looked as though he was not going to approve the plan. As he had feared would turn out to be the case, the problem was the number of side chambers.

"As I indicated on my last visit, six is far too many," stated de Perrelle.

"Why?"

"No passage-dolmen has that many side chambers."

"So? Is that a reason for this one not to have that many? It is, after all, a special one – as I reminded you before."

"It will create a prec'dent," stated Mannequin. He sniffed noisily. "In my opinion, too many prec'dents are set these days."

"What about innovation?" protested Gastelois. "Surely there's room for that?"

The P. & E. man looked at him as though he had just used a dirty word. "Cut the number by half," he said.

"By half?" Gastelois looked at the other incredulously. "You can't be serious."

"By half," repeated Mannequin. "Three side chambers – no more. And even *that's* more than's normal for here."

"But that will create an imbalance," protested Gastelois.

De Perrelle thought about this. "Yes, that's true," he agreed. He stroked his chin pensively. "All right, then, two."

"Two! That's ridiculous!" said Gastelois with feeling. "I am trying to create something special here," he reiterated.

The Planning man was unmoved. "Two side chambers." Then a thought occurred to him: "You could still have three if you reduced the size of the terminal part of the main chamber and made it the same size as the lateral ones." A pensive expression crossed his face. "Yes, that would work."

"But I don't want to reduce the size of the main chamber," said Gastelois.

The other shrugged his shoulders. "It's up to you. I'll be back tomorrow afternoon to inspect your revised plans."

Gastelois opened his mouth to say something, but decided it was pointless.

"I bid you good day!" With that, Mannequin de Perrelle left the site, sniffing noisily.

Once he was safely out of earshot, Gastelois turned to Pierre. "This is getting absurd!" he fumed. "How am I supposed to produce something worthy of the occasion if that fool won't let me build what I want?"

The DRAGON of ANGUR

His assistant shrugged his shoulders, not knowing what to say.

"I've had enough," Gastelois went on. "I'm going to see Branleur de Bitte."

"D'you want to do any more today?" ventured Pierre.

"What's the point, mmm?" He angrily kicked a small stone that was lying nearby, minding its own business. Then he looked at Pierre. "I'm sorry," he said. "Come on. Let's all go for a drink."

* * *

From his concealed vantage point in the branches of the oak tree, Piton chuckled merrily to himself. His master would be pleased with what he had to tell him – Gastelois' plan had not been approved. This meant a further delay, which was just what they wanted.

Once Gastelois and his team had left and the coast was therefore clear, Piton dropped out of the tree and scurried home to report to Grosnez.

* * *

Swinging slowly over his seaweed fire, Vraicer T'loch watched the goblin-like figure of the Le Malin hurrying homewards in the fading evening light and permitted himself a satisfied smile. He was looking forward to the coming night's entertainment. It promised to be rather amusing...

* * *

It was late into the evening when the two figures furtively approached Gastelois' site. To their relief, there was nobody about; in fact they had not encountered a soul on their way from the north-west of the island. Apart from the lateness of the hour, the indifferent weather was probably keeping people indoors, either in homes or in pubs.

"Right, mon vier," said Grosnez once they were standing inside the staked-out area of the new dolmen's main chamber. "Let's try to work out exactly where this vial's supposed to be buried and then you can start digging."

After some thought, Grosnez started from one of the outer of the three surviving elm trees standing nearby while Piton did so from the other outer one. As 'Stone-Ears' Meade had not been precise, they first walked twenty paces in such a way that their paths would cross. Grosnez marked the resulting crossing point with a small stone he found lying nearby. They then returned to the elms and repeated the exercise; only this time they measured out twenty-five paces. Again the relevant spot was marked with a small stone. Grosnez reckoned that if they dug in a line joining the two points, they would stand a reasonable chance of finding the vial – if indeed it was buried in that area.

Of course, there were other possibilities depending upon which tree or tree stump you measured from, and Grosnez fully intended to exhaust them all before the night was out.

On his master's orders, Piton set to work close to the second point they had marked, carefully loosening the ground with an antler pick. Gastelois' men had already deturfed the area, which made his job somewhat easier. Once he had broken up a sufficient amount of soil, he scooped out the earth and stones with a shovel fashioned from the shoulder blade of a young aurochs, depositing the spoil nearby.

Grosnez stood by, silently watching in anticipation as the hole grew.

After a few cycles of picking and shovelling, Piton had attained quite a respectable depth. He stopped and looked up at Grosnez.

"Well?" demanded the latter.

"I... I can't see anything yet, Grosnez."

"Let me have a look." He knelt beside his servant and groped around in the hole.

It was difficult to see clearly. Although the Moon was still full, intermittent cloud cover prevented its light from consistently illuminating their surroundings. Grosnez found himself wishing that he had brought a firebrand, but on reflection knew why he had not – it would have been too risky to use as it would have alerted anyone who happened to be in the area to their presence.

"Keep digging, mon vier," Grosnez instructed after a few moments of fruitless groping. "We'll give it a bit longer before we try another spot."

But more digging produced nothing. After a while, Piton flopped down on the ground, dropping his tools beside him. He stared forlornly at the hole, shaking his head.

Grosnez stroked the point of his chin pensively. "Right. Dig another one just here." He indicated a spot nearby, on the line between the two points. "But fill in that one first."

Piton slowly got to his feet, morosely contemplating the heap of spoil from the first hole.

Grosnez glared at him: "Hurry, fool! I haven't got all night!"

A second hole was dug and turned out to be as barren as the first, as did a third.

At that point, Piton ventured to suggest that if Grosnez had brought one of his dowsing switches with him, the locating of the elusive vial might have been easier.

"Shut up!" was the curt response to this. "Try again. There!" Grosnez waggled a long, bony finger at a spot about a foot's length away from the third hole, still on the line between the two marker stones. He knew that his servant had a perfectly valid point, but would never have admitted it. The truth was that he had been so convinced that they would find the vial just by following Stone-Ears' directions, despite their lack of precision, that it had never occurred to him to bring along any other aid.

While Piton worked, Grosnez looked around, searching for something with which he could dowse. After a while, however, he gave up – there just was not anything suitable. Cursing beneath his breath, he went back to see how his servant was getting on.

Not very well, as it turned out. The latest hole revealed no vial, nor indeed any other form of container. Piton had dug almost right to the first marker stone. He looked helplessly at his master, who favoured him with a look that left him in no doubt that he, somehow, was to blame for their ill luck.

"Right," said Grosnez after a long silence broken only by the sound of the leaves of the three elm trees rustling in the wind. He shivered, for the wind had recently grown chilly. A rain drop struck his forehead. Then another. And another. He drew his cloak up around his neck and glared malevolently at the sky. The Moon was disappearing behind a large bank of cloud.

Piton looked at him, waiting for his next words. Rain spattered his forehead.

"We'll wait until this shower passes and then we'll carry on," decided Grosnez.

Piton had hoped that Grosnez would have decided to abandon the search for the night and go home. Clearly he was not prepared to give up just yet.

The elm trees afforded some shelter from the rain and they stayed there until it stopped and the Moon showed signs of putting in an appearance again. Grosnez, deep in thought, did not say a word during the whole time they were taking cover.

"Right, come on!" he said once the weather had improved and moonlight was once again bathing the scene. "Let's get on with it."

"Get on with what, Grosnez?"

"Digging, fool, digging!"

"But *where*, Grosnez?" Piton looked at his master helplessly.

The other made exasperated clicking sounds with his tongue. "We'll start from this tree behind me and pace out the distances again, first twenty and then twenty-five, heading in a straight line. Then we'll dig between the two points like before. After that, we'll repeat the process with the two outer trees." He nodded to his right and then to his left. "Then we'll do the same with those over there." He again nodded to his right, towards the two tree stumps standing forlornly in the moonlight.

"But Grosnez, that will take all night!" protested Piton.

"Per'aps so." He gave his servant a disparaging look. "And if we don't have enough time tonight, we'll come back tomorrow, and, if nec'ssary the night after, until we find it."

Grosnez then proceeded to walk twenty paces forward, as before ending up in the chamber area. He marked the spot with a small stone and then walked five paces further, again marking the spot with a stone. Piton followed disconsolately behind him.

"Dig here!" he commanded imperiously, pointing at the second stone.

Piton picked up his tools from where he had left them when it had started to rain and went over to where Grosnez was standing.

"Right, get on with it!" ordered Grosnez, pointing at the ground.

His servant cast a glance at the sky. Although there were still clouds about, they were not presently obscuring the Moon. Looking at her face, he could have sworn that the Moon goddess was laughing at him, mocking his efforts.

He was even more convinced of this by the time he had dug the latest series of holes and it had proved to be as fruitless an exercise as the previous one.

Without a word, Grosnez headed back to the elm trees, stopping at one of the outer ones. Again the twenty and twenty-five paces were measured out, the line running parallel to the previous one, and again the relevant points were marked with stones.

Halfway through the digging of this latest series of holes, it began to rain again.

To Grosnez' relief, they did not have to shelter under the trees for long before the skies began to clear and the rain stopped. He glanced at the Moon, emerging from behind a cloud. It was just beginning to occur to him that there was something not quite right about her face when he was distracted by a sudden high-pitched yelp from his servant.

"Aieeh!" Piton dashed from the trees, frantically running his hands through his hair.

"What the...?" began Grosnez. Then he noticed the bat gliding and swooping as it cavorted silently around the area in the moonlight. He realised that the creature must have brushed against Piton's hair as it dived out of the tree where it had been resting.

"It's only a bat, mon vier," said Grosnez, laughing at the other's discomfort.

"A... a bat?" said Piton, stopping and looking back at his master.

"Yes, a poor, harmless bat. Now let's get on." He began to walk in towards the staked-out dolmen area from the other outer elm tree, counting the paces as he did so.

"Grosnez!" called Piton suddenly.

"What now?" demanded the other in exasperation.

"Th... there's something here, Grosnez."

Grosnez walked over to where his servant was standing, just inside the curving line of stakes marking what would become the wall at the western end of the new dolmen's main chamber.

"What?" he demanded irritably.

Piton pointed to a square patch of ground where signs of recent disturbance were clearly evident in the moonlight.

"You didn't do that, did you," said Grosnez in a slightly accusatory tone.

"No!" declared Piton, looking hurt.

His master crouched and examined the area in question, scooping up a few handfuls of soil with his hand and each time letting it sift through his fingers. He looked around at the holes Piton had already dug (and carefully back-filled) and frowned.

Then he looked at the elm trees and smiled. Piton watched him nervously.

"Well," said Grosnez at last as he stood up, "this is quite recent. If it has been dug by someone searching for the vial - and if that's the case, I'd love to know who - I think they've been digging in the wrong place."

"Why's that, Grosnez?"

"Too close to the trees, fool."

"Ah yes. Of course, Grosnez."

"It's probably something else, though, and nothing to do with the vial. But just in case, we'd better investigate it."

"You want me to dig it up, you?"

"No, I want you to sit on it and keep it warm," was the sarcastic response.

Unprintable thoughts materialised in Piton's mind as he set to work with his antler pick, some of which involved the effect of said pick on his master's head.

Soon the disturbed area had been excavated. Once it had been cleared of all the loose earth and small stones filling it, it turned out to be a cavity about a foot square and the same in depth. If there had been anything of interest there, there was no sign of it now.

"Oh well," said Grosnez resignedly. "I expected as much. And we can't tell if there was anything here or not."

"What do we do now, Grosnez?"

"Carry on with our plan, fool."

With that, he returned to the elm tree from where he had been measuring when Piton had called him, and started the process again. Soon yet another series of holes was being dug as before.

Grosnez was kneeling by the second one, examining its interior, when:

"Gr... Grosnez," said Piton suddenly. "Wh... what's wrong with the Moon?"

"What're you saying you?" Grosnez looked up, expecting to see a brilliant white orb.

Only it was no longer brilliant, nor was it white. The Moon's face was assuming a reddish hue as if the shenanigans she was witnessing below were beginning to embarrass her.

It did not take Grosnez long to figure out what was going on.

"It's a ruddy eclipse!"

"I didn't know there was one predicted," said Piton, squinting at the Moon.

"I b'lieve there is," said Grosnez. "But I didn't think it was tonight. I thought it was due at the next full Moon, not this."

"The priests have got it wrong before, them."

"That's true, that." He looked at the other: "You know what this means though? As soon as people realise what's happ'ning, they could come up here for a better view."

Piton gulped. "Are we going then, Grosnez?" he asked hopefully.

"Yes. I think that would be the best course of action." He glared at the Moon. "It's a ruddy nuisance! We'll just have to come back tomorrow night and carry on then. Come on!" He began to walk smartly away from the site.

"What about this hole?" asked Piton.

Grosnez stopped and looked back. "You'd better fill it in – and quickly! Then you can catch me up – I'm not hanging about."

Piton glared flint daggers at his master's back as the latter resumed his departure from the area. Then he set to shovelling the soil back into the freshly-dug hole, working in haste and not caring how shoddily he did it. Once he judged it to be adequately full, he stamped on the earth to flatten it. Then he hurried after Grosnez, occasionally casting anxious glances behind him to see whether he was being followed.

In his haste, he left his antler pick behind...

CHAPTER FOURTEEN
A MEETING AT MONT MADO

Gastelois and his team arrived at the dolmen site early the next morning. It was again overcast and a persistent drizzle was wrapping the countryside in its damp blanket.

No sooner had they got there than one of them noticed that something was amiss.

"What's *thees*?" he cried.

"What you seen, you?" asked one of his colleagues as the others came over to join him.

"Someone's been mucking about here," said the first.

"*Mucking about*, Tapin? What're you saying, you?"

"Look for yourself," replied Tapin Le Large, pointing at the ground, a slight tone of annoyance in his voice.

They all followed the direction of Tapin's outstretched arm. There, plainly visible on what was destined to be the floor of the main chamber, were patches of disturbed soil, as if someone had been digging and then back-filling the resulting cavities. What was more, there were a series of parallel lines of holes, suggesting that whoever had been digging had been doing so with a set plan in mind.

"And look here!" exclaimed Pontrel Le Porc. "I've just found this lying on the ground, it." He held Piton's antler pick aloft for all to see.

Gastelois stroked his chin pensively. "What d'you think, Pierre?" he asked his assistant without taking his eyes off the area of ground in question.

"Well, someone's clearly been digging," said the other. He walked over to one of the patches and crouched next to it, fingering the soil with his right hand. "Definitely a filled-in hole," he concluded as he let the loose earth cascade through his fingers. "The question is, who and why?"

"That's what I was wondering," said Gastelois, looking puzzled. "Why should anyone want to dig holes here?"

"Per'aps they were looking for something," suggested Pierre, stating the obvious.

"Yes, but *what*?"

The other shrugged his shoulders.

"Maybe they've been burying something, not trying to dig it up," suggested one Martin, a burly individual with a heavy brow ridge and thick, black eyebrows that belied a not inconsiderable intellect.

"I hadn't thought of that," admitted Pierre.

"Seems unlikely they'd dig so many holes just to bury something," observed Gastelois. He sighed. "I suppose there's only one way to find out. Let's dig out the holes and see if there's anything there – although I doubt we'll find anything."

"*All* of them?" asked one of the other workmen, who shared his boss's suspicion that they would be wasting their time.

"Yes," confirmed Gastelois. "All ten of them. It shouldn't take too long."

They set to and excavated the enigmatic holes. As Gastelois had predicted, it hardly took any time at all as none of them was particularly deep. It also came as no great surprise that each and every one of them was empty, containing nothing but the earth that had been dug out of them in the first place.

Gastelois asked for the holes to be filled in again and then said to Pierre: "Well, whoever's responsible undoubtedly did it last night while we were off site. I'm going to ask for a couple of volunteers to stay overnight and keep a lookout - just in case our friend, or friends, pays us a return visit."

"That's a good idea, that," said Pierre.

"Right, let's get on with some work. Can you continue sorting out the plan?" He looked at the other who nodded. "I've got to go to Mont Mado to select a suitable piece of granite to keep Planning happy and I want to be back in time for that pain Mannequin de Perrelle's inspection this afternoon."

* * *

Grosnez had been pacing back and forth across the floor of the main living chamber of his home for ages – at least it seemed that way to Piton, who had been watching his master apprehensively, not daring to breathe a word, especially after having been thoroughly lambasted by him for having left the antler pick behind. Occasionally Grosnez would mutter something incomprehensible under his breath followed by a loud sigh of exasperation.

Eventually he stopped, turned to his servant and said: "Piton, mon vier, we have to do something. I don't want to waste another night digging pointless holes, me."

"But Grosnez, if the vial is buried, how're you going to find it without digging, you?"

Grosnez shot him a venomous look. "I know that! But before we do any more digging, I'll dowse first."

"Supposing we still don't find anything?"

"We will," said Grosnez confidently. "It's just a question of finding the right spot. It's a ruddy nuisance that that fool Meade's directions were so vague."

"Aw, but you have a point there, you," agreed Piton.

Grosnez stood looking up at the corbel-vaulted roof of his living room as if there were something there of particular interest, his features illuminated by the pale grey daylight filtering through the hole in its apex.

"Right," he said after a few moments, "I'm going to Mont Mado to see La Cloche. You can go back to the new dolmen and keep an eye on things again."

Piton looked crestfallen; another day spent cramped in that oak tree did not appeal to him in the slightest. Apart from that, he did not like the idea of these surreptitious activities at Gastelois' site. The sooner they found that vial, the happier he would be, as he was sure that the longer they took to locate it, the more likely they were to get caught.

* * *

Vraicer T'loch chuckled to himself as he partook of a late breakfast of shellfish, bread and cider. The previous night's activities had been as entertaining as he had hoped; the lunar eclipse an unexpected addition to the fun. He was now looking forward to what the day would bring...

* * *

The sacred site of Mont Mado was a large outcrop of fine-grained pink granite situated a little distance inland from the centre of Angur's north coast. Rising proud of the surrounding countryside, it glowed like a beacon when the sunlight struck it in the right way on a fine day.

As with most of these sites, nobody could remember exactly why this one was sacred; it was sufficient to know that it was. As a result of its status, its granite was used only for religious or very important secular erections and even then only sparingly, as the more the outcrop was quarried, the smaller it would become. It was not considered desirable that it should be reduced in size at anything other than a very gradual rate. There were many who viewed the *Pouquelaye and Earthworks Committee's* current obsession with every new dolmen having to have at least one stone of Mont Mado granite as the thin end of a wedge causing an increase in the rate of quarrying that could only hasten the outcrop's demise.

The sounds of the quarry reached Grosnez' ears before he set eyes on it. Despite the inclement weather, there was clearly much activity. The path he was walking along rounded a corner and led up on to a ridge, and there ahead of him stood the sacred outcrop of pink granite with its ring of encircling standing stones, quarrymen swarming over it like bees on a honeycomb.

As he neared it, he could see that the workers were trying to persuade it to part with a particularly large chunk of rock, hammering wooden wedges into the naturally occurring cracks in the granite. Once these had been rammed in as far as possible, water would be poured on to them to make them swell, which would hopefully cause the rock to split further. Eventually, after several cycles of wedge hammering and water pouring, the desired piece of granite would be separated from the remainder of the outcrop.

He wondered why they were trying to break off such a large piece of rock. He was sure it was not destined for Gastelois' new site; it seemed too big, even for the largest capstone that dolmen's builder might have in mind. Then he remembered the La Tanche Menhir, a giant standing stone to be erected in the High Elder's honour and intended to be used as the foresight of a new lunar observatory planned for the south-west of the island. It had been hoped to have it up in time for the Flint Jubilee celebrations, but this was looking unlikely as the project was somewhat behind schedule.

When Grosnez reached the outcrop, Clychard La Cloche was standing next to one of the stones comprising the ring around it, deep in conversation with the priest in charge of the site, Maître Abatfalaise Le Gripert.

"Ah, Grosnez, mon vier," said the union chief, noticing his arrival. "What brings you here?" He had to shout to make himself heard above the din of the nearby quarrying.

"I need to see you," said Grosnez, trying to tone down the note of urgency that threatened to dominate his voice – he did not want Le Gripert to think that he had come to see La Cloche on anything other than some matter of no great import.

"That project?" said La Cloche openly, as if there was nothing to hide.

The other nodded. "Indeed so," he said, taking his cue. He jumped slightly as a particularly loud bang resounded from the sacred outcrop as it was struck a particularly forceful blow. He glared in that direction. "There are a few details I need to discuss with you before I go."

"Ah, of course! You're off to Lesur." La Cloche extended the fiction.

"That's right. As soon as poss'ble. So if you could spare me some time now, mon vier, I'd be grateful."

La Cloche grunted. Turning to Le Gripert, he said: "Excuse me for a moment, Maître Abatfalaise, this shouldn't take long."

The priest quarry-manager smiled and made a gesture with his right hand as if to say *go ahead, be my guest*.

The union chief put a hand on Grosnez' back and gently propelled him away from the ring of stones and the din within so that they could talk more easily. He also wanted to be out of earshot of Le Gripert, although that worthy had turned his attention to the quarrying and was not paying any attention to him and Grosnez.

"You just missed Gastelois," said La Cloche once he judged that they had gone far enough.

Grosnez frowned, then smiled. "Ah, of course - doubtless organising a piece of Mont Mado granite for his new dolmen."

La Cloche nodded. "So," he said, after a moment's pause, "how did it go last night?"

"Very frustrating," said Grosnez, shaking his head agitatedly. "Very frustrating indeed. We dug quite a few holes and found nothing."

"Nothing at all?" La Cloche sounded surprised.

Grosnez nodded: "Nothing at all." His face assumed a pensive expression. "There was one spot, though, where someone else had been digging, but that was too close to the trees."

"I see."

"And we couldn't stay for as long as I wanted to as there was a ruddy eclipse of the Moon, and people might have come up from Gor for a better view."

"So, you're going back tonight?"

"That's the plan." Grosnez gave the other an intense look. "But time is getting on and I think you need to come up with some ideas to delay work on the dolmen should that prove nec'ssary."

La Cloche nodded slowly. "Mmm," he mumbled pensively. "You're sure you were following that chap – what's his name – Meade's directions precisely?"

The other clicked his tongue in irritation. "Of course," he said. "Not that they turned out to be as precise as I would have liked. But we tried every permutation poss'ble."

"And still found nothing."

"That's right."

"Supposing," said La Cloche after a few moments' reflection, "that his directions were wrong, them."

"What you saying, you?"

"That would mean you were digging in entirely the wrong place."

"I'm sure I wasn't," said Grosnez, looking miffed. "Anyway, why would they be wrong?"

La Cloche shrugged his shoulders. "Don't know. Just a thought." He scratched his head. "Right," he said, examining his fingernails, "you're going to have another go tonight?"

"Yes," snapped Grosnez. "I've just told you that! I have no intention of giving up. And you'll give some thought to ways of delaying Gastelois?"

La Cloche nodded. "That I will; don't worry," he said reassuringly.

The weather was showing signs of improving, the Sun beginning to break through the clouds. Shafts of sunlight played with shadows on the reddish granite of the sacred outcrop and the ring of standing stones encircling it.

"You know," he went on after contemplating the rock and the workers busily labouring on it for a few moments, "we might just be able to turn the fact that Gastelois has to use a piece of that granite to our advantage."

* * *

Gastelois, Pierre and Sylvia stood watching Mannequin de Perrelle as he walked away from the site. Sylvia had arrived during the course of the latter's visit to see how the dolmen was progressing and had remained quietly in the background while he had carried out his inspection.

"Well, thank goodness for that!" declared Pierre, breathing a sigh of relief as Mannequin left the site. "I'd thought we were never going to get this thing approved."

"Nor did I," said Gastelois. "It's not what I wanted, but I suppose two side chambers are better than one, or none at all."

"True," agreed Pierre. "I know he'd have agreed to three if you'd gone along with his suggestion for the end of the main chamber, but I understand why you didn't." He paused, looking pensive. "Let's just hope he doesn't give us any more grief while we're actually building the thing."

Gastelois shrugged his shoulders, but did not comment.

"So, how did you get on at Mont Mado?" asked Sylvia, gazing at him.

"Fine. I told Abatfalaise what I need and it should be quarried and ready to be moved by the next half Moon." He stroked his chin pensively. "La Cloche was there."

"The union chief?" queried Pierre.

"Yes. I had to wait while he finished discussing some business with Le Gripert. Teus knows what it was, but when he left I could've sworn he gave me an odd look."

"I don't trust that one," declared Sylvia emphatically.

"Me neither," said Pierre.

"Oh well, no point in dwelling on it," said Gastelois. "Come on, the weather's cheered up and we've got a dolmen to build."

* * *

A large number of potentially suitable megaliths for the new dolmen had been located in the vicinity of Gor and near the foreshore about half a mile to the south of the site. During the remainder of the afternoon, Gastelois and his assistant were shown the majority of them by Martin Le Blancq and Lucien Roche-Fendeur. The latter was a particularly burly individual who would be in charge of the eventual quarrying operations. They examined the megaliths thoroughly, considering their shape and carefully measuring their length and width. Some were selected, others rejected.

Each chosen stone was marked with a white blob by one of Gastelois' team, Eustin Le Mince, who stood by with a pot containing a singularly edifying mixture of guano and powdered chalk while each lump of rock was being examined. Once one had been selected, Le Mince liberally daubed it with some of the 'paint', applying it with such enthusiasm that it splashed everywhere.

Accompanying these five was the priest Esclenquier Le Digot, who was there to consider the levitation of those megaliths too large to be conveniently moved by manpower alone. Absent-mindedly standing too close to the first stone picked, he very nearly caught a face-full of guano mix as a quantity of it ricocheted off the uneven surface of the rock and headed in his direction. He managed to jump clear in the nick of time and from then on made sure that he kept well clear of Le Mince's artistic endeavours.

While Gastelois and his companions were contemplating megaliths, the remainder of the team, led by one Rougetête de la Cloche, started work on clearing a route up the hill from Gor to the site along which the stones selected from that area could be transported. Once that had been done, another path would be forged from the foreshore for the boulders from there. The other priest, Asceline Le Doublier, accompanied them. He had to ensure that the routes chosen would be as suitable for levitation as they would be for the dragging of the sleds upon which the stones would be transported.

There were a lot of trees to be felled and cleared out of the way as the nearby slopes were thickly wooded. Some, at least, of the felled trees would come in useful. There were the sleds to be constructed and the tracks to be laid for the moving of stones, and A-frames and levers to be made for their positioning.

The tracks along which a sled and its megalithic cargo would be pulled consisted of a series of logs cut in half lengthways and laid end to end in parallel pairs. The upper surface of each log was trimmed and greased with animal fat to ensure the smooth, easy running of the sled over it. If necessary, stakes would be driven into the ground on either side of a log to help anchor it, the parts of them protruding above the surface shortened so as not to interfere with the sled's travel. To save labour, no more than four or five pairs of logs were generally used, the rear ones being moved to the front once the sled had cleared them. As far as could be ascertained, this now commonly employed system was first used by Taranis de Téviec when he was building the passage-dolmen of Kercado in Armor and as a result was known as a *Kercadoan-Téviec* trackway (usually shortened to Kercadoan or K. T. trackway).

The men went about their work with gusto, singing lustily about the joys of being a dolmen builder as they swung at tree trunks with flint axes hafted in wooden handles, two men to a tree.

One particular song extolled the virtues and successes of their leader...

> *I erect dolmens everywhere,*
> *Building them with the greatest care.*
> *I'll build you a pouqu'laye over there,*
> *As fine a one as anywhere.*

...while another their own skills and achievements:

> *We move large stones with the greatest skill*
> *Over land and up the hill.*
> *No rock's too big for us.*
> *Tall or short,*
> *Thin or squat,*
> *We go right in and shift the lot.*

By the end of the afternoon, everyone was ready for a good session in *The Quernstone*. After eating a hearty meal of roast deer, which Hacquoil Le Buvet had obtained and prepared especially for them, Gastelois and his team settled down to an evening's imbibing of ale or cider.

The two priests retired immediately after eating, saying that they had their evening ancestral communings to perform and that too much consumption of beverages alcoholic would interfere with this. It did not go unnoticed, however, that, shortly after they went up to their sleeping quarters, the landlord followed them with two jars and a large flagon of something you could have bet your last limpet shell was not plain water.

"I'm sure the ancestors will be pleased to see them," said Pierre de Lecq sarcastically once the priests were out of earshot.

"They'll probably all be as befuddled as each other," observed Gastelois irreverently. It was a well-known fact that the ancestors were not averse to a tipple or ten, which often made communication with them somewhat difficult, but this was not something you were supposed to comment on.

"You know I didn't see many rocks today that I would want to use as capstones," he said changing the subject, after taking a swig of cider.

"Come to think of it, nor did I," said Pierre. His face assumed a pensive expression. "I seem to recall that there's a rocky outcrop not very far from the site that might be worth investigating."

"Ah yes," said Gastelois, nodding slowly. "I know the one you mean. We'll look at it in the morning." He drained his jar. "You ready for another one?"

"Yes," said Pierre, draining his own. "Thanks." He handed it to Gastelois.

When Gastelois returned from the bar with the duly replenished drinking vessels, after stopping on the way there to have a brief chat with two salt-seasoned fishermen at a nearby table, who interrupted their game of *shove limpet* to ask him how the new dolmen was progressing, Pierre said:

"I was just thinking about the levitation of the large stones – any news yet on those two priests with the cold?"

Gastelois shook his head as he sat down. "No. I asked Maître Esclenquier about that earlier and he hadn't heard anything."

"Well, time is hardly on our side, so I hope we get some good news soon."

"So do I, mon vier," said Gastelois. "So do I."

Pierre contemplated his drink in silence for a few moments and then he asked: "What's the plan for tomorrow – continue with the clearance?"

"Yes. With any luck we should finish that by tomorrow evening. Then we can get on with quarrying and transporting the stones."

"Well, I hope it all goes smoothly," said Pierre, lifting his jar to his lips.

"You and me both, mon vier," said Gastelois with feeling. "You and me both."

Sinclair Forrest

* * *

It was very late when a more than half asleep Clychard La Cloche opened the door of *Levitation House* and peered out into the night, having been roused from his slumbers by a loud, persistent knocking.

Grosnez pushed past him, telling Piton to wait outside.

"What d'you want now?" demanded La Cloche grumpily as he followed him along the passage to the main chamber. He had not long retired to bed and was not at all pleased at having been woken so soon after falling asleep.

Grosnez waited until he had seated himself in the chamber before saying anything. He was almost as familiar with the layout of the dolmen as its resident was, and so the lack of light in the interior did not hinder his locating one of the wooden stools to be found there.

"So," said the union chief after Grosnez had told him, "you can't do any more digging because Gastelois has posted lookouts." If there had been adequate illumination, he would have been able to see the look of total frustration etched into the other's face.

"That's right." A loud sigh of exasperation escaped from Grosnez' mouth. "I think, mon vier, the time has come for some action from you. I've helped you out enough times in the past – the union's acquisition of this place, for instance."

"I know," agreed the other. "But..."

"Work on the site must be delayed so we have time for a proper look."

"That's easier said than done," said La Cloche, yawning. "And if I do manage to pull something off, you'll probably only have one shot at it. Gastelois is suspicious, him. He knows someone's int'rested in the site, so he'll be keeping a close watch on it. It might be poss'ble to keep him away for a little while, but you won't be able to return there night after night, digging away until you find the thing." He paused and scratched the top of his balding head with dirty fingernails. "And another thing," he went on, examining his nails in the gloom. "How sure are you that the vial is still buried there?"

"What're you saying, you?" Grosnez glowered at the other.

"That other hole you found, the one you told me about this morning that someone else had dug, what of that? The vial could already have been r'moved."

"As I said before, that hole was too near the trees – totally the wrong place."

"If the directions were correct," said La Cloche.

"I'm well aware of that, Clychard," hissed Grosnez between clenched teeth.

The two men fell silent for a few moments. Then Grosnez said: "I'm going to see T'loch."

"Why?" asked La Cloche.

"He knows about the glowing liquid and the vial. In fact, I think he probably knows where it's buried, despite what he told us before, so I pr'pose to ask him."

"If you're right, what makes you think he'll tell you where it is?"

"There's only one way to find out, mon vier."

With that, Grosnez bade the other goodnight and made his way out of *Levitation House*. He would seek out Vraicer T'loch first thing in the morning.

CHAPTER FIFTEEN

PLOTTINGS AT SUNSET

Work continued the following morning in earnest. Fortunately, after the way it had been on the previous few days, the weather was now cooperating. An early start was made on continuing to clear the route from Gor along which the megaliths from that area would be transported. After that had been completed, the route from the foreshore would be tackled.

Gastelois' men were helped in their endeavours by a group of stalwart individuals from the settlement, who turned up to offer their assistance. This was gratefully accepted.

While Rougetête de la Cloche and Asceline Le Doublier were supervising the clearance, Gastelois, Pierre and Esclenquier Le Digot went to look for rocks that would be suitable for use as capstones. They decided to investigate the area Pierre had mentioned in *The Quernstone* the previous evening – a prominent outcrop of pinkish rhyolite sticking conspicuously out of the middle of a field to the north of the new dolmen. Not only was this fairly close to the site, it was also on more or less the same level, thus making transportation of rocks from it a relatively straightforward process. In addition, there were no trees in the way.

"This looks fine to me," said Gastelois, contemplating the outcrop from atop it.

Pierre was examining some of the fissures running through the rock. "Yes," he said, "we should be able to split off what we need without too much trouble."

"There are some rocks near the base that might do for the smaller capstones," remarked Gastelois, pointing at the ground near the bottom of the outcrop where smaller chunks of rhyolite were jutting out.

Pierre looked down from where he was standing next to Gastelois, having climbed up to join him, and nodded.

The DRAGON of ANGUR

"What do you think, Maître Esclenquier?" Gastelois then asked the priest, who was standing on the ground a little way away from the rock.

Esclenquier Le Digot looked at the outcrop, then in the direction of the dolmen site and then at the rock again, all the while slowly massaging his chin.

"If it's suitable for you, I don't see a problem," he said. "In fact, to save time, we could probably levitate the stones from here to the dolmen without using sleds – it would be a lot quicker."

And a lot more dangerous, thought Gastelois. He and Pierre exchanged knowing looks. "We'll see how it goes," he said. "Right, let's get back to the dolmen."

* * *

In the end, it was not Grosnez who found T'loch, but T'loch who in effect found Grosnez. Considering that T'loch knew that the other was looking for him and deliberately put himself in a location where he was sure that Grosnez would find him with very little effort, this was not altogether surprising.

Grosnez had arisen at the crack of dawn and, after a hastily consumed breakfast prepared equally hastily by a not fully awake Piton, he had headed for Ang-Lenn. Piton had been sent off, grumbling, to do his daily stint in the tree overlooking Gastelois' site.

On reaching the settlement, Grosnez had gone straight to *The Old Vraic and Coracle*. Boileau Le Gobel had given him a suspicious look when he had walked in, which had grown even more so when Grosnez had asked him if he had happened to have seen Vraicer T'loch recently.

As the luck would have it, T'loch was already in the pub, partaking of a breakfast there before catching the next boat to Lesur.

"He's here," said Le Gobel, nodding past Grosnez' shoulder as he poured him the jar of ale he had ordered.

Grosnez looked round. His eyes fell on a thin, dark-garbed figure ensconced at a table at the far end of the pub, to one side of the entrance.

"Thanks," he said. Casting the exact number of limpet shells on to the bar to pay for the drink, he picked up the jar and headed for T'loch's table.

"Greetings, mon vier."

Vraicer T'loch looked up. "Ah, Grosnez Chatel, greetings," he said cordially. "Sit down, sit down."

As Grosnez did so, he could not help but notice that the other was looking more youthful than ever. What was his secret?

The two magicians of greatly disparate abilities faced each other across the table.

"How was Piltdown?"

The question took Grosnez by surprise. How had he known?

"Verman Clouet told me," said T'loch, smiling.

"Ah!" breathed Grosnez. "It was, er, very interesting."

"Good. And have you found the vial, then?"

"The vial?"

"Of glowing liquid."

"Oh yes, the vial." There was something about T'loch's manner that Grosnez found disconcerting. He took a gulp of ale to steady his nerves. "No," he said, putting his jar back down on the table. "I haven't. In fact, I'm glad I bumped into you, mon vier. Maybe you can help."

"What's the problem?" T'loch took a spoonful of seaweed stew from the bowl before him.

"I, er, couldn't find it," confessed Grosnez.

T'loch studied the other intently. "I take it you followed the directions you were given?"

"Yes, but they were a bit vague. There were a number of poss'ble starting points."

"That's always the way, it seems," observed T'loch, playing with another spoonful of seaweed stew.

"What if the directions were wrong?"

T'loch shook his head. "They wouldn't be wrong," he said emphatically.

Grosnez wondered how he could be so certain. "In that case," he said, "I'm sure that it's on the site of Gastelois' new dolmen."

"So why don't you ask him if you can have a good look? I don't suppose the work is too advanced, at least not yet."

"Er, I don't want him to know," said Grosnez, avoiding the other's gaze. "I want to keep my plans for the Jub'lee as secret as poss'ble."

The DRAGON of ANGUR

"Ah!" breathed T'loch, drawing the word out.

"I went back last night, but he'd posted lookouts so I couldn't do anything."

"Lookouts?" T'loch feigned surprise.

"Yes, mon vier, lookouts."

"Why?"

Again Grosnez avoided T'loch's eyes. "I pr'sume because he'd noticed that someone had been digging there the night before."

"You?"

Grosnez nodded. "Could you, er, help, mon vier?" he then asked hopefully.

"*Me*?" replied T'loch. "What good would I be? I told you before that I don't know where the vial is." He smiled. "Well, I suppose I now know that it's somewhere on the site of the new dolmen, but that's only because you've told me."

"But, with your powers, surely you could find the exact location?"

T'loch shrugged his shoulders. "Perhaps I could. Perhaps I couldn't." He finished the bowl of stew. "Anyway, as you've just said, Gastelois has posted lookouts, so that rather scuppers any attempt to look for the thing if you won't say anything to him."

Grosnez frowned. "It's rather difficult, mon vier."

That I can well believe, thought T'loch. "Look, I tell you what I'll do," he said. "I'm going to Lesur for a few days. I'll think about it while I'm there and, if I come up with any ideas, I'll contact you when I get back." He smiled at Grosnez. "Us magicians must help each other out whenever possible, eh?"

* * *

By the end of that day, the route from Gor to the dolmen site had been completely cleared of trees and other vegetation, apart from the tree trunks that would be used for the *Kercadoan-Téviec* trackway and which now lay at the start of the path. Gastelois inspected it with Pierre de Lecq and the two priests, walking up it towards the site and then back down it to check for any obstacles that might have been missed and that could interfere with the transportation of the megaliths.

Apart from three or four projecting tree roots that would probably prove very difficult to remove and were therefore best left alone, the path was clear.

"Pierre, first thing tomorrow, we'll paint those," said Gastelois, referring to the roots. "That way they'll be easier to see – we don't want anyone tripping over them."

"No, that we don't," wheezed Asceline Le Doublier, breathless from the exertion of walking up and down the hill between Gor and the dolmen.

His fellow priest, Esclenquier Le Digot, watched him as he struggled to catch his breath, the expression on Le Digot's face more one of irritation than concern.

"You're getting too old for this, Maître Asceline," he said. "Per'aps you should spend tomorrow having a good rest, you."

"I'll be fine," said the other, resenting the implication that he was past it.

"We've had a hard day," said Gastelois quickly, anxious to defuse the developing tension between the two priests. "Time to unwind. Let's join the others in *The Quernstone*."

"That's a good idea," agreed Pierre, nodding his head.

With that, Gastelois led the way down to Gor, the priests following and his assistant bringing up the rear. It had indeed been a tough day and the ale and the cider would slip down very nicely.

* * *

That evening, while Gastelois and his team were relaxing in *The Quernstone*, Grosnez went to see Clychard La Cloche. As it was a particularly fine evening, La Cloche had suggested that they climb on to the first tier of *Levitation House's* oval mound and chat outside while watching the sunset.

Now they were sitting near the western end of the mound, jars of ale in hand, their backs against the reddish-pink granite megaliths facing the second tier. The Sun was still warm, its gradually reddening rays bathing the two men and their megalithic surroundings in a ruddy orange glow.

"So, what did T'loch have to say?" asked the union chief.

Grosnez related his discussion of earlier in the day.

"Not a lot then!"

"No, not really. Said he'd think about it while he's in Lesur."

La Cloche took a drink of ale and contemplated the scene before him.

Ang-Lenn was visible beyond the forest cloaking the plain below the high ground upon which *Levitation House* stood, its buildings silhouetted against the glare of the western sky. The steep sided bluff that was the Town Mount stood out as a dark mass to the left of the settlement, the rotunda of the Elder's Assembly Hall clearly visible on its northern summit.

"I wonder what words of wisdom have been spouted in that place today," said the union chief sarcastically, nodding in the direction of the Hall.

"Nothing of any consequence," said Grosnez. He looked at his companion. "So, what are we going to do about the vial?"

"I thought you were going to wait for T'loch to come up with some ideas," replied La Cloche, still contemplating the Town Mount.

"No I didn't. In any case, I haven't time to wait for him."

"Well, *I* may have a plan," said La Cloche, looking into his ale jar. "But it will take some time to achieve its objective."

"What plan? I need to get that vial *now*."

"Patience, mon vier, patience."

"So, tell me about this plan." Grosnez was feeling anything but patient.

"Well, apart from another little scheme I've been dreaming up..." began the union chief.

"What other scheme?" interjected Grosnez, interrupting him.

"Well," said La Cloche, "as you know, I was up at Mont Mado yesterday. You may recall that, as you were about to leave, I made a remark about turning Gastelois' need for a piece of Mado granite to our advantage."

"Yes, I seem to r'member that."

"Well, this morning I paid a visit to that commune at Geonnais."

"Why did you want to do that?" asked Grosnez, a puzzled look coming over his face.

La Cloche scratched a chubby cheek with the tip of the middle finger of his left hand, which he then proceeded to suck noisily as if tasting something nutritious it had picked up from the aforementioned cheek. He then examined the fingertip closely, his piggy eyes nearly going cross-eyed in the process.

Grosnez watched this performance with mounting irritation. "Well?" he demanded.

"For a donation of, er, int'resting substances, that lot can be persuaded to do almost anything. When Gastelois goes to collect his block of Mont Mado granite..."

"I don't see how that can poss'bly help us," stated Grosnez in exasperation.

"No, I agree. But the more disruptions, the better."

Grosnez frowned at the other. He had no idea what the union chief had organised for Mont Mado, but whatever it was, he had a feeling that it would not be of much use as far as his plans were concerned. The only disruptions he was interested in were those that would clear the dolmen site completely so that he would have undisturbed access to search for the vial. He said as much to La Cloche.

"As it happens, I do have an idea that may just work," said the latter. "The important thing is to get the site cleared of people. The best way to do that is to get it offic'lly closed down and our own lookouts posted."

"And how d'you pr'pose to do that?"

"First of all," said La Cloche, pausing to noisily slurp some more ale, "we need to replace some of Gastelois' men with our own." He furrowed his brow contemplatively. "Three or four should do."

"How're you going to do that?" queried Grosnez.

"Supposing a few of Gastelois' men were to become, er, unwell," said La Cloche, "and were unable to continue working."

"So you intend to make them sick."

"That's the gen'ral idea."

Grosnez looked doubtfully at the union chief: "How?"

La Cloche swilled what was left of his drink around in the jar. "Oh, per'aps a few dodgy shellfish, or something like that." He lifted the vessel to his lips and drained it. "Or per'aps you could come up with a suitable potion or something."

"I dare say I could," said Grosnez. "But once you've got your men on the site, what then?"

"We can engineer some kind of, er, accident," stated La Cloche in a tone of voice that suggested that this would be the easiest thing in the world to accomplish.

"What will that do?" asked Grosnez. "I mean, other than cause a temp'rary disruption."

"Oh, if it's serious enough, it will be more than temp'rary, mon vier."

"How so?"

"*Health and Safety* will get involved, the site will be closed down and made a no-go area pending a full invest'gation."

"Excellent!" declared Grosnez. Then an expression of doubt came over his face: "But how will they find out?"

"They'll find out, mon vier. They'll find out."

Grosnez smiled, nodding slowly. La Cloche's plan had merit; it might just work. He contemplated the scene ahead of him. The trees of the forest and Ang-Lenn's buildings beyond these were taking on a sort of greyish purple, almost misty aspect with the approach of twilight as the Sun sank lower in the western sky. A chill, seaborne breeze had sprung up and Grosnez shivered involuntarily as it ruffled him. He drained his jar.

"Right," he said, "I'm heading for home. Piton wasn't back, him, when I left to come here. It'll be int'resting to see if he has anything to report from the dolmen." He frowned. "And he'd better have pr'pared me something to eat." He looked at La Cloche: "You'll keep me informed of progress?"

"That I will, mon vier," confirmed La Cloche. "That I will."

CHAPTER SIXTEEN

THE GEONNAIS COMMUNISTS

The next morning, while Rougetête de la Cloche and Asceline Le Doublier were off supervising the clearance of the route from the foreshore to the new dolmen, a start was made on quarrying the first stones to be used in its construction. Under the enthusiastic direction of Lucien Roche-Fendeur, the men worked quickly and efficiently, using hefty stone mallets to hammer stout wooden wedges into natural fissures in each of the selected rocks.

The wedges were then thoroughly soaked with water to swell them and thus force the two sides of each crack apart, after accomplishing which, each piece of wood was driven deeper and given another dousing to further widen the split. Once the first wedges were thoroughly saturated and could be hammered in no deeper, the whole process was repeated using larger pieces of wood.

When a gap of sufficient width had been achieved between two pieces of rock, log levers were inserted into it to persuade the required boulder to separate from its parent outcrop. This was not always successful at the first attempt, but a combination of wedges of the right size and persistent levering eventually persuaded the most stubborn chunk of rock to break free.

At the same time as the quarrying operations were taking place, the socket holes for the uprights were being partially excavated – the final depth and extent of each hole could only be determined once the relevant megalith had been laid alongside it with its base adjacent to it.

By the end of the day, four megaliths had been quarried, and early the following morning, the first two stones were brought up to the dolmen site from the area immediately to the north of Gor where they had been located. As they were smallish ones destined for the entrance to the passage, their size did not warrant the use of levitation. In fact, it was decided to move both of them at the same time on one of the wooden sleds that had been built for the purpose.

This was sitting on the first of four pairs of half logs forming the *Kercadoan-Téviec* trackway which had been laid the previous day, and which just needed the application of liberal quantities of animal grease to make it fully operational.

Once the two roughly cuboid blocks of dark red granite had been levered on to the sled, which creaked in protest at the weight, they were lashed securely to it with ropes of hemp and vegetable fibre. Similar ropes were attached to the front of the sled to enable teams of men to pull it.

While all this was being done, half a dozen men with buckets of animal grease were making their way along the trackway, plunging their hands into the contents of their buckets and slapping copious quantities of the friction-reducing substance on to the upper surface of each log. They then spread it out evenly with their fingers and palms so that it had a consistent thickness. It was a mucky job, but at least it was an honest one – unlike the greasing of certain higher placed palms that was commonly believed to take place. To the average Angurian, this was the only explanation for certain governmental decisions, particularly some of those of the *Pouquelaye and Earthworks Committee.*

When all was ready and the men were in position, Gastelois gave the order to move off. Traditionally, the chief dolmen builder always accompanied the first stone to be moved, be it large or small, and thus it was on this occasion, Gastelois walking to one side of the sled and keeping a wary eye on its progress.

This particular load his men managed to pull easily, despite an uphill gradient that in places was quite steep. Three men walked behind the sled, pushing when necessary, but always ready to jump clear should the stones slide backwards off it.

As soon as the sled had cleared the first pair of logs, they were quickly lifted and moved to the front of the leading pair. More grease was smeared on them to keep them lubricated. Then, when the sled had passed over the now rearmost pair, these were moved into pole position, and so the process was repeated again and again as the transportation of the megaliths progressed up the path.

The men often had to run the gauntlet of local kids who, on these occasions, were in the habit of hiding in the branches of nearby trees from where they would hurl anything conveniently to hand that would serve as a missile at the workmen as they passed by. These brats were especially fond of pelting priests engaged in the levitation of megaliths, which was a particularly rewarding pastime as any disruption of the levitation process had potentially spectacular consequences.

If any children were hiding in the trees on this first run, they were conspicuous by their lack of action, and the sled reached its destination without incident. The two blocks of granite were then off-loaded at the entrance to the new dolmen's passage.

"Thank the Teus that's done!" exclaimed one Gérard, who had been one of those moving the logs of the K. T. trackway. "I wonder how many more times we'll have to shift these things," he added somewhat morosely as he rested a booted foot on one log of the last pair to have been transferred to the front of the trackway.

"Don't worry about it," said Haysie Fiott, one of those working with him. He wiped his greasy hands on his leather tunic. "Just think what we've got to look forward to when it's all finished."

He was referring to the great celebratory feast that took place upon the finishing of a new dolmen. It commenced early in the evening of the day of completion and only very rarely did it last any less than the whole night.

Gérard nodded slowly and a smile cracked his swarthy, weather-beaten features: "That's true, that!"

The work of placing the uprights always started with the passage, progressing inwards from the entrance. The walls of the passage utilised the smallest megaliths in the structure, and once completed, it could help channel energies to assist with the movement of the larger stones of the main chamber at the western end. These had to be very carefully positioned by means of ropes, levers and levitation, and it could take a full day to place just one upright chamber megalith.

Gastelois stood next to the two stones, a pensive look on his face, his eyes moving from them to the staked-out site and back again. The stakes had been temporarily replaced in those sockets that had been partially dug out so that the overall layout of the dolmen was still clear. He had already formed a good idea of which stone would go where. Now he was certain. "This one on the left side," he said, tapping the one nearest to him with his right foot, "and the other facing it."

The two boulders were then manhandled into position next to the first two sockets of the passage, being lined up so that the correct end was immediately adjacent to the hole in question.

Gastelois removed the stakes from the two holes and then knelt down and examined each hole in turn, while his men watched him intently. "Right," he said, standing up and turning to them. "These need to be enlarged. Fortin, Tapin, can you deal with that?"

Fortin La Berfote and Tapin Le Large walked over to Gastelois, each carrying an antler pick and an aurochs shoulder-blade shovel. Fortin took the socket to the left of the entrance while Tapin busied himself with that to the right. Gastelois looked on while they alternately picked and shovelled, occasionally giving them directions or advice. Eventually, he was satisfied that the holes were the right depth and shape to accommodate the lower third of the two stones.

"That's fine," he said. "Témoins?"

Near the entrance was a pile of stones of assorted shapes and sizes, but none bigger than a man's hand. These were the *témoins* or witness stones, which had been gathered earlier. A number of them would be deposited in the socket hole of each upright of the dolmen before it was manoeuvred into its hole.

First, though, the témoins had to be blessed. Asceline Le Doublier, who had been waiting at the site for the sled and its cargo to arrive, now performed that service. He walked over to the pile, his pudgy hands clasping a large jar of ale specially brewed by his fellow priests for the purpose, muttered a few barely audible, arcane words and then poured half its contents over the stones. After waiting for a few moments, contemplating the pile in silence, eyes half closed, he passed his hands over it from left to right and back again several times in broad sweeping movements, uttering more arcane mutterings at the same time.

Then he turned to Gastelois: "It's done. You may proceed."

"Thank you, Maître Le Doublier."

Gastelois, Pierre de Lecq and Martin Le Blancq picked up a stone each from the pile and dropped it in the left-hand hole. Asceline Le Doublier then sprinkled some more of the specially brewed ale over these stones and mumbled arcanely for a few moments. When he had finished, three more pieces of rock were deposited in the right-hand socket. Again, Asclenquier performed his priestly duties, as he would with every hole on the site destined to receive an orthostat once the témoins had been placed in them.

Now the first megalith could be levered into its cavity and pulled upright, a straightforward process with the smaller orthostats, but often rather more fraught in the case of the larger ones. Ropes were looped around it and, as it was slowly pulled upright by one group of Gastelois' men, another inserted log levers under it to help manoeuvre it into its socket. Check ropes, pulled in the opposite direction to those of the first group, ensured that the stone did not overbalance.

As soon as it had attained the vertical, a couple of men held it steady while the ropes and logs were removed. Then Gastelois checked its alignment, eyeing the new orthostat's internal face in relation to the stakes along that side of the passage. After a few adjustments, he was satisfied.

"Right," he said. "Pack it."

'Packing' an orthostat was the term used to describe the filling of its socket with stones and soil which were then compacted with the ends of logs to ensure that the megalith was securely located.

Gastelois carried out a final check. "Excellent!" he declared, standing back and regarding the orthostat with satisfaction.

His men cheered. This was traditional after the first megalith of a new dolmen had been safely positioned.

"Let's get the next one up."

The raising and positioning of the second orthostat was as drama-free as the first.

It was traditional for the entire workforce to be on site for the raising of the two orthostats that formed the entrance to a new dolmen's passage, but once both of these had been successfully located and packed, the team would split up, with each group going to its respective stations.

So it was that, once the second upright had been positioned and secured to his satisfaction, Gastelois turned to his men and said: "Very good. Right, let's get the next two stones brought up. Lucien, you can continue supervising the quarrying, if you wouldn't mind."

Lucien Roche-Fendeur nodded. "Come on, men," he said. "Let's go to it!"

As Lucien and the quarrymen left the site, Gastelois said to his assistant: "Pierre, can you keep an eye on the transportation? You know the order I want the stones in."

"Yes. Leave that to me. You staying here?"

Gastelois nodded: "Yes. I'll look after things at this end."

The DRAGON of ANGUR

By the time they broke for lunch in *The Quernstone*, the next two passage orthostats were in place and the quarrying of a further four was well underway. By late afternoon, when Gastelois called a halt for the day, two of these were standing in line with their already-erected companions in the dolmen and the other two lay freshly quarried, ready for transportation to the site.

"Not a bad day's work," remarked Pierre de Lecq as he and Gastelois contemplated the partially constructed passage. They were on their own, the others having already set off for Gor.

"No, indeed," agreed Gastelois. "Let's hope it continues to go as smoothly."

"I'm sure it will," said Pierre encouragingly.

Gastelois slowly massaged his chin, a pensive expression on his face. "Tomorrow, I'll go to Mont Mado and see whether Maître Abatfalaise has our upright quarried. It won't be long before we're ready for it."

"He should have," said Pierre. "He's had enough time."

"True," said Gastelois. He glanced up at the sky, which was beginning to take on the tinges of evening. "Well, we'd better get to *The Quernstone* before our worthy workers drink the place dry!"

* * *

As soon as the coast was clear, Piton Le Malin clambered down out of his oak tree and scampered off homewards as fast as he could. Not only was he hungry, but he was anxious to give his report on the day's progress. Work had gone well – too well – and that would not please Grosnez. No, that would not please Grosnez in the slightest.

* * *

As Gastelois approached Mont Mado after lunch the following day, the sounds of some species of commotion reached his ears. Much shouting filled the air and some of the language being used was not of the most polite variety.

When he emerged into the sacred area from the tree-lined pathway that approached it from the east, the reason for the hullabaloo became all too apparent. A crowd had gathered in front of the reddish-pink granite outcrop and the ring of standing stones encircling it and was chanting noisily. Some people appeared to be clambering over the rock itself and one individual had climbed on to the summit and was standing there waving some form of banner over his head for all he was worth.

Confronting this lot were the quarrymen, who were evidently being prevented from accessing the outcrop to do their job. Invective was being hurled liberally back and forth between the two groups, with references lewd and bawdy to the participants' nearest and dearest.

Gastelois went up to one of them. "What's going on here?"

The burly individual whom he had addressed turned. "Ah, Gastelois! This is ridic'lous! Those fools are stopping us from working."

"Oh? Why, Pierre?"

"I don't know, me," replied Pierre Le Carrier. "We got 'ere this morning to find this lot encamped around the rock. They say that we're vandalising a sacred site by r'moving rock."

"What?" Gastelois looked at him. "Who are they anyway?"

The other shrugged his shoulders.

"I think they might come from that dodgy commune over at Geonnais," said Grandin de la Roche, a colleague of Pierre's.

"Ah!" said Gastelois, nodding slowly. He stared pensively at the demonstrators. "I wonder who put them up to this," he said, half to himself.

The other two looked at him, a puzzled expression on their faces, wondering what he had meant by that remark.

"Is Maître Le Gripert around?" he asked.

"Hiding over there in his hut," said Grandin. He spat contemptuously on the ground. "Been in there the whole time. Hasn't dared come out."

"Well, I'd better see him."

Casting a quizzical glance in the direction of the demonstration, Gastelois walked smartly over to the quarry manager's hut. He knocked on the door.

"Who... who is it?" enquired a voice nervously from within, barely audible above the din outside.

"Gastelois de Bois," said that worthy, raising his voice.

A few moments passed, the door creaked open and a pale, haggard face peered cautiously out.

"Come in, come in," said Abatfalaise Le Gripert with a degree of impaticnce.

Gastelois did as instructed, closing the door behind him. "What's going on, Maître Abatfalaise?" he asked.

"I'm not sure," said the quarry manager, returning to the table where he had been counting piles of payment shells, having earlier separated them into their various denominations. He exhaled a loud sigh: "When I woke up this morning, they were already here. They must've crept up in the night, them."

"I gather they're upset about a sacred site being used as a quarry."

"Apparently so." Le Gripert sighed again.

"Bit stupid, isn't it?" Gastelois looked at the other, who was moving shells around to no apparent purpose. "I mean, the stones from here are destined for sacred or important sites themselves."

"That's true, that," agreed Abatfalaise. He picked up a limpet shell and examined it closely.

"What d'you intend to do about it?"

"Don't really know, mon vier," said Le Gripert. "Per'aps if we ignore them they'll get bored and go away." He put the limpet shell back down on the table and picked up another one.

"That's all very well," said Gastelois impatiently, "but I've come to inspect the stone for my dolmen and I can't afford to hang around all day."

The other rubbed his eyes.

"I take it it's ready?"

"We were going to, er, quarry it this morning," said Le Gripert in apologetic tones. "I mean, it's all marked out ready."

"But not cut out yet." Gastelois sighed in exasperation. "I saw you about it ages ago. I'd have thought you'd have had it quarried by now. You knew how urgent it was."

"Yes, yes, I'm sorry. We had hoped to do it yesterday, but something came up."

"And now you can't get at the stone because of that lot out there."

"I'm afraid so."

"Right, we'll see about *that!*"

So saying, Gastelois turned and walked out of the quarry manager's hut, not bothering to close the door properly behind him. Ignoring the group of angry quarrymen, he marched straight up to the line of demonstrators, holding up his hand to get their attention and a modicum of quiet so he could make himself heard.

They were now singing a somewhat abusive song about the quarry manager, which hopefully for that worthy's sake would not turn out to be prophetic:

> *Abatfalaise last went out*
> *When the ale was drainèd,*
> *But a menhir fell on him,*
> *Left him stiff and brainèd.*

"People! People!" shouted Gastelois. "Can we talk about this?"

There was no response; no indication that he had even been noticed. The singing continued.

"*People!*" he shouted again, louder, whilst vigorously waving both arms to draw attention to himself.

Then one of the three demonstrators perched on the summit of the outcrop, a tall, rather thin individual with a particularly lean and hungry look about him, evidently noticed Gastelois, for he began to motion with his arms for the others to quieten down. Gradually his fellow protesters became aware of the dolmen builder's presence and the commotion began to subside.

"This is a sacred site," said the thin, hungry one, looking straight at Gastelois. The other demonstrators raised their voices in agreement until more motioning of the thin one's arms silenced them again. He was clearly their leader.

"I'm aware of that," said Gastelois. "That's why stone from here is so important."

"If we let this continue, soon there'll be nothing left," stated the leader, one Fanigot Le Bétyle, emphatically.

"I doubt that one or even two blocks per dolmen and the odd menhir or two is going to make much impact on this," Gastelois described the outcrop with a sweeping movement of his right arm, "at least not for some considerable time."

"But it will eventually."

"Yes, I suppose it will – eventually."

"That must never be allowed to happen!"

"No, never!" chorused the protesters in unison.

You've got this lot well trained, thought Gastelois. Then, after a few moments reflection, he asked: "Who put you up to this?"

The demonstrators exchanged puzzled glances. Their leader looked at the two standing next to him on the summit, possibly his deputies.

"What're you saying, you?"

Gastelois shrugged his shoulders. "It just seems odd to me that, considering how long this place has been operating as a quarry, you should wait until now before trying to do anything about it," he said matter of factly. "Or has word only just reached Geonnais?"

"Of course we've known about it," said Le Bétyle, looking somewhat hurt at the implication that his community lived in some backwater with little contact with the outside world. Which, of course, was precisely what it did do.

"Well, why haven't you done this before then?"

"We haven't felt the need to."

"But you do now."

"Yes."

"Why?"

"The La Tanche Menhir."

"The La Tanche Menhir!" repeated Gastelois with emphasis. "What's *that* got to do with this?"

"Its size, mon vier, its size."

"So?"

"Well, it's going to be big."

"Yes, so I believe."

"Bigger then anything that's ever been quarried from here before."

"With good reason, I understand."

"That's not the point, that!" retorted Fanigot Le Bétyle. "If the priests need something that big, why don't they get it from elsewhere, rather then bugg'ring up this place?"

"I presume because they have need of this particular type of rock," countered Gastelois.

"It was fine when smaller blocks were being quarried," said Fanigot, ignoring what Gastelois had just said, "but we feel that this menhir marks a whole new direction that will ultimately lead to the destruction of the site."

"This is ridiculous!" protested Gastelois. "One special menhir is hardly a whole new direction, as you put it. I mean, it's not as if all the streets in Ang-Lenn were going to be paved with Mont Mado granite."

"I wouldn't be so sure," said Fanigot. "That time might come."

Gastelois snorted. Glowering at the other, he said: "So, you're trying to stop the quarrying of the La Tanche Menhir?"

"That's right. As I said, it's too big." He paused momentarily. "And the union don't like it."

"The union?"

"Yes. The *Dolmen and Granite.*"

Ah! thought Gastelois. *So was that why Clychard La Cloche was up here that day?* Out loud, he asked: "And how do you know that?"

"La Cloche said so. He was up here earlier to see what was happening." He gave Gastelois a smug look. "We have union backing."

"I see. And how long do you intend to keep this up for?"

"As long as it takes. Why?"

"Because I need a block of granite for my new dolmen, which has to be finished in time for the Flint Jubilee."

The three on the summit looked at each other and exchanged mutterings that were inaudible from where Gastelois was standing.

"We appreciate what you're saying, mon vier, and we're sorry that this causes you a problem," said Fanigot Le Bétyle, and his two companions nodded in evident sympathy. "But we're staying here until this matter is r'solved, and no work will take place until that happens."

"Right!" said Gastelois, gritting his teeth. "We'll see about that!" He turned on his heels and headed back to the quarry manager's hut.

"I've had enough," said Gastelois to Abatfalaise Le Gripert as he walked into the hut. "Give me a small lump of granite that I can take with me now. You must have something lying around that those idiots can't stop me from getting at. Have you anything *bétyle*-like?"[8]

"But... But it's supposed to be for your dolmen, isn't it?"

"Yes. So?"

"Won't Planning want something more, er, substantial?"

"Tough!"

"As you wish," said Abatfalaise with a sigh of resignation. "Come with me, then, and I'll find you something."

With that, he got laboriously to his feet and headed slowly towards the door of the hut, moving as if every step was a major effort. Clearly he had no wish to go outside as to do so would mean that he would have to face the demonstrators.

Gastelois followed him, glaring at his back. He needed all of this like the proverbial trepanation. He just wanted to grab a piece of Mont Mado granite – any piece would do as long as he could carry it, or at least drag it – and get back to his dolmen without any further ado.

When the two men emerged from the hut, the demonstrators were in the throes of delivering another number of dubious musical merit with the same lusty enthusiasm that had characterised the production of the previous one:

> *Menhirs are cheap today,*
> *Cheaper than yesterday.*
> *Menhirs are half a clam,*
> *Cheaper than half a lamb.*

As they walked towards the outcrop, Abatfalaise cast nervous glances in the direction of the demonstrators who, as soon as they spotted him, started on a repeat rendition of *Abatfalaise last went out*, much to the chagrin of its subject.

"Ignore them," said Gastelois.

"I'm trying to," responded Le Gripert. "I'm trying to."

---

[8] A bétyle was a slender piece of rock, usually from one to three feet in length and tapering to a pointed or rounded end, rather like a miniature menhir. They were used as movable markers to record the progress of the Sun's rays inside a passage-dolmen at the approach of the solstices and equinoxes.

Sinclair Forrest

As they approached the standing stones encircling the outcrop, Abatfalaise hailed one of the quarry workers standing around helplessly watching the demonstration: "Grandin!"

At the sound of his name, Grandin de la Roche turned and, seeing his boss, said: "Yes, Maître Abatfalaise?"

"Gastelois needs a small piece," said Le Gripert as he walked up to him.

"A small piece?" queried the other.

"Yes, something bétyle-like. It's for his new dolmen."

"Ah! There's a bétyle up there, it," said Grandin, glancing up at the summit of the outcrop where Fanigot was exhorting his followers to "stick with it" because the "struggle" was worthwhile. "Why don't you brain that and plant it in your dolmen. I'm sure it would make a splendid..."

"Yes, yes," said Abatfalaise, interrupting him. "I'm sure Gastelois doesn't have all day."

"It's an interesting idea, though," said Gastelois, smiling at the thought of Fanigot rooted permanently in the passage or chamber of a dolmen.

They walked part way round the circle of standing stones until they reached a heap of rocks of various sizes piled up just outside it. These were cast-offs or 'seconds' – quarried pieces of granite that were flawed in one way or another and which would be sold at around half the price of a perfect specimen, or even less in some cases.

Grandin de la Roche pointed at one particular stone lying on the ground at the edge of the pile. "How about this one?" he suggested.

Gastelois looked down at the rock in question, a piece of granite a little under three feet long and shaped like a rough-hewn cone. He squatted next to the stone and, with a bit of an effort, turned it over, examining it carefully. Still squatting, he then lifted its thicker end off the ground to get a better feel for its weight. After a few moments, he put it back down and stood up.

"This should be fine," he said. "How much?"

Le Gripert shook his head: "No, no, mon vier. Have it on the house."

"Are you sure?"

The DRAGON of ANGUR

"Yes, yes. It's the least I can do under the, er, circumstances." He stroked his chin pensively. "You'll need a sled to transport it."

"I think there's one on the other side of this lot," said Grandin, nodding at the rocky heap. "I'll get it."

"Right, thanks," said Gastelois.

Grandin duly returned, pulling a rather crude-looking wooden sled behind him. He then helped Gastelois manhandle the bétyle on to it.

"That seems fine," said Gastelois once the stone had been positioned lengthways on the sled. He cast a look at the demonstrators, still vociferously trying to make their point from within the stone circle and the various parts of the sacred outcrop on to which they had climbed. "I'll be off then; leave you to the tender mercies of that lot."

"Will you be able to manage that?" asked Grandin, nodding at the lump of granite reposing on the sled. "I mean, if you like I can walk back with you and help you pull it."

"I should be all right, but," Gastelois hesitated for a moment, "why not? I'd be glad of the company."

"Good. It's not as if I can get much done around here." Grandin glared at the demonstrators before turning to Le Gripert: "Is that all right with you, Maître Abatfalaise?"

The quarry manager nodded: "Yes. As you say, there's not a lot you can do here." He let out a long sigh. "Maybe they'll get fed up soon and go home – back to that ramshackle excuse for a dolmen at Geonnais."

"Not one of the better examples of the breed, I must admit," observed Gastelois. "But it *was* a do-it-yourself effort, so it's hardly surprising it turned out the way it did."

Then, bidding Abatfalaise Le Gripert farewell, he and Grandin de la Roche left Mont Mado. As the two men headed eastwards, pulling the sled and its load behind them, the sacred outcrop glowed in the afternoon sunlight, its unwelcome visitors still crawling over it like maggots on a hunk of meat.

CHAPTER SEVENTEEN

A CHANTING OF LEVITATIONS

It was fortunate that Gastelois was using relatively small blocks for the passage orthostats, which could be transported to the site by manpower alone, as there was still no sign of the team of levitation priests. After much cajolling and pleading on Gastelois' part, Esclenquier Le Digot was eventually persuaded to go to the priestly centre in the west of the island to ascertain the state of play.

When he returned, two days later, the news was not good.

"I'm afraid," he said, "that, while the priests that had the cold have r'covered, them, they've given it to two of the others."

"Great!" declared Gastelois. "Any idea when we can expect to see them here, Maître Esclenquier?"

Le Digot shook his head.

"Didn't think so," muttered Gastelois, half to himself.

"Hopefully it won't be too long," said the priest, trying to sound reassuring.

"Hopefully not," said Gastelois. "We'll have fun moving some of the chamber stones without your help. I've chosen some pretty large ones, as you well know, and the assistance of you and your colleagues would be rather, er, welcome to say the least."

* * *

"What're you doing to my rock? You leave my rock alone, you!"

It was later that afternoon and some of Gastelois' men were working under his direction on the outcrop of pinkish rhyolite rising out of the field to the north of the dolmen site. They looked down from the outcrop to see a gnarled old man waving a stick at them that was as crooked as his physique.

"What? What d'you mean *your* rock?" queried Gastelois staring at him.

"It's my rock. I put it there, me."

Expressions of incredulity came over the faces of Gastelois and his companions.

"What...what do you mean you, er, put it here?" asked Gastelois looking at the others, who were trying their best not to smile or snigger.

"I put it there to keep the Kerions in."

Somebody hastily stifled a guffaw that had inadvertently slipped out.

The old man glared in his direction. "It's no laughing matter, mon vier," he declared firmly. "If you break up the rock, you'll let the Kerions out and that will mean disaster for the neighbourhood."

Three of the men, being of a more superstitious disposition than their colleagues, ventured to suggest that the old boy might have a point.

"Well," said Gastelois after thinking about this for a few moments, "if that's how you feel, you don't have to stay." He smiled at them. "But if you do decide to go, I don't suppose I'll be buying you any drinks in the pub tonight."

Being sensible fellows who invariably had thirsts to quench, it did not take them long to decide to stay.

"No good will come of this," insisted the old man, frustrated by the obvious reluctance of these unbelievers to leave *his* rock alone.

"What makes you so sure?" asked Gastelois.

"Got first hand experience of Kerions, have we?" said one of the others, smirking at the two perched next to him on the rock. They grinned approvingly.

The venerable one waved his stick threateningly in their direction. "Not exactly," he said, glaring at them.

Smug looks appeared on faces.

"But my grandfather had."

Smug looks disappeared from faces.

"Oh?" said Gastelois, intrigued to learn more. It was not often that you met someone who knew of an encounter with the supposedly mythical *Kerions* or little people.

"Yes." The old man eyed his audience closely, looking for any more signs of mockery. None, however, met his gaze. There was nothing but rapt attention. He went on:

"When my grandfather was a small boy, he used to spend a lot of time walking along the cliff tops at Sor. One day, so he told me, he thought he saw some figures in a rock pool way below him. He climbed down for a closer look, taking care not to be spotted. He got as close as he dared and, hiding behind a rock, watched them for some time. There were five Kerion girls and they were playing in the waters of the pool without a care in the world."

"The *Lavoir des Kerions*!" said Rougetête de la Cloche, who was standing next to Gastelois. "The Kerions' bathing pool."

The old man nodded slowly. "Yes. Not many people have seen them there, but my grandfather did."

"What were they like?" asked Eustin Le Mince, who was sitting on a narrow ledge near the base of the outcrop.

"According to my grandfather, they were the most beautiful girls he had ever seen – slender, graceful creatures with flowing hair falling to their waists. But it was their eyes he remembered more than anything else." His own eyes assumed a misty, far off look. "Yes, their eyes. He always used to tell me about their eyes."

"What was so special about them?" asked Gastelois.

"They were a very bright green and seemed to glow as if lit with a light of their own. He said they were magical, spell-binding eyes, unlike any he had ever seen on an ord'nary person."

"Kerion eyes!" exclaimed Rougetête de la Cloche, who seemed to be more convinced by the old man's tale than any of his colleagues perched on the rhyolite outcrop.

"So what happened?" asked Gastelois.

"Well, he watched them for ages. Time seemed to stand still – he said it was like being in a trance. Eventually, he dragged himself away and went home. But he went back the next day. He went back three more times and then he got caught."

"He got caught?" repeated Eustin Le Mince excitedly.

The old man nodded: "Yes, one of the Kerions spotted him and pointed him out to her sisters. He said he then left rather hurriedly. But he did go back again."

"He went back *again*?" Le Mince stared at the old man, eyes wide in surprise.

"Yes, a few days later, when he had summoned up sufficient courage. But this time, when he tried to get down to the pool, he found the path blocked by a huge black dog with great, glowing, blood red eyes that he said seemed to burn into him. He stood, rooted to the spot, until this creature started towards him and then he turned and fled. He never went there again." The old man paused, staring intently at his audience. "So do not meddle with the Kerions – no good will come of it!"

"I'll tell you what," said Gastelois, breaking the silence that ensued when the other had finished. "If we do find a cave entrance or any other kind of hole or opening during the course of quarrying this rock," he thumped the rhyolite next to him with the palm of his right hand, "we'll leave a large jar of cider and some bread for the Kerions. That should keep 'em happy."

"Time will tell," said the old man. "Time will tell."

After further reassurances from Gastelois that he and his men would take the greatest of care not to upset the Kerions, the old man was eventually pacified and finally wandered off muttering to himself: "What a forkful for the little people!"

* * *

"So, Mannequin de Perrelle didn't like Gastelois' piece of Mont Mado granite," said Grosnez sarcastically. "What a shame!"

It was early that evening and Piton had just related to his master how, as work on the dolmen was winding down for the day, the aforementioned worthy from the *Pouquelaye and Earthworks Committee* had arrived unexpectedly to see how the new structure was progressing. He had found little to criticise until he had been shown the contribution from Mont Mado.

"No, he was far from happy with it," said Piton. "He said that a bétyle was not big enough and that Gastelois would have to go back to the quarry and get something at least as big as one of the nearby uprights. Gastelois flatly refused, saying that he didn't have the time and that in any event there was nothing in the Planning regulations that stipulated what size the Mont Mado stone had to be. Mannequin said he would check the regulations with Branleur de Bitte and then stormed off, threatening dire consequences if Gastelois was in breach, as he was sure he was, and didn't rectify it."

"Excellent!" said Grosnez, rubbing his bony hands together gleefully. "I might have a word with a certain friend of mine in the Planning Department." He prodded the boar roasting over the hearth in the centre of the room with a flint knife. "On the other hand," he went on, examining the point of the knife in the firelight, "a bétyle is easy to r'move."

"If it's r'moved, Grosnez, Gastelois will have to get another piece of Mont Mado granite."

"Exactly, mon vier. Exactly."

"Aw, but you have a good idea there, you."

"I know I do." Grosnez hacked off a small sliver of meat from the boar, blew on it to cool it down and then popped it in his mouth. "Ah, nearly done! Now tell me again about that old fool who gave Gastelois grief earlier in the day."

"As I said before, I was too far away to see or hear much," said Piton, his mouth watering as he eyed the boar sizzling over the hearth. "But from what I overheard later, it was something to do with the Kerions getting out and causing trouble if that rocky outcrop near the site was quarried."

"Even better!" said Grosnez. "Another way we can get work delayed if necessary."

"Oh? How's that, Grosnez?"

His master did not elaborate. Instead, he muttered something about there also being La Cloche's plan, which meant nothing to Piton as so far he was not a party to it, and then told his servant to help himself to some meat.

This the Le Malin gratefully did. The evening was drawing on and he was rather hungry. The satisfying of the stomach was rather more important than the plottings of his master. Doubtless all would be revealed in due course.

* * *

A few days later, Maîtres Esclenquier Le Digot and Asceline Le Doublier turned up at the dolmen site with five of their colleagues, together with three assistants bearing drums, bone trumpets, tapping sticks and a hide painted with magical symbols (the usual accoutrements required for the levitation ritual). Gastelois was so overjoyed to see the full complement of levitation priests that he greeted them like long lost friends, almost forgetting to show them the deference their station demanded. Not much progress had been made since the last passage upright had been positioned a couple of days earlier, but now, at last, the larger stones could be moved and the construction of the chamber begun.

Around mid-morning the following day, after spending the night in *The Quernstone* (to the considerable inconvenience of at least fourteen members of Gastelois' team), the priests assembled on the beach to the south-west of Gor and arranged themselves in an arc behind an eight-ton block of seaworn, dark red granite destined to be used as one of the uprights in the new dolmen's chamber. It lay prone on the sand next to the outcrop from which it had recently been separated. Four other similar stones lay nearby, awaiting their turn.

As prescribed by tradition borne out by experience, the three drummers formed the centre of this arc, Maître Esclenquier Le Digot in the middle, with Bertholin Le Bandé and Pétard de Quen'vais to his left and right respectively, their drums suspended from their necks by leather straps which had seen better days. Next were Fielebert Sottevast and Griesensacq Le Gripert; these two had the trumpets, and would be responsible for producing the unearthly braying that would soon be issuing from their instruments. The left arm of the arc was completed by Songeur Le Rêveur, the right by Asceline Le Doublier, each of whom held a tapping stick. It was they who, together with Le Bandé and de Quen'vais, would intone the requisite chant for the occasion.

The priests then sat on their haunches, laying their instruments on the ground in front of them, and leant forward, eyes closed, fingertips together as if in prayer. After a while, Le Digot muttered a few incomprehensible words, then reached forward and lifted the large drinking vessel he had with him to his lips. He took a few sips of its contents – a special brew to help focus the mind – and then passed the jar to his left. In a low voice, Le Bandé uttered something equally unintelligible before drinking some of the vessel's contents, after which he handed it to Maître Sottevast, who continued the ritual. Once all the priests had drunk the prescribed quantity of the brew, the vessel duly found its way back to Le Digot, who put it down on the ground in front of him.

"Right!" he said, standing up. "I need someone to pull the hide."

Gastelois looked at his men: "Any volunteers?"

For a few moments, no one said anything. Eyes either shifted to avoid contact with Gastelois', or remained firmly fixed on the ground. The truth was that nobody wanted to be anywhere near the boulder while it was being levitated, and pulling the hide involved walking directly in front of the thing. Once the stone had been raised off the ground, the hide with the magical symbols would be slipped underneath, a risky business in itself. It would then be pulled along as the stone was moved, always staying directly beneath it, the power of the symbols helping to keep it off the ground.

"I will!" declared someone eventually. It was Philipot du Moncel, a veteran of Gastelois' team. He had pulled the hide before and knew the risks involved.

You had to make sure that you kept ahead of the stone while ensuring that the hide remained in the right position under it. On not a few occasions in the past, hide-minders, as they were known, had been knocked over by levitated stones through not paying sufficient attention. Amazingly, there had not been that many serious injuries. Although there had been quite a few bruises and cracked bones, and one victim had spent several days aimlessly wandering the countryside tying to remember where he had been after a blow to the head, nobody had actually been killed.

"Good man!" said Gastelois.

His fellow workers cheered vociferously as the courageous du Moncel walked over to the priests.

"You've done this before, haven't you?" asked Le Digot, recalling that he had seen Philipot perform the service on at least one previous occasion.

"That I have!" confirmed that worthy proudly as Le Digot handed him the rolled-up hide.

"Good, you know what to do then."

Philipot nodded, unwinding the drawing rope from around the hide and then unrolling the latter, walking towards the front of the boulder as he did so.

"Right," said Le Digot, "we can begin." He raised his right hand: "On my mark!"

With that he started beating a slow, regular rhythm on his drum. The other drummers joined in as did the two trumpeters, blowing long, low notes, all the instruments aimed at the stone. The chant priests began a deep bass ululation, barely audible above the other sounds. Gradually, Le Digot stepped up the level and the tempo of his drumbeats, the other two drummers following suit. The chanters increased the speed and volume of their delivery, while the trumpeters blew harder.

Imperceptibly at first, the boulder began to shake. Then the shaking became a pronounced wobble until, at the height of the priestly cacophony, with drums rolling, trumpets blaring and voices wailing, it lifted slightly off the ground as if raised by unseen hands.

At that moment, Philipot quickly slipped the hide under the stone, symbol-painted side facing upwards, and took the free end of the drawing rope in his right hand. As he was doing this, four men with a rope net pulled it over the boulder from the rear. This rope cradle would be fastened around the megalith to help keep it under control while it was being levitated. It was big enough to be used for all but the largest of the dolmen's stones (a second net would be specially made for those), and could be tightened or loosened to account for the differences in size among them.

The positioning of this was always a fraught stage in the proceedings: the men had to move in front of the priests to perform the operation and, although they kept as low as possible, this inevitably interfered with the sound waves produced by their holinesses. To minimise the effect of the interference, the two priests with the tapping sticks began to rhythmically tap the front part of the stone, keeping to the same tempo as that of the drummer at the rear. Even so, the boulder wobbled alarmingly, but stayed airborne.

The four quickly positioned the net and then ran from the stone, again keeping low. Each was holding an end of one of the four guidance and stabilising ropes attached to the net, which they uncoiled as they ran; two went off to either side while the other two went forwards, each of the latter at about forty-five degrees to the intended direction of travel. Eight more of Gastelois' men joined the rope team, so there were three to a rope.

"Take up the strain!" shouted Le Digot above the general din, and the ropes were pulled taut.

He then speeded up the rhythm slightly and the other priests matched their contributions accordingly. Slowly, inexorably, the rock began to move forwards, remaining no more than a foot or so above the ground. To the accompaniment of the rhythmic beating of the drums of Maîtres Le Digot, Le Bandé and de Quen'vais, the braying of Maîtres Sottevast and Le Gripert's trumpets, and the crescendos and diminuendos of the priestly chanting, the levitation party advanced with it, heading inland over the sand of the beach and making for the steep slope that led up to the plateau and the dolmen site.

Sinclair Forrest

The priests kept to their semi-circular formation, Songeur Le Rêveur leading one arm of the arc, Asceline Le Doublier the other, these two occasionally striking the stone with their tapping sticks to ensure that it behaved itself. Gradually the pace increased to that of a steady walk. Gastelois went ahead of the others, using his arms to signal slight course changes to the right or to the left to avoid the odd rocky outcrop that jutted up through the sand.

Philipot du Moncel alternated between walking backwards and walking forwards so that he could keep an eye on the hide and ensure that it stayed in the right position under the stone. The twelve men on the ropes kept a wary eye on the boulder, watching for the slightest deviation and using the ropes to compensate and keep it on course.

They managed to get the rock to the desired spot at the base of the slope without incident. Here a wooden sled was waiting, its runners greased with animal fat. It was sitting on the first pair of the greased logs of the K.T. trackway, at the start of the path previously cleared through the trees and which ran straight up to the top. The megalith was positioned over the sled and allowed to drop gently on to it. It creaked ominously under the weight, but did not collapse.

Philipot rolled up the hide, which he had pulled clear just before the stone was placed over the sled, wrapped the rope around it and handed it to Esclenquier Le Digot, its job done for the time being.

"Thank you," said Le Digot, handing it to one of the other priests for safekeeping. "Right, let's get ready for the next stage."

This involved dragging the sled with its cargo up the slope and over the ground to the dolmen site along the greased trackway. The priests would walk behind it, modifying their vocal and instrumental performance so that the stone would effectively lose weight, without actually lifting off the sled, thus making it easier to drag, particularly uphill.

The priests could, if required, make a rock leap from the bottom of a moderately high cliff to the top, but too often in the past its flight path had proved dangerously unpredictable and as a consequence this method was resorted to only if no other was possible. Fortunately, this was a very infrequent occurrence indeed.

Levitation was normally only used on its own to move a megalith over very soft ground, such as beach sand, or over uneven terrain which would render the use of a sled impracticable. Otherwise a combination of the two was generally employed, dolmen builders having decided long ago that this was far safer than relying solely on levitation.

"All right," said Gastelois. "Take up your positions everyone."

His men moved to the front of the sled and picked up the four ropes attached there, three to a rope as before. The priests meanwhile arranged themselves in two concentric arcs behind the sled, the route through the trees being too narrow to permit a single one as before. Maître Le Digot was in the centre of the front row, the two trumpeters on either side of him, while the four chant priests formed the second arc behind them. Right at the back, so they would not get between the levitation priests and the megalith, were the men who would move and reposition the logs of the K.T. trackway as and when required.

"Ready?" asked Le Digot when he thought everybody was in position.

Everybody nodded, Esclenquier gave the signal and the priestly cacophony erupted once again.

Soon the sled was proceeding uphill along the trackway to the accompaniment of drum, trumpets and chanting from one end and the groans of straining men from the other. The priests' efforts might have considerably reduced the effective weight of the stone, but even so it was hardly the lightest object on the face of the planet.

Le Digot, seeing that Gastelois' men were having a bit of a struggle, increased the tempo of his drumming, the trumpets were immediately blown harder and the chant chanted faster. The megalith, happy to assist, promptly lifted off the sled, which was very nearly pulled out from under it. Le Digot at once slowed his drumming slightly and the others followed suit. The adjustment worked: the rock settled back on to the sled.

After a short period of trial and error, Le Digot hit just the right tempo; a happy medium that ensured the stone was heavy enough to remain on the sled while being light enough to enable it to be pulled with the minimum of effort.

Without any further ado, they reached the top of the slope and manoeuvred the sled on to level ground. From there, it was only a relatively short distance to the site of the new dolmen where Pierre de Lecq and the rest of the construction team were waiting.

There was a spontaneous outburst of cheering from certain members of the latter when they saw the sled and its load emerge from the trees. This had the unfortunate effect of interfering with the priests' levitational sound waves and the stone suddenly put on the weight that it had lost. The twelve on the ropes were jerked off their feet while the back row of priests collided with the front row, which in turn stumbled into the rear end of the rock as the sled came to a sudden standstill.

Le Digot glared at those responsible for this disruption of the progress, while Gastelois and Pierre both favoured them with a 'you-should-have-known-better' look.

Apologies quickly followed and soon the sled and its cargo were underway again, completing the final leg of the journey without further incident.

The sled was stopped on the southern side of what would become the new dolmen's chamber, and the new boulder manhandled into position next to its destined socket immediately adjacent to the inner end of the passage. Gastelois removed the wooden stake from the hole, and then knelt down to examine the latter carefully.

"This needs to be bigger," he said, standing up.

Armed with antler pick and aurochs shoulder-blade shovel, Fortin La Berfote and Tapin Le Large did the honours. Before long, the socket was the right depth and shape to accommodate the lower third of the megalith. Three témoins later, duly blessed by the priestly ale and Asceline Le Doublier's arcane mutterings, and the new upright was being persuaded into its cavity. Although this had been a straightforward process with the smaller orthostats of the passage, it could be rather more fraught with the larger ones.

The erection principle was, however, the same. One group of men heaving on ropes looped around the stone slowly pulled it upright, while another shoved log levers under it to persuade it to enter its socket, and a third used check ropes to make sure that it did not topple over.

"Excellent!" exclaimed Gastelois once the megalith had been safely positioned and he had checked its alignment. "Let's pack it and get the next one up. I'll buy you all an extra round in *The Quernstone* if we get three erected by the time we stop this evening."

* * *

The DRAGON of ANGUR

Safely concealed in the branches of the nearby oak tree, Piton had been watching the proceedings with interest. He was, however, feeling rather more nervous than usual, not because of a fear of being discovered – although that did engender a fair degree of anxiety whenever he was up the tree – but because Grosnez had ordered him to follow Gastelois' and his team to *The Quernstone* after they finished for the day. He was not looking forward to this in the slightest.

He had been told to stay in the pub until closing time and to watch the dolmen workers carefully. Grosnez, being his usual helpful self, had not informed his servant of exactly what he was supposed to be looking out for. But he had given him some limpet shells – enough for him to buy himself some drinks, but not so many as to run the risk of inebriation or serious impairment of the senses.

He had to wait up the tree for longer than normal as Gastelois and his men worked later than on previous occasions. Clearly spurred on by the promise of the extra round, they were determined to get the third orthostat of the chamber erected before they were prepared to 'down tools' and leave the site.

Eventually, they achieved their aim and exhausted, but content, began to make their way down to Gor, chatting and singing happily.

Piton waited for a short while and then followed them at a discrete distance, stopping every so often when he thought that one of those at the rear might have heard him and be about to turn around. Why he should have been worrying was anybody's guess – Gastelois' men were making so much noise that a herd of stampeding aurochs could have been coming up behind them and they would not have heard anything.

When they reached the pub, Piton stayed outside for a little while before entering himself. Thankfully, it was pretty busy and he was able to lose himself amongst the crowd. Once he had bought himself a jar of ale, he found himself a shadowy spot by one of the carefully trimmed tree trunks serving as a wall pillar. From there, he could keep an eye on the dolmen builders, just as his master had instructed.

* * *

Piton was now on his third ale and beginning to feel just a little light-headed. If anything untoward was going to happen, it was certainly taking an age to make itself apparent. Gastelois and his men were clearly having a convivial time, but this was no more than you would have expected under the circumstances.

Then, just as Piton was coming to the conclusion that nothing out of the ordinary was going to occur, his attention was caught by a sudden commotion over by the bar.

There appeared to be some species of struggle in progress: two men were evidently wrestling with a third in the doorway behind the bar, which led to the pub's storeroom. One of these Piton recognised as the landlord, Hacquoil Le Buvet, the one assisting him he did not know, and the object of their affections he could not at first see clearly. He decided to move in closer to get a better view, following the example of a good number of the pub's clientele who had become aware of the commotion behind the bar.

Standing on tiptoe to see past the people in front of him, Piton observed that the one being grappled with was a small, middle-aged fat man in the final stages of baldness. With a shock, he realised who it was – Clychard La Cloche! What had *he* been up to?

Hacquoil Le Buvet soon provided the answer:

"So, you thought you'd improve the taste of my seafood stew, did you?" said the landlord between gritted teeth, as the other man gripped the union chief tightly by the scruff of the neck. He held up a small, narrow-necked jar of evidently dubious content, pointing at it with his free hand.

La Cloche tried to wriggle free, but the man's grasp was too strong.

"I don't know what you're on about, you," he said, feigning innocence as he squirmed in the vice-like grip of his captor.

"Well, what were you doing in my storeroom with this, then?" demanded the landlord, waving the jar in front of the union chief's face.

"I..."

At this point, Piton decided that it would be best not to hang around for the outcome and that therefore a speedy, but discreet exit was called for. He was not looking forward to telling his master about what he had just witnessed. He was sure that he would not be pleased.

* * *

The DRAGON of ANGUR

"*So, you thought you'd improve the taste of my seafood stew*"

Grosnez was indeed far from pleased. In fact, Grosnez was furious.

"What was the fool thinking of?" he fumed, his face livid with rage. "How the Teus did he manage to get himself caught?"

"I don't know, Grosnez," said Piton quietly. He yawned. It was now very late and he was exhausted. He longed for his bed.

"Well, first thing in the morning we're going to see him. He'd better have a good explanation!"

"Yes, Grosnez," said his servant disconsolately. Not only would it be late before he put his head down for the night, but now it seemed that he would have to get up at the crack of dawn as well. What a life! Not for the first time did he rue the day that his path had crossed with his master's.

* * *

Swinging slowly over his seaweed fire, Vraicer T'loch could hardly contain his mirth. With his remote viewing abilities, he had watched the incident in *The Quernstone*, from the time when Clychard La Cloche had sneaked surreptitiously into the pub's storeroom via its back entrance to his ignominious ejection from the premises with the encouragement of Le Buvet's booted foot. He had observed with not inconsiderable amusement the moment that the union chief had been apprehended on the verge of pouring the contents of the small jar he had been carrying concealed in the folds of his cloak into the vat of seafood stew simmering on the storeroom's hearth.

He did not envy La Cloche when Grosnez visited him in the morning. He would not be in the best state to be on the receiving end of his partner's venom. Apart from the hangover that he would undoubtedly have after what he had consumed on returning to *Levitation House*, his rear end would probably still be sore from the kicking it had received.

But all this was no more than the union chief deserved after what he had been up to. It would now be interesting to see what replacement scheme he and Grosnez would concoct between them to incapacitate some of Gastelois' workmen with the thwarting of the original one that evening.

Yes, very interesting. T'loch could hardly wait.

CHAPTER EIGHTEEN

A BETYLE FOR THE KERIONS

The crowd of onlookers from Gor and elsewhere that now gathered on a daily basis to see how work on the new dolmen was progressing mostly stayed at a respectful distance. Some of the children, however, most notably those who had wandered along on their own without parental support, frequently ventured in for a closer look and had to be told repeatedly to keep clear in case they got hurt. Gastelois did not relish the thought of having to tell little Pierre or little Jean's parents that their errant offspring had been crushed by some falling megalith.

One particular individual, a thin, gangly specimen with a flat-topped head that seemed too large for his body and overlong arms that seemed to hang limply by his sides, hands almost touching the ground, wandered from onlooker to onlooker to no apparent purpose.

This was Escogriffe Le Manquais, a simple soul whose beetle brow and shallow, sloping forehead fronted an intellect of quite formidable dimness. A man of equally simple needs, his favourite pastime was pushing strands of seaweed into one ear to see whether he could thread it through his head and pull it out of the other. When using one ear as the entry orifice failed to produce the desired result, the expression on his face would grow even more bemused than normal and he would forthwith switch to the other ear. If he was in the right mood, this sequence of events could be repeated many times in the course of a single morning, and whenever people spotted him, they would point and say: "Oh look! There's poor Escogriffe vraicing his brains again!"

On this occasion, after spending some time going from one member of the crowd to the next, he suddenly stopped by one and pointed at the dolmen:

"It's a dolmen," he announced, a slight note of triumph in his voice.

The man he was addressing nodded slowly, trying not to smile.

"There are stones," continued Escogriffe. "Passage stones."

The man nodded again. It was becoming more difficult to suppress visual expression of his amusement.

"One stone, two stones..." In slow, deliberate tones, Escogriffe began to count the passage uprights from the entrance inwards, pointing at each of them in turn. "Three stones..." He faltered.

"Four?" offered the man. Unable to contain himself any longer, a broad smile spread across his weather-beaten face.

"Four," repeated the afflicted one, his face assuming an expression of immense satisfaction.

* * *

While Escogriffe was showing off his arithmetical prowess, a somewhat sheepish Clychard La Cloche was being lambasted by a still irate Grosnez on the matter of the incident in *The Quernstone* the previous evening. What with a thumping headache, and a bottom and ego bruised in equal measure, the last thing he needed was Grosnez haranguing him, no matter how much he deserved it.

"You realise, you, that you may have ruined any chance we had of taking out some of Gastelois' men," Grosnez was saying, wagging an accusatory finger in the union chief's face. "Unless I can think of some other way."

"It wasn't easy, mon vier," said La Cloche defensively, backing away from Grosnez. "I waited until I was sure the coast was clear before going in."

"Well evidently it wasn't," snapped the other. "You should've been more careful."

"I spent some time watching that storeroom and the movements in and out of it," said La Cloche in mortified tones. "How was I to know that Le Buvet and that other idiot would come back in only moments after leaving?"

"Indeed, how *were* you to know!" said Grosnez sarcastically. He glared at the other for a few moments, the flickering torchlight illumination of the interior of the main chamber of *Levitation House* dancing on his features. Then he sighed. "We'll just have to think of another way of removing the workmen, but in the meantime I have an idea how we can give Gastelois another headache and buy us some more time."

"Oh? What's that then?" asked La Cloche, relieved that Grosnez appeared to be calming down.

"It involves a certain bétyle, just like the ones you have in here, which came from Mont Mado and which is presently standing in the new dolmen. One effect of that demonstration you persuaded those idiots from Geonnais to hold was that Gastelois didn't get the rock he should have, because it wasn't ready, so he took a bétyle-size one. From what Piton tells me, Mannequin de Perrelle was far from happy when he saw it as he was expecting Gastelois to use a considerably larger piece of Mont Mado granite. Gastelois apparently told him that there was nothing in the Planning regulations to dictate what size he had to use, at which point Mannequin went off to consult his boss on the matter."

"So?" said La Cloche, unsure of where all this was heading.

"Well, I feel pretty sure that *P. & E.* will insist that Gastelois use something rather more megalithic than a mere bétyle, but..."

"Supposing they don't," said the union chief interrupting him. "Supposing they let him use this bétyle, what then?"

"I was coming to that," said Grosnez irritably. "We'll pre-empt that by removing it. Then he'll have to get another piece of Mont Mado granite – Planning *will* insist on it."

La Cloche nodded slowly. "I see," he said. "And just how do you intend to, er, remove this bétyle? I mean, how are you going to get past Gastelois' guards?"

"I'll find a way," said Grosnez. "I'll find a way."

* * *

The days passed and gradually the new dolmen took shape. To the onlookers watching and those assisting with its building, it appeared to be progressing well. All the orthostats had been set up with the minimum of hassle, and work on the construction of the encircling stone mound was well under way. Many people, including women and older children, were helping Gastelois and his men by bringing basketloads of rubble from a quarry to the north of Gor, not far in fact from where some of the megaliths had been obtained.

Despite all this evident progress, Gastelois was far from happy. The work was actually way behind schedule and he knew it.

Although some of the capstones had been quarried, not one of them had been transported to the site and positioned on the uprights.

Gastelois remarked ruefully upon this point to Pierre de Lecq as the two men contemplated the site at the end of yet another long, tiring day. "I was hoping we'd have had at least two or three of the capstones up by now," he said.

"What you need," said Pierre, "is a good feast. Some good food and drink will soon cheer you up."

"Don't think it would," was the morose reply. "I've got a bad feeling – can't seem to shake it off."

His assistant frowned. Gastelois was normally pretty unflappable, but the pressure of this particular project was clearly getting to him. "Look," said Pierre, "we're all exhausted. I know we don't normally break for a feast until the mound's at capstone level, but under the circumstances I feel this is as good a time as any and I know that the men would appreciate it. I'll start making arrangements this evening."

Gastelois smiled weakly. "Yes, I suppose you have a point. Come on then, let's get down to Gor."

* * *

Piton Le Malin watched them leave. So, they were going to hold a feast. Maybe this was the opportunity his master had been waiting for; the chance to accomplish what La Cloche had failed to do in *The Quernstone*. As soon as they were out of sight, he dropped out of his tree and scampered homewards. Grosnez would be pleased with him. Yes, Grosnez would be *very* pleased with him.

* * *

It took two days for preparations for the feast to be completed and during that time work on the dolmen carried on apace. While the mound rose slowly but steadily around the orthostats as basketload after basketload of rubble was brought to the site, the quarrying of the capstones continued at the rhyolite outcrop in the nearby field to the north.

As the venerable individual with the concern about the Kerions had paid him and his men a return visit to see whether they were indeed doing anything to placate the little people, Gastelois had decided that it would be best to humour him. He had therefore arranged for a jar of cider and a bowl containing a hunk of bread to be left next to the outcrop when work on it finished for the day, as an offering for the Kerions should they emerge from their cave

The DRAGON of ANGUR

beneath it. He had assured the old man that, from then on, fresh drink and food would be left there at the end of every day until the new dolmen was finished. This had seemed to satisfy him.

On the day of the feast, tools were downed early and the workforce trooped down to Gor en masse. They were in good spirits, singing lustily and laughing heartily. All were looking forward to much engulfing of things edible and imbibing of liquids drinkable, preferably alcoholic.

Gastelois had already resigned himself to the fact that he was unlikely to get much out of them in the way of constructive work on the morrow due to the state they were bound to be in. Little did he know that the condition of a number of them would not be blameable entirely on the amount they had consumed, but rather on *what* they had consumed...

* * *

Grosnez and Piton reached the outcrop to the north of the dolmen site undetected, at least as far as they were aware. It was a beautifully clear, starry night with barely a whisper of a breeze to disturb the prevaling stillness. There was no moon to illuminate their nefarious activities, for which Grosnez was grateful – while a bright moon would have aided visibility as far as they were concerned, it could have done so for others they would have preferred not to have been seen by.

As they crept up to the pale mass of rock, they could see evidence of recent quarrying, and four large blocks, scheduled to be used as capstones, lay prone on the ground nearby. Piton spotted the jar and the bowl reposing at the base of the outcrop.

"There they are!" he squeaked excitedly. "Just as I said."

"Quiet, fool!" hissed his master. "Do you want to wake the whole of Gor?"

"No, Grosnez. Sorry, Grosnez," apologised Piton, although he could not see what the other was worrying about. On this particular night, with no lookouts at the dolmen and the feast well under way down at the settlement, there was no real chance of either of them being heard, no matter how loud they spoke. In the unlikely event that their voices did carry as far as Gor, they would be drowned out by the sounds of merrymaking currently rising up from there.

"Right," said Grosnez, nodding towards the two vessels by the rock, "eat that bread. As for the contents of that jar, you can either drink them or pour them away – I don't really care which you do."

"Why do you want me to eat the bread, Grosnez?"

His master made a clicking noise with his tongue to show his irritation. "As I explained to you earlier, fool, we are trying to give the impression that the Kerions have consumed the food and drink before taking the bétyle. Now get on with it!"

"Yes, Grosnez." Piton put down the antler pick and aurochs shoulder-blade shovel he was carrying and picked up the hunk of bread. He examined it for a moment and then bit into it. He promptly made a face that indicated that something was not to his liking.

"Problem?" asked Grosnez.

"It's stale!" complained Piton.

"Too bad!" said Grosnez unsympathetically. "Eat it!"

Piton chewed the mouthful of bread, masticating it laboriously for a few moments before attempting to wash it down with a swig of cider from the jar. He immediately spat it out, grimacing.

"What's wrong now?" asked Grosnez in a tone of some annoyance.

"There's things in it!" moaned Piton.

"Aw, what a pity!" said the other unsympathetically.

Like the bowl with its bread, the jar and its cider had, of course, been sitting out in the open, attracting each and every insect that flew close enough to pick up the scent. Some of these had landed in the drink and, unable to escape, had subsequently expired, to remain floating lifeless on its surface until Piton inadvertently ingested a number of them with a mouthful of the golden liquid.

Although there was nothing wrong with the cider *per se*, he decided to discard the rest of it rather than risk ingesting more deceased insects. Grosnez insisted that he eat all of the bread, however, and he reluctantly did so as they proceeded to slink cautiously across the field from the outcrop to the dolmen. With his left hand, he carried the bowl and the now empty jar.

As they neared the site, Grosnez kept his eyes peeled for any indication that the place was guarded, although Piton had assured him that, because of the feast, no one had remained behind when work had stopped for the day.

"Right, mon vier," said Grosnez when he was satisfied that they were indeed on their own, "the coast is clear. Come on!"

They entered the dolmen via the temporary passage that led through the unfinished mound to the gap in the south wall of the main chamber. Once inside, they stopped and looked around. It did not take long for Grosnez to spot the bétyle. It was standing near the chamber end of the passage, between two of the megaliths of the latter's northern wall, where it had been erected just before Mannequin de Perrelle's last visit.

"I'll start digging this thing up," said Grosnez, inclining his head towards the bétyle, "while you take this down to the feast." He produced a small, narrow necked, wooden-stoppered jar from within the folds of his cloak and held it up in front of Piton. "Pour it into the food or drink of – let's see – at least four or five of Gastelois' men."

"Will there be enough there?"

Grosnez nodded: "Oh yes, mon vier, more than enough. A few drops per person will more than suffice." He handed the jar to his servant.

Piton put down the bowl and jar he had been carrying on the floor of the dolmen's passage and took the vessel from Grosnez. "Supposing there's some left over?" he asked, running his thumb over the surface of the jar as he held it in his right hand.

The other thought about this for a few moments, stroking his chin pensively. Then his face twisted into a malevolent leer. "There'll be large pots of seafood stew. Tip the remainder into one of those – or two, if you think you've enough."

"Yes, Grosnez. As you wish, Grosnez."

"In fact, make sure that you do. At least that way some people other than Gastelois' lot might fall ill – it'll make it look less suspicious."

"That's true, that," agreed Piton.

"Right, give me the pick and shovel and be off with you."

Piton lowered his eyes. "I... I left them by the rock, Grosnez."

"Fool! Hurry up and get them, then. I haven't got all night."

While Piton dashed back to the outcrop to retrieve the tools in question, Grosnez contemplated the bétyle. Hopefully he would be able to extract it with the minimum of difficulty and it would be out by the time his servant returned from the feast.

* * *

The people of Gor had put on a fine spread for the dolmen builders, a large number of whom were, of course, their own. The feast was held on the col overlooking the settlement, next to the large gallery-dolmen that stood there.

Roasting pits had been dug, over which wild boar and deer hung, suspended from wooden spits, sizzling in the heat of the fires beneath them. Large earthenware cauldrons brimming with seafood stew stood over other fires, their contents carefully watched and stirred when deemed necessary. Flagons, skins and jars were arranged in rows on wooden tables, for people to help themselves from the nearby vats of ale and cider. These would be replenished when empty from *The Quernstone*, the landlord of that establishment having got in extra supplies for the occasion.

Gastelois' men attacked the fare as if they had not eaten for weeks, washing it down with copious quantities of the proferred brews. He himself behaved in a rather more restrained fashion, despite Pierre de Lecq's attempts to persuade him to let his hair down.

"Oh come on," Pierre said at one stage. "Loosen up and relax. Forget about the dolmen for tonight and just enjoy yourself."

"I'm getting pleasantly mellow," was Gastelois' response.

* * *

As he descended the wooded slope leading to the col overlooking Gor, Piton's heart beat faster the closer he got to his destination and the louder grew the sounds of the merrymaking below. When he reached the edge of the trees, he waited for a few moments before emerging from the safety of their cover. An owl suddenly hooted, startling him. A couple of bats, also taken by surprise, flew over his head and disappeared into the night.

Ahead of him, he could see that the feast was in full swing. He was relieved to note that it was very well attended – he would be able to lose himself among the throng and this would make his task that much easier.

Fingering Grosnez' jar under his goatskin tunic, he left the wood and walked towards the revelry, his heart thumping in his chest. No one noticed him approaching, nor did they pay him any attention as he made his way through the crowd. He glanced around for members of Gastelois' team. At first, he could not see any of them, then he perceived two he recognised. One of them was Raté Le Grossier, but he could not recall the name of his companion. They were standing next to a table of drinking vessels, jars in hand. From the way they were swaying on their feet, Piton correctly deduced that they were not on their first drink of the evening.

As he approached them, they each took a swig from their jars and then put them down on the table. Seeming to ignore the two men, he casually brushed against Le Grossier as he reached for a jar for himself from one of the many lined up on the tabletop. Then he filled it from the nearby vat of cider and gulped some down, all the while keeping an eye on Le Grossier and his companion.

Judging his moment, he reached inside his tunic with his right hand and pulled out Grosnez' jar. Then, quick as a flash, he deftly removed its wooden stopper and tipped some of the potion into the two dolmen workers' vessels.

Despite his alacrity, however, he only just managed it, for no sooner had he done the deed than his unsuspecting victims picked up their jars and downed a goodly portion of their contents.

Piton retreated from the scene, wondering how long it would be before the potion took effect – Grosnez had not been forthcoming on this point.

Flushed with the success of the first encounter of his mission, he looked around for his next hapless victim. After a few moments, he spotted Martin Le Blancq walking in the general direction of the gallery-dolmen that dominated the col. The term *walking* is used advisedly, as he was clearly experiencing navigational problems due to having already indulged in a few brews too many.

Piton followed him, planning his next move. Just as he was contemplating the best way to get the potion into Le Blancq, the answer presented itself, for that worthy staggered straight into one of the orthostats forming the dolmen's western wall and promptly crashed backwards on to the ground. Except by Piton, this feat appeared to go unnoticed, even by the small group of revellers standing in the vicinity.

As he went up to Le Blancq's motionless figure, Piton tipped a small, but sufficient quantity of potion into his own jar of cider and shook the vessel vigorously to thoroughly mix its contents. He then splashed some of the cider over Le Blancq's face and, as the latter stirred, slipped an arm under his back and helped him to sit up.

"Here," he said, holding the jar to Le Blancq's lips, "drink some of this. It'll make you feel better."

The recently senseless one regarded Piton with the bemused expression of someone not entirely sure of what was happening, where he was or indeed who he was, but drank some of the proferred liquid anyway as Piton tipped the jar towards his mouth. Eventually he had had enough, for he pushed the vessel away, rolled his eyes and capsized on to his right side. Piton left him lying there on the grass, snoring loudly.

He found victim number four sitting cross-legged and cross-eyed with his back resting against the huge granite megalith that constituted the rear wall of the dolmen. A jar of ale or cider – it was of no consequence which as far as Piton was concerned – stood on the ground in front of him, at an angle that suggested that it could tip over at any moment.

There was now no stopping Grosnez' servant. Without a moment's hesitation, he approached the diminutive figure reposing against the dolmen – Brie Le Petit was not known for his stature – and asked: "A refill, mon vier?"

A head raised itself with painful slowness. Glazed eyes contemplated him through a mist of alcoholic stupor. An animalistic grunt escaped from Le Petit's lips, followed by "Pleash."

Piton handed him the fresh jar he had already collected from one of the tables. Naturally, it contained some of the potion.

Le Petit took it from him with shaky hands, raised it unsteadily to his lips and gulped down some of its contents. Despite the fact that a goodly proportion of the ale cascaded down his chin and the front of his tunic, Piton felt confident that enough had gone down his gullet to ensure the efficacy of the potion.

Le Petit burped. "Th.. thank you," he said appreciatively.

"You're welcome," said Piton insincerely. He then bade him good night and walked away, smiling. Four down. This was going much better than he had dared hope. Should he leave it at that or seek out a fifth? Grosnez had said four or five. As far as he could judge by shaking the jar, there was a reasonable quantity of the potion still left inside it – certainly enough for another person with sufficient over to go into the seafood stew.

He made a decision. Yes, he would find a fifth member of Gastelois' unsuspecting workforce. Now, who was there?

He had not got very far from the dolmen when a sudden commotion, audible above the general feastly hubbub, reached his ears. He turned around to see three of the levitation priests

The DRAGON of ANGUR

struggling with a gangly specimen just outside the trilithon portal at the dolmen's south-eastern end. This was its main entrance, and what Piton saw taking place there clearly indicated that the lanky one was in the process of being evicted from the premises. Unbeknown to Piton, Mordu Le Tapin, hearing the sounds of revelry emanating from the edifice's hallowed interior and with inhibitions reduced in direct proportion to amount of alcohol consumed, had ventured inside to join in the fun.

Unfortunately for him, the building was currently the abode of Maîtres Le Digot and Le Doublier and the other levitation priests. After just one night crammed into the sleeping quarters at *The Quernstone*, which had been cramped enough with just the first two and Gastelois and his men in residence, the priests had decided to use Gor's spacious gallery-dolmen as their home for as long as was necessary, and had therefore appropriated it without as much as a by your leave or thank you.

What had enticed the inquisitive Le Tapin to venture inside was the noise of the priests' own private party, which they had decided to hold to the exclusion of the common people. Naturally, being one of the latter, his arrival on the scene was not welcome, which was why he now found himself being forcibly ejected from the dolmen. That he considered the priests' attitude to be unreasonable was evidenced by the struggle he was putting up.

The weight of superior numbers soon scored a victory for the priests, however, and Mordu was duly deposited in an undignified heap on the ground in front of the dolmen's entrance. Hurling abuse at the holy posteriors of his assailants as they headed back inside, he sat up and glared malevolently at anyone and everyone who happened to be within eyeshot.

This included Piton, who, seizing the opportunity presented, grabbed a jar from the nearest table, dunked it quickly in the cider vat standing alongside and walked casually over to the fuming Le Tapin, surreptitiously adding potion on the way.

"Here, have some of this," he said, offering the jar to Mordu, who was still sitting where he had been unceremoniously dumped.

"Did you see *that*?" croaked Le Tapin hoarsely, taking the drinking vessel from Piton. Then, before the latter had a chance to answer: "I just wanted to join in the fun." He took a large swig of potion-enhanced cider. "Miserable bastards!" he shouted at the dolmen. He drank some more and then turned around to hand the jar back to Piton, but Piton had melted into the crowd.

* * *

"Well?" demanded Grosnez as his servant walked up the passage towards him. He was looking extremely pleased with himself.

"It's done," confirmed Piton, nodding. "I managed to give five of his men a dose of the potion. I slipped it into their drinks. They were so pissed, them, that they didn't notice a thing."

"Any left over?"

"In the seafood stew, as you instructed."

"Excellent! Right, help me with this."

"You haven't got it out yet, you?" said Piton, stating the obvious since the bétyle was still in position.

"No I have not!" hissed his master irritably.

While Piton had been spiking drink and stew, Grosnez had been attempting to dig up the bétyle. It had been as well located as you would have expected from the standards of the builder in question, and, although not the largest of stones, was proving somewhat reluctant to part company with the patch of ground into which it had been set. Additionally, Grosnez' efforts were hampered by the fact that it was pretty tightly wedged between the orthostats on either side of it.

He had dug quite a deep hole in front of it, on the passage side. He would have liked to have dug one behind it as well, but to have done so would have entailed removing the stones of the mound abutting against it on that side, a rather time consuming task. He had tried pushing it from behind, but it had resolutely refused to budge.

He handed Piton the antler pick and aurochs shovel he was holding: "Get digging!" he commanded. "It needs to be much deeper."

Piton set to work.

"Right, let's see if it'll come free," said Grosnez after a little while. "You pull it and I'll push it."

With that, he clambered on to the mound from where he had been standing in the passage and knelt behind the stone, the top of which was barely protruding above the present upper surface of the mound. Then, while Piton, squatting in front of it, took hold of it with both hands and tried to pull it towards him, Grosnez pushed with all his strength. After a few moments, it gave slightly, displacing two or three small stones of the tumulus in the process.

"Ah!" exclaimed Grosnez. "We might be getting somewhere."

"I think you're right, you," agreed Piton.

They tried pulling and pushing the bétyle again, but to no avail. It evidently did not want to move any further.

"By the Teus!" swore Grosnez, glaring at the object of his exasperation.

"Shall I make the hole bigger?" offered Piton.

"Yes, yes. And be quick about it. I don't want to hang around here longer than is nec'ssary."

While his servant excavated, alternating between pick and shovel, Grosnez intermittently pushed at the bétyle from his position atop the tumulus, seeing whether it would shift.

Nothing much happened for a while and then, as Grosnez pushed at it for the nth time, the stone came free unexpectedly, taking both of them by surprise. Piton fell backwards with the suddenness of it, landing on his back with the uprooted bétyle on top of him. Freed of the buttressing effect of the stone and with Grosnez' weight on top it, the edge of the mound collapsed beneath him, toppling him forward. He landed spreadeagled on top of the stone in an undignified heap.

"Aieee!" wailed Piton, who now had his master to contend with as well as a reasonable mass of best Mont Mado granite. "You're crushing me!"

Grosnez got to his feet and stared at the bétyle, brushing himself down as he did so. At just under three feet in length, it was a little bigger than he had thought it would be, but he was sure that they would be able to remove it from the site.

Piton managed to extricate himself from under the stone and stood beside Grosnez, looking down at it while he massaged his bruised chest with his right hand.

"We'll move this thing clear and then backfill the hole," said Grosnez after a few moments' contemplation. "The Kerions are tidy beings – they wouldn't leave a mess. Once you've done that, we'll put the empty bowl and jar where the stone used to be."

"So Gastelois and his men will think that the Kerions have had a little feast before making off with the stone?"

"That's the general idea." He glared at the other. "Don't just stand there gaping at it – help me move it."

"Yes, Grosnez."

They dragged the bétyle away from where it was lying and Piton quickly filled in and tidied up the area of disturbance. Then Grosnez carefully placed the bowl and the jar in front of the stone's erstwhile location.

"Right, mon vier, that looks fine," he said, standing up and stepping back a couple of paces. "Now, let's get the bétyle out of here."

"Where are we taking it, Grosnez?" asked Piton.

"Back home."

The other's jaw dropped. "You mean we've got to carry it all the way *home*?"

"No, fool, not *carry* it. We'll drag it on a sled." Grosnez peered around him, his eyes probing the nocturnal gloom. "There's bound to be one here somewhere."

"I'm sure there is," said Piton, who recalled noticing a few such objects here and there on the site. He was relieved that they would not be attempting to carry the wretched bétyle to the other end of the island. In any case, he could not see how the two of them would have managed it. Although not exactly the easiest task in the world, lugging it on a sled was a far better idea. "I'll get one."

"Be quick about it then," said Grosnez as his servant hurried off down the dolmen's passage towards its entrance.

Piton duly returned, hauling a stout wooden sled behind him back along the passage, which was just wide enough to permit unhindered progress through it.

"Excellent!" said Grosnez as the other parked the sled alongside the bétyle. "Right, let's load up and get the Teus out of here!" No sooner had these words left his lips, however, than a pensive expression spread across his face, followed by a smile. "Wait a moment. I have an idea."

"What's that, Grosnez?"

"We won't take it home. We'll take it to *Levitation House* instead. La Cloche can look after it. He can put it with the others he has littering the place."

"Aw, but that's a good idea, that. If anyone looks there, it'll never be spotted amongst the other ones."

The DRAGON of ANGUR

"Exactly, mon vier." His countenance had assumed a look of smug self-satisfaction. "Exactly."

* * *

Vraicer T'loch waited until they were out of sight before coming out from behind the elm tree. He had been watching the proceedings with some amusement, very nearly bursting out laughing when the bétyle had come free and Piton had ended up underneath it with Grosnez on top. So, they were going to take it to *Levitation House*. La Cloche would certainly welcome *that*!

He walked over to the dolmen, heading for the break in the rim of the tumulus that signified the entrance of the temporary passage. When he reached this, he began to head slowly inwards along the corridor, carefully studying the borders of the mound along either side of it. These had been faced with small orthostats as temporary revetments to safeguard against the risk of collapse.

On the eastern side, near the junction with the gap in the south wall of the chamber, he noticed what appeared to be a recess. He reached inside his long, grey cloak and withdrew a small cylindrical vial that glowed with a yellowy-green light. He then bent down and peered in, using the light from the vial to illuminate the depths of the recess. It was quite large, certainly big enough to take an average-sized person lying down curled up. He was not sure what it was for, nor whether it was permanent or temporary, but it would suit his purpose admirably.

He crawled in as far as he could, removed a few stones, carefully placed the vial in the space thus created and then put the stones back. Smiling, he backed out of the cavity, stood up and wiped his hands on the folds of his cloak. Most satisfactory. Most satisfactory indeed.

Now, all he had to do was insinuate his desires into a certain person's mind, a mind as vacant as the empty chambers of an unused passage-dolmen.

CHAPTER NINETEEN

A DAY BEST FORGOTTEN

To describe Gastelois' mood as ill-humoured would be something of an understatement to say the least. His latest problems had first manifested themselves in the middle of the night, when the first member of his team to have taken Grosnez' potion started to demonstrate its effects with a quite spectacular eruption of the guts.

The unfortunate Raté Le Grossier was soon followed by the next to succumb, Drouet de Drédillet, his drinking companion of the evening. Then it was the turn of Brie Le Petit, and not long after him, Piton's fifth victim, Mordu Le Tapin.

With this quartet of retching wretches giving a gala performance in the sleeping area of the pub, not much time passed before the atmosphere there was not of the freshest. Their companions, however, being as full of drink as they were free of potion, slept through their moans and groans in a state of alcoholically-induced anaesthesia, blissfully unaware of their suffering.

Gastelois, however, having spent the evening exercising a commendable degree of restraint, was not sharing his workforce's state of terminal stupefaction and was quickly roused from his slumbers by the hapless Le Grossier's oral and anal explosions. He did what he could to help, waking up Pierre to assist him when he realised that Raté was not the only casualty of whatever malady this was.

Piton's third victim, Martin Le Blancq, did not make it back to *The Quernstone*, but spent the night crashed out next to the gallery-dolmen, every so often forced into a sort of semi-awake daze by the demands of his convulsing stomach. He had been found in the morning unsure whether he was alive or dead, but wishing that he were the latter, by Asceline Le Doublier when that worthy had emerged from the dolmen after sleeping off the excesses of the previous night's party. Shortly thereafter, two of his fellow priests had carried the ailing Le Blancq down to the pub where they were sure he would be well looked after.

The day had dawned in as bad a mood as Gastelois, with squalls of driving rain propelled by south-westerly gusts, and now, early in the afternoon, it was showing no sign of becoming better tempered. After the clement conditions of the previous few days, it was a somewhat sudden and dramatic change, but island weather patterns are like that and the locals were used to it. The fine weather could return just as quickly the following day.

Gastelois was at the dolmen site with Pierre and those of his team who had managed to make it there from *The Quernstone*. He had given everyone the morning off to recover from the previous night's excesses. Not that he had had much choice in the matter – the five sick ones would clearly be incapacitated for some time and none of the others would have been capable of moving very far, let alone working, had he insisted on an early start. Even now, of those who were on site, some would have been better off staying in the pub for all the use they were.

He wondered how his five indisposed workers were faring. He had left them in the care of Hacquoil Le Buvet's wife, the aptly named Jeanette Les Deux-Hougues[9], who had promised to look after them and do what she could to nurse them back to health. He had uttered profuse apologies for the inconvenience, but she had brushed these aside, insisting that, being the wife of the landlord of a busy pub, she frequently had to deal with worse.

Gastelois had known that he was up against it as regards finishing the dolmen on time before the mysterious illness had claimed Martin Le Blancq and the others. Now the situation was worse. How worse it would get would depend not just on how long it took them to recover but also on whether, in the interim, he would be able to replace them.

This was a question he agonised over with Pierre: "How *do* I replace them?"

His assistant shrugged his shoulders and favoured him with a blank look.

"I need skilled men. It's not going to be easy to find five at short notice."

"True," agreed Pierre. Then a thought struck him: "How about the Tourvel brothers?"

---
[9] Two Mounds.

Gastelois stroked his chin pensively. "Yes, they're a possibility. I'd forgotten about them." Then he frowned and shook his head.

"What's the problem?" asked Pierre.

"They're not union members. If you recall, that's why we couldn't employ them before."

"I know, but they could always make themselves scarce if La Cloche, Pipon or any of their cronies turned up."

Gastelois' face assumed a doubtful expression.

"Look, what have you got to lose?"

The other sighed: "Yes, I suppose you're right."

"That's settled then. I'll see if I can find them."

* * *

While Pierre was away attempting to locate the Tourvel trio, the construction of the new dolmen's mound continued in what could best be described as fits and starts. It was not just Gastelois' workforce that was under the weather, but the majority of the inhabitants of Gor as well. All were paying the price, to a greater or lesser degree, of their excesses of the previous evening. As a result, there were rather less helpers on hand than usual, and this combined with the inclement weather, was not helping progress.

Not only that, but the priests were notable by their absence, and therefore no levitation of megaliths was possible. While this might on the surface have seemed an inconvenience, as it meant that none of the capstones could be moved, it was in fact a good thing. Considering the amount of alcohol they had consumed the night before, not to mention interesting substances smoked, no one in their right mind would have let the levitation priests anywhere near a large rock.

It was not until some time after Pierre had left on his mission to find the Tourvel brothers that another problem manifested itself. Considering what it was, you would have thought that it would have reared its head earlier, but then again, taking into account the general state of the workforce, you might not have been so surprised that it remained unnoticed for as long as it did.

It was Rougetête de la Cloche who spotted it first. He was walking along the passage of the new dolmen, on his way to retrieve a stone maul he had left in the chamber the day before, when his eyes fell on the jar and the bowl.

The DRAGON of ANGUR

"What's this?" he muttered to himself as he bent down to examine them. "Gastelois!" he called, looking around for that worthy.

Gastelois broke off from the conversation he was holding with Pontrel Le Porc in the new dolmen's forecourt area. "Yes?" he called back.

"Come and look at this!"

"What is it?" asked Gastelois as he walked up the passage towards Rougetête.

"I'm not sure," replied the other. "Somebody's left these here." He picked up the two vessels and sniffed them. "This one's had cider in it." He handed the jar to Gastelois. "Don't know about the other."

"Yes, you're right," said Gastelois after likewise sniffing the jar. He took the bowl from Rougetête. "Might've been some food in this one – bread or something."

"But who would have left them? None of us lot, I'm sure."

"True." Gastelois stroked his chin pensively as he continued to examine the two vessels. "Wait a moment!" he then said as realisation dawned. "Aren't these the ones we left by the outcrop, to keep that old man happy?"

"Aw, but you could be right, you," said Rougetête as Gastelois handed them back to him. "But what're they doing here?"

"Search me!" said the other, staring at the ground where the bowl and the jar had been found. Then he went pale as he noticed something that up to that point had escaped his attention. "By the Teus!" he exclaimed.

"What's the matter?" asked Rougetête.

"The bétyle! It's gone!"

"What?"

"The bétyle I got from Mont Mado – it's not there!" Gastelois waved his right hand at a gap in the north wall of the passage.

Rougetête followed his boss's wavering arm. "By Ker! You're right, you."

"It's the Kerions. They've taken it," announced a voice from behind them.

They both turned around. Pontrel Le Porc was standing there, having followed Gastelois to see what was going on.

"The Kerions?" queried Gastelois, brows furrowed as he regarded him.

"Yes," said Le Porc nodding. "That would explain the empty jar and bowl. They obviously took the stone and helped themselves to the food and drink into the bargain."

"They must've got out from under that rock," said Rougetête, nodding in the direction of the rhyolite outcrop to the north of the dolmen. "They would've seen the bread and cider we left for them, and prob'bly scoffed that first before coming here to remove the bétyle."

"Exactly!" agreed Pontrel with the satisfied air of one certain that the right explanation had been found. "They delib'rately left the empty jar and bowl here so that we'd know they were r'spons'ble."

"And look how they've left the bit where the stone was – all neat and tidy. That's the Kerion way."

"Exactly!" agreed Pontrel again, nodding.

"But why would they take it in the first place?" asked Gastelois, who had been listening to the other two with a slight grin on his face despite growing feelings of concern and annoyance at the bétyle's disappearance.

Pontrel shrugged his shoulders. "Who knows?" he said.

"What the Kerions want, the Kerions get," remarked Rougetête matter-of-factly.

"Exactly!" agreed Pontrel for the third time.

Gastelois shook his head slowly. "No, I don't think that this has anything to do with the Kerions. I have a feeling that this was done by someone who wanted us to *believe* that they were responsible."

"But who would want to do that, Gastelois?" asked Pontrel, looking doubtful.

"I don't know," muttered Gastelois. "But I intend to find out."

* * *

As the day wore on, Gastelois was interested to learn that it was not only his own men who had been taken ill in the night, but that some of the villagers themselves had also been struck down. No one was sure of the cause, but the blame was being laid at the door of those responsible for the preparation of the seafood stew. This was hotly denied by those accused who, while admitting that the symptoms of the stricken were broadly similar to those exhibited in the past by others who had consumed seafood that was not,

The DRAGON of ANGUR

shall we say, of the freshest, vigorously maintained that there had been nothing wrong with the ingredients that they themselves had used.

Gastelois did not, however, dwell on the matter of the mysterious affliction. Although he was of course concerned about the well-being of his sick workers, he was certain that if nature were allowed to take its course, helped along by the ministrations of Jeanette Les Deux-Hougues, they would soon be on the mend.

Uppermost in his mind at the moment was the disappearance of the bétyle. He had organised a search party to look for it soon after its absence had been discovered, but, despite scouring the neighbourhood for some considerable time, the dozen members of said party eventually returned to report that no sign of it could be found anywhere.

It was not long after the last man came back from the search that Philipot du Moncel suggested that perhaps the stone had been taken further afield than had originally been thought.

"If a sled was used, then it could have been taken anywhere," he added.

It then occurred to someone to check to see whether any of the sleds on the site were missing. As there had been no transportation of megaliths that day, no one working on the dolmen had bothered about the vehicles in question.

A quick check confirmed their fears. Whereas there had been six sleds when they had left for the party the previous evening, there were now five.

"Some bugger's pinched one!" declared Ernaud Le Grand, voicing what everyone else was thinking.

"It certainly looks that way," agreed Gastelois.

At that point, Pierre de Lecq arrived back at the site. So involved were the others in discussing the matter of the disappearing bétyle and now the missing sled as well, that they did not see him turn up let alone notice that although he was looking tired, he also appeared to be somewhat pleased with himself.

"What's going on?" he asked, sensing at once that something was amiss.

"Ah, Pierre!" said Gastelois, turning to meet him. "You're back. Any luck?"

Sinclair Forrest

"Yes," replied Pierre, staring past the other at the gathering behind. "I found the Tourvels. They can start in a couple of days or so – they've got something to finish first. What's going on?"

"We've got a problem. Someone's stolen the Mont Mado bétyle."

"*What?*" Pierre looked at Gastelois in disbelief.

The latter nodded slowly. "I'm afraid so. During the course of last night."

"But how?"

"Well, whoever it was, probably just dug it up and then took it off on one of our sleds – there's one missing. I'd say there were at least two of them involved - no one could have done it on his own."

"Let me have a look," said Pierre.

They went up the passage to the area in question. The jar and bowl were lying where Rougetête de la Cloche had left them on top of the mound behind the spot where the missing stone had once stood.

"We found these on the floor just here," said Gastelois, rubbing the area in question with his right foot.

"They're the ones we left at the outcrop," observed Pierre astutely.

"Precisely. Our friends obviously intended us to think that the Kerions were responsible. They also left the area neat and tidy – just as the little people are supposed to do."

Pierre laughed: "Do they think we're that stupid?"

"It fooled some people," said Gastelois, glancing over at Pontrel Le Porc and Rougetête de la Cloche.

Pierre stroked his chin slowly. "But who would want to take the bétyle and why that one as opposed to any other stone?"

"Don't know. But I've been doing some thinking and I'm sure that whoever it was must have known that we were all going to the feast and that the place would be unguarded."

"Yes, that was obviously a mistake – leaving no one here to keep an eye on it."

Gastelois sighed: "Yes, no good crying about it now, though."

"So, what are we going to do?" asked Pierre.

"Well, I suggest we talk about this further in *The Quernstone*. It's getting late and we're not going to achieve much more here today."

"Good idea. But we should reinstate a couple of guards – we don't want to risk anything else happening."

"True." Gastelois frowned. "We now have another problem."

"Oh?"

"We're going to have to get another piece of Mont Mado granite."

"Yes, of course."

"Teus knows how long that's going to take."

"Maybe, under the circumstances, Planning will waive the requirement for a Mont Mado stone," suggested Pierre.

"I'd have thought that was highly unlikely," retorted Gastelois.

"Just an idea."

"Sorry, I didn't mean to snap." Gastelois apologised. He sighed: "Well, we'll see what happens when they next turn up, which could be at any time. We know friend Mannequin was unhappy with the bétyle and went off to discuss it with de Bitte. I fully expect a deputation to descend upon us imminently."

"Yes, that will be something to really look forward to, I'm sure," remarked Pierre sarcastically.

"Right, let's sort out the guards and close down for today." Gastelois glanced up at the overcast sky. It was a while since it had last rained and he felt hopeful that the weather was improving. "Maybe some food and drink will help us work out who took the bétyle."

"Even if it doesn't," said Pierre, "it will still be most welcome."

CHAPTER TWENTY

THE VIAL

The next day dawned bright and sunny, as Gastelois had hoped, with everything more or less back to normal. Grosnez' victims, however, remained off sick, still recovering from the effects of his dreaded concoction.

The construction of the mound continued during the morning, as did the quarrying of the capstones at the outcrop to the north of the site. All the levitation priests were present, having got over the effects of their party, and were standing by ready to assist with the transportation of said coverstones to the new dolmen.

The positioning of these was always a particularly fraught part of the construction process and probably the most dangerous. Members of the public who came to watch were always kept well clear, particularly children and total liabilities like Escogriffe Le Manquais.

A capstone would be placed over the relevant orthostats using a combination of levitation and men manoeuvring it with ropes. A framework of carefully trimmed logs, wedged between the uprights on either side of the passage or chamber directly below where the capstone was to sit, would guard against the risk of these either being forced inwards if inadequately located, or displaced by any unexpected, violent contact with the capstone. It would also hopefully hold the latter if for any reason it tried to fall between opposing uprights.

Another way of guarding against these hazards was to completely fill the passage and chamber of a new dolmen with earth, which would be dug out once all the capstones had been safely positioned. With the advent of the wooden bracing frame, however, this method was now hardly ever employed, as not only was it much more labour intensive, but it also left the interior of the dolmen in a rather mucky state necessitating a thorough clean-up operation before it could be deemed fit for use.

As the Sun rose inexorably in the sky above the toiling workers, some building up the mound, some taking part in the quarrying operations, others cutting and trimming logs to brace the dolmen's walls, the usual crowd of onlookers gathered to watch the proceedings. Present amongst them as ever was Escogriffe Le Manquais, as enthusiastic in his support of the workers and their project as he was slow of wit.

He spent the morning either exhorting Gastelois' workers to greater efforts, which they tolerated with commendable patience, or explaining, with much dribbling from the mouth, the finer points of dolmen building to his fellow spectators. Most people ignored him and therefore did not notice that, towards the end of the morning, he was nowhere to be seen.

By midday, another large block destined to be a capstone had been freed from the rhyolite outcrop and the first of those already quarried moved to the site and positioned atop the three uprights forming the walls of the southern side chamber, its journey there having been completed with an amazing lack of drama. No wooden frame had been used to buttress the walls of this chamber, nor would one be employed in its northern counterpart, Gastelois having taken the view that the arrangement of the side chambers' orthostats meant that these would brace each other more than adequately. With the southern one now completed, he was confident that the afternoon would see the successful roofing of the other side chamber.

At this point, he called a halt to the proceedings and everyone, including the onlookers, but excluding Escogriffe, trooped off to Gor for refreshments, only a couple of the workers remaining on site to guard it.

* * *

Sylvia d'Arass was sitting at a table in *The Quernstone* waiting for Gastelois. In front of her were three jars of cider, two of which had been poured ready for him and Pierre.

"Ah, Sylvie!" Gastelois greeted her, beaming. "That's very decent of you." He nodded towards the drinks.

"I thought you'd probably both be in need of at least one," said Sylvia. "Busy morning?" she added as the two men sat down at the table, Gastelois alongside her and Pierre opposite.

"Yes," replied the latter, picking up one of the cider jars. "We got quite a lot done. The first of the capstones is in position – on one of the side chambers."

"And we should have the other side chamber roofed later this afternoon," added Gastelois. "Seafood stew, anyone?"

"Excellent idea!" said Pierre, and Sylvia nodded her wish to be included.

Gastelois stood up. "While I'm about it, I'll ask Jeanette how our ailing companions are faring."

While he was away obtaining the food and enquiring after the health of his sick workers, Sylvia resurrected the question of the missing bétyle, which the three of them had been discussing in the pub the previous evening.

"I've been thinking about it," she began, after taking a sip of cider. "Do you think its disappearance has anything to do with those backfilled holes you found that morning not long after you started work on the dolmen?"

Pierre looked at her intently as if she had just suggested a solution to an age-old problem. "D'you know, I hadn't thought of that!"

"It's just an idea. *Someone's* obviously been taking an interest in the site."

Pierre regarded her over the rim of his jar. "You have a point, you," he said as he put the vessel down on the table. "The question is, who?"

"And why?" added Sylvia. She brushed her long, black hair away from her forehead with her right hand. "There's got to be some motive behind all of this."

"That's true," agreed Pierre. "It's pretty obvious that whoever dug those holes was looking for something – what, is another matter – but why take a piece of Mont Mado granite?"

"Perhaps because it *was* Mont Mado granite."

"Yes, but why take it from our site?" said Pierre. "Why not just get a piece from the quarry?"

Sylvia shrugged her slender shoulders. "Who knows?" She took a sip of cider. "Who knows?"

* * *

When they returned from *The Quernstone* suitably satiated, Gastelois' men found that, while they had been away, the new dolmen had been honoured by a couple of visitors. These two were standing next to each other in the main chamber near the junction with the passage. Both were tall, skinny individuals, so similar in their terminal thinness that you would have been hard pressed to decide which was the more emaciated. The one with the straggly brown hair falling over his shoulders, who was gesticulating towards the north side of the passage with a particularly knobbly walking stick, was evidently a good few years older than his companion, who could be also be distinguished from him by the mop of straggly black hair that adorned his head.

"But it's not there now!" the first was saying as the dolmen workers returned to the site.

Gastelois' heart had sunk as soon as he had seen them. This was the expected deputation from the *Pouquelaye and Earthworks Committee*, and it had materialised in the shape of that committee's president, Branleur de Bitte, and one of its support staff in the guise of Mannequin de Perrelle. He of course knew why they had turned up. They were obviously discussing the Mont Mado granite stone and it was equally obvious that they now knew that it was missing.

Taking the aurochs by the horns, he walked up to the two gentlemen from Planning and confronted them.

"Good afternoon!" he greeted them. "What can I do for you?"

"We've, er, come to inspect the piece of Mont Mado granite that you are, er, required to have in your dolmen," said Branleur pompously, "but we see that it is not to be found. Mannequin tells me that it was here, but it's obvious that it has now gone. Why is that?"

"Somebody's taken it," said Gastelois nonchalantly, as if such a thing were an everyday occurrence.

"What d'you mean somebody's taken it?" demanded Mannequin de Perrelle.

"Precisely what I say," replied Gastelois. "It was there two days ago, but when we arrived on site yesterday, it had gone. Some blame the Kerions, but…"

"Don't be r'dic'lous!" De Perrelle interrupted him. "You knew that we weren't going to approve that pathetic little stone you had installed, so you r'moved it to save yourself embarrassment." He sniffed noisily. "I take it you have a replacement ready – one that will meet with our approval?"

"I do not!" retorted Gastelois. "The stone has been stolen. And," he went on, his eyes narrowing, "there was nothing wrong with the one I did have. There's nothing in your regulations to say what size the piece of Mont Mado granite has to be."

"Er, that is where you are wrong, Gastelois," said Branleur de Bitte, waving his stick at him. "When Mannequin came to tell me about your stone and ask my advice, I told him that, in the view of the current committee, size *is* important. A Mont Mado orthostat is an important feature of any dolmen and therefore a large erection is better than a small one as clearly it will stick up more." More shaking of the stick. "Although I was sure of what I would find, Mannequin's description having been more than adequate, I decided to come here to see it for myself." He paused for a moment before continuing: "I have to say that I am most disappointed to see that you have *no* Mont Mado stone of *any* size to show me. Yes, most disappointed."

"How many times do I have to tell you," said Gastelois, making no attempt to hide the intense irritation he was feeling, "the stone has been stolen."

"By the Kerions, I suppose," said Mannequin de Perrelle sarcastically.

"Not at all!" said Gastelois hotly.

"By who then?"

"I have no idea."

"No matter," said Branleur after a few moments' reflection during which time Gastelois and Mannequin exchanged glares of particular vehemence. "If the stone has gone, the stone has gone." He sighed. "You'll just have to get another one and that's all there is to it."

"I haven't got time for that," said Gastelois. "We're already behind schedule as it is."

"That's not our problem," said Branleur. "It is imperative that this dolmen has at least one large stone of Mont Mado granite. And, as it's for a special occasion, count yourself lucky that we're not insisting on *two* stones."

"Well," said Gastelois, "when the Jubilee celebrations are taking place, *you* can explain to Cou-Cou La Tanche and to the winner of the dragon contest why the prize dolmen isn't finished."

"As I said, that's not our problem." Branleur glanced at de Perrelle, who was smiling smugly next to him. "Is it, Mannequin?"

"Indeed it is not. Our job is to ensure that all dolmens are built according to strict planning guidelines. If that means they can't be completed on time, or even have to be rebuilt, so be it."

"What d'you mean, rebuilt?" queried Gastelois, suddenly worried that they were going to come up with something else to cause him grief.

"Simply that were you to use an unsuitable piece from Mont Mado, you'd have to replace it with something we deemed acceptable," said de Perrelle.

"That clearly means large," said Gastelois through gritted teeth.

The two planning men nodded in unison.

"I still don't see why."

"As I told you," said Branleur, shaking his walking stick at him, "large erections are to be preferred to small ones. The committee has decided that."

"Well, I was never told," retorted Gastelois.

"That is not our concern. It is up to those in the building trade to familiarise themselves with all planning requirements. Ignorance is no excuse."

Gastelois looked at both of them despairingly. Clearly, arguing the point was going to be a pointless exercise. He exhaled a long, loud sigh: "Well, I'll see what I can do."

"Excellent!" said Branleur. "Let us know when you have a new stone and we'll come back to inspect it." He favoured the dolmen builder with a facetious look. "And this time, try to hang on to it. Come, Mannequin!"

With that, the two visitors left the site, Gastelois glaring daggers at their backs.

* * *

By the end of the afternoon, the northern side chamber had received its coverstone in an operation that had proceeded without a hitch. With the two side chambers now complete, the workers could get on with roofing the rest of the monument, starting at its western end with the inner part of the main chamber – once, that is, the relevant capstone was on site. This, a particularly large specimen, was still being quarried and unlikely to be ready for at least another day.

By the time Gastelois and his team were ready to leave the dolmen for the day, the buttressing of the orthostats at its western end had been completed. He inspected his men's handiwork with Pierre.

"These should do fine," he said as he pushed against one of the horizontal bracing logs with both hands and then against another and neither showed any inclination to move. "Right, let's call it a day."

"Excellent idea!" said Pierre, who was feeling somewhat thirsty after the afternoon's work.

Just as they were all preparing to set off for *The Quernstone*, the workmen became aware of a strange noise. It was Philipot du Moncel who heard it first, a sort of pitiful whining that seemed to be coming from within the mound on the dolmen's southern side.

"It's coming from over there!" he cried, pointing in the direction of the sound.

They all trooped over to the area in question – a recently constructed part of the mound near the gap in the south wall of the main chamber.

"Shh!" said Gastelois, putting a finger to his lips.

They all listened intently.

The sound came again, and this time they thought they could make out a word; muffled, yes, but a word nonetheless: "Help!"

They all looked at each other.

"Help!"

"By Ker!" exclaimed Pontrel Le Porc. "Some bugger's in the mound!"

"Help!"

Sure enough, the voice was coming from within the mound, seemingly from a spot just outside the gap and on the left-hand side of the the escape trench, the temporary passage leading away from the main chamber.

"Come on!" said Gastelois. "We'd better get whoever it is out."

"How could there be someone in the mound?" asked Pierre de Lecq.

"Search me," said Gastelois, shrugging his shoulders.

"Let's move this stone first," suggested Fortin La Berfote, going up to one of the smallish uprights that had been placed as a

The DRAGON of ANGUR

temporary revetment against the mound bordering the eastern side of the escape trench.

Ernaud Le Grand and Bertholet La Grosse-Barbe went to help him. Being three particularly stout fellows, they pushed the stone over without too much difficulty. It fell forward to reveal a small recess with a figure hunched up inside. A pale face peered out, eyes blinking in the sunlight.

"Well I never!" exclaimed Bertholet, bending down to help the prisoner out.

"Escogriffe!" said Gastelois as Le Manquais was half lifted, half dragged out of the mound. "How the Teus did you get in there?" Then, seeing the vacant expression on the other's grimy face: "Oh never mind!"

"What's that you've got?" asked Pierre de Lecq, noticing that Escogriffe was clutching something to his chest, something that appeared to be glowing.

"Can I have a look at that?" asked Gastelois. "Come on, it's all right," he added, seeing Escogriffe's reluctance. He stretched out his right hand. "Come on," he said again, gently.

The afflicted one slowly handed over what he had been holding. "Pretty," he said.

"What is it?" asked Pierre.

"Don't know," said Gastelois as the others crowded around him for a better look. "It seems to be some form of container, but nothing like I've ever seen before. You can see what's in it." He held it up to the light. "Some yellowy-green liquid."

"Pretty!" declared Escogriffe again.

At that point there came the sound of something falling through the branches of a tree, followed by a loud thump.

They all turned and looked in the direction of the noise. A small, goblinesque figure had picked itself up off the ground and was in the process of trying to conceal itself behind the tree in which it had been hiding.

"Piton Le Malin!" cried Rougetête de la Cloche. "What's *that* been up to?"

"Let's get 'im and find out," said Ernaud Le Grand. "Piton!" he yelled. "Come 'ere, you! We want a word with you."

Sinclair Forrest

Escogriffe was clutching something to his chest

Whilst Gastelois and the others watched, Le Grand and La Grosse-Barbe set off in pursuit of the now fleeing Le Malin. As these two were not the most sylphlike of individuals, Piton would have escaped from them easily had he not tripped over a large stone and fallen flat on his face.

Bertholet reached him just as he was about to run off again and knocked him to the ground with what one day would become known as a rugby tackle. Ernaud arrived a moment or two later, as Bertholet was hauling Grosnez' unfortunate servant to his feet, and together they frogmarched him back to the dolmen site.

"Piton Le Malin! Well, well, well!" said Gastelois looking down at Piton as he stood before him, wriggling and squirming, but held by the vice-like grip of Le Grand and La Grosse-Barbe. Even if he had managed to free himself from them, he would not have got very far as the others had formed a tight circle around him, hemming him in.

"Well, what have you got to say for yourself?" demanded Gastelois.

"I... I was..." stammered Piton, trying to look past Gastelois to where Escogriffe was sitting cross-legged on the ground fingering the vial of liquid.

"Why were you in that tree?" asked Pierre.

"I... I... I was, er watching..." said Piton, still craning his neck first one way and then the other as he tried to get a better view of Escogriffe.

"Watching what?" asked Gastelois.

"Just your, er, work."

"From up a tree?"

"Er... yes." Piton thought quickly. "I'm a small person," he whined. "I wanted to have a better view."

That seemed a reasonable enough explanation, although Gastelois was far from satisfied. If it had come from any other small person, he would have been happy enough, but this was Piton le Malin standing in front of him, Grosnez Chatel's servant. There was bound to be a hidden agenda. For a moment, he wondered whether he might have known something about the missing bétyle, but he did not pursue it. He knew that he would not find out much from Piton about that – or indeed any other devious scheme the latter and his master might be involved in - at least not without a great deal of time and effort, and time was something he did not have a lot of. He therefore decided just to send him on his way with a warning:

"If you want to watch, stand somewhere we can see you. If I catch you skulking around, I'll personally throw you off the site – permanently. Do you understand?"

"Yes, Gastelois. Perfectly, Gastelois," said Piton, nodding quickly and looking suitably contrite.

"Good. Be off with you then!"

As Piton scurried away, occasionally glancing back at Gastelois and his men to see whether he was being followed, Sylvia d'Arass stepped forward. She had accompanied Gastelois back to the site when they had left *The Quernstone* after lunch, and had spent the afternoon studying the interior faces of the dolmen's uprights with a view to deciding which ones would be most suitable for decoration.

"I'd have asked him if he knew anything about your missing stone," she said quietly to Gastelois, one eye on Le Malin's diminishing figure.

He looked at her. "That thought occurred to you too, then?"

She nodded. "Yes. Why didn't you say anything?"

"No point. He'd have denied it and, even if it was him or Grosnez, I don't see how we could prove it – short of finding the bétyle in their possession."

"True," agreed Sylvia.

"Hopefully we'll find out who's responsible sooner or later," said Gastelois. "But in the meantime it's more important that I get a replacement stone. I'll go to Mont Mado in the morning."

"Yes, I suppose that's the best thing to do in the circumstances," said Sylvia. She sighed: "It's just that," she hesitated for a moment, "I have this feeling..."

* * *

"I've got it, Grosnez, I've got it!" shouted Piton as he burst into the main chamber of his master's home, beside himself with excitement.

"What have you got?" Grosnez sneered at his servant without looking up from the table at which he was sitting.

"The container, Grosnez, the container!" Piton was now standing right in front of his master, smiling from earhole to earhole, hopping from one foot to the other unable to keep still.

"What?" Grosnez' manner changed completely.

"I have it, Grosnez, I have it!" Piton was feeling extremely pleased with himself.

"Well, give it to me, then!" demanded the other impatiently.

Piton reached inside his tunic and then carefully passed the vial to his master, who snatched it out of his hands.

"How... How did you get it, mon vier?" asked Grosnez incredulously as he turned the vial over in his hands.

"It wasn't easy," said Piton. He proceeded to tell his master how the container had come into his possession, embellishing this detail and exaggerating that detail. He related how Escogriffe Le Manquais had been retrieved from the mound with the vial, which he had apparently found while stuck in there. He left out the bit about falling out of the tree, saying that he had waited until Escogriffe had left with the vial, which Gastelois for some unfathomable reason had allowed him to keep, before following him. He had caught up with Escogriffe and had managed to wrest the vial from his possession.

"Excellent!" said Grosnez. He stared hard at his servant. "And no one saw you?"

"Er, n.. no, Grosnez, n.. no one," stammered Piton, avoiding his master's gaze.

"Don't lie to me!"

"W.. Well, actu'lly... Gastelois did. And some of his men." He eyed Grosnez fearfully.

"What!" exploded the other. "You fool!" He advanced menacingly on his servant.

"B.. But no one saw me get it from that fool Escogriffe," said Piton, backing away. "They sent me packing before he left the dolmen. I just hid and kept an eye on things. Then I followed Escogriffe."

"Well, I hope for your sake, mon vier, that you're right." He massaged his chin. "Escogriffe knows that you've got it, but we can prob'bly handle that."

"So, what do we do now, Grosnez?" asked Piton, relieved that his master appeared to have calmed down.

"We put this somewhere safe and then we bide our time."

"Bide our time?"

"Yes, mon vier. Until the dragon contest."

CHAPTER TWENTY-ONE

A BREACH OF RULES

When Gastelois and his team arrived on site the following morning, they found Escogriffe Le Manquais sitting cross-legged in the main chamber, rocking backwards and forwards on his heels and sobbing quietly. How long he had been like this, they could only guess.

"What's the matter, mon vier?" asked Pierre de Lecq, going up to him and putting a hand gently on his shoulder.

Escogriffe looked up at him; tear streaks had formed river channels in the dusty grime on his face. "It's gone!" he sniffed noisily.

"What has?"

"My light, my pretty light!"

"You mean that thing you found yesterday?" asked Gastelois.

"Yes. *He* pinched it!"

"What? Who?" asked Pierre.

"That Le Malin!" replied Escogriffe, sobbing loudly.

Gastelois and Pierre looked at each other.

"He attacked me," continued the distraught Le Manquais, "on my way home."

"What d'you mean he attacked you?" asked Gastelois, frowning.

"He set upon me from behind," said Escogriffe, and sniffed snottily as he wiped his nose with the back of a grimy hand. "He grabbed my light and ran off with it before I could stop him."

Gastelois stroked his chin pensively as he contemplated the pathetic figure still rocking backwards and forwards on the ground in front of him to the accompaniment of much sobbing and sniffing. "Don't fret," he said softly. "We'll get it back." He looked at his assistant: "Won't we, Pierre."

"That we will," said Pierre de Lecq confidently and closed a reassuring hand on Escogriffe's right shoulder, shaking it gently but firmly.

"In the meantime," said Gastelois, "why don't I get one of my men to take you down to *The Quernstone* for a few nice drinks? You'd like that, wouldn't you?"

Escogriffe nodded.

"Good." Gastelois scanned the faces of his workmen, who had been standing nearby observing the proceedings with the occasional muttered comment and knowing nod. "Anyone want to do the honours?" He hoped that he would not have to volunteer one of his men for the task, but any reluctance on their part he could quite understand – the afflicted one was hardly the most stimulating of drinking companions.

"I will," said Haysie Fiott, stepping forward. To him, no time in a pub was ever a hardship, no matter with whom it was spent.

"Good man," said Gastelois and handed him some limpet shells from the pouch slung from the belt around his waist to pay for the drinks. "Stay with him for as long as you think necessary."

Fiott nodded and then went over to help Escogriffe to his feet.

"Now we know what that peeping so-and-so Le Malin was after," said Gastelois grimly as the still distraught Le Manquais was gently led away to drown his sorrows in *The Quernstone* and the workforce minus Haysie drifted off to get ready for the day's tasks.

"Yes," said Pierre. "And maybe that explains those holes we found, too."

Gastelois nodded slowly, stroking his chin pensively. "Indeed. I think it's safe to assume that Grosnez and Piton were responsible for those. They've obviously been after that vial for some reason – goodness knows why – and must've found out that it was buried on this site."

"Seems odd that we never found it ourselves, considering all the digging we had to do for socket holes."

"Just one of those things, I suppose."

"Perhaps they took the bétyle as well," suggested Pierre. "Maybe they thought it was buried underneath."

Gastelois shook his head. "No, I don't think so," he said. "Even if it had been under there, why take the stone? Why not just take the vial and put the stone back? That way they would've covered their tracks."

"You have a point there, you," agreed Pierre. "In that case, maybe somebody else took the bétyle?"

Gastelois shrugged his shoulders. "Who knows?" he sighed. "But I wouldn't put it past those two. I'd say they were capable of anything."

The two men fell silent for a few moments, a silence then broken by Pierre asking: "I wonder what's so special about that vial?"

"More the liquid in it," responded Gastelois. "You noticed the way it glowed?"

"Mmm," said Pierre, nodding. "I wonder where it came from?"

"That's a very good question." Gastelois paused. "I think we should seek the opinion of an expert, someone who knows about these things."

"Who do you have in mind?"

Gastelois looked at his assistant. "Vraicer T'loch."

"T'loch?"

"Yes. There's more to this than meets the eye. If anyone can throw any light on it, he can."

* * *

Gastelois had intended to go to Mont Mado that morning to see about a replacement for the stolen bétyle, but what with one thing and another, he did not make it. Halfway through the morning, he had an unexpected visitor, or rather visitors, for it was not just one but four individuals who turned up at the site.

The small, balding man with the porcine optics, who led the new arrivals, he knew only too well.

"Ah, Clychard La Cloche! What brings you here on this fine morning?"

The union chief smiled condescendingly. "Good morning, Gastelois. I heard you've been having a spot of bother, so I've come to offer you some assistance."

"Oh?" Gastelois regarded La Cloche suspiciously.

"Yes. I understand that some of your workers have fallen ill."

"How d'you know that?" demanded the other.

The DRAGON of ANGUR

La Cloche scratched his head and then examined his fingernails. "Oh, I have my sources," he replied, avoiding Gastelois' gaze. "Especially where labour matters are concerned."

Gastelois favoured him with an even more suspicious look, but did not comment. "So," he asked, "who are these three?"

La Cloche introduced them. First of all, there was Armand Le Bricateur, a dark-haired individual of nutmeg complexion whose surliness was in direct proportion to his burliness, neither of which was insignificant. Because appearances can be deceptive, the union chief was at pains to point out that he was a good, reliable worker.

The next to be introduced was a thinner, paler specimen called Pelletier de Merde, whose name was singularly appropriate as he was prepared to shovel anything.

One Pierre Le Bécheur completed the group. A seemingly quiet, unassuming person, who from his appearance and general demeanour you would have thought would have been incapable of saying "Boo!" to a goose, he was in reality made of far sterner stuff than his peacefully bland countenance would suggest.

"They are yours if you can make use of them," said La Cloche. "And they can start immediately."

Gastelois looked the three of them up and down, and decided that they would do. All things considered, though, he had very little choice – he was hardly in a position to refuse the proferred assistance.

"Right," he said, "I'll get Philipot to find something for you to do." He called du Moncel over and introduced him to the three newcomers. They duly went off with him and it was not long before that worthy ascertained that none of them had ever worked on a dolmen before. Hopefully they were quick learners, but if not, there was bound to be something they could do.

* * *

By the end of that day, the first of the main chamber capstones was ready to be transported to the site. Weighing some twenty-five tons, this beast would have to be moved and positioned with the greatest of care. It was not, however, the largest that would be used in the new dolmen. That honour would go to the one that would span the outer part of the main chamber, where it would extend over the two side cells, resting on their capstones as well as on three nearby uprights of suitably substantial proportions.

This would be the last of three stones to roof the chamber area, the middle one being rather smaller than those on either side of it, but a sizeable chunk of rhyolite nonetheless.

Gastelois knew from experience that it would take a full day to move and position just one of these capstones. It was not the actual moving of each stone from quarry site to dolmen that consumed the time, but the period of preparation the levitation priests insisted was necessary before they attempted to shift such a large block.

To make matters worse, there had been occasions in the past when, after spending the best part of a day supposedly preparing themselves, the priests had announced that they were not ready. In each case, their lack of readiness had undoubtedly been caused by overindulgence in the mind-altering substances that were supposedly an essential part of the preparations.

Knowing their propensity for overdoing it, Gastelois was dreading what the following day would bring.

"I hope they behave themselves," he remarked to Pierre and Sylvia as the three of them sat in *The Quernstone* that evening, the ubiquitous jars of cider on the table in front of them.

"So do I," said Pierre. "We're short of time as it is, without them causing any further delays."

"I'm sure they'll be fine," said Sylvia, ever the optimist. "Mind you, from my point of view the longer the thing is without its capstones, the better – I'll have more light to paint by."

"You should be about done by now, though, shouldn't you?" said Pierre.

"More or less." She sipped some cider, moistened her lips with the tip of her tongue. "Just a couple of stones to finish and some touching up to do here and there."

"Whatever," said Gastelois. "But I don't want you anywhere near the chamber or the passage when we start to move their capstones."

"Don't worry, I know when I'm not wanted."

"I didn't..." began Gastelois, but broke off as her smile told him that she was just teasing.

She took a drink of cider, put the jar back down on the table. "Do you think they'll have started their preparations yet?"

"Well, I believe they're all ensconced in that dolmen up there." Gastelois gave a quick nod of his head in the direction of the col overlooking the pub. "They're bound to be drinking and smoking that weed of theirs. Let's just hope there's some restraint being shown."

"Yes," agreed Pierre. "But of course they won't start preparing themselves properly until the morning." He drained his jar. "Anyone for a refill?"

Gastelois accepted, but Sylvia declined. While Pierre was up at the bar, she turned to Gastelois: "I know getting the dolmen finished on time is important to you, but you're worrying too much about it. You're looking very tired these days."

"I know, I know," he said, a trifle impatiently. "But finishing it on time *is* important to me – I don't like letting people down."

"I realise that, but it can't be helped if it's through circumstances beyond your control."

Gastelois sighed. "I suppose you're right." He massaged his forehead, moved his hand down to rub his eyes, then looked at her with a careworn expression. "This is one dolmen I really will be glad to be shot of."

Sylvia reached across the table and gently stroked his left wrist. "I know," she said softly, nodding her head. "I know."

* * *

To Gastelois' relief, the Tourvel brothers arrived the following morning. After being reassured by him that he would deal with any comeback from the unions - the three still did not belong to any - they went off to assist with the transportation of the first main-chamber capstone from the outcrop.

The priests had, amazingly enough, been at the rhyolite outcrop since the crack of dawn. The seven of them were sitting on their haunches in the usual semicircle behind the first stone that was to be moved, facing the intended direction of travel in the normal way. Nearby, lay the traditional trappings of the levitation ritual: drums, bone trumpets, tapping sticks and the hide with its magical symbols.

They were leaning forward in silence with closed eyes, fingertips together before their faces, Maître Esclenquier Le Digot in his customary position in the middle of the arc, the vessel containing the special pre-levitation drink on the grass in front of him.

After a while, he muttered incomprehensibly, took a few sips from the jar, and then passed it to Bertholin Le Bandé, who continued the ritual. Soon all the priests had partaken of a drink and the vessel was back on the ground in front of Le Digot. The seven holy men then returned to their trance-like state. It was not long, however, before Le Digot initiated another round of muttering and imbibing, its completion heralding another session of silent rumination, to be followed yet again by more mumbling and drinking. And so it continued for the remainder of the morning.

While the priests were thus engaged preparing themselves for the task ahead, a number of Gastelois' men were readying the nearby rhyolite block for its journey from outcrop to dolmen site.

The rope cradle that would be fastened around the megalith to help keep it under control while it was being levitated had already been made. Larger than the one that had been used for the passage orthostats and those walling the side chambers, it was commodious enough to be used for all of the dolmen's bigger capstones, and, like its smaller counterpart, could be tightened or loosened to account for variations in size among these. The four guidance and stabilising ropes attached to this netting were systematically uncoiled and both these and the strands of the cradle were checked for signs of fraying or other defects. Particular attention was paid to the attachment points, where the ends of the ropes were looped and knotted around the netting, as any flaw here could potentially have disastrous consequences.

At the same time as these checks were being carried out, other members of the workforce were walking the route from outcrop to dolmen, making sure that it was free of any obstacles that might hinder the megalith's progress. Although the way had already been cleared for the transportation of the side-chamber coverstones and in readiness for moving the ones destined for the chamber and passage, it was still important to check it before any stone was levitated along it in case anything had either been missed or had ended up there since the previous time it was used. So important was this that Gastelois himself, accompanied by Pierre de Lecq, walked the route as well. They could not afford to take the risk of overlooking any item that might trip up either one of the men on the ropes or, worse, one of the priests.

By midday, all was ready. The priests had completed their preparations, the net and the guide ropes found to be in satisfactory condition and the path to the dolmen free of any likely stumbling block (in the truc sense of the term).

A buzz of excitement ran through the usual crowd of onlookers from Gor and elsewhere. Not only were they standing around the dolmen, but they were also lined up all the way from the latter to the outcrop, on either side of the levitation route. Following his instructions, some of Gastelois' men acted as minders, stationing themselves in front of the spectators to keep them well back from the pathway. Once the levitation of the megalith was underway, the bystanders would also have to remain quiet until it was safely in place atop the relevant uprights of the dolmen.

Once the netting had been secured over the top and down the flanks of the capstone, the guidance and stabilising ropes were run out from either side of the net. Each of these would be kept taut by a group of three men pulling on its end. The Tourvel brothers made up one of these teams, working together as they always did.

As soon as the men holding the ropes were in position and the priests arranged behind and partly alongside the megalith in the traditional levitation arc, Maître Esclenquier Le Digot raised his right hand above his head. The crowd fell silent, eyes on the priests in eager anticipation. After glancing around to double-check that all was ready, Le Digot gave the signal to proceed by quickly dropping his hand.

As the usual levitational litany of drums, trumpets and chanting grew in intensity, Philipot du Moncel kept a wary eye on the rock from his position directly in front of it, ready to unroll the symbol-adorned hide he was holding in both hands and slip it under it the moment it lifted off the ground. He was doing his best to remain calm - as this was a particularly large specimen, the consequences of being in its way should it not be kept under control did not bear thinking about. He recalled just such an occasion during the building of the Varde passage-dolmen in the north-west of Lesur, which utilised some particularly large stones in its construction. He had been visiting that site and had been present when the priests had lost control of one of the uprights as it was being lowered into its socket in the main chamber. As a result of their incompetence, it had fallen on two workmen unfortunate enough to have got in its way. Once it had been lifted off them, it had taken some time to clean up the rather gruesome consequences of its descent, and in fact some wag had suggested pushing them into the socket and leaving them there as a sort of foundation burial.

Fortunately, no such disaster befell the capstone Philipot was in front of during its journey from outcrop to dolmen. As soon as the rock parted company with the ground, he unravelled the hide and slipped it beneath it with great dexterity, being careful not to let go off the rope with which he would pull it.

Once the megalith had been levitated a few feet, the procession began to advance slowly towards the dolmen, the priests keeping to their semi-circular formation, the faces of the chanters and the instruments of the trumpeters aimed at the rock, as they would be constantly throughout its journey so that it received the full benefit of the soundwaves emanating from mouths human and bony.

The puller of the hide led the way, his eyes regularly darting looks back at the symbol-adorned rectangle of animal skin to make sure that it was always in the correct relationship with the huge lump of rhyolite above it.

The capstone and its entourage duly reached the dolmen and, giving the northern perimeter of the mound quite a wide berth, turned in towards the forecourt. This manoeuvre involved a fair degree of activity by those on the ropes, while the priests had to ensure that the stone stayed aloft. This it did, although there were a couple of hairy moments when it wobbled alarmingly and another when it dropped to within a foot or so of the ground, but fortunately the priests managed to levitate it back to the required height.

The procession entered the forecourt and halted in front of the passage entrance. The rhyolitic lump hung suspended in mid-air, held aloft by the continuing priestly music. While the workers on the ropes moved cautiously to either side of the mound, Songeur Le Rêveur and Asceline Le Doublier stepped up on to it, the former to the north of the passage, the latter to the south. They walked over the tumulus, being careful not to dislodge any of the stones that composed it, until they were opposite the northern and southern orthostats of the western end of the main chamber. Gastelois and Pierre were already up there and they nodded towards Maîtres Songeur and Asceline in silent greeting. Below them in the chamber, the bracing frame stood ready - just in case. Then the two priests turned to face the megalith in the forecourt, their colleagues maintaining their semi-circular formation behind it.

While all this was going on, members of Gastelois' team were doing their best to keep the crowd watching in the vicinity at a safe distance; not always an easy task, as the curious frequently try to get closer than they should, believing that they are in less danger than they actually are.

As soon as Maîtres Le Rêveur and Le Doublier were in position, Esclenquier Le Digot gave the signal to advance, a sudden, particularly loud *thwack* on his drum, and the procession moved slowly towards the dolmen's passage. Once the megalith was above the first orthostats of this, the earth force spiralling upwards through them from the blind springs below provided extra lift and so the priests toned down the level and tempo of their music-making to compensate.

They remained just outside the passage entrance, watching the capstone intently as they levitated it over the uprights of the dolmen towards the end of the main chamber. When it had reached its destination and was hovering over the relevant orthostats, they skilfully lowered it on to these, keeping an eye on Songeur Le Rêveur and Asceline Le Doublier who, with the assistance of Gastelois and Pierre, were directing the positioning from their vantage point on the mound.

Once the capstone was safely and securely atop its uprights, Le Rêveur and Le Doublier rejoined their companions. Esclenquier Le Digot walked along the passage, looked up at Gastelois and Pierre and excused himself and his fellow priests: "We're leaving now," he said. "We've done enough for today. We have to recuperate after our exertions."

"As you wish, Maître Esclenquier," said Gastelois, briefly taking his eyes off the capstone to glance at the priest.

"We'll be back tomorrow morning," Le Digot assured him.

"Excellent."

Le Digot gave a slight nod of his head, turned and walked away. Gastelois gave a courteous nod in return. The priests' departure for the rest of the day came as no surprise to him. He knew from past experience that, where very large megaliths were concerned, the priests would only levitate one a day. They claimed that to attempt any more would be beyond their powers, and it was no good trying to persuade them otherwise.

The afternoon was spent dismantling the wooden bracing frame that had now done its duty at the western end of the main chamber and then reassembling it a few feet to the east between the orthostats that would support the second capstone.

While this was going on, other members of the team continued to work on the mound, which was by now almost complete. It had reached the point where the peristalith, the ring of megaliths that encircled the outer edge of a dolmen's mound and acted as a revetment, could be put in position.

Originally, Gastelois had had the idea of using quartz for the peristalith, although he would have had to import it. The Elders had quickly vetoed that scheme, however, on the grounds of cost. He had known all along that they would, but it had been worth suggesting it to them for the resulting looks of downright horror on their faces alone.

* * *

By noon the next day, the priests were ready to levitate the second capstone of the main chamber. All the rope components of the transportation paraphernalia had again been checked and found to be in satisfactory condition. Likewise the pathway between the outcrop and the dolmen. And all the preparations were helped by the continuing fine weather, with clear, almost cloudless skies and very little wind.

"If this carries on," said Pierre de Lecq, referring to the weather, "we should make excellent progress."

"True," agreed Gastelois. "Let's just hope that nothing happens to upset the cider barrel."

* * *

When Gastelois awoke at the crack of dawn the following morning, he was in a very good mood. The previous day had seen the successful placement of the second chamber capstone, and he had no doubt that this new day would see the equally successful positioning of the third one.

He was back on site before anyone else, giving the two coverstones now partially roofing the main chamber a quick examination to ensure that they were still safely located and that there were no problems with them. It was not unknown for cracks to develop after a capstone had been sitting on its supporting uprights for a while, which, if extensive enough, could lead to serious consequences. After satisfying himself that they were all right, he turned his attention to the bracing frame, now awaiting the arrival of the next capstone. Neither its positioning nor its overall condition gave him any cause for concern. It seemed to be standing up to the task in hand very well.

The priests arrived as Gastelois was completing his checks of the frame. While the others went off to the outcrop, Le Digot stayed behind to have a word with him.

The DRAGON of ANGUR

"Another nice day," he remarked when the latter had finished.

"Indeed it is, Maître Esclenquier," said Gastelois, glancing up at the sky and then smiling at the priest. "You all ready for the next one?"

"We will be, we will be," Le Digot assured him. He stroked his chin pensively. "We should get them all in place in time."

Gastelois' face assumed a puzzled, slightly alarmed expression: "What do you mean? In time for what?"

"The levitation contest."

Gastelois was none the wiser and favoured the other with a blank look.

"We're holding a contest for our High Elder's benefit as part of the Jubilee celebrations," explained Le Digot. "Therefore we have to practise to make sure we're properly prepared – we'd lose too much face if we lost, especially on such an occasion."

"And who are you competing against?" Gastelois realised what the answer was even before he finished asking the question.

"Lesur," replied Le Digot, confirming what Gastelois was thinking. "You can therefore see why it is important that we win."

"Yes, indeed."

Maître Esclenquier smiled. "I must now join the others. You will excuse me."

Gastelois nodded. "Of course." He stared thoughtfully at the priestly back as its owner walked off in the direction of the outcrop. He felt he should have known about this levitation contest, but he could not recall it having been mentioned before. He just hoped that the priests would be able to complete their work at the site before having to leave to practise for it. Not that he thought they needed to - in his opinion all this levitational activity they were currently engaged in was surely preparation enough.

By midday, the priests had attained the right frame of mind, all checks had been completed and everything was once again ready for capstone transportation.

While Gastelois, Pierre de Lecq at his side, was keeping a wary eye on the proceedings in general, Clychard La Cloche was having some final words with Armand Le Bricateur and the other two workers he had brought along to supposedly assist the dolmen builder. He had turned up about halfway through the morning, ostensibly to see how the three men were doing. But they had been expecting him, for there was another reason for his visit.

"Right," he concluded, speaking in the same low voice he had used throughout their meeting, having only raised it when anyone passed close by, simultaneously changing the subject to allay suspicion, "you know what to do."

The three standing before him nodded slowly. They had already gone over the plan several times and knew precisely what to do.

"Good," said the union chief and walked away to melt into the crowd that had gathered to watch the day's events.

As he did so, and with the levitational cacophony starting up over by the outcrop, the three agents of his scheme moved into position to execute it. Pelletier de Merde shinned up a conveniently placed tree overlooking the site from its northern side, while Armand Le Bricateur ascended another on the opposite side. Pierre Le Bécheur sauntered over to the edge of the nearby forest and concealed himself behind a tree from where he had a good view of the forecourt and entrance to the dolmen's passage. Thus ensconced, the three men settled down to wait.

With some thirty-five tons of rhyolite capstone aloft, the procession, led by that worthy puller of the hide, Philipot du Moncel, once again began its slow journey towards the dolmen, to the familiar musical accompaniment of beating drums, braying trumpets and the rising and falling of the priestly chanting.

As on the two previous occasions, their holinesses were arranged behind and partly alongside the capstone in the classic levitation arc, with Songeur Le Rêveur and Asceline Le Doublier at the head of these as before, occasionally striking the megalith with their tapping sticks to remind it who was boss.

Gaston, Gaetan and Gerard Tourvel once again made up one of the teams of three men on the four stabilising ropes running out from either side of the net draped over the capstone, ensuring that these were kept taut and using them to check any wayward movement of the block.

To Pelletier de Merde, watching from his tree, the procession resembled a gigantic spider creeping up on its prey. He smiled as he thought this, for this spider was in for a shock.

Once the tricky manoeuvre into the forecourt had been successfully completed, the procession halted in front of the passage entrance. While the continuing priestly music kept the megalith stationary in mid-air and the men on the ropes made their way to either side of the mound, Maîtres Le Rêveur and Le Doublier walked up the passage. They clambered on to the already positioned second capstone of the main chamber, giving a courteous nod of the head to Gastelois and Pierre who were standing on the mound to either side of that part of the chamber about to be roofed.

In their trees, Pelletier de Merde and Armand Le Bricateur reached inside their leather tunics and carefully drew out a small catapult. Each was then loaded with a pebble, one of several that had been selected earlier. By his tree at the edge of the nearby wood, Pierre Le Bécheur did likewise. All three held their breath.

With Maîtres Songeur and Asceline ensconced on their capstone, Esclenquier Le Digot gave a loud *thwack* on his drum and the procession moved slowly towards the dolmen's passage. As before, the priests toned down the level and tempo of their music-making once the megalith was over the first uprights of this, to compensate for the lifting effect of the earth force spiralling upwards through them.

Then, when the new capstone was about halfway along the passage, Pelletier de Merde aimed and loosed the stone from his catapult. The missile struck Fielebert Sottevast on his left thigh. He let out a cry of pain, which was translated into a strangulated bray by his trumpet. The leading edge of the capstone reared up alarmingly. Dropping the instrument, Sottevast clutched at his leg. Le Digot shot him a perplexed look as he and the other priests quickly brought the megalith under control. Gastelois and Pierre exchanged puzzled frowns.

No sooner had they done this than Armand Le Bricateur fired his catapult. His stone found Griesensacq Le Gripert's right hand, with which that worthy was holding his trumpet. Another strangulated bray and that instrument was tossed unceremoniously into the air. Again the capstone reacted by rearing up.

Gastelois and Pierre looked at each other. Something was clearly very wrong. They decided that perhaps it would be wiser not to hang around where they were. Keeping a wary eye on the antics of the new arrival, they climbed down off the mound and walked smartly away from the dolmen towards the watching crowd.

The onlookers had also come to the conclusion that, on this occasion, discretion was definitely the better part of valour. Although panic had not yet set in (after all, many of them had seen the priests do silly things before), they were becoming increasingly nervous at what they were witnessing. They began to retreat, encouraged by Gastelois' men who thought that it would be better if they were to move back out of potential harm's way.

Shortly after Le Gripert's trumpet left his hand, Pierre Le Bécheur fired his catapult, aiming for the backside of Bertholin Le Bandé. Despite the easy target provided by the ample dimensions of this, the stone somehow managed to miss it. Continuing on its way, it hit one of the uprights of the northern side-chamber, ricocheted off this and flew towards the southern chamber. Having the decency to enter this by its entrance, it found a pile of sacking lying on the floor.

The stone hit hard. The sacking suddenly came to life as a bewildered Escogriffe Le Manquais, who had been sleeping peacefully underneath it, was roused from his slumbers. He sat up, rubbing his eyes. Then, as he became aware of the levitational din outside, one eye followed by the other slowly opened to be greeted by the louring shadow of the third capstone as it came into view overhead.

A blood-curdling shriek rang out from the depths of the side chamber and, with an agility born of sheer terror, Escogriffe leapt out of it, negotiated the logs of the timber bracing-frame and dashed for the cover of the nearby elm trees.

Still trying to bring the capstone back under control after the strike on Le Gripert, the shriek followed by the sight of the fleeing Le Manquais took the priests completely by surprise and broke their concentration totally. Asceline Le Doublier and Songeur Le Rêveur, still standing on the second capstone of the main chamber, both went pale as thirty-five tons of best rhyolite careered unchecked towards them. They pointed their tapping sticks at the new arrival, frantically shaking them at it in a vain attempt to arrest its progress. Then, fearing the worst, they decided that it would be better not to stay where they were and so, while Maître Songeur jumped off to one side, Maître Asceline took a headlong dive to avoid the looming megalithic menace. Unfortunately, he chose the wrong direction, and plunged between the second and first capstones. But the gap was of insufficient width to accommodate his more than ample proportions and he got stuck halfway, priestly legs waving frantically in the air to the accompaniment of muffled imprecations from the dolmen's interior.

Moments later, the new capstone collided with the second and bounced back. It then rose in the air as the priests tried to regain control of it while those on the ropes did their best to assist. It duly stopped its ascent, hovered for a few moments, wobbling as if uncertain what to do next, and then plunged earthwards. There was the almighty din of large mass of rock meeting rock as the great bulk of rhyolite landed on the capstones covering the two side chambers, followed almost immediately by an ear-splitting *crack* as it broke in half. The bracing frame creaked in protest as the fractured ends pressed down on it and then, unable to stave off this two-pronged attack any longer, collapsed in a cacophony of snapping and splintering wood.

The ensuing silence was suddenly broken by a solitary voice:

"I really do not believe you wanted to do that!"

It belonged to one Gaston L'Enmerdeur, a smug-looking individual whose main business was everybody else's business.

Gastelois glared at him. "Anyone got a bétyle?" he asked grimly.

Messrs. La Berfote and La Grosse-Barbe obliged, selecting a particularly pointed specimen, and shortly afterwords Gaston L'Enmerdeur waddled uncomfortably off the site like a duck that had impaled itself on an unnoticed reed.

Gastelois did not bother to watch what was done with the bétyle. He did not need to - the shriek followed by the peals of laughter from those who did witness it was sufficient to tell him that the nosey one had been suitably dealt with. In any event, now that he was over the initial shock of the accident to the capstone, there were more pressing things to attend to.

* * *

La Cloche, who had been standing quietly in the background, had watched the disaster unfold with an impassive expression on his face. Now, as he slipped surreptitiously away, he permitted himself a smile. He knew exactly who to contact about what had just happened. Indeed, in the circumstances there *was* only one person...

* * *

Having quickly ascertained that the only thing injured in the accident was Asceline Le Doublier's pride, Gastelois started to assess the damage with Pierre de Lecq whilst the priest's companions

Sinclair Forrest

As he slipped surreptitiously away, he permitted himself a smile

attempted to extricate that worthy from his undignified position between the two capstones.

An incident of the sort that had just occurred was quite the last thing that Gastelois needed. As he remarked to his assistant, it was probably the hole that would sink the coracle.

Pierre, who was examining the southern side chamber, did his best to reassure him: "It may not be as bad as it looks."

"I don't see how it could be much worse," returned Gastelois ruefully. "Apart from rebuilding the bracing frame, we'll have to quarry a replacement capstone - none of the others we already have will be big enough."

"That's true, that," agreed Pierre. "But perhaps the two halves of the broken one could be re-used elsewhere?"

Gastelois nodded. "That's certainly a possibility."

"Well, at least this side cell appears to be all right. I'll check the other one."

While Gastelois studied the fractured capstone, Pierre carefully negotiated the wreckage to examine the other side chamber. He was relieved to find that that, too, had somehow survived unscathed. He imparted the good news to Gastelois.

"Well that's something, I suppose," remarked the latter, a wan smile flickering briefly across his face. "Now let's get this mess cleared up quickly," he paused, looked around, "before Health and Safety find out about this."

* * *

Toubib Le Véroleux, the Chief Inspector of the *Committee for Health and Safety* arrived at the site accompanied by two assistants and one other. Although anticipated, his appearance was quicker than anyone had expected. The one other was Clychard La Cloche, who, having left the site just after the incident with the capstone, had gone straight to Le Véroleux to report the mishap, which he had proceeded to do with much glee.

"Gastelois de Bois!"

The thin, reedy voice hit the dolmen builder like a sudden blast of chill air. He gave an involuntary shiver and turned to face the newcomers.

"Ah, Toubib! How are you?"

"I am well, thank you."

"And la Petite Vérole?" asked Gastelois.

"My daughter is well also."

"I am glad," said Gastelois. Then, recognising one of Toubib's assistants and remembering the incident Sylvia had told him about, he went on: "And how are you, François? Recovered from your ducking at Handois' quarry?"

François Le Modeste, a man small in the stature but large in the ego, went red with embarrassment at the recollection of the event in question and glared at Gastelois.

That worthy smiled, turned to Toubib: "What can I do for you?"

Toubib Le Véroleux scratched a spot near the tip of his nose, one of many that graced his face. "We have been informed of an accident on this site."

"Ah yes, the accident," said Gastelois. "At least this time it actually did happen here. I seem to recall that on the last occasion you arrived to look into an accident on one of my sites, it turned out that it had occurred some considerable distance away. I was in the midst of building the *Pouquelaye des Marécages* and one of my men brained himself on a beam in *The Bog and Bétyle*, if memory serves." He regarded his visitor through narrowed eyes: "You got here quickly."

"It is my job to investigate these things as quickly as poss'ble," said Toubib in a superior voice, ignoring the reference to the earlier incident Gastelois had just related. "Now show me what happened."

"Quite so. Please come this way."

With that, Gastelois led the three *Health and Safety* men over to where the two halves of the broken capstone lay in the main chamber, the bracing frame a mass of displaced and splintered timbers beneath it. La Cloche followed, smirking.

"I really don't know how it happened," confessed Gastelois, scratching his head.

"That's what we're here to find out," said Toubib, stating the obvious. "Mourant!"

"Yes?" Mourant Le Crevé, the other assistant, was a particularly thin, almost skeletal, figure with a complexion so exceptionally pale that you would have sworn that he spent all his time avoiding the sunlight.

The DRAGON of ANGUR

"You and François start questioning everyone who saw what happened. I want as much information as poss'ble."

"I can tell you what happened," said La Cloche. "I saw it all, me!"

"Go on, then," said Toubib. "You've already told me, but I'm sure Gastelois will want to hear your version of events for himself."

The dolmen builder shot the union chief a filthy look, but desisted from saying anything.

La Cloche proceeded to give an accurate account of what he had witnessed, leaving nothing out and lingering over the more spectacular parts with obvious relish. To be fair to him, he did not exaggerate – although the temptation must have been great - but then again he did not need to.

"...and those three were assisting on the ropes, them," La Cloche finished off in an accusatory tone, pointing at the Tourvel brothers. "And they're not even union members!"

"Is that so?" said Le Véroleux, steely eyes glinting coldly in the sunlight as he favoured the three stalwarts with an icy stare. "Did you know this, Gastelois?"

That worthy shrugged his shoulders. "Yes," he admitted, "I was aware of that. But under the circumstances I didn't see that it would be a problem. After all, I wasn't going to need their services for all that much longer."

"That's not the point," said La Cloche. "You know perfectly well, Gastelois, that non-union men are not to be employed as part of a dolmen construction team. I shudder to think what would happen if we relaxed the rule – it would set a most undesirable prec'dent."

"Indeed," agreed Toubib. "Gastelois, you have flagrantly flouted the rules!"

"I'm sorry," apologised Gastelois, "but it's important that this thing is completed in time for La Tanche's Jubilee, as you well know..."

"But look what's happened," interjected La Cloche. "Those idiots have set you back days!"

The Tourvel brothers exchanged frowns.

"What d'you mean?" asked Gastelois.

"Well, their incomp'tence caused that stone to fall."

"How d'you work that one out?" demanded the dolmen builder.

"I'd have thought that was obvious," declared La Cloche, making clicking sounds with his tongue to show his irritation at Gastelois' obvious lack of savvy in the matter. "You used unqualified people on the ropes."

"They were not unqualified. I can assure you..."

"But they're not union members," La Cloche interrupted him.

"That doesn't make them unqualified."

The union chief sniffed noisily and glared at the other.

"Whatever," said Le Véroleux, looking at each of them in turn. "The fact remains that there's been a serious accident, which will have to be invest'gated." He paused for a moment, then continued: "And pending the outcome of the invest'gations," he paused again, studying Gastelois' face, trying to gauge the likely reaction to what he was about to say, "I shall have no altern'tive but to close the site down."

Gastelois stared at him incredulously. "What d'you mean, close it down?"

"Precisely what I say. There's no way I can allow it to stay open after something like *that*." He nodded towards the broken capstone resting forlornly on the crushed bracing-frame.

"But you can't shut us down," protested Pierre de Lecq. "How are we supposed to complete the dolmen in time for the Jubilee?"

"That's not my problem," said Toubib. "As I said, I have no altern'tive."

"The Elders aren't going to like this," said Gastelois.

Le Véroleux shrugged his shoulders. "It's not me that's got to explain it to them."

"We'll see about that!" retorted Gastelois between gritted teeth.

Toubib called over to his two assistants: "Come!" he commanded, snapping his fingers at them. "We've seen enough for today. We'll start our invest'gations properly tomorrow." He turned to Gastelois: "In the meantime, nothing is to be touched. I want everything left exactly as it is at the moment."

* * *

Almost beside himself with glee, Clychard La Cloche left the site for the second time that day. He was again going off to see someone. On this occasion it was Grosnez, whom he had not seen for a good few days. He was looking forward to telling him what had happened. Now, with work on the dolmen being suspended, Grosnez should have no problems searching for that vial.

CHAPTER TWENTY-TWO

A DOLMEN IN THE DOLDRUMS

As Cou-Cou La Tanche's Flint Jubilee drew nearer, the people of Angur busied themselves making final preparations for the great event.

Each settlement was to put on something special during the course of the seven-day celebrations. There would be a variety of contests and games, including a coracle race from Sersur to Angur and a trial of strength involving the hauling of a megalith over a specified distance, while every pub in the island would hold a drinking competition of one sort or another. As for the levitation contest between the priests of Angur and Lesur, the mere thought of it filled most normal people with dread. This would be one event during which the spectators would stand well back, and one wag had even suggested that Lesur would be a good place from which to view it.

In the settlement of Grantez-sur-Montais in the west of the island, they were planning to hold a tree-felling contest using trees from a nearby limb of the great forest as the hapless victims. Once felled, the trees had to be stripped of their branches and the trunks then carried over a set distance, the winning team being the first over the finishing line. The locals fully expected to come home first, although there would be stiff competition from the men of Bagot-de-Lecq.

As for Bagot-de-Lecq itself, its inhabitants intended to host a fishing competition in the waters to the north of the settlement. Its best known resident would not be taking part, however; Leoville de Vinchelez would be too busy fine-tuning his latest creation to go fishing.

The whole thing would culminate in the dragon contest. While all the other tournaments were open for anyone to participate in, Angurians and even inhabitants of the other nearby islands were barred from competing in that involving Old Mauger. The object was to attract desirable, high profile individuals from foreign parts and encourage them to settle on Angur in the hope that their presence would enhance the island's status, the prize for winning the contest being, of course, residency in the island and a brand new dolmen to go with it, which, naturally, everyone was expecting to be built in time.

* * *

It was now some days after Toubib Le Véroleux had shut down the dolmen in question and there was still no sign of his inquiry reaching a conclusion.

It was a particularly hot afternoon and its builder was ensconced in the cool, dim interior of *The Old Vraic and Coracle* along with Sylvia and Pierre de Lecq. They were sitting in silence, contemplating the drinks on their table and oblivious to the general hubbub around them. It was as if each was waiting for one of the other two to break the silence first.

It was Gastelois who did break it: "I think I'll tell the Elders to stuff their project. If they want this dolmen built, they can find someone else."

"Isn't that a bit drastic, mon vier?" queried Pierre, picking up his cider jar to take a drink.

Gastelois shook his head. "No, I don't think so," he said. "I just don't see the point of carrying on."

"Well, you can't anyway," Sylvia pointed out. "At least not until you've heard the outcome of that idiot Le Véroleux's inquiry. You've been closed down."

"I know that!" said Gastelois tetchily. He did not need to be reminded of the fact. Then, seeing the hurt look on Sylvia's face: "I'm sorry. I didn't mean to snap at you."

"No problem," said Sylvia, smiling reassuringly at him.

"Look, even if Toubib wound up his inquiry tomorrow and gave me the go ahead to continue, I don't see how we could get it finished in time for the contest. Le Digot and his cronies are off practising for that levitation contest, so we would have to do all the remaining moving and lifting ourselves."

Sylvia sipped some of her cider. "So, apart from moaning at the Elders, what are you going to do?"

Gastelois shrugged his shoulders. "Don't know." He stared disconsolately at his own cider jar.

"Well, we can't just sit here and do nothing," said Pierre. "Anyway, I thought you were going to see T'loch".

"Yes, I am. But I haven't been able to yet. You know what it's like when you want to see him - can't find him anywhere."

"Not unless he wants to be found," pointed out Pierre.

"True," said Gastelois.

"Why don't you see him at home?" suggested Sylvia.

"*No-one* ever sees him at home," stated Gastelois emphatically. He sighed. "No, I'll just have to wait until I spot him here in Ang-Lenn, or wherever."

* * *

As was his way, it was T'loch who effectively found Gastelois, rather than the other way round. He was sitting in his favourite corner of *The Old Vraic and Coracle* when the dolmen builder walked in and strode up to the bar.

As Boileau Le Gobel poured Gastelois a jar of cider, he nodded past him to T'loch's table by the entrance: "We don't often see him," he said. "I wonder what brings him here?"

Gastelois turned and saw the magician. *Ah!* he thought. *Vraicer T'loch. Just the person I need to see.* Out loud he said: "I expect he's thirsty, like me."

He paid for the cider and walked over to join T'loch.

"Ah, Gastelois!" said the magician, looking up. "Good morning. Nice to see you. It's been a long time."

"Yes, that it has."

T'loch motioned to the vacant chair opposite him: "Please."

Gastelois put his jar on the table and sat down.

"You want to ask me about a vial of glowing liquid," said T'loch, eyeing him intently.

"Yes." Gastelois' rapidly elevating eyebrows registered his surprise. "How did you know?"

"It is my business to know these things," said T'loch in an enigmatic tone.

It was then that Gastelois recalled that the magician was rumoured to have the power to read people's minds. Out loud, he said: "We found one on my dolmen site recently. Well, actually it was Escogriffe who discovered it."

"Le Manquais? The afflicted one?" asked T'loch, knowing very well whom Gastelois meant.

"Yes." The dolmen builder took a drink of cider, smacked his lips in satisfaction as he put the jar back down on the table. "Things have happened at the site which, looking back, seem altogether rather suspicious. Now, of course, we've been closed down - you may have heard?"

The magician nodded. "Yes, it had come to my attention - an accident with a capstone, I believe." He peered at Gastelois. "What suspicious things?"

Gastelois proceeded to tell him what he knew already: about the enigmatic holes and the missing bétyle; about how Piton Le Malin had been skulking in that tree near the site, how he had fallen out of it when Escogriffe had found the vial and how the simple one had been deprived of his "pretty light" by Piton.

Gastelois concluded by asserting his belief that Grosnez was behind what had been going on, that he, aided and abetted by his servant, was responsible for the digging of the holes and that they had done so because they had been searching for the vial.

When he had finished, T'loch contemplated him in silence for what seemed to Gastelois to be an eternity, but in reality was only a little while.

"You are quite right," he said eventually. "Grosnez and Piton did indeed dig those holes, and they *were* after the vial."

"But why? What's so special about it?"

"Have you heard of sea-dragon milk?"

Gastelois frowned. "Yes. Legends tell of such a substance. Is it not known as 'the milk that glows'?"

"Indeed so." T'loch drank some ale. He continued, now speaking in a low voice: "And that is precisely what is in that vial. In the right hands, it has powerful properties. Mixed with certain herbs, it can be used for curing sicknesses and healing wounds. It can also assist with the reading of divination shells, and it is in this capacity that friend Grosnez is particularly interested."

"Ah!" exclaimed Gastelois, staring at him over the rim of his cider jar.

T'loch nodded slowly. "Yes," he said. "You may have heard of the divination properties of certain turtle shells?"

Gastelois nodded. He had indeed heard of such things, although he had never actually seen one.

"Those skilled in the reading of turtle shells look at the lines marking their inside surface," T'loch went on, "and from these they can predict the future, foretell people's destinies." He took another drink of ale. "But sometimes the lines are faint, making them difficult to see clearly and thus interpret, and this is where the sea-dragon milk comes in. A small quantity placed in a shell and allowed to flow along the lines will reveal them more clearly, particularly in a darkened room where they will glow due to the properties of the milk, thus showing them up better and making their interpretation easier."

"I see," said Gastelois. "Clearly, from what you say, Grosnez is interested in these shells, and hence why he was after the vial. Has he got one?"

"No, but he knows where one is."

Gastelois wondered whether T'loch was going to tell him. The magician took a long, slow drink from his jar of ale, put the vessel back down on the table and then sat back with his eyes closed, resting his chin on his fingertips. Gastelois waited patiently.

"The dragon has one," T'loch said eventually.

"Old Mauger?"

"The same."

"How did he get it?"

"Oh, I believe someone gave it to him many years ago," said T'loch vaguely. "Somehow Grosnez found out that he had it and that's why he..."

"Suggested the idea of the dragon contest to the Elders," Gastelois interrupted him, "so that he could get Mauger out of his cave and get the shell."

"Exactly!"

"And to use it properly he had to get some sea-dragon milk." Gastelois drank some more cider. "But how did he know where to look for the vial? How did he know it was buried on my site?"

"I, er, had something to do with that," confessed T'loch, smiling as he anticipated the other's reaction.

"*What?*"

The magician nodded. "Yes. I set him on the right path, so to speak."

"But why?"

T'loch took a few unhurried sips of his drink, relishing each mouthful of ale as if it were his last. Gastelois watched him as patiently as he could.

"He needs to be caught with the evidence," said T'loch eventually.

Gastelois frowned. "I don't understand. Other than predicting people's futures - and I grant you that's a pretty useful thing to be able to do - what use will the shell be to him? I mean, why all the fuss?"

"My dear Gastelois," said T'loch in a slightly condescending tone, "Grosnez is after far more than the ability to predict people's futures. What he desires is *control* of their destinies." He paused for a moment. "And by controlling theirs, he'll be able to keep control of his own."

"Well, I suppose that's something we'd all like to try to do," observed Gastelois matter of factly.

"True, but we should not do so at other people's expense," stated T'loch. He stayed Gastelois with a raised hand as the latter opened his mouth to say something, continued: "What Grosnez wants above all else is power. He thirsts for it like a man who has gone without water for days, and he believes that with the aid of the turtle shell and the dragon milk he will get it."

"And what will he do with it if he does get it?" asked Gastelois.

"Control Angur - at least for starters."

"How's he going to do that?"

"First of all, he gains control of the priesthood by using the shell to predict their destinies. Then, once he has accomplished that, he can influence and control the Elders."

"Could he do it? I mean, is he capable?"

T'loch slowly massaged his bearded chin. "Regrettably, yes. His abilities as a magician may leave a lot to be desired, but I believe he has sufficient knowledge." He paused to take another drink. "In any event, mediocrity can bring its own dangers."

"How d'you mean?"

"Whether he achieves his ambition or not, he could do untold damage on the way. Turtle shells are not to be trifled with, and their use by inexperienced hands can result in immeasurable harm."

"So that's another good reason to stop him."

T'loch nodded. "Indeed."

Gastelois contemplated his cider jar for a few moments while he let what he had been told sink in. Then he took a quick swig and said in a scornful voice: "He'd never get away with it. Someone would surely suspect something before it went too far."

"One would hope so, but one cannot be certain, and in that uncertainty lies the danger. I've seen it before."

Gastelois looked at T'loch expectantly, but the other was clearly not going to elaborate.

"Is anyone else involved in Grosnez' scheme?" he asked after a few moments which T'loch spent regarding him with an impassive stare that he found somewhat unsettling.

"I think you already suspect someone."

Gastelois frowned. Then realisation dawned: "Ah yes, our dear union chief. I was sure he was up to no good."

"That he is. But he has his own agenda."

"Oh?"

"Yes. He's as greedy for power as Grosnez."

"That doesn't surprise me."

"They're using each other for their own ends, and the one will stab the other in the back at the first available opportunity."

"I see. So how do you propose to stop them?"

"I have a plan, which I cannot reveal at the moment. I know it is small comfort considering what you have been through, but I hope that our meeting will at least have explained what has been going on and that the disruption of work on your dolmen has been a necessary, if unfortunate, consequence of…"

T'loch broke off, interrupted by a sudden commotion at the *Vraic's* entrance next to them.

The two who were attempting to enter the pub were clearly related, albeit separated in age by a good twenty years. Behind them came the third member of their party - as fine a specimen of aurochs as ever roamed the island. But while Boileau Le Gobel was perfectly willing to allow Désiré Arsène Le Cocq and his son, Arsène Désiré, into his establishment, he drew the line at bovine quadrupeds. He had enough problems clearing up after some of his human customers without worrying about other species. The cow could be tethered outside and he said as much.

The DRAGON of ANGUR

"But she's carried us all the way from Grantez!" protested Arsène Désiré. "She deserves a break, her."

"That's right," said his father. "She always gives us a good ride, her."

"She's not coming in here!" said Boileau emphatically.

At this point, Vraicer T'loch stood up. Gastelois did likewise without even thinking.

"Time to go, I think," said T'loch. He motioned to Gastelois to sit down. "Stay and enjoy the rest of your cider. Don't concern yourself about Grosnez. I have things well in hand." He smiled enigmatically at the other. "The dragon contest should prove very interesting. And as for your dolmen, don't worry about it. There will be others."

He made to leave *The Vraic*, but his way was blocked by the aurochs, which was half in, half out of the pub, its owners still arguing the toss with the landlord. The magician fixed his eyes on first the cow and then the two Le Cocqs. Immediately, the animal began to back out, encouraged by her owners. T'loch followed them outside.

"Well I never!" exclaimed Boileau Le Gobel.

A few moments later, the Le Cocqs returned, *sans* aurochs.

Gastelois smiled and drained his jar. He thought about leaving, but decided to have another drink first. The encounter with T'loch had left him feeling strangely relaxed. There was no reason to dash off anywhere. There was nothing to do other than let events take their course.

* * *

The three gnarled, weather-beaten specimens drinking at one of the tables in *The Old Vraic and Coracle* had been spending the morning putting the world to rights.

"I see that Gerard's been caught again," remarked the round-faced individual with the ruddy complexion two shades short of apoplexy.

"What's he been doing now, François?" asked one of his companions as he lifted his beer jar to his lips and noisily slurped some of its contents.

"They found some of those figurines in his boat, René," said François. "They were piled high under an aurochs skin!" He gulped down some of his own beer, dribbling a quantity of it down his chin.

"The fat ones?" enquired the third man, Jean.

François nodded.

"Ah me!" exclaimed René. He ran a hand through his tousled hair, swigged a quantity of beer and then wiped the back of a sweat-stained, grimy hand across his sun-cracked lips. "I s'ppose he was trying to import them from Armor."

"So I b'lieve," said François.

"You'd 'ave thought he'd 'ave learnt his lesson by now," said René. "Espec'ally after that time he was caught trying to bring in those slates with the suggestive carvings."

"Ah, but some people just can't 'elp themselves," stated François.

"And him an Elder an' all," said Jean. "That's not a good example to be setting to the young people, them!"

Sitting at a nearby table, a broad smile spread across Pierre de Lecq's face as he listened to this conversation. Considering the Elder in question, what he had just heard came as no surprise to him.

Just then, Gastelois walked into the pub, spotted his assistant and came over to him.

"Morning, Pierre."

"Morning, mon vier."

"I've seen T'loch." Gastelois said this in a low voice.

"So, what did he have to say?"

"Let me get a drink first." He nodded towards the other's jar. "Another?"

"Yes please." Pierre drained the vessel and handed it to Gastelois.

Gastelois duly returned with the replenished jars and set them down on the table. "Well," he began as he took the seat opposite his friend, "T'loch confirmed what we all suspected: that Grosnez's behind it all, assisted by friend La Cloche."

"What a surprise!"

Gastelois then summarised the conversation he had had with T'loch the day before, ending by saying: "Something tells me that

The DRAGON of ANGUR

Old Mauger will have a bigger part to play than merely taking part in the contest."

"Well, it will certainly be interesting to see what happens," remarked Pierre. He took a drink. "Any news from Toubib?"

"Ha!" exclaimed Gastelois. "What do you think?"

Just then, René, leaning over from the nearby table, interjected: "I heard you fell foul of that bugger Le Véroleux."

The two dolmen builders looked at each other and smiled.

"Yes," admitted Gastelois. "We've had a few problems."

"I've heard a few things about that one, things he wouldn't want to become common knowledge."

"I dare say," said Gastelois, who had a pretty good idea of how the other would have come by the information he was referring to and therefore its reliability.

"Well, if I can 'elp, just let me know," offered René. "A word in the right ear might be all that would be nec'ssary to persuade Le Véroleux that..."

"Thanks," Gastelois interrupted him. "I'll bear that in mind."

"Don't let the bastards get you down!" contributed François, while Jean, sitting next to him, nodded slowly in agreement, his eyes somewhat glazed and out of focus after the morning's imbibing.

"No indeed," said Pierre. "We won't."

Gastelois noticed that René was wearing a rather hurt expression. He correctly deduced that that worthy had taken umbrage at his less than enthusiastic response to his offer of help. "Let me get you all a drink."

"Aw, but that's very kind of you," said René, his features softening.

While this move clearly placated René and was also appreciated by his companions, it would not have been the wisest thing to do had the two dolmen builders been in a hurry to leave. But with work on their dolmen remaining at a standstill, they had time on their hands. So they just relaxed and whiled away the rest of the morning listening to René and his friends sorting out the problems of the island.

* * *

During the seven days prior to the start of the celebrations, the various contestants as well as visiting spectators from other lands and islands began to arrive in Angur. They were put up in the homes of those Angurians who had agreed to offer them accommodation.

Amongst these were the Rollrights, a troupe of travelling acrobats from Alb whose bodies' ability to perform all manner of contortional activities was quite amazing to behold.

Also hailing from Alb, but from further north than the Rollrights, was a particularly tall lady who went by the name of Long Meg. She came with five of her daughters. It was rumoured that there were many more, sired by a variety of fathers, and if these others were even half as attractive as the ones that accompanied her, then the young men of her settlement had no grounds for complaint whatsoever.

The problem, however, from their point of view, fine upstanding specimens of manhood though they undoubtedly were, was that Long Meg considered them unworthy suitors for her darling offspring. Where her aspirations for her daughters were concerned, she was decidedly upwardly mobile, and travelled to any event where there might be a half-decent possibility of setting up a worthy match. For logistical reasons, she only took some of them with her on any given trip, but they all got to accompany her sooner or later.

In all the time she had been doing this, only two satisfactory partners had been found for the girls. But this had everything to do with their mother's impossibly high standards and nothing to do with the condition of the merchandise.

Amongst the visitors from Lesur for the festivities was Thière de Guérin. His arrival in the island cheered Gastelois up immensely. Although his coming had not been unexpected, the actual day he was due to turn up was unknown, so his appearance at Gastelois' home early on the evening of the following day was a very pleasant surprise.

He was accompanied by Gastelois' half-sister, Marie-Hélène, who, having spotted him going into *The Old Vraic and Coracle* soon after making landfall, had parted him from the jar of cider Boileau Le Gobel had been in the process of pouring for him, insisting that she take him straight to Aube.

Of course, there was no question that during his visit to Angur Thière would stay anywhere other than the residence of that island's chief dolmen-builder, but he had hoped for a quick restorative after what had been a rather choppy crossing from Lesur before going to see his friend. Marie-Hélène's determination had been difficult to resist, however, and he had only managed a quick slurp from the half-filled jar before apologising to the landlord as he was dragged away.

The reason for the hurry, she had explained, was that Gastelois had big problems with his new dolmen, was very disconsolate as a result, and therefore the sooner he saw Thière's cheery face the better.

As he had not been on Angur since his overnight stay after the Carnac megalithic conference, Thière knew nothing about the new dolmen let alone the trials and tribulations that had attended its attempted construction. But by the time they reached Aube and the entrance of Gastelois' home, he had learnt all about it – or at least as much as Marie-Hélène herself knew.

Initially, Gastelois' face looked drawn and pale when he opened the door, but as soon as he saw who was there, it brightened into a broad smile.

"Thière!" he exclaimed and then hugged his friend in a tight embrace. "Come in, come in!"

As he followed Gastelois into the living area of that worthy's home, Marie-Hélène close behind him beaming so widely that you would have thought her face would split, Thière felt himself begin to relax after the rigours of the day.

Sylvia d'Arass got up when Thière walked in with Gastelois and embraced the Lesurian warmly. Her aroma was more wholesomely pleasant than he remembered, and for a moment he found himself envying his friend's good fortune.

After Thière had had a chance to unwind after his sea journey and the walk from Ang-Lenn, Gastelois suggested that they go to *The Prancing Pouquelaye* for a few ciders and something to eat. The pub had a reputation for producing some particularly savoury dishes, in spite of the presence of such unsavoury characters as Morpion Le Crasseux amongst its clientele.

When they walked in, the place was pretty busy. The aforementioned Le Crasseux was there as usual, ensconced on his own on a stool by the bar, a noticeable space between him and the customers on either side. He was not entirely unaccompanied, however, as attached to the leather belt around his waist was a thin rope, the other end of which had been looped around the carapace of a chancre crab that was reposing - one can only assume contentedly – at his feet, a shallow bowl of water in front of it.

Glancing around, Gastelois saw that Soulard's chamber was presently unoccupied, but from the appearance of him after whom it had been named, it would not remain so for long. Louvel was looking particularly unsteady on the pins, even through it was still early in the evening, and was swaying backwards and forwards with the glazed, vacuous expression of the truly inebriated.

Despite the crowded appearance of the pub, the four of them found a table easily enough, and while Sylvia, Marie-Hélène and Thière settled themselves at it, Gastelois went off to get refreshments.

At the table next to them, a well-rounded young woman was nursing what appeared to be a particularly rosy baby, but which on closer inspection turned out to be a piglet. The animal grunted contentedly as it suckled on her nipple.

Gastelois cast an eye in the piglet's direction as he returned with the drinks. After the recent incident at *The Old Vraic and Coracle* with the aurochs, he wondered whether Boileau Le Gobel would allow the nursing of wildlife in his pub, but on balance thought that, under certain circumstances, he probably would. Gastelois had never actually seen this in *The Vraic*, however.

Just as he was sitting down with his friends, a particularly tall woman entered *The Prancing Pouquelaye* accompanied by five younger women of particularly arresting appearance. Despite the busyness of the establishment, they did not have to wait long for a seat at a table, as one near the entrance was speedily vacated and offered to them by the group of suddenly hopeful young men who had been sitting at it.

Their arrival did not go unnoticed by Gastelois, Pierre and Thière.

"By Teus!" exclaimed Pierre, his jaw dropping.

"Seen better," said Thière. "But not very often."

"Not bad!" declared Gastelois. "Not bad at all!"

Sylvia elbowed him in the ribs. "Be thankful for what you've got!" she said firmly. "Men!" she added, looking at Marie-Hélène.

"Can't take them anywhere!" said Gastelois' half-sister.

"They are attractive," Gastelois gave Sylvia a reassuring hug, "but not a patch on you!"

"They're not from these parts, though," observed Thière.

At that point, the landlord, the ever-jovial Gaston Le Remplieur, arrived with the food Gastelois had ordered.

"They're from Alb," he said as he began to put the bowls of steaming seafood stew down on the table. "Here for the festivities. Michel Langlois is putting them up."

"He's that artist fellow, isn't he?" queried Thière.

"Yes," confirmed the landlord, nodding. "He lives up the street. I believe he's hoping they'll sit for him while they're here."

"Bet that's not all he's hoping," remarked Pierre with a lascivious grin.

Now it was his turn to receive a dig in the ribs, courtesy of Marie-Hélène.

As they began to tuck into their stew, Thière looked at Gastelois and said: "Right, tell me all about your new dolmen. I couldn't get much out of you back at your house, and you promised you would reveal all once we were here."

"Yes, so I did." Gastelois swallowed a mouthful of stew, took a drink of cider and then launched into the whole sordid tale. He skimmed over some details such as the difficulties with the Planning Department (that, after all, was a foregone conclusion), but lingered over others, especially the capstone disaster and the subsequent visit of Toubib Le Véroleux and his cronies from *Health and Safety*. He ended with the meeting with T'loch and the pointing of the finger at Grosnez and Clychard La Cloche.

"Why don't you complain to the Elders?" suggested Thière when Gastelois had finished. "I mean, it's their project, so surely they'd do something about it."

"Thought about it," said Gastelois, "but I didn't see the point. It would've taken them too long to agree on a course of action. Anyway, it's too late now."

"So there's no way it's going to be finished in time for the dragon contest?"

"Not a chance!" declared Gastelois emphatically. "I'll have to finish it afterwards."

"Well, they'll just have to give the winner his prize when it's ready," remarked Pierre. "He'll simply have to be patient, that's all."

As he finished speaking, he happened to glance towards the pub's entrance. He froze, nudged Gastelois. "Don't look now," he muttered, "but a certain little friend of ours has just walked in."

Despite Pierre's advice, Gastelois did look. "Piton! What's he doing here?"

"Probably been sent by Grosnez to spy on us."

All four of them were now staring at Grosnez' servant, who was nervously glancing about him. It was unclear whether he had seen them, but it did not bother them one way or the other.

Suddenly, a stentorian voice rang out, slicing through the general hubbub: "Bah Teus! There's that little *branlant* Le Malin!"

The sound of that voice transfixed Piton. He went pale as its owner, a swarthy, powerfully-built giant of a man with a swarm of black hair and an expression to match strode across the pub towards him.

"Ne Touchepas!" muttered Pierre. "If Piton's done something to upset him…"

Tchiard des Ne Touchepas was reputedly the strongest man in Ang-Lenn, if not the whole of Angur, and one whose temper was never far off boiling point. The place quietened down, all eyes on him, as he marched up to Piton.

The latter backed away, a look of sheer terror on his blanched features.

Next second, a large hand was closing around his scrawny throat. He struggled for breath, legs kicking futilely as he was lifted off the ground. The vice-like grip holding him airborne, he was propelled backwards through the pub's entrance and out into the balmy evening. Some thundering invective, followed by a distant splash.

Ne Touchepas came back in on his own. *The Prancing Pouquelaye's* customers returned to what they had been doing, judging it best to mind his or her own business.

"Oh well," smiled Gastelois. "I don't think we'll have to worry about Piton for the time being."

* * *

Grosnez and Clychard La Cloche were sitting by the hearth in the central living area of the former's' home, rehearsing their plan to relieve Old Mauger of the turtle shell.

"So," said the union chief, taking the hunk of wild boar the other had just sliced off the carcass roasting on the spit straddling the hearth, "we make our way to his cave while he's otherwise engaged and just help ourselves to the shell."

"That's about the size of it, mon vier." Grosnez bit into the piece of boar he had cut for himself. "And Piton," he added between mouthfuls, "can keep a lookout at the entrance."

"Then, once we've got it..."

"We bring it straight back here," Grosnez interrupted him.

"And we start using it!" La Cloche rubbed greasy hands together as he gleefully contemplated forthcoming riches.

"All in good time," said Grosnez. "As I told you before, we've still got to get hold of the vial."

La Cloche gave a grunt. "Still don't see why you couldn't have got it by now," he grumbled. "You've had plenty of time – the dolmen's been shut down for days."

Just then, the sound of the entrance door opening and then banging shut reached their ears. A few moments later, a wet, bedraggled and somewhat miserable looking excuse for a servant was in the presence of his master.

"Ah, Piton!" said Grosnez, ignoring the other's state. "Learn anything useful?"

"I... I didn't get a chance, Grosnez." Piton looked hopefully at the hearth, wanting to get closer to dry off and get warm.

"Why not?" What happened?"

"Tchiard was there, him."

"So?"

"He must have realised it was us who scuttled his boat."

"Why?"

"He grabbed me and threw me in the harbour."

Grosnez laughed heartily: "I wish I'd seen that, mon vier!"

A loud rapping sounded on the entrance door.

Grosnez frowned. "Piton, see who that is and then get rid of them!"

"Yes, Grosnez. At once, Grosnez."

His servant cast a mournful look at the fire and then disappeared along the passage leading to the entrance. He duly opened the door to reveal a stocky, ruddy-faced man standing there wearing the expression of one about to demand something with menaces.

"I've come for my rente,"[10] stated this individual in a tone that brooked no arguments.

---

[10] Rentes were a form of loan or mortgage where whatever had been borrowed was repaid by regular payments of some substance, the nature and amount of which was decided by the lender or *rentier*. Almost anything could be stipulated, but cider, beer, fish, birds' eggs, guano, vraic (seaweed) and vraic ash (a good fertiliser) were the most common.

"What rente's that, Girard?" asked Piton innocently.

The other's expression climbed a notch on the belligerence scale. "My skinful of cider," he hissed between gritted teeth.

"Ah yes. You'd better come in then, you."

Piton led the way into the main chamber of Grosnez' home. His master broke off from his discussions with the union chief and glared at him.

"Well?" he demanded.

"Gr... Grosnez," began Piton nervously, "G... Girard's here for his, er, for his rente."

"I haven't got time for that now. Tell him to come back tomorrow when I'm not so busy."

"I'm here now and I've come for my skinful." Girard emerged from the shadows behind Piton.

Grosnez studied his visitor's complexion, made even ruddier by the firelight from the hearth in the centre of the room. "Seems to me you've already had a skinful, mon vier," he remarked unkindly, a smirk spreading across his features.

The other glared at him. "I've come for my cider. You know very well that a goatskin of cider is owed as rente on this property once a year and falls due at this time."

"So, this year I'll buy you a couple of jars in a pub."

"That would not be right, that. The rente has to be paid in the proper manner."

"I really haven't got time for this right now."

"And I haven't got time to come back."

"Oh all right!" Grosnez let out a long sigh of exasperation. "Piton! Fetch the man his cider."

As his servant walked past him, Grosnez laid a hand on his shoulder and bent to mutter in his ear: "I'm sure you must need to relieve yourself. Why don't you use the goatskin. That probably couldn't tell the difference."

Girard, unfortunately for Grosnez, had hearing whose acuteness rivalled that of a bat. "I wouldn't try pulling a stunt like that on me, Chatel!"

While Piton was away filling up a goatskin, hopefully with the requested liquid, an uncomfortable silence prevailed in the living room. Girard regarded Grosnez and La Cloche suspiciously. Quite why the union chief should be in the company of this self-styled magician he did not know, but he was sure that nothing good would come of it.

Piton returned after a short while and handed Grosnez the goatskin.

"I trust you haven't filled it too full," the latter remarked acidly. He turned to Girard, the dripping skin held at the end of an outstretched arm: "Your rente, mon vier."

"About time!" said the other, grabbing the reluctantly proffered container. He weighed it carefully in his hands, a suspicious look on his face. Then, the expression deepening, he opened it and sniffed its contents.

"As much as I would have liked to," said Grosnez, watching Girard's actions, "my good nature got the better of me."

"Just making sure," said Girard. "Until next year then."

"I can hardly wait, mon vier," said Grosnez sarcastically.

With that, Girard bade the others a good evening and then he and his rente left Grosnez' residence.

Once he was out of the way, La Cloche, suddenly concerned, said: "You don't think he suspected anything, do you?"

"How could he suspect anything? He has no idea what we're up to. You could be here for any number of reasons."

The union chief relaxed. "Aw, but you're prob'bly right, you."

"I am right," said Grosnez. His eyes narrowed. "And once I'm in control, there will be certain changes. Next year it will be that fool Girard paying *me* rente!"

* * *

Over the course of the next few days, the competitors for the dragon contest arrived in the island, having come from near and far, but none, of course, from Angur itself or the other islands in the vicinity. As with those foreign contestants already on the island, the new arrivals were housed in the homes of hospitality-inclined Angurians.

There were three from Armor: Hugo de Hambye, Jean Le Flecheur and Anquetil L'Efflanqueur. A further three had journeyed up from Iberia: Manuel de Viera, Miguel de Millares and Rodrigues de Menga. One George, who hailed from the southern part of Alb, had arrived later than the others, blaming a troublesome dragon at home as the reason he had been delayed.

There was also a certain McTavish who had travelled from Alb's more northerly, colder climes accompanied by a strange contraption consisting of an animal-skin bag from which sprouted a variety of hollowed and holed cabbage stalks. Despite the firm opinion of most of those who saw it that it was clearly some strange kind of communal drinking container, McTavish insisted that it was a musical instrument. When, however, he played the thing for the benefit of the locals, they begged to differ, being only prepared to agree on the 'instrument' part of the description.

Finally, the line-up of contestants was completed by four powerful, thickset individuals, square of head and blue of eye, who hailed from the dark, mysterious forests of the Teutons, a good month's travel to the east of the islands. Gunz, Mindel, Riss and Wurm von Rotsteinen were brothers whose prowess in fighting dragons and other creatures was legendary.

Mindel, the second oldest, had a reputation for being particularly fearless; before every encounter, he would don a headdress made from a pair of bison horns and daub himself with copious quantities of red ochre to make himself look as ferocious as possible. This get-up had earned him the nickname of *The Red Bison*, a soubriquet of which he was especially proud.

In the opinion of those who considered themselves to be in the know, which collection included the von Rotsteinens, it was a foregone conclusion that one of the brothers would win the contest, the only question being which one. Fate, however, might well decree otherwise.

CHAPTER TWENTY-THREE

A FESTIVE ISLAND

From the first day of Cou-Cou La Tanche's Flint Jubilee celebrations, the foreshore of the Bay of Aube was a hive of activity. A variety of displays and sideshows had been set up on the beach above the high tide mark prior to the start of the festivities. The air was vibrant with excitement as a hustle of humanity bustled around, locals rubbing shoulders with visitors as they watched jugglers and acrobats or participated in bouts of wrestling, trials of strength or games of wit.

There were stalls of food and drink, conveniently located near the various areas of activity along the length of the beach, and from these a variety of seafood, animal and bird dishes was obtainable. People were therefore never short of somewhere to get sustenance and refreshments as they moved from one place to the next.

Teams from Angur's settlements competed both against each other and against teams of foreigners in heats of *tug-of-war*, during a number of which the rope broke due to the enthusiasm of the contestants and had to be replaced. Amongst those taking part was the successful tree-felling team from Grantez-sur-Montais, who had beat their close rivals, the men from Bagot-de-Lecq, to take first place when that particular contest had been held near their home settlement on the second day of the celebrations. There had been stiff competition from other areas' teams, however - in particular one group of powerful, blond-haired men from the ancient Teuton forests and another from Hampwood in Alb.

Other people took part in tournaments of *seven-bétyle bowling*, organised by the proprietor of *Nouaux's Bowling Allée Couverte*[11], a large gallery-dolmen designed for the purpose and conveniently situated not far inland from the bay.

Like the aforementioned tree-felling contest, competitions were held in parts of the island other than the Bay of Aube. The

---
[11] Allée couverte – literally 'covered way' – another term for a gallery-dolmen.

inhabitants of Bagot-de-Lecq managed to regain their pride by winning the fishing tournament that took place on the third and fourth days of the celebrations. It no doubt helped them that they were on home ground, or rather water - the stretch of sea immediately to the north of their village. Clarry Le Brocq, who had been convinced that he would win, accused them of cheating, but without being able to muster a shred of evidence. A forced ducking in Bagot-de-Lecq's harbour was his reward for his troubles.

While the hapless Le Brocq was thus being dealt with, other stalwart seafarers were competing in the Sersur to Angur coracle race. This was convincingly won by the team from Lesur, who arrived in the harbour of Dragon Rock Bay on the north coast of Angur several coracle lengths ahead of the boat from Sersur. To the chagrin of the host island, the Angurian boat sprang a leak halfway between start and finish and had to be abandoned, its woebegone crew rescued from the foamy brine by two vessels from the flotilla that accompanied the competitors on the crossing.

Each day, the Elders deigned to grace the festivities with their presence from about mid-afternoon onwards. The mornings were spent recovering from the excesses of the night before, during which the Angurian Elders had entertained their colleagues from Lesur, Sersur and Ortac. This over-indulgence was resumed every lunch-time in *The Granite Cabbage*, when copious quantities of roast aurochs, roast boar and various seafood delicacies were consumed, washed down by even more copious quantities of beverages alcoholic. A procession of somewhat bloated and well-oiled sages would then slowly wend its way down the Town Mount and out of Ang-Lenn to the canopy-covered stand that had been erected on the beach about halfway between the town and Aube.

On the fifth afternoon, they were entertained to a megalith-hauling competition. This involved five teams, each of whom had to drag a ten-ton block of granite over a fifty-yard distance on the beach in front of the Elder's platform. Each team was provided with logs with which to build a *Kercadoan-Téviec* trackway and buckets of animal fat with which to grease it.

The Armorian squad was first over the finishing line, but only just, as it was very nearly a tie between them and the Angurians, captained by Gastelois himself, while the brave band from Lesur, led by Thière de Guérin, came a very close third. The Teutons did their best, but they were completely outclassed by the men from those areas where the moving of megaliths was in the blood, and there was a considerable gap between them and the Iberians, who finished fourth, not far behind the Lesurian contingent. For reasons best known to themselves, the Sersurians did not enter a team.

Sylvia d'Arras cheered the Angurian team on, but she had to be discreet about encouraging Gastelois personally because Albert de Richolet was on the Elders' stand and she felt that he was watching her every move.

At least the men from Angur lost honourably, which is more than can be said for the members of that island's priesthood who were to take part in the levitation contest against Lesur on the afternoon of the sixth day. To put it bluntly, they were disqualified. Somebody, who preferred to remain anonymous, had somehow discovered that at least two of the Angurian priests had partaken of a performance-enhancing potion not permitted in competition. This came to light just before the start, and as a result the contest was promptly cancelled. The Lesurian priests therefore won by default and went off looking decidedly smug, while the menhir that was due to have been levitated remained where it lay (it would be moved from the beach after the end of the festivities).

During the evenings, drinking contests were held in the island's pubs. As is invariably the case, the object of these was to drink as much as possible before all but one contestant had collapsed comatose on the floor, the survivor being declared the winner. Various stalwarts of local establishments took on visiting stalwarts of foreign establishments, and the ale and the cider flowed copiously. Fortunately all the landlords had anticipated the amount that would flow down the gullets of the competitors and had therefore bought in extra supplies. Needless to say, the mornings after saw some pretty spectacular hangovers, and very few of those taking part were fit to leave the scenes of their successes, or failures, much before midday – in some cases the midday of the second day after their contest!

* * *

The seventh day, the day of the dragon contest, dawned warm and sunny. Old Mauger awoke about halfway through the morning, having slept late. Once he realised what day it was, he began to feel decidedly nervous, but Vraicer T'loch, who had been sitting just inside the cave entrance, patiently waiting for him to wake up, reassured him.

Sinclair Forrest

"Don't worry, you'll be fine," he said in a soothing voice. "You'll feel better once you've had some breakfast. I've brought you something special." He reached inside his cloak and produced a wineskin, only it did not contain wine but a special brew T'loch had concocted for the occasion.

"I'll feel better once this business is over," said the dragon morosely. "Being shot at isn't my idea of how to spend a nice summer's day."

"Just remember that you're doing it for a good cause," said T'loch. "Now open wide!"

Mauger did as he was bid and T'loch carefully poured the contents of the wineskin down his gullet. A warm, vibrant feeling coursed through the dragon's body.

"Feel good?"

Mauger nodded.

"It'll give you extra energy and keep your spirits up," explained T'loch. "I take it myself from time to time."

That reassured the dragon, although he knew that T'loch would never give him anything that was not perfectly safe.

"It takes a little while to work," continued the magician, "but by the time the contest starts this afternoon, it will have reached its full potency." He put the wineskin back inside his cloak. "Now, while you're eating, I'll go over my plan with you so you're clear about what I want you to do."

As the dragon proceeded to eat some pieces of limestone from a pile that reposed nearby, crunching them noisily, Vraicer T'loch told him what he had in mind in relation to the day's events. If all went according to plan, the crowd already gathered on the large crescent beach between Ang-Lenn and Aube was in for a big surprise...

* * *

Meanwhile, in a cove on the north coast, a strange double-hulled craft, the likes of which had only once before been seen in these waters, and never in any other waters, was being readied for sea. It was designed to be the launching platform for a sea-going catapult, the purpose of which was to protect Angurian fishermen in the event of disputes with any of the neighbouring islands getting out of hand. It was the intention of its builder, the indefatigable Leoville de Vinchelez, to demonstrate its capabilities in front of the dignitaries, local populace and visitors currently gathered on the shore of the Bay of Aube to watch the dragon contest.

The DRAGON of ANGUR

The first occasion on which the vessel had put to sea (so far the only one) had not been a success, to put it mildly. The outward leg of the voyage along Angur's north coast had gone without a hitch, but the return journey had proved to be a rather different cauldron of fish. All had been going reasonably well, although the rowers in one hull had been experiencing difficulties synchronizing their efforts with those in the other, and Leoville had been certain of making port without incident. Then suddenly, and for no apparent reason, the catapult arm had broken free of its restraining ropes with catastrophic results; the craft performing a maritime cartwheel to finish upside down in the water.

It was this incident, in fact, that Old Mauger, Grosnez and Piton had witnessed as they neared the north coast of Angur on the last leg of the flight back from Alb.

Unfazed by this disaster, Leoville had managed to get his vessel towed back to its home cove near Bagot-de-Lecq, where he promptly set about modifying, and hopefully improving, its design.

The fifty-foot-long twin hulls, each of which had seating space for some thirty rowers two abreast, were connected to each other by three sections of decking made from thick planks of oak running at right angles to the hulls. By far the largest of these sections was the midships one, the central part of which was dominated by the catapult support tower: four stout logs, braced by a criss-cross network of thinner ones, rising some fifteen feet above deck level. The port and starboard ends of the deck now sprouted a mast, each carrying a square, leather sail. A third mast, with a slightly larger sail than the other two, was also a new addition and rose from the middle of the deck section joining the hulls at the bows, while the one connecting them at the stern housed the redesigned anchoring points for the securing ropes of the catapult arm.

Leoville was directing preparations for his vessel's departure from amidships. He was looking towards the stern, making lowering motions with his arms, eyes focused intently on the team of men standing on the planks of the rear deck. They were hauling on the ropes attached near the aft end of the catapult arm, a long yew trunk chosen for its pliant qualities. It extended from about twelve feet in front of the central deck section to a little way aft of the stern, where it terminated in a sort of bucket formed from animal hides stitched together with thongs of leather.

Once Leoville judged that the bucket end of the arm had been pulled down as far as was necessary, he shouted to his men to secure the ropes. These were quickly passed through eyes set into the rearmost plank of the aft deck and then looped around nearby log bollards in such a way that they could be easily and speedily freed when the catapult came to be fired.

Satisfied that that end of the arm had been adequately secured, Leoville made his way around the support tower to the forward part of the central deck. As he passed the triangle formed by the two main logs of that side of the tower, he glanced up at the arm's pivot assembly attached to its top. As far as he could tell, all was in order, but he would check it properly before the boat left harbour. He then clambered on to the box-like construction at the forward end of the deck. When the catapult was fired, this would halt the downward motion of the anterior part of the arm - its heavily padded front face designed to cushion the impact - and from its top he could supervise the loading of the wooden counterweight box attached to the front end of the arm.[12]

This - a considerably more substantial affair than the basket of the earlier design - was filled with stones from the nearby beach, the yew trunk straining as the weight increased.

"Right, that should be enough!" Leoville shouted to the loaders when he estimated that there were a sufficient number of stones in the box. "How are we doing with the boats?"

He was referring to the four flat-bottomed, barge-like cargo-coracles that, filled with rocks, large pebbles and other suitable missiles, would accompany the catapult-catamaran on its journeys. Although they could have travelled independently of the larger vessel, as each had a sail and a crew of oarsmen, they would be towed by it, two behind each of its hulls. Having all the boats thus connected would obviate the risk of them becoming separated from the main craft, for whatever reason.

"Nearly there, I think," one of Leoville's men responded. He was standing waist deep in water next to one of the coracles, in which he had just placed a large, sea-smoothed stone obtained from the nearby pebble-covered strand. "Just a few more to put in this one." He motioned with his hand to where two of the other three boats, laden with projectiles, were being rowed towards the stern of the catamaran, which was moored further out to sea, the first having just been attached. "Those two are on their way."

---

[12] In some ways, the design anticipated that of the medieval *trebuchet* many, many centuries later.

The DRAGON of ANGUR

"Excellent!" Leoville jumped down off the box at the front of the midships deck. "You finish off there. I'm just going to check the pivot assembly." As he walked towards the central tower, he glanced up at the Sun, smiling benignly down on them from a virtually cloudless azure sky. "I have a feeling we're going to arrive at just the right moment," he said, half to himself.

Soon all the preparations had been completed, the crews were on board and the strange flotilla was ready to put to sea.

* * *

The arrival of the Elders that afternoon was heralded by a series of blasts on seven aurochs horns, as it had been on the six previous afternoons. To describe these as fanfares might give you the impression that there was an element of musicality involved, but this would be misleading. At the head of the procession was the subject of these Flint Jubilee celebrations, the man for whom everyone had gone to so much trouble, the High Elder himself, Cou-Cou La Tanche.

In his youth he had been a tall, imposing figure, with jet black hair framing sharp, piercing eyes set in taut, angular features; but although extreme age had turned the hair silvery grey, dulled the fire in the eyes, creased the features, and caused him to walk with a pronounced stoop, relying heavily on two stout canes, he maintained an air of some dignity.

Behind him came the other Elders. Not only was the entire Angurian Assembly present, but also those of Lesur and Sersur, the all-female one from the latter island headed by La Dame Blanche, one of the most formidable politicians of these parts. Despite her advanced age – she was only a few years younger than La Tanche – she had maintained the beauty of her youth to a remarkable degree and seemed to be eternally sprightly. A few put this down to something in the Sersurian water; more suspected the island's alcoholic beverages; while there were those who were certain that it was due to a potion supplied by Verman Clouet, a potion that evidently slowed the ageing process.

The Elders climbed the few steps on to the large wooden platform with much wheezing and grunting from the more corpulent members and not a little creaking from the more arthritic ones. They settled their well-fed forms on the three rows of tiered benches, shaded from the Sun's rays by a hide-covered canopy.

Cou-Cou La Tanche eased his ancient, leather-covered frame into the high-backed oaken chair that, along with two similar chairs one to either side of it, divided the front row of benches. La Dame Blanche, High Elder of Sersur, occupied the seat on La Tanche's right, while her Lesurian counterpart, Torteval Le Grospétard, took the one on his left.

Once they were all comfortably ensconced in their places, Gaetan Le Sterc, Chairman of the Angurian Assembly, got up from his seat in the front row between the Lesurian and Sersurian chairpersons, Ernaud de Langetot and Vivienne de Vaurocque, a woman almost as redoubtable as La Dame Blanche. Walking to the edge of the platform, he faced the gathered multitude and raised both arms high above his head.

Another series of blasts from the aurochs horns. The watching crowd subsided into silence.

"Honoured guests, friends, visitors and fellow Angurians, welcome!" he began in a voice well practiced to making such pronouncements. "We come to the final day of these festiv'ties in honour of our esteemed High Elder." He turned and bowed respectfully to La Tanche, who gave a nod of his head.

"For your pleasure and enjoyment, your Highness," he continued, "we have arranged a special dragon contest."

Muttering broke out amongst the crowd. "Hope it goes better than yesterday's levitation one!" quipped someone.

Haut-Maître Hacquebuttier Le Grandin, High Priest of Angur, heard this remark and went red with a mixture of anger and embarrassment.

Le Sterc ignored it and went on: "A number of contestants, who will shortly be presented to your Highness, will fire soft-tipped arrows dipped in coloured dyes at the dragon, and he who scores the most hits will be declared the winner."

He faced the crowd: "Let those who are partic'pating come forward and present themselves!"

The competitors for the dragon contest, who had been hastily schooled in how to comport themselves for the occasion, assembled in front of the Elders' platform, bowed, and introduced themselves one by one.

The first to come forward were the three from Armor: Hugo de Hambye, Jean Le Flecheur and Anquetil L'Efflanqueur. Next were the three Iberians: Manuel de Viera, Miguel de Millares and

Rodrigues de Menga. These were followed by the two Albians, George and McTavish, the latter clutching his strange, animal-skin bag with its holed cabbage stalks, clearly unwilling to entrust its safekeeping to anyone else.

Finally, the four blond-haired Teutons, Gunz, Mindel, Riss and Wurm von Rotsteinen completed the line up. Although they greeted Cou-Cou La Tanche and the other Elders with all due deference and respect, you could see from the rather smug expressions on their faces that they had already decided who was going to win the contest. To them, it was a foregone conclusion.

When the introductions were over, Le Sterc explained the rules of the contest. These had been drawn up some time previously and Gastelois himself had been on hand to ensure that they were fair and did not put Old Mauger at undue risk. The competitors would have thirteen arrows each (one for each month of the year), dipped in a dye of a colour peculiar to the individual contestant. Only strikes on the dragon's body would count. On no account were they to aim for his head, his eyes in particular - that was a definite no-no and would result in instant disqualification.

The explanation completed, Le Sterc wished them all the best of luck. They were then directed to a spot lower down the beach where twelve clay vessels stood in a row, an assistant standing next to each one holding a quiver of arrows.

When the contestants were ready, the seven aurochs horns emitted a series of six short blasts followed by a final longer one. Everyone waited in eager anticipation.

* * *

Old Mauger heard the seven blasts and looked up from the limestone pile.

"That's the signal," said T'loch, smiling.

Mauger knew this as it had been pre-arranged. His double heart was thumping in his chest. He glanced back at the pile, and decided that he had consumed enough to give him the buoyancy he needed. He belched and a jet of flame shot out from his mouth, narrowly missing incinerating a bumblebee that had been buzzing around in close proximity to the dragonly snout. The insect, clearly enraged by its near immolation, thought about stinging said snout, but on this occasion evidently decided that discretion was the better part of valour and flew off, buzzing angrily.

"Well, that seems to be working all right," observed T'loch, still smiling.

The dragon looked at him. "I think I'm about as ready as I'll ever be," he said, the tone still a trifle morose, but less so than it had been when the magician had first arrived, thanks to the effects of the potion given to him earlier.

"Right then. Off you go and good luck! I'll see you later when the fun's over."

Without further ado, the dragon crawled to the mouth of the cave, eased himself out into the open, flapped his wings and headed skywards.

T'loch stood in the entrance and watched Mauger depart, keeping an eye on him for a few moments to make sure that he was all right. Then he left the cave, concealed himself behind a suitable rock a short distance away and settled down to wait.

* * *

Grosnez, Piton and Clychard La Cloche saw Old Mauger fly off as they made their way through the marsh towards his home. After stopping briefly to watch him, they hurried on, Grosnez insisting that there was no time to lose. They duly reached the foot of the scree slope and scrambled up it to the cave's entrance.

Once there, Grosnez turned to his servant: "Right, Piton, you can stay outside and keep watch."

Piton gladly complied with his master's orders; skulking around inside dragon lairs was not high on his list of favourite activities.

The other two entered. Grosnez reached inside his cloak and pulled out a small, reddish ball. He muttered a few words, incomprehensible to the union chief, and then tossed the ball towards the roof of the cave with a deft movement of his right arm. There was a loud crack, and the gloom of the cave's interior was dispelled by light; not a blinding, overpowering light, but sufficient for them to see their surroundings clearly.

With visibility thus improved, they started to make their way towards the back of the cave.

"By Ker! Look at those!" exclaimed La Cloche, his piggy eyes growing wide with greed as they alighted on the pile of jadeite axes, their finely polished surfaces shining in the yellowy-orange glow from the ball, now hovering near the cave's ceiling. "That lot must be worth a fortune!" He strode over to the axes and began to stuff some of them into the large leather pouch slung from his waist.

"I dare say," said Grosnez, his face wearing an exasperated expression. "But we haven't time for those now."

"There's always time!" declared La Cloche as he added another two axes to those already in his pouch.

Grosnez clicked his tongue in annoyance. "Look, he said, "if things go according to plan, we'll be richer than we've ever dreamt."

"Supposing they don't?" said La Cloche.

"Why shouldn't..." He broke off, a smile temporarily softening his sharp features. He had spotted a recess in the back wall of the cave.

"What is it?" asked the union chief.

"Over there," said Grosnez pointing towards the nook in question. "The shell should be in there."

"What're we waiting for then?"

"Indeed!"

Grosnez strode over to the rear wall. Despite the light from the glowing ball, the interior of the recess was deep in shadow. He could have moved the ball closer to illuminate it better, but he couldn't be bothered. Instead, he reached inside and felt around with both hands. They touched something cold and a little clammy. Instinctively he withdrew them, but even as he was doing so, he realised that it was nothing more than seaweed. He resumed the search.

"Well, is it there?" demanded La Cloche impatiently.

Grosnez ignored him. The fellow annoyed him. Still, all being well, he would not have to put up with him for much longer. Rummaging around, he found something hard wrapped up in the weed. *Ah!* he thought. *This must be it.* He pulled the object out and, brushing off the few strands of seaweed sticking to it, held it up to the light.

He slowly turned the turtle shell around in front of his eyes, scrutinizing its every feature. He was glad that it was a small example, measuring only six thumbs or so by four, and thus easily concealable. He found himself thinking of the particularly large specimens he had heard that the priests of certain distant lands used – apparently they were so big it required two people to carry them.

He paid particular attention to the lines criss-crossing the shell's inside surface. He imagined the sea-dragon liquid coursing through these grooves, revealing them with unparalleled definition. The shell was now his, his alone. The power he would now be able to wield.

"Is that it, then?"

The union chief's voice broke into his reveries. He had forgotten he was there. "Yes," he said, without taking his eyes off the shell.

"Give it to me. I want to look at it."

Grosnez frowned, handed the other the shell without saying anything.

La Cloche grabbed it greedily from Grosnez' grasp. His eyes once again grew wide as he in turn held it up to the light.

"I'll have it back now, mon vier," said Grosnez firmly after a few moments. "We haven't time to hang around here."

The union chief hesitated, then gave it back. The other parted the front of his cloak and carefully put the turtle shell into his waist pouch.

Having got what he had come for, Grosnez took one last look around Mauger's home. Just as he was on the verge of retrieving his illumination ball and leaving, he suddenly noticed something, something that in his single-minded determination to get the shell he hadn't spotted before.

"Aha!" he exclaimed, and strode over to where a distinctive ovoid object was reposing next to a pile of white chunks of dragon food. "So *this* is where it's got to!"

"What?" queried La Cloche, staring at him blankly.

"My egg," replied Grosnez, carefully picking up the sea-dragon egg that T'loch had entrusted to Old Mauger's care. He began to gently stroke its leathery surface. "You recall I told you it had been stolen from my cave. I wonder how it ended up here."

"Ah yes," said La Cloche. "You mean the one you took from old Verman Clouet."

"That's not the point, that!" snapped Grosnez.

He knelt on the ground, gingerly putting the egg down beside him and extracted a hide bag from inside his cloak. He pulled it open and carefully put the egg into it. He then took hold of the two ends of the leather thong laced through eyelets set into the bag's rim and drew them together, tying them in a secure knot. He got

The DRAGON of ANGUR

to his feet and, looking up at the ceiling where the glowing ball was still hovering, muttered a few words. It promptly spiralled down towards him, growing dimmer as it did so, and when it was within reach, he grabbed it and put it back inside his cloak. Then, picking up the bag and clutching it to his chest, he headed for the mouth of the cave.

La Cloche followed reluctantly. He had stuffed as much as he could into his pouch, but wanted to take more and bitterly regretted not having brought sacks of sufficient capacity to cope with his greed.

"Right," said Grosnez as soon as they were outside the cave, "let's get this lot home."

CHAPTER TWENTY-FOUR

THE CONTEST

Such was his popularity that Old Mauger's arrival over the Bay of Aube was greeted by a tremendous outburst of cheering from the crowd gathered on the beach. To show he appreciated their support, he let out a roar of approval and looped the loop directly over their heads. Then he flew over to where the contestants were lined up further down the beach next to the row of large clay urns filled with dyes, and hovered above them at what he judged to be a reasonable height – not too high for their first shot to have no chance of hitting him, but not so low that he would present a ridiculously easy target.

Philipot du Moncel, who had the, in his opinion dubious, honour of acting as referee (at least, though, he could look out for the dragon), dropped his right hand and the first batch of arrows was loosed in Old Mauger's direction. Despite the size and relative proximity of the target, they all missed. The crowd cheered and clapped. Mauger began to slowly circle the contestants while they reloaded their bows with arrows dripping with dye from the urns. To the crowd's delight, the second salvo missed as well.

In fact, it was a while before any of the arrows got anywhere near the dragon. The contestants were not helped in their endeavours by the offshore breeze that seemed to gust just when they let fly their arrows. All the shots from the first few rounds went well clear of their mark and quite a few landed in the watching crowd, several members of which ended up on the receiving end. The soft tips ensured that there were no injuries, but the coloured dyes left a vivid impression on skin, hair or clothing.

One of those hit was Philoche du Tus, the renowned Lesurian adventurer, and the stentorian bellow he let out as a result was almost audible above the din of clapping and cheering. To those standing next to him, it most certainly was. Some of them had to physically restrain him (not the easiest of tasks with someone of his build) from charging off to the archers and committing a mischief on one or more of them.

* * *

"You found it, then?" asked Piton when the other two emerged from the cave's mouth. He had been nervously waiting for them just outside, occasionally peering inside to see how they were getting on, and was relieved that they would all soon be leaving the area.

Grosnez nodded. "Yes, mon vier." He clutched his bag a little more tightly to his chest.

Piton looked at it suspiciously. It seemed to be bulging rather more than he thought it should have done with only a turtle shell in it. Maybe it was a larger shell than he had anticipated. He thought about making a comment, but instead asked: "Are we going home now?"

"Yes."

"Are we going back the same way?" his servant then enquired in a worried tone.

"No," said Grosnez bluntly. "I want to get back as quickly as poss'ble, so we'll go up through the Beauval - that's our most direct route. I doubt we'll bump into anyone on the way – they should all be watching the contest."

"We won't have to go into the, er, forest, will we?" Piton was terrified at the prospect.

"Well, as you know, parts of it do spread into the valley," said Grosnez. "So, yes, we will." His mouth twisted into a malicious leer. "Don't worry, mon vier. I doubt you'd be considered much of a meal, so they prob'bly won't bother with you. Clychard, on the other hand, has more meat on him, so they'd go after him instead, especially as he can't run very fast and so would be easy to catch."

Piton went pale and La Cloche shot Grosnez a nervous look. The union chief had only ventured into the great forest once, and even then more by accident than design, but it had been an experience he had never forgotten. He had had a run in with a wild boar that he had inadvertently disturbed, and had only just managed to escape by clambering up a tree, a feat not facilitated by his less than athletic body shape, to which Grosnez had just alluded. He had waited in the tree for what had seemed like ages until the animal had finally grown bored with hanging around at its base and had disappeared, snorting with frustration, into the crepuscular depths of the forest.

"Come on! Let's get going!" ordered Grosnez imperiously as he slung the bag with the sea-dragon egg over his right shoulder to make it easier to carry.

They half climbed, half slid down the slope of loose earth and stones in front of Mauger's cave, turned right at the bottom and set off smartly along the path through the marsh. A thin mist was hanging over its black, brackish pools and Piton kept casting anxious looks at these, dreading to think what eldritch horrors might be lurking in their dark depths. He would be glad when they got home – *very* glad indeed.

* * *

Mauger wheeled to avoid another arrow and then went into a dive, heading straight for the beach. Four arrows had by now found their mark and the dragon's belly bore green, ochre-brown and blood-red splodges from their sponged tips. Of the twelve contestants involved, Hugo de Hambye had scored two hits and the fellow called George from Alb one. The tips of George's arrows were soaked in a blood-red dye, which tonally was very similar to the ochre-brown one, especially when viewed from a distance. He was sure that two of his arrows had hit home, but in point of fact one fired by de Hambye's fellow Armorian, Jean Le Flecheur, using the brown dye, had been responsible for the fourth strike.

Despite their absolute belief that one of them was going to win the contest, none of the von Rotsteinens had as yet scored a hit. One of Gunz's arrows had come very close, but had been deflected off course by one of Rodrigues de Menga's. This had not been a deliberate tactic on the part of the Iberian, but the result of one of those million to one chances that in all probability neither contestant would ever encounter again. As for Mindel, if the dragon was finding the *Red Bison*'s supposedly ferocious appearance in any way intimidating, he certainly wasn't showing it.

Mauger pulled out of his dive a matter of feet above the sand and flew directly in front of the Elders' canopied rostrum, his slipstream buffeting the structure and causing the venerable sages to utter gasps of surprise. The archers ran along the beach in hot pursuit, frantically trying to reload their bows as they did so. One, the lanky Armorian Anquetil L'Efflanqueur, was so busy watching the dragon that he failed to notice that Manuel de Viera, who was a particularly swarthy Iberian, had stopped to attend to his bow. The resultant collision sent both of them flying and the air in the immediate vicinity was promptly filled with liberal quantities of international invective.

The dragon began to climb, gaining height with considerable speed. Then he dived towards the contestants, who released their arrows just as he levelled out. Three managed to hit his belly, making a tally of seven. Despite the softness of their tips, the force of the arrows' impacts had initially taken Old Mauger by surprise, but by now he was used to them. In fact, he was beginning to rather enjoy himself and was now trying to think of ways he could make this contest more interesting.

Then, as he climbed away from the beach for what seemed like the umpteenth time, an idea occurred to him and he smiled a dragonly smile...

* * *

As they hurried along the path, it seemed to Grosnez that the mist over the marsh was growing thicker. Perhaps there was a sea fog coming in, in which case that would wreak havoc with the dragon contest if it were dense enough. The others had noticed it too, and before long they could all feel its cold, clammy fingers caressing the exposed parts of their skin and trying to grope through their clothing. They increased their pace, having no desire to stay in the area for longer than was absolutely necessary.

It was Piton who saw the lights first. They struck his peripheral vision, causing him to stop and turn in their direction. "Wh.. what's *that*?" he asked in a shrill voice, pointing at the column of glowing dots that had begun to rise out of the swamp on his left.

The others stopped too. They watched as the lights swirled upwards in a spiral of twinkling luminosity, which then moved en masse towards the path where it hovered behind them for a few moments. Then slowly, inexorably, it began to advance towards them. Something about it filled them with unease and they broke into a run, Grosnez keeping a tight grip on his bag to safeguard its contents. Every so often, they looked nervously over their shoulders to check on the column's progress.

"Faster!" yelled La Cloche breathlessly. "It's gaining on us."

The resultant collision sent both of them flying

Running as fast as he could, driven by sheer terror, Piton failed to spot a small patch of bedrock projecting from the surface of the track. Catching his right foot on it, he stumbled and fell headlong. Temporarily winded, he lay still for a moment, sprawled face down, tasting dirt. Then he eased himself into a sitting position, twisting round to look fearfully at the approaching cylinder, the luminous dots composing it a swirling blur of yellowy-white light. It was almost on top of him.

"Come on, Piton!" called La Cloche, who had seen him fall. "Get up!"

Still running, Grosnez glanced back over his shoulder. His face creased into a frown. "Piton, move!" he bellowed.

But the hapless Le Malin remained rooted to the spot, transfixed by the luminous column. He opened his mouth to scream as it reached him, but no sound came. He shut his eyes. Next moment, it passed harmlessly over him, leaving him unscathed, and continued along the path.

The other two stopped running, stood and stared at it, mouths agape.

"Quick!" said Grosnez. "Stand aside and let it through."

He and the union chief stepped to opposite sides of the track and the phenomenon passed swirling between them. As it went by, Grosnez noticed that a vaguely familiar, pungent odour emanated from it. He realised on reflection that he had smelt this before, during a particularly intense thunderstorm when a bolt of lightning had struck a tree uncomfortably close to where he had been sheltering.

"Well, what do you make of that?" La Cloche's face wore a somewhat bewildered expression as he watched the cylinder spinning away from them along the path.

"No idea," replied Grosnez. "I've seen lights over marshes before, but nothing as, er, organised as that thing."

As they stared after it, the lights forming the mysterious column began to grow dim, and then the whole thing suddenly evaporated, vanishing into thin air.

"Wh... what was that?" asked Piton, who had rejoined his companions.

His master ignored him. "Right, let's get a move on. I want to get this lot home and we've wasted enough time already."

So saying, he swung the bag with the sea-dragon egg over his left shoulder, adjusted the pouch around his waist containing the turtle shell and strode off along the track.

Piton Le Malin and Clychard La Cloche followed, both continually casting nervous glances at the marsh on their left, wondering what fresh horror would next erupt from its depths.

* * *

Old Mauger had decided that the contestants were having it too easy, particularly Hugo de Hambye whose green dye constituted five out of the ten splodges now adorning the dragon's belly. Of the remainder, two (one red and one brown) were the result of strikes by the Albian, George and the Armorian, Le Flecheur (still on one apiece), while the Iberian, de Menga, using a blue dye, was responsible for the other three. The Teutons still had not scored a hit, and their frustration, not to say annoyance, grew with every missed shot.

To make things a little more difficult, the dragon moved out to sea, to a position just out of range of the competitors' bows - as they found out when the next volley of arrows fell short, landing harmlessly in the water. Now, to stand a half-decent chance of hitting the target, they were forced to wade in until more or less waist deep.

This was all very well for those who lived in maritime environments and were used to bathing in the sea, such as the three Iberians and the trio from Armor, but for the others it was a rather intimidating experience. This was particularly true of the von Rotsteinens, hailing as they did from the Teuton forests many days travel from the nearest stretch of salt water. In fact, they had been distinctly nervous during the whole crossing from Armor to Angur, which had only added to the misery caused by the seasickness from which they had all suffered.

Although the two Albians, George and McTavish followed the Armorians and the Iberians into the waves, albeit warily, the four Teutons stood on the shoreline, protesting vigorously, insisting that Mauger's actions gave the others an unfair advantage and demanding that he come back closer to the beach.

As they were vociferating in their own tongue, the dragon did not understand a word of what they were saying, but worked out from the beckoning motions of their arms what they wanted him to do. However, he responded by doing a spectacular belly flop into the water, sending a series of waves of respectable height in the direction of the contestants, nearly knocking some of them off their feet and relieving George of his bow. That worthy now splashed and spluttered around in a frantic attempt to retrieve his weapon as the sea played games with him, washing it clear just as he had it within his grasp, although he did manage to get it back in the end.

But the more significant effect of Old Mauger's immersion was that it successfully washed most of the dye off his belly, wiping the score card almost clean, as it were. *Almost*, because for some reason Hugo de Hambye's green dye seemed to be more waterproof than any of the others as three out of his five strikes remained, diluted admittedly, but still there nonetheless.

"Way to go, Mauger!" called Pierre de Lecq, who was watching with Gastelois, Sylvia, Thière de Guérin and Marie-Hélène.

"Most of the marks seem to have been washed away," observed Thière.

"Yes, that will have upset them," said Gastelois, smiling. "Good old Mauger! And they probably thought they'd have an easy time."

"Do you think he did that deliberately, then?" asked Sylvia. She was standing very close to Gastelois, her excitement at watching the competition overriding any concerns she might have about her husband seeing where she was. Albert de Richolet, however, was himself too engrossed in the contest to notice what she was up to.

"Yes," replied Gastelois.

"Ooh, this is exciting!" exclaimed Marie-Hélène, grabbing Thière's arm.

He looked at her and smiled, then said: "I think that the one using the green dye could well win now, as his marks are the only ones that seem to have survived the ducking. What was his name again?"

The others performed a collective shrug of the shoulders.

"Not sure," said Pierre. "Hamb something, I think."

"Well, he's going to want his dolmen if he does win," said Sylvia.

"I know," said Gastelois. "It'll be interesting to see what the Elders do about it."

"Yes," agreed Thière, nodding. "It most certainly will."

* * *

Grosnez, Piton and Clychard La Cloche had reached a fork in the path. The right-hand one led up to the mouth of the Beauval, a densely wooded, steep-sided valley that opened up in the southern slopes of the main Angurian plateau.

"We go that way," said Grosnez, pointing towards the valley. "'Through there and up on to the high land above. Then we'll skirt round the edge of the forest, keeping as close to it as poss'ble, and be home before you know it!"

Although it was bad enough that they would be going into part of the great old forest while making their way up through the valley – Piton, like many of his compatriots, believed without question the tales of nameless terrors lurking within its depths – he was relieved that they would be staying outside it once they reached the plateau.

"Come on!" ordered Grosnez. "There's no time to dawdle." With that, he strode off up the right-hand path in the direction of the Beauval, his servant and the union chief following reluctantly. Then, just as they were nearing it, a series of all-too-familiar glowing dots materialised in the gloom between the trees crowding the valley mouth, and then flowed out into the open where they formed themselves into the strange, swirling cylinder of all-too-recent memory. It hovered above the track, barring their entry into the valley.

"What *is* that thing?" demanded Grosnez, addressing no one in particular.

"Wh... what are we going to do, Grosnez?" whined Piton.

"Shut up, fool! I'm thinking." He moved to one side and then to the other, seeing whether he could bypass the object by going around it, but each time it moved so that it was directly in front of him.

"Well, we're not going to get very far by going ahead," observed La Cloche, a touch of sarcasm in his voice.

"No, it appears not," agreed Grosnez, stroking his chin pensively. Then an idea occurred to him: "Last time, it passed over Piton without harming him, yes?"

The union chief nodded. "So?"

Being blessed with a sixth sense in these matters, Piton looked at the two of them, dreading what was coming next.

"Piton, mon vier," said Grosnez somewhat slimily, "I want you to see whether you can crawl under that thing."

The word 'doubtful' fails spectacularly to describe the look that came over the unfortunate Le Malin's face. But he knew that it would be pointless to argue, and so, dropping onto his hands and knees, he began to crawl towards the swirling, luminous column.

He had not gone very far before the latter began to emit a deep hum. He froze, rooted to the spot. Suddenly, a bolt of lightning rent the air with a violent 'crack' as it shot forth from the cylinder and incinerated the ground not very far from his head.

"Aieee!" he shrieked, and hugged the path, involuntarily covering his head with his hands in the subconscious hope that this would offer it some protection, presumably against another bolt. The smell of what we now call ozone hung in the air.

"You okay, mon vier?" queried Grosnez with mock concern. "For one moment there, I thought you were going to be turned into a steaming black pile!" He gave an evil chuckle. "You know, the sort people step over."

His servant got to his feet and hastily retraced his steps. He did not want to tempt fate by staying too close to the speedily rotating column.

"What do you suggest?" asked La Cloche.

Grosnez frowned. "Don't know," he muttered, and lapsed into silence. The other two looked at him, waiting for him to come up with an idea, Piton casting anxious glances at the swirling luminosity nearby.

"Well," Grosnez said eventually, "there are two other valleys we can try – Haule and Valmont. Come on!"

He set off back down the track, his servant and the union chief hot on his heels, neither of them wanting to stay in the vicinity of the strange column for any longer than was absolutely necessary.

When they reached the fork, they rejoined the path they had taken from the dragon's marsh and continued westwards. Behind them, the cheering and shouting from the crowd watching the contest was clearly audible, but, although they could see Old Mauger in the sky above the bay, the marram-cloaked sand dunes that lay between the path and the beach prevented them from seeing either the competitors or the onlookers; not that this bothered them, as it meant that they were themselves hidden from the view of those on the beach.

They duly reached another fork, but no sooner had they taken the turning for the Val de la Haule, its wooded mouth a mere fifty yards or so ahead, than the glowing dots once more appeared amongst the trees, and moments later the swirling, luminous cylinder was yet again barring their way.

"The Teus take that thing!" swore Grosnez, glaring at it. Then he made a decision.

"We won't bother trying Valmont," he said. "I don't see the point. We'll head for Aube instead. There's bound to be a boat there we can, er, borrow."

"A boat?" queried Piton.

"Yes, a boat. We'll sail around the coast and get home that way."

"But, Grosnez, supposing someone sees us," said Piton.

"He has a point, him," said La Cloche, nodding slowly.

"No one will see us, mon vier. They're all too busy watching the contest. Now come on!"

"I hope you're right," muttered La Cloche as he started to follow Grosnez, who was already hurrying along the track towards Aube, the bag with the sea-dragon egg still slung over his shoulder. Piton brought up the rear, continually glancing behind him to see whether the luminous cylinder was following them. But it remained hovering in front of the Haule valley mouth.

Over in the east, the noise from the throng was as loud as ever, Old Mauger still performing aerial acrobatics as he tried to avoid the contestants' arrows.

Eventually, they reached Aube, and, to their relief, found that the place was indeed deserted, as Grosnez had suspected would be the case. They made their way to the harbour, where a number of boats lay, bobbing gently at their moorings. Grosnez was relieved to see this. The inlet connecting the settlement to the sea, being tidal, could dry up completely at the harbour end at low water, but fortunately the tide was currently in flood and, although it had only turned relatively recently, it meant that there was sufficient water in the harbour to float the boats.

With no one around to challenge his actions, Grosnez jumped into the water and waded, waist deep, to the nearest craft, a leather-hulled coracle capable of taking six people.

"Piton, untie the rope!" he shouted to his servant as La Cloche, following him, tripped over the root of a nearby alder and entered the harbour with an undignified bellyflop. "Way to go, mon vier!"

he called over to the union chief as he grabbed hold of the side of the boat. Then leaning in, he carefully put the bag containing the sea-dragon egg in the vessel's bottom before clambering aboard. "Piton, hurry up!"

Spluttering and coughing, La Cloche duly reached the coracle. He made a valiant attempt to heave himself into it, but once again his shape mitigated against such athletic activities, and he managed to get himself stuck half in and half out, his rotund torso weighing down on the port side so that the craft listed alarmingly. Grosnez, realising the danger, pulled him in before the threatened capsize could take place and La Cloche flopped into the bottom of the boat like a blubbery seal sliding off a rock.

Grosnez grabbed one oar of a pair lying lengthways across the three wooden planks placed across the interior of the leather-hulled vessel and which served as seats. Settling himself on the middle one, he slotted the oar into one of two niches on the starboard side and then repeated the operation with the second oar on the port side. He began to row.

A sudden yelp from the harbour side followed by a splash reminded Grosnez that his servant was not yet in the boat. Glancing in the direction of the noise, he saw Piton frantically swimming in his direction, but rather than stop and wait for him to catch up, he decided to keep rowing, although to be fair, he did slow down a little. The unfortunate Le Malin had still been holding the mooring rope when his master had set off; the rope had tautened and he had been jerked off his feet and into the harbour.

Piton, though, was a good swimmer and he soon caught up with the coracle. La Cloche, sitting in the stern, helped him aboard.

"Right," said Grosnez, "you can take over the rowing. Clychard, you go up front." He pulled the oars in, then got up and made his way to the stern seat while La Cloche gingerly moved towards the bow, the boat rocking from side to side in response to this sudden unexpected activity and shipping some water in the process.

"Get a move on!" Grosnez said irritably to Piton when he reached the stern. He pulled his hapless servant roughly from his seat and propelled him forward, sending him sprawling towards the centre of the boat.

"Give me a chance!" moaned Piton, as once again the coracle rocked in response, taking on board some more of the harbour's liquid contents.

Sinclair Forrest

"I'll give you a chance to swim back to shore if you don't shut up and start rowing," snapped his master, holding on to each side of the boat and trying to dampen the rocking motion. "Now get on with it!"

Piton sullenly took the oars and reluctantly did as he was bid. The boat headed along the tree-lined inlet leading away from Aube, making for the open sea.

* * *

Unseen by the three fugitives, Vraicer T'loch had followed them to Aube. The lights he had summoned from the marsh and the forest had done their job, forcing them towards the settlement. He now shadowed them, walking stealthily along the path that snaked through the trees on the eastern side of the inlet as Piton rowed the stolen coracle down it. Although the boat was only a matter of a few feet away and he could see its occupants clearly, they had no idea that he was there. Away to his left, sounds of cheering and clapping erupted from time to time as the contest continued apace. The trees blocked his view of it, but it was obviously going well.

When the craft eventually emerged from the inlet into the open sea, T'loch watched its progress for a little while longer from the cover of an alder tree standing very close to the shore. Once he was sure that its occupants were too far away to see him, he walked out from behind the tree and sat down in front of it, his back resting against the trunk. Then he lowered his head, closed his eyes and concentrated hard.

Gradually, the image of a large, predominantly bulbous form with a long, sinuous neck began to take shape in his mind's eye, materialising from dark, murky surroundings. As the thing came into better focus, a head appeared at the end of the neck, while along either side of the creature's body, just below the level at which the front and rear flippers protruded from each flank, there ran a row of luminous dots, glowing with a spectral, yellowy-green light.

T'loch concentrated harder...

* * *

From his vantage point high above the bay, Mauger could see a large, odd-looking vessel approaching Le Mont Noircissant from the west. It was nothing less than Leoville de Vinchelez's strange catapult-carrying catamaran, barely under control and listing to

The DRAGON of ANGUR

port as it sailed wallowingly towards the headland, its four projectile filled cargo-coracles still miraculously under tow behind it.

Now bored with the contest, the old dragon decided to fly over for a closer look at Leoville's marine contraption.

Grosnez spotted him. "Faster!" he shouted, casting an anxious look at Mauger wheeling over the bay. "Row faster! I think the bloody dragon's seen us!"

"I'm rowing as fast as I can, Grosnez," protested Piton breathlessly, peering fearfully at the approaching dragon.

Grosnez shot him a disbelieving look; he was sure his servant was not trying hard enough. At his feet, the bag with the sea dragon egg rolled from side to side in time with the motion of the boat, bathed in the seawater sloshing around in the bottom.

"It would help if the wind was in our favour," observed La Cloche. "Then we could have used the sail."

"What sail?" said Grosnez in a sarcastic tone. "If you bothered to look, you'd see this boat doesn't have one."

"Aw, but that's true, that," said La Cloche. "I would've taken a boat with one, me."

"There wasn't time to pick 'n' choose," snapped Grosnez, glaring at him.

Old Mauger flew overhead, patently not the slightest bit interested in them, heading for the southern tip of Le Mont Noircissant.

"Where's he off to?" asked La Cloche, staring after the dragon.

"Who knows?" replied Grosnez, a pensive look on his face.

"Oh well, if we still want to go faster, why don't we use these?" suggested the union chief, kicking a spare pair of oars lying in the bottom of the craft.

"You can if you like, mon vier. I've no intention of doing any more rowing."

"Well, I will," said La Cloche. He reached down and pulled the oars out, laying them lengthways to one side of Piton and Grosnez. Then he stood up quickly – too quickly - to move closer to Piton. The boat rocked alarmingly, shipping a quantity of water that washed over Grosnez' bag, which was by now well on its way to becoming thoroughly saturated.

"Sit down!" commanded Grosnez. "Before you capsize us."

La Cloche sat down, ashen faced. Leaning forward, he lifted one of the spare oars by its blade, intending to slot it into a nearby niche in the starboard side. As he did so, it swung round and the handle clouted Grosnez on the shoulder.

Grosnez let out a cry of pain. "By Ker!" he swore, clutching at the injured part. "Be more careful!"

"Sorry!" apologised the union chief. He managed to get the oar slotted into place while Piton did his best to keep the boat on an even keel and on course. La Cloche then attempted to position the second oar, Grosnez watching him warily from the stern, leaning as far back as he could to minimise the risk of being struck again.

"Right," said Grosnez, once the oar was successfully located in its port side slot, "you and Piton change places – it'll balance the boat better."

This manoeuvre was carefully undertaken, Grosnez holding on to the sides of the boat until the other two were settled and the rowing resumed.

It was a little while before La Cloche and Piton managed to synchronise their efforts, and until that occurred, the craft progressed through the water with a sort of drunken, corkscrew motion akin to that of Louvel Le Soulard weaving his way homewards after a typical session in *The Prancing Pouquelaye*.

Grosnez stared passed the two rowers at Le Mont Noircissant headland approaching off the starboard bow. Its southernmost point was getting steadily nearer. Soon they would be rounding it and heading away from the Bay of Aube. Then it would not be long before they would be out of sight of the assembled throng on the beach.

A dull, tapping sound caught Grosnez' attention. La Cloche heard it too and stopped rowing. Both men looked at the bottom of the boat where the bag with the sea dragon egg was almost floating in the water collected there.

The noise came again, clearly from the bag.

"It's hatching!" exclaimed La Cloche. "The egg's hatching!"

"Let's see, shall we?" said Grosnez calmly, but his heart was thumping in his chest as he picked up the bag, untied it and carefully removed its contents. Now he was holding the egg, he could feel the tapping through its leathery surface.

"What's happening?" squeaked Piton anxiously, trying to peer over the union chief's shoulder. "What's going on?"

"Nothing!" snapped Grosnez. "Keep rowing!" He gently placed the egg at his feet, watching it intently.

Piton favoured him with a sullen look, but did as he was told.

The tapping sound was continuing with increasing vigour. The egg's occupant had clearly had enough of its confinement and was determined to get out as quickly as possible. A section of the leathery shell split open and a long, bluish-green snout pushed its way through, widening the crack further. Soon the rest of the head was out, two black eyes surveyed the new world now encountered and a toothy mouth opened to emit a piercing squawk.

Piton let go of both oars in alarm.

"Help it!" said Grosnez.

"I'm not touching it!" said La Cloche emphatically.

"Scared it might bite?" sneered Grosnez.

"You help it, then."

"I think it can, er manage," said Grosnez hastily as the baby sea dragon pushed itself further out of the egg.

"Thought you'd say that," said La Cloche smugly.

"Is it a boy or girl dragon?" asked Piton, craning forward to get a better look, curiosity overcoming his initial fear.

"How should I know?" said Grosnez. "I'm not an expert."

The creature gave another loud squawk and finally broke free of the egg, flopping on to the bottom of the boat where it lay, panting and spluttering in a pool of seawater.

"Per'aps we should give it a name," suggested La Cloche.

At that precise moment, the baby dragon looked up at the union chief, squawked in what seemed like delight and leapt on to his knees. La Cloche recoiled, raising both arms in alarm. Then he slowly lowered them again as the animal settled itself in his lap, making gentle croaking noises, and he realised that it was not going to attack him.

"Aw look at that!" said Grosnez. "It thinks you're its daddy!"

La Cloche grunted, but before he could make any articulate comment, from out of the blue there came a stentorian voice shouting an urgent warning:

"Get out of the way!"

A large shadow began to fall over the boat, blocking out the sunlight.

"Out of the way!" The voice was frantic, desperate even.

Grosnez looked up, his jaw dropped with great rapidity and the blood fled from his face to his feet. La Cloche wheeled around where he sat, inadvertently knocking the poor baby dragon off his lap from where it fell to the bottom of the boat with a yelp mingling surprise with fright. Piton turned around at the same time as the union chief and what his eyes beheld caused him to let rip such a piercing shriek of alarm that the sea dragon instinctively covered its head with its front flippers to protect itself.

Bearing relentlesly down on them under full sail, its crew barely able to control it, was Leoville de Vinchelez' marine catapult. So engrossed had the occupants of the smaller craft been with watching the hatching of the sea dragon that they had failed to notice not just that the larger vessel had rounded the headland, but that they had drifted straight into its path. Its twin-hulled bulk now loomed over them, the catapult arm and its bucket arched back like a scorpion's sting poised to strike, the bow sail and the sails on either side of the arm flapping noisily in the stiff breeze.

What happened next was as spectacular as it was inevitable. Before Grosnez and his two companions had a chance to take any avoiding action, or even to jump clear, the two vessels collided. Leoville's lumbering monster tossed Grosnez' small, fragile craft into the air, flipping it over like a cat playing with a mouse and causing all three of its occupants to be flung unceremoniously out.

Being the heaviest, Clychard La Cloche travelled the least distance, doing a stunning bellyflop into the foaming brine a matter of feet from the starboard hull of Leoville's boat. Piton's headlong progress was arrested by the vessel's forward sail, which cushioned the impact, but he then slid off this and landed heavily on the deck below, which did not. He bounced off the deck and slid under the water. The boat, still under way, passed safely over his head as he came up, spluttering and gasping for air, between the two hulls.

Grosnez inadvertently performed the most sensational aerial display. Having been in the stern of his boat and thus the furthest from the point of impact with Leoville's contraption, the trajectory of his flight was higher and longer than that of either of his two companions. Passing to port of the catamaran-catapult's foreward sail, which he managed to avoid by a matter of inches, and just missing the central tower, he then landed heavily in the bucket, which shook under the impact. The catapult arm, iffily secured at best, promptly burst its restraining twines and shot skywards, flinging a dazed and confused Grosnez towards the heavens.

Old Mauger, who had been hovering nearby watching the unfolding events with some considerable amusement, now saw the hapless magician head straight for him. Waiting for just the right moment, he opened his mouth, yelled "Howzat?" (a term he had learnt from Otis) and snatched Grosnez out of the air, closing his jaws firmly but gently before his prize could fall out.

"Put me down!" demanded Grosnez, struggling in Mauger's maw. "Put me down at once!"

The dragon was in no great hurry to oblige. He would deposit his prisoner when he was good and ready, and in a spot of *his* choosing. He executed a one hundred and eighty-degree turn and flew towards the shore, heading for the multitude assembled there.

Meanwhile, all was not well with Leoville's catamaran. The force of the arm's release was so great that it ripped the vessel in two, destroying the support tower in the process and scattering timbers and crew with equal indiscrimination. Separated from the transverse decking that had held them together, the two hulls slowly turned turtle. The port one, punctured in several places, filled with water, rising up like a duck taking a dive, and then headed for the seabed emitting gurgling and sucking sounds in evident protest. Those crew members who had been clinging to it, slid or jumped off before it disappeared and swam towards the starboard one, which was still afloat and taking on human flotsam, Clychard La Cloche included.

The union chief was lucky to have made it that far. When he had been flung into the water, he had still been wearing his waist pouch. Under normal circumstances, that should not have posed a problem, but on this occasion the pouch had contained the jadeite axes he had purloined from Old Mauger's cave, and the weight of these had overcome the natural buoyancy afforded by his shape. Faced with the choice of sinking or swimming, he had reluctantly jettisoned the pouch and its valuable contents before they had taken him to a watery grave.

Leoville de Vinchelez himself was clinging to a large piece of timber, wondering what had gone wrong. His initial feeling of disconsolation at what had happened had been replaced by scientific interest. Clearly he had miscalculated the forces involved in firing the catapult. The funny thing was that, although the three attempts during the previous week at launching the thing had not gone exactly according to plan, the vessel had remained intact. On reflection, he could only conclude that the earlier trials had somehow weakened the structure.

As for Piton, he was holding on to another piece of wood not very far from Leoville, pushing it ahead of him as he tried to paddle towards land, all the while looking around him in a state of considerable nervous anxiety.

His plan was to make for the nearby headland of Le Mont Noircissant. Once safely ashore, he would head for Grosnez' place as fast as he could and then take one of his master's boats from the cave below. He would probably sail to Lesur, as he felt reasonably sure that he would find sanctuary there. Certainly he rated his chances as better there than if he stayed on Angur; he had seen Mauger flying off with Grosnez and felt positive that his master would not be in for an easy time once he had been delivered to the Elders - Piton was pretty sure that that was what the dragon had in mind.

All hope of a safe landing on the shores of the headland was soon dashed, however. He suddenly became aware of what appeared to be a great, dark, bulbous mass rising from the depths directly below him. As it drew relentlessly nearer, yellowy-green lights along its sides twinkled into view. He now knew exactly what the thing was and the knowledge paralysed him with fear, but even if he had been capable of movement, he would not have been able to swim clear in time.

The head broke surface first, about ten feet ahead of him, quickly followed by a long, bluish-green neck, trailing seawater. As the head turned towards him, it brought the ventral side of the neck into view; this was paler than the dorsal, more a sort of milky green colour. The great hump of the creature's body surfaced soon after, raising Piton into the air with it.

There was a sudden squawk from behind him and he swung round, heart beating as if fit to burst from his chest, to see the baby sea-dragon perched on its mother's back regarding him inquisitively, head cocked to one side.

He turned back to face the front. Black eyes met his with a cold, unblinking stare as he clung, trembling uncontrollably, to the mother sea-dragon's smooth, blue-green back. Then, before the hapless Le Malin had time to do anything to prevent it, the head swept down towards him, mouth open, and picked him up by the scruff of his neck.

The huge creature then began to swim for the shore, not of the nearby headland, but of the central part of the Bay of Aube where everyone had gathered to watch the contest, Piton dangling helplessly from its mouth, too terrified to do anything.

Old Mauger, also heading for the shore, had seen what had happened to Piton. Grosnez, who had been complaining vociferously since his mid-air hijacking, had by now grown quite hoarse and was on the point of losing his voice entirely when the dragon landed in front of the Elders' canopied platform and dropped him unceremoniously at their feet.

Grosnez landed in an undignified heap. As he staggered somewhat drunkenly to his feet, the people, who had moved back to make space for Old Mauger to land, now crowded in around him and the dragon, intrigued to find out more. Most of them had witnessed the destruction of Leoville's vessel and the more eagle-eyed among them had spotted Old Mauger catch something in mid air. Now that that object had been dropped in their midst and they could see what, or rather who, it was, they wanted to know what was going on.

The Elders likewise wanted some answers. This was a most unusual situation, without precedent in point of fact. Gaetan Le Sterc called repeatedly for the crowd to be silent, but he had little chance of being heard above the general din.

Old Mauger could see that the Elders' chairman needed some assistance and so he pointed his long snout up in the air and let out a great roar. A jet of flame shot skywards. It had the desired effect and the crowd fell silent.

But just as Le Sterc was about to give forth, the hubbub started again, for some people had noticed the dragon's marine cousin heading for the beach. At first, the unfamiliar sight of this creature had filled the onlookers with something between awe and downright terror. The less brave amongst them, not knowing what to expect but fearing something dire, turned on their heels and beat a hasty retreat, deciding to watch the proceedings from a safe distance. Those that stayed began pointing wildly out to sea, shouting excitedly to attract the attention of their more unobservant fellows.

As the animal approached the beach, the watchers realised that something appeared to be dangling from its jaws, something that wriggled and squirmed incessantly.

When the sea-dragon was as close in to shore as she dared without beaching herself, she spat Piton contemptuously into the shallows in front of her. Then, as several brave souls waded in to drag a coughing and spluttering Le Malin out, she backpaddled for a few yards before turning and heading out to sea. One she had reached water of sufficient depth, she plunged quickly beneath the waves amidst a cloud of foam and spray.

Piton was taken to stand alongside Grosnez in front of the Elders. He looked around him, wild-eyed and bemused, still traumatised by his recent experience.

"Right," said Le Sterc as the crowd once again fell silent. "Would somebody mind telling us what exactly is going on?"

But before his question could receive an answer, twelve stalwart fellows, led by Hugo de Hambye, pushed their way through the throng.

"Oh, what is it now?" sighed Le Sterc as they purposefully strode up to the Elders' platform.

"I take it," said de Hambye, hands planted firmly on hips, "that the contest is now over?"

In all the confusion, everyone had forgotten about the dragon contest, except for the competitors themselves, that is.

Le Sterc glanced over to where Old Mauger was standing quietly amidst the crowd, scratched his head and then examined his fingernails. "I suppose it must be," he said non-committally.

"Well," continued de Hambye, who evidently either had been elected or had elected himself as the contestants' spokesman, "if it is, it would be nice to know who the winner is."

"Can't you see we've got more important issues to deal with just at the moment?" said Le Sterc irritably. "We'll deal with the contest later."

"When?" demanded de Hambye, and his fellow competitors reiterated the question.

"As soon as we're ready," said Le Sterc firmly, and the Elders behind him on the platform nodded and muttered in agreement.

Hugo de Hambye was about to say something he might live to regret when, at that precise moment, another voice cut in, a deep, rich, sonorous voice not native to these parts: "Perhaps I can help?"

Everyone looked as a tall, cloaked figure emerged from the crowd and stood in front of the Elders. He bowed courteously and then pulled back the hood that had been covering his head.

It was Vraicer T'loch.

CHAPTER TWENTY-FIVE

SHENANIGANS ON THE SEASHORE

There were a quite few gasps from the assembled multitude when T'loch revealed himself. Although he was a familiar sight in some parts of Angur and to some people, his appearances at public gatherings were extremely rare. On this occasion, he had surreptitiously joined the throng, just one of the many people who had gathered to watch the contest.

Grosnez breathed a sigh of relief when he saw T'loch. At last, here was someone who could vouch for him and verify his story. But he was in for a rude shock.

"If I may be permitted," said T'loch, stepping forward in front of the Elders' platform.

Gaetan Le Sterc looked at Cou-Cou La Tanche, who nodded. "Proceed," said Le Sterc.

Those of the other sages who had not fallen asleep during the contest or its immediate aftermath were regarding the magician with looks that ranged from mild interest bordering on indifference to intense fascination.

"Grosnez," began T'loch, "I must congratulate you on your idea for the dragon contest - it has been a most splendid event." He favoured the other with a bow, a faint, some would have said slightly mocking, smile on his face.

Grosnez acknowledged the compliment with a nod of his head.

"You may have wondered why our friend here would suggest such a contest," continued T'loch.

Grosnez gave him a puzzled look, wondering where this was leading.

"Well, I've been watching the activities of these two for some time now," said T'loch, inclining his head towards Grosnez and Piton, "and as soon as I found out, I knew precisely why he had suggested it."

The DRAGON of ANGUR

He paused, as if collecting his thoughts. Grosnez was regarding him intently, an increasingly worried expression on his face. He dreaded to think what revelation was going to materialise next.

"Go on," prompted Le Sterc.

"To get Old Mauger out of his cave."

"And why would he want to do that?"

"So that he could search it," stated T'loch matter-of-factly.

"What for?" enquired Le Sterc.

"A turtle shell."

Grosnez went pale. Piton was staring at the ground, shaking uncontrollably.

"A turtle shell?" queried Le Sterc. There was some mumbling and muttering from the Elders seated behind him. He glanced back at them. They were all now staring at Grosnez intently.

"Yes indeed, a turtle shell, repeated T'loch. "But a special one from a particular type of turtle, and used, amongst other things, for divination purposes. I will tell you in due course why Old Mauger had one, but for now suffice it to say that he did.

"Friend Grosnez knew about the shell and its capabilities, and somehow found out that there was one in the dragon's cave. Being greedy for power and influence, he wanted to possess it so that he could foretell the future and be able to control people and their lives."

He paused, his eyes sweeping from left to right across the Elders. "In particular," he continued, "he wanted to control you!"

"*Us?*" queried Le Sterc, clearly startled by the revelation. There was much expressing of surprise and amazement, not just by the sages behind him, but also by the gathered populace who had been listening to T'loch with rapt attention, hanging on his every word.

"Yes, all of you." He waited while the implications of what he had said sank in.

The Elders all looked at one another, exchanging remarks of incredulity. The very idea that someone should seek to gain power over *them*, the chosen leaders of the people!

The people themselves found the notion equally unbelievable, although it has to be said that there were those who felt - quite strongly in some cases - that certain of the Elders should have at least some of their powers taken away from them and that in general they should be held more accountable for their actions.

Le Sterc called repeatedly for quiet and the hubbub duly subsided.

Grosnez, who had until now remained silent, found his voice. "This is absolute nonsense!" he protested.

"You're denying it, then?" asked Le Sterc.

"Absolutely!"

"Well then," said T'loch, "perhaps you would like to show us what you have in that pouch there?"

Grosnez fingered the pouch he was still wearing around his waist, clearly undecided as to what to do next, but before he could reach a decision, his mind was made up for him. Three worthy onlookers marched up to him, and while two of them held his arms, the third attempted to wrest the pouch from his person. Grosnez struggled, telling them to leave him alone and to mind their own business, but to no avail. The object was duly removed and handed to Vraicer T'loch.

"Right," said he. "Let's see what's in here."

With that, he opened the pouch and extracted the shell Grosnez had earlier placed inside it in Old Mauger's cave. He held it up for all to see.

Excited chatter broke out amongst the crowd, those further back craning past their fellows in front to get a better view. Le Sterc raised his hand and the people quietened down.

"Can I see it please?" he asked.

"Certainly." T'loch handed it up to him. "On the face of it, it doesn't appear particularly interesting, but if you look, you will see a number of lines criss-crossing the inside surface."

The chairman held it up in front of him and nodded slowly.

"It is those lines that are read by those with the right skills and used for divination," T'loch went on as Le Sterc gave the shell to Cou-Cou La Tanche. The High Elder examined it and then passed it without comment to La Dame Blanche on his right.

"And Grosnez has the necessary abilities?" asked Le Sterc.

"I believe he does," replied T'loch.

"I remember my father telling me about these years ago," said Torteval Le Grospétard, the Lesurian High Elder, who had just been handed the shell by La Dame Blanche. "He said that there was one on Lesur once."

"That may very well be true," said T'loch.

The DRAGON of ANGUR

"They're very ancient, aren't they?" said La Dame Blanche.

"Indeed they are," confirmed T'loch, bowing politely to the Sersurian High Elder.

"Well, Grosnez, what do you have to say for yourself?" asked Le Sterc, staring hard at the other.

That individual stared back at the chairman, holding his gaze unwaveringly. He had thought about concocting some weird and wonderful story and bluffing his way out of the situation, but in the end had decided that, under the circumstances, telling the truth was probably the best course of action. Whether that meddler T'loch would believe him, time would tell.

"Well?" demanded Le Sterc.

Grosnez stroked his chin pensively, glanced at Piton who was still cowering nearby, then returned his gaze to the chairman.

"I don't know where T'loch gets this idea from that I'm trying to control everybody," he began. "No matter - let him think what he likes. The important thing is, I was only retrieving my own property. You see, that turtle shell actually belongs to me!"

This statement took everyone except Vraicer T'loch completely by surprise. He studied Grosnez carefully, a thoughtful expression on his face, while another verbal cacophony broke out around them as everybody from the Elders downwards noisily discussed the revelation with his or her neighbour.

It took Le Sterc a little while to restore order, but eventually he succeeded. "So it's yours, is it?" he said, peering hard at Grosnez. "How did it end up in Old Mauger's cave, then?"

"My father lost it on a visit here many years ago," the other replied. "I'm not sure how it ended up in the dragon's possession, but it was Piton who managed to find out that he had it."

His servant looked up at him. Surely Grosnez did not expect to get away with this.

"Can you prove any of this?" asked Le Sterc.

Grosnez shrugged his shoulders: "Yes, but I don't see why I should have to - it's up to *him* to make his accusations stick." He glared flint daggers at T'loch.

That worthy stroked his beard with slow, deliberate movements. All eyes were upon him as people waited for some species of a response. Grosnez had called his bluff. Making the accusations stick might not be as easy as he had thought. There was, however, the glowing liquid. The vial was still in Grosnez' possession, doubtless hidden away in a safe place - in his home more likely than not. He could tell the Elders how he had hidden it in Gastelois' new dolmen, how Escogriffe had found it and had subsequently been robbed off it. Gastelois was a reliable witness, but would the afflicted one's testimony be believed? He needed to get hold of the vial, but somebody independent would have to accompany him otherwise Grosnez could just say that he, T'loch, had planted it in his home.

"Well?" asked Le Sterc, trying to elicit a response from T'loch.

The latter stopped stroking his beard. It was now time to introduce Grosnez' main accomplice. He had so far been reluctant to do so, as the individual in question was not present to defend himself, but he now felt that he had very little choice. And it would be interesting to see how Grosnez reacted.

"Grosnez has not been operating alone," said T'loch. "Apart from the unfortunate Le Malin, there is another." He was watching Grosnez carefully as he spoke.

All eyes were on T'loch. Who could this accomplice be?

"I have been keeping an eye on the activities of the *Dolmen and Granite Workers' Union* for some time now, and in particular those of the head of the local branch." He noted that Grosnez did not bat an eyelid as he said this.

Several of the onlookers nodded knowingly and some exchanged equally knowing looks. They evidently had an idea that what the magician was about to say would come as no surprise to them.

And indeed it did not!

"Clychard La Cloche has been using the union as a front for certain nefarious activities to help Grosnez further his ends. It was due to his, er, efforts that work on Gastelois' new dolmen was..."

"Quite so," said Le Sterc, hastily interrupting him. The chairman did not want the contestants to find out about the unfinished prize dolmen until the Elders had come up with an alternative, which so far they had not.

T'loch got the message and changed tack: "To pay for these, er, activities, La Cloche has been appropriating union dues - building up a sort of slush fund, if you like."

At that point, the surviving hull of Leoville's catamaran came ashore. Still upside down, it beached towards the eastern end of the bay, on the outskirts of Ang-Lenn. Its human cargo wasted no

The DRAGON of ANGUR

time sliding, climbing down or simply jumping off it, glad to have reached dry land safely.

One of these 'passengers' was, of course, Clychard La Cloche. Having seen what had happened to his two partners in crime and surmising that in all probability he himself had by now been implicated in what had been going on, he decided that the situation called for a disappearing act.

Carefully climbing down the side of the upturned hull, he reached terra firma and began walking away from the scene as casually as he could, not wanting to draw attention to himself by departing the scene with unseemly haste.

He had barely reached the bow of the hull when there was a sudden shout:

"Look! There he is! Grab him!"

La Cloche looked in the direction of the voice. One glance was enough. He broke into a run. Bearing down on him were Clarry Le Brocq and two of his fishermen friends.

"No you don't, mon vier!" shouted Le Brocq as he caught up with the fleeing La Cloche and launched himself at his legs, quickly bringing him down.

"What're you doing, you?" demanded the union chief, feigning indignation.

"You seem in a bit of a hurry," said Le Brocq, pulling the other roughly to his feet by the scruff of his neck.

"Let... let me... go!" spluttered La Cloche between choking noises.

"Why? Got somewhere we have to go, have we?"

As one of his friends grabbed the union chief by his right arm, Clarry transferred his grip from his neck to his left arm and together they frogmarched a struggling and cursing La Cloche in the direction of the Elders' platform.

"Aha!" exclaimed T'loch. "Grosnez', er, partner, I believe. We were just talking about you. So nice of you to join us."

The union chief tried to look as though he did not have a clue what was going on.

"Clychard La Cloche," said Gaetan Le Sterc gravely, "some very serious all'gations have been made against you, and from what we have heard, we b'lieve that there is a case to answer."

"Wh... what're you saying, you?" stammered the union chief. He glanced at Grosnez, who was standing nearby with an air of nonchalance, doing his best to ignore the fact that the union chief was even there.

"Yes," said T'loch, eyes flitting from La Cloche to Grosnez and back again. "Amongst other things, we were discussing your slush fund."

"Wh... what slush fund?" said La Cloche. He was making a big effort to look all innocent, but the harder he tried, the guiltier his demeanour appeared.

"The one your union draws on from time to time to, er, help in certain negotiations," said T'loch.

"We don't have such a fund," stated La Cloche as if this were incontrovertible fact.

"In that case," said T'loch, "you won't mind if we search *Levitation House.*"

"Be my guest," said the union chief. "But you'll be wasting your time." His smug expression hid the fact that he was feeling distinctly nervous. This was not a good situation. He wondered what they'd got out of Grosnez. Had they found out about the turtle shell or indeed the vial of glowing liquid?

"What do you know about this?" asked Le Sterc, holding up the shell.

The union chief peered at it. Well, that answered that question. After some quick thinking, he decided that total denial was the best course of action. "Never seen it before in my life," he said. "What is it?"

"A shell," said Le Sterc. "A *turtle* shell." He put particular emphasis on the word 'turtle'.

"Fascinating," said the union chief. "Where did you get it?"

Le Sterc frowned at him. "We got it from Grosnez," he said.

"*Really?*" La Cloche feigned surprise. "And where did he get it from - the beach?"

"No," replied Le Sterc, doing his best to remain calm, "Old Mauger's cave."

La Cloche shrugged his shoulders. "So, Grosnez likes turtle shells. I don't see what that's got to do with me."

Le Sterc looked helplessly at Vraicer T'loch, who had been impassively watching the union chief.

"I think I need to present you with more evidence," said T'loch, stroking his chin slowly. "And witnesses."

Witnesses! This remark took Grosnez completely by surprise and, caught off guard, he glanced at the union chief, having so far successfully managed to ignore him. La Cloche, equally surprised, glanced back at him. *What witnesses? Had they been seen going into or coming out of Mauger's cave? Or taking the boat from Aube?*

The exchange of glances had not gone unnoticed by T'loch, who permitted himself a faint smile.

"And you can provide us with these?" asked Le Sterc, looking hopeful.

"Indeed I can," confirmed T'loch.

"When?"

"By tomorrow morning," stated the other emphatically.

"Good," said the chairman. "One moment." He turned to Cou-Cou La Tanche and the other Elders and held a brief consultation with them.

He then addressed Grosnez, La Cloche and Piton: "We have decided that this matter does indeed warrant further examination. We will therefore meet at the Green Motte tomorrow morning after the solstice ceremony to deal with it. In the meantime, you will remain with us as our, er, guests."

"Your guests?" queried Grosnez, finding his voice.

"Yes. Take them to the Chamber!"

Grosnez' heart sank, as did those of his companions. The *Chambre des Dames* was a dark, dank dolmen perched rather precariously on the eastern slope of the Town Mount. It had originally been the home of a rather eccentric priest, who had claimed to be able to communicate with the Kerions and receive their advice (dubious at best, due to their propensity for mischief). He had shared it with a number of young ladies with whom he had an understanding and who, it was generally believed, were the reason he had lived to an exceptionally advanced age. After his death, the Elders had taken them under their wing and continued the 'arrangement', as well as finding them better accommodation. As for the *Chambre*, it subsequently served various functions before its current one of town prison.

While Piton seemed to meekly accept his fate without protest vocal or physical, the other two were not quite so acquiescent.

"You're making a big mistake!" hissed Grosnez as two burly individuals who had been standing near the Elders' platform approached him.

"You'll regret this!" stated La Cloche emphatically, struggling to get free as his arms were pinioned behind his back by another two. "I have the support of the *Dolmen and Granite*."

"That we will see!" said Le Sterc. "Take them away!"

"Right," said T'loch turning to the Elders after briefly watching the three miscreants being led away, "if I may be so bold, perhaps you would like to deal with the results of the dragon contest. I think poor old Mauger would rather like to get home."

"About time too!" declared Hugo de Hambye.

Le Sterc glared at him. "Er, yes," he said. "Excellent idea. If Old Mauger can, er, come forward, we can count the strikes and announce the winner."

The crowd parted to allow the dragon room to get through. After dropping Grosnez before the Elders, he had retreated a little way from the scene as he did not want to get in the way. He now waddled slowly towards them, wheezing noisily as he was still feeling somewhat exhausted following the afternoon's events. He stopped in front of their platform and let his bulk sink to the ground.

"Will the Referee step forward," commanded Le Sterc.

Philipot du Moncel did as he was bid.

"Let the marks be counted!" ordered the chairman.

Philipot asked Old Mauger to show his belly and the dragon obligingly - and noisily - rolled over, like a dog wanting its tummy tickled.

The result was so obvious that it could be seen without the marks having to be counted. Although all the contestants, even the von Rotsteinens, had scored hits since Mauger's deliberate self-ducking and the dragon's underside was looking rather variegated as a result, the predominance of green splodges meant that the decisive winner was Hugo de Hambye.

"I therefore declare Hugo de, er, Hambye the winner!" announced Gaetan Le Sterc in a suitably pompous tone of voice.

The majority of the losers accepted the result gracefully and applauded the winner along with the Elders and the crowd, but the Teuton contingent went into a huddle and muttered teutonically amongst themselves.

"Ve do not think zat zis is satisfactory," stated Gunz von Rotsteinen when the huddle broke.

The other three nodded slowly, Mindel clutching his bison-horn headdress to his stomach.

"Why?" asked Le Sterc, looking puzzled.

Gunz glanced at his brothers and then stared the chairman in the eye: "Because ve suspect zat ze contest vas fixed."

"*What?*" Le Sterc's face began to assume a purple hue.

"Ven ze dragon vent in ze sea, he knew zat all ze markings other zan zose of zis Hambye vould be vashed off."

"What *are* you talking about?" demanded Le Sterc.

"It vas decided zat Hambye vould vin before ze contest vas beginning," Gunz went on.

"This is ridiculous!" asserted the one who had been declared the winner. Hugo was standing nearby, hands planted firmly on hips, glaring at the Teuton contingent in general and Gunz in particular.

"Ve do not think so," said the other. "How is it zat your markings vere not vashed off?"

Hugo shrugged his shoulders: "I have no idea."

"Vell, ve haf!" Gunz glared back at him. "Ze dye zat you haf been using has treated been so zat it vill be proof against the vater."

"Vater?" queried Le Sterc

"Water," interjected Philipot du Moncel, who had understood.

"Ah," said Le Sterc, nodding slowly. "So, if I understand this correctly, what you are suggesting is that the winner was decided before the contest began; that something was added to his dye so that when the dragon went into the sea it would not wash off whereas the others would, thus giving him an advantage; and that Old Mauger knew this and deliberately dropped into the water to wash off the marks of the other contestants' strikes."

"Zat is exactly vat ve are suggesting," said Gunz, nodding slowly. His brothers did likewise.

Much muttering broke out among the assembled multitude and the Elders. Hugo seriously considered committing an act of gross unfriendliness on one or all of the von Rotsteinens, but was physically restrained by Philipot before he was able to do something he would undoubtedly have regretted. Le Sterc raised both arms above his head and motioned to everyone to be quiet.

"I can assure you," he said when order had been restored, "that there was no such, er, arrangement." He paused, then continued: "Now, we should be happy if you and the other competitors would stay and join us in cel'brating the summer solstice, which takes place, I b'lieve, tomorrow." He glanced at Hacquebuttier Le Grandin, who nodded in confirmation.

The von Rotsteinens went into another huddle. Gunz emerged from it and faced Le Sterc. "No, ve do not vish to remain here," he said. "Ve are returning to ze land of our vater and ve go now. But," he cast his eyes over the crowd, then the Elders, "ve vill be back!"

With that, all four von Rotsteinens lined up in front of the Elders' platform, clicked their heels together, bowed, did an about turn and marched smartly off in the direction of Ang-Lenn, where they had been staying.

The crowd silently let them pass but as soon as they had gone, broke out into excited chatter. Again Le Sterc raised his arms to restore order.

"What about my prize?" called Hugo de Hambye, trying to make himself heard above the din.

"What was that?" asked Le Sterc, cupping a hand around his right ear and making agitated movements with his left arm for the crowd to quieten down.

"My prize," repeated de Hambye, a look of considerable irritation on his face. "What about my prize?"

"Ah yes, your prize," said Le Sterc as the babbling of the rabble subsided. He glanced back at the Elders as if looking for assistance or support. They knew he was playing for time. He turned to face Hugo: "After we celebrate the solstice sunrise, which, as I said, you are most welcome to attend, you will be presented with your prize at a special ceremony at the Green Motte - once we've dealt with Grosnez and his accomplices."

"I hope it's worth waiting for," said de Hambye.

Le Sterc glared at him, but made no comment. He did not like this man and found himself wishing in spite of himself that the von

Rotsteinens had been right, that he had cheated. But he knew that that was not the case.

"Right," said the chairman. "That concludes that." He frowned at the dragon, who was snoring contentedly nearby, still on his back, having drifted off to sleep while Gunz had been making his allegation of contest fixing, then said to T'loch: "Do we wake him, or shall we just leave him be?"

The magician shrugged his shoulders. "I'd let him sleep - he looks exhausted. He'll wake up in due course and go home."

"Fine," said Le Sterc. He then addressed the crowd: "As you are aware, today is the last day of our dear High Elder's Flint Jubilee celebrations. I am sure he has found them most enjoyable and is very appreciative of all your efforts." He turned and beamed at Cou-Cou La Tanche, who gave a slight nod of his head and smiled at everyone in a vacuous manner suggestive of Escogriffe Le Manquais.

"There are more displays and competitions for you to watch or take part in before the day is done," continued the chairman, "and this evening there will be much feasting." He then struck a cautionary note: "I would, however, remind you that tomorrow is the summer solstice and that therefore it will be necessary to rise early to get to the ceremony on time. So enjoy yourselves, but don't overdo it!"

As the assembled gathering began to disperse in search of fresh entertainment, Gastelois turned to his companions: "I don't know why he bothered saying that. Those who are going to overdo it, as he put it, will do so anyway."

"True," said Pierre de Lecq. "Look! There's an aurochs riding competition going on over there. Let's have a go."

"You can, " said Gastelois. "I'll watch - I value my bones."

"Oh don't be such a wimp!" said Sylvia with feeling.

"Oh all right then," sighed Gastelois. "If it makes you happy." He reluctantly followed the others in the direction of the aforementioned competition. He did not share his assistant's enthusiasm for attempting to ride a snorting, bellowing, bull aurochs, the very idea of which filled him with a not inconsiderable amount of dread. Still, he would do it to please Sylvia.

* * *

Later that afternoon, two worthy residents of Ang-Lenn were standing before the remnants of Leoville de Vinchelez' marine catapult and debating its likely fate.

"That seems a bit drastic, mon vier," the first observed in response to his companion, who had just stated that the best thing you could do with it would be to break it up for firewood.

"Well what would *you* do with it?"

The other massaged his chin slowly, contemplating the upturned hull in front of him. "It's quite big. I don't..." He broke off in mid sentence.

"I know," he then said after a few moments' silent reflection. "You could put some windows and a door in it and turn it into a drinking establishment. I mean, it's not as if the town has an abundance of them at the moment."

"That's true, that," agreed his companion, nodding slowly. "Aw, but you have a good idea there, you."

CHAPTER TWENTY-SIX

TRIAL AND TRIBULATION

As Gaetan Le Sterc had reminded everyone, the next day was the summer solstice, and therefore the entire population of Angur (locals and those visitors who had stayed on) was up and about well before the crack of dawn. From their observations at their ritual centre in the south-east of the island, the priests had worked out some time before that this would be the day of the solstice, and Hacquebuttier Le Grandin had duly informed the Assembly of Elders of the fact. The priest of each settlement thereafter told the people.

As the people converged on the centre from all over the island, many of them holding flaming torches to help illuminate the way, the indications were that it was going to be another fine day, which was just as well as clear skies were rather essential if you wanted an unhindered viewing of the sunrise.

In contrast to the general festive atmosphere, the procession slowly wending its way eastwards from Ang-Lenn was a rather sombre one. At its head was the full Angurian Assembly of Elders (the visiting Elders having gone home the previous evening) and immediately behind them came Grosnez Chatel, Piton Le Malin and Clychard La Cloche, marching in single file, arms bound behind their backs. Each was accompanied by two burly volunteers (there had been no shortage of applicants), one on either side, to ensure that they did not try to make a run for it.

Among those in this particular procession were the competitors from the dragon contest, apart from the von Rotsteinens who had left the island in a huff the evening before to return to their native land.

As the column made its way along the path over the southern tip of the Town Mount, Hugo de Hambye noticed the dark mass of what appeared to be a rather fine gallery-dolmen sited on the low promontory to its right. Mindful of what he was to be awarded as a prize for winning the dragon contest, he commented favourably on the structure in question.

"That's the *Pouquelaye des Pas*," said a local within earshot. "But if you think you're getting that as your prize, forget it."

"Oh?" Hugo looked somewhat crestfallen, for he had indeed been thinking that. "Why?"

"Because it's the subject of an on-going land dispute," explained the other. "The Elders commissioned Gastelois, our chief dolmen-builder..."

"He's the one who's been, er, building the prize dolmen," interjected another, but was prevented from expanding on the subject by the look he received from the first.

"Yes," continued the latter. "Gastelois built the one over there for the Elders, but no sooner was it finished than Alphonse Le Tombeur, who had been away from the island during its construction, returned and accused the Assembly of building it on his land.

"He insisted that that headland had belonged to his family since a distant ancestor arrived here and claimed it for his own. Not only that, but he said that you could see his ancestor's footprints preserved in the rock."

"Really?" Hugo was intrigued.

"Apparently so, although I've never seen them myself. Not that there's much chance of seeing them now."

"Oh, why?"

"According to Alphonse, the dolmen's been built right on top of them - now that really did upset him."

"So what's going to happen?"

"Depends on who wins the dispute. If the Elders do, then it will stay where it is, but if Alphonse does, then it will probably have to be knocked down and moved elsewhere - I can't see Alphonse wanting it to stay."

"Is the dispute anywhere near being resolved?"

The other shrugged his shoulders. "Who knows? But Gastelois for one will be glad when it is."

"Why?"

"He's still to be paid for building the dolmen, and apparently won't be until the matter's been sorted." He paused, stared pensively at the edifice in question for a few moments, then went on: "And if in the end the Elders don't win, he may never be paid."

"I'm sure he'll be happy about that!" said Hugo grimly, frowning at the dolmen as the path began to descend the eastern side of the promontory.

At a place known as Dicq des Pas, a little further on down near sea level, the procession passed close to an establishment called *The White Dragon*. As this was a hostelry and some of the walkers were feeling quite peckish and thirsty – especially those who had not had a decent breakfast - you would have thought that time would have been found to make the slight detour required to visit it. There were some lights showing, indicating that the landlord, Harpagon Le Grigou, was up and about. But this was one pub that was deemed best avoided, especially first thing in the morning. It had once been very popular, but that was until someone had stumbled on the landlord's habit of re-using those leftovers from the night before, drink as well as food, that he did not give to the resident swine. It would have been bad enough had these just been the remains of what the customers had been consuming, but all too frequently he recycled what the pigs left as well. 'Waste not, want not' may have been Le Grigou's motto, but it was hardly doing wonders for his business.

In any event, at this precise moment Harpagon was more concerned with joining the solsticial procession than with potential customers. Therefore, as soon as he heard it passing by, he went outside to join it.

And so the column continued on its way. Although there was much chatter and heckling from the islanders bringing up its rear, the three prisoners walked in silence, grimly contemplating what lay ahead.

Grosnez looked over to the south-east, to where the grassy hillock of the Green Motte rose above the surrounding dune-dominated landscape. He had glanced at it periodically ever since it had first come into view from atop the promontory on which the *Pouquelaye des Pas* stood. As he stared at its summit, at the strange megalithic structure silhouetted against the night sky where the stars had yet to be extinguished by the pre-dawn glow over in the north-east, not for the first time did he wonder what fate had in store for him. He suspected that he would most likely be banished from Angur - perhaps for life.

And not for the first time did he curse himself for having trusted Vraicer T'loch. Why on earth had he ever believed that he was with him as opposed to against him? If only he had seen through him.

He now thought it highly likely that T'loch had been masterminding his downfall from the word go. Who else had been involved that he was unaware of? Maybe he was about to find out.

As for his servant, the hapless Le Malin was more than ever rueing the day he had the misfortune to get involved with his master. He had always known that no good would come from it; now he was about to find out to what extent. Unlike his master, though, he had no real idea of what punishment to expect, but he was sure that whatever it was it would be horrible.

During the previous night in the dark, dank interior of the *Chambre des Dames*, he had slept only fitfully, endlessly tossing and turning on the pile of straw that passed for a bed. His sleep had been plagued by nightmares, and when he had awoken, his stomach had been too full of butterflies for there to be any room for the meagre breakfast that had been on offer.

Now, as he stumbled along behind Grosnez, his legs like jelly and seemingly reluctant to obey the commands from his quivering and quaking brain to walk, one nightmare in particular continued to gnaw at his mind. Try as he might, he could not blot out the image of a strange, unknown land where scores, if not hundreds, of Kerions were mocking him, taunting him, jabbing at him with long, pointed fingers because he had yet again failed to complete yet another task they had set him. Was his punishment to be an eternity of toil in some faraway land? Would the Elders really condemn him to such a fate?

But in the dream he had been offered an alternative. A tall, grey, wraith-like figure with indiscernible features had come over to him, put one cloak-enveloped arm around his shoulders and had pointed at Grosnez and La Cloche with the other while muttering suggestions in his ear. The aim of these had been all too clear, but, if push came to shove, would he be able to find the necessary courage to do that which the figure in the dream had tried to persuade him would be in his best interests to do?

Clychard La Cloche continued to do what he had spent most of the previous night doing - blaming everyone but himself for his current situation, particularly his two associates. He peered up at the tree-cloaked headland of Le Mont Tubelin, which dominated the landscape in front of him, its dark mass overlooking the coastal plain to its south on which stood the Green Motte. If it had been daylight, the mound of *Levitation House* would have been clearly visible on the ridge just below the headland's summit, but for now it had been swallowed up by the nocturnal gloom. He found himself wondering when, if ever, he would be seeing it again.

As the procession rounded the southern tip of Le Mont Tubelin, it passed the pair of tall standing stones that marked the entrance to the path leading over the dunes to the Green Motte. The three prisoners all stared at the two monoliths as they walked by them, Grosnez grimly, Piton with dread and La Cloche with a feeling of foreboding mixed with self-pity at what he believed to be the unfairness of his situation.

They were now halfway between Ang-Lenn and the priests' centre in the south-east of the island. Over in the north-east, the sky was gradually brightening, but sunrise was still some way off and there would be plenty of time to get to the centre before the Sun's disc actually put in an appearance above the horizon.

When they duly arrived at their destination, the people were offered the traditional bowls of warm seafood broth from large vessels that had been set up over open fires at the megalithic trilithon that marked the entrance to the ceremonial area. As was the norm on such occasions, they were also all given a specially prepared drink to help them get into the right frame of mind for the proceedings. All except the three prisoners, that is. Much to their chagrin, they were told that, while they could partake of some food, mind-altering drinks were out of the question. They were informed that this was for their own good, as they would need clear heads to answer the questions that would be put to them in their forthcoming examination at the Green Motte.

As with the previous equinox, the solstice ceremony took place without a hitch. The Sun obligingly appeared at the anticipated spot on the north-eastern horizon, its arrival welcomed with the blast of horns and much chanting by priests and populace alike.

Once all the elements of the solstitial ritual, prescribed by tradition and modified by experience, had been observed and performed, the populace made its way en masse to the Green Motte for the next big event of the morning - the keenly anticipated trial of Grosnez Chatel and his accomplices.

* * *

The structure that crowned the summit of the Green Motte was unlike any other on Angur. A short entrance passage of granite uprights roofed by four roughly rectangular capstones of grey diorite led into an oval enclosure just over twenty-seven feet in diameter at its widest point. This consisted of fifteen regularly spaced standing stones, alternately tall and short, the former of the pink, fine-grained granite that composed the Town Mount, the latter of white quartz that gleamed in the sunlight. Abutting against the granite uprights was a series of small chambers, each with its own capstone and with the open side facing the centre of the main enclosure.

The western half of the latter was now occupied by the Assembly of Elders, who were arranged in a tightly packed semi-circle on wooden benches in front of and to either side of Cou-Cou La Tanche. That worthy was perched, somewhat precariously, on a seat atop the capstone of the westernmost side cell, which was also by some measure the largest. There had been a few nail-biting moments while two of his colleagues had helped him into his chair, but he was now safely ensconced in it. The term 'safely' is used advisedly, for the chair wobbled alarmingly every time he moved due to the uneven surface of the capstone upon which it had been placed.

Facing the Elders were the three prisoners, their guards and Vraicer T'loch. Everyone else, including the visiting dignitaries had to remain outside.

"You may proceed," said Gaetan Le Sterc, after receiving the necessary confirmatory nod from the High Elder.

"As I informed you yesterday, began T'loch, "Grosnez wished to obtain the turtle shell so that he could divine the future and control people's lives."

"Rubbish!" stated Grosnez emphatically, interrupting him. "I was only retrieving what is rightfully..."

"Silence!" commanded Le Sterc, cutting him short.

Grosnez glared at him in mute defiance.

"He found out that, to make full use of the shell and enhance its properties, a special liquid is required - one that glows. It can only be obtained from a creature known as a sea-dragon, a beast that very few people ever get to see. You are all very fortunate to have seen one in the Bay of Aube yesterday."

Something made T'loch glance up at the sky. Was it his imagination or was there something happening to the light? He returned his gaze to Le Sterc and the Elders.

"Grosnez discovered the connection between the sea-dragon and the liquid when he and Piton were forced to divert to Sersur on their way back from Alb."

"What were they doing in Alb?" asked Le Sterc, and some of his colleagues nodded, the same question evidently having occurred to them.

"Patience," said T'loch, holding up his hand. "All in good time." He stroked his chin pensively, collecting his thoughts, before continuing: "When they were on Sersur, they were shown hospitality by two locals - they're not as bad as their reputation would have you believe," he added, seeing the expression on some of the Elders' faces, "as I'm sure your own High Elder can confirm." He smiled courteously at La Tanche, who nodded.

Grosnez thought about denying that he had been on Sersur.

"I'd like to call my first witnesses," said T'loch.

Grosnez' face fell.

"Proceed," said Le Sterc.

"Philoche, Philippe," called T'loch, eyes searching the multitude eagerly following developments from outside the circle.

Philoche and Philippe d'Ane, the Sersurian twins who had shown hospitality to Grosnez and his servant during their enforced stopover on Sersur, now stepped into the enclosure via a gap between two of the standing stones. They faced the Elders and bowed courteously to them.

"Have you seen these two before?" asked T'loch, pointing a long, bony finger at Grosnez and Piton.

The twins did not need to think twice before responding. "Yes," they said, nodding their heads in unison.

"Would you like to tell us what happened?"

"We met when we were walking near home," said Philoche. "They and their dragon had just landed in a field. We invited them back to our place for refreshments."

"And they noticed our paintings," continued Philippe. "The tall one..." He hesitated.

"Grosnez?" offered T'loch.

"Yes, Grosnez," said Philippe, nodding. "He seemed very interested in the painting of the sea-dragon our grandfather did, and especially in his use of the milk that glows."

"Sea-dragon milk," stated Le Sterc knowingly.

"Exactly," said T'loch.

Le Sterc motioned to Philippe with his hand: "Do go on."

"Grandfather used some actual sea-dragon milk to paint the luminous spots on the body of the creature in his painting. We told Grosnez that grandfather probably got some of it from our magician, old Verman Clouet."

"I rather think we may have said too much," said Philoche. He jabbed a finger in Grosnez' direction: "But *he* seemed to know about magicians and their dragons."

"Yes, he does," confirmed T'loch. "Rather more, I fear, than is good for the rest of us."

"I don't know what you're talking about," said Grosnez.

T'loch shrugged his shoulder: "Don't worry, we'll see whether you do in due course." He turned to Le Sterc and the Elders: "It was when he found out that sea-dragon milk had been used to paint the luminous spots in the painting that Grosnez probably made the connection between it and the glowing liquid he needed for the turtle shell, realising that they were one and the same."

"This is ridic'lous!" protested Grosnez.

"Silence!" commanded Le Sterc. "You will be given a chance to speak when we have heard T'loch. Until then you will remain quiet. Is that understood?"

Grosnez bowed obsequiously: "As you wish."

Le Sterc favoured him with a withering stare. Turning to T'loch, he said: "You mentioned that Grosnez and Piton had been in Alb."

"Indeed so," confirmed T'loch. "I thought it might be interesting if they were led to believe that they could get information on the whereabouts of some sea-dragon milk from someone in Alb. So I hatched a little scheme with the connivance of the aforementioned Verman Clouet, who is an old friend of mine, whereby they would go there. This necessitated them visiting Verman at his home on Sersur where they found out that they would have to go to a certain Albian village called Piltdown to get the information they wanted."

He paused at this point and massaged his chin for a few moments before commenting: "I have to say that Grosnez really knows how to repay someone's help and hospitality."

"Oh?" said Le Sterc, looking puzzled.

"Yes. While he was a guest in old Verman's home, he saw fit to steal a rather valuable egg."

The DRAGON of ANGUR

Le Sterc opened his mouth.

"Later," said T'loch, raising a hand before the chairman had a chance to speak.

"What nonsense!" declared Grosnez with as much conviction as he could muster, forgetting what Le Sterc had told him. The revelation that Verman Clouet was clearly in league with T'loch in this affair had left him feeling rather flustered.

Le Sterc glared at him. He glared back. The chairman decided not to say anything this time.

"Grosnez decided to get the dragon to fly him and Piton to Piltdown," continued T'loch. "At first Old Mauger wasn't very keen on the idea, but I managed to persuade him to go."

"Why didn't he go by boat?" asked Le Sterc.

"It would have taken too long."

"He was obviously desperate enough to get hold of some of this, er, sea-dragon milk to risk his and Piton's lives - not to mention Old Mauger's," observed Le Sterc. "Pretty selfish, don't you think?"

The Elders and the crowd muttered in agreement.

"Yes," said T'loch, nodding. "I wouldn't have let Mauger go if I hadn't been able to give him something to sustain him on the flight."

"No indeed," said Le Sterc. "Do go on."

"Well, with the aid of my directions, Mauger got them to Alb, landing a safe distance from Piltdown so their arrival, or more particularly their mode of transport, would hopefully go unnoticed by the villagers. They met the local dragon, Otis – Mauger had come down in a marsh by his home – who fortunately for them is a hospitable soul. They rested there until sunrise and then Otis gave Grosnez and Piton directions for Piltdown."

Grosnez was regarding T'loch impassively, trying not to let his feelings show. *You seem to know everything in a remarkable amount of detail, my friend,* he thought. *I wonder how?* This was not the first time he had wondered this. Of course Old Mauger could have told him – he had already come to the conclusion that T'loch and the dragon were in league – but there was something more. Remote viewing? Was it possible that T'loch had mastered that most esoteric of skills? Very few had. If he was capable of it, then that was a disturbing thought, for it meant that he most likely knew a great deal more about what had been going on than he, Grosnez, realised. In fact, he could well know everything. Time would tell.

"Once they reached the village," T'loch continued, "they sought out an old friend of mine, one 'Stone-Ears' Meade."

An old friend of yours, thought Grosnez. *Why doesn't that surprise me?*

"Verman had given them his name when he saw them on Sersur," explained T'loch. Again his eyes searched the crowd gathered outside the circle. "Eddie, can you and 'Stone-Ears' come forward please."

'Hand-Tongue' Eddie and 'Stone-Ears' Meade made their way through the press and rather nervously entered the enclosure.

"As I needed them here in a hurry, I persuaded Otis to fly them here," explained T'loch, noticing the puzzled looks on the Elders' faces and correctly deducing the reason for their puzzlement. He then turned to the Meade and his interpreter: "Can you tell the Assembly what happened in Piltdown?"

Eddie and 'Stone-Ears' both bowed before the Elders. "Certainly," said Eddie and repeated T'loch's words with hand signals for the deaf one's benefit. The Meade smiled broadly at the sages, displaying his fine set of gums with their scattered population of crooked teeth. His halitosis breath could fell the stoutest individual at a good half-dozen paces.

Then the two of them proceeded to relate, with much signing and repetition, what had taken place during Grosnez and Piton's visit to their village. During their tale, Grosnez watched the Meade closely, still as unconvinced as he had been in Piltdown as to how deaf 'Stone-Ears' actually was.

"So, as you have just heard," continued T'loch, "'Stone-Ears' told Grosnez that a vial of sea-dragon milk was buried on Angur, and gave him directions to find it."

"How did 'Stone-Ears' know where it was?" asked Gaetan Le Sterc, looking puzzled.

"*I* told him."

"Of course, I should've realised." He massaged his chin pensively. "But what I don't understand," he said, "is why get Grosnez and Piton to go all the way to Alb to learn the whereabouts of the liquid when all the time there was some here on Angur. Surely if you wanted them to discover it was here you could have arranged for them to find out without them having to make such a huge detour."

"I wanted to see the lengths to which Grosnez would go to lay his hands on it," explained T'loch.

He glanced up at the sky again and frowned. Something was definitely affecting the light - either it was growing dim like the gradual onset of twilight, or there was something wrong with his eyesight and that was growing dim. A thought suddenly occurred to him and he looked to the north-east, squinting up at the Sun for no longer than was absolutely necessary. Then, as realisation dawned, he smiled. Should he say something? No, he decided that he would not. It would be interesting to see the priests' reaction, in particular Hacquebuttier Le Grandin's, when they, too, realised what was going on.

"Everything all right?" enquired Le Sterc, who had been watching him.

"Yes, er, fine," said T'loch, returning his gaze to the chairman and the other Elders. He resumed his monologue: "Once Grosnez and Piton were back here, they wasted no time in finding out where the vial was buried. Imagine their surprise when the directions led them to the site of Gastelois' new dolmen, the one he was constructing as the prize for the dragon contest."

At this revelation, much excited chatter erupted from the watching crowd.

Le Sterc glared at them and called for silence. Once the din had subsided to a level above which he could make himself heard without having to raise his voice, he asked T'loch: "So what did they do next?"

"They went back that night and started digging."

"And did they find it?"

T'loch shook his head. "No, though not for want of trying - ask Gastelois about the number of hastily backfilled holes he and his men found when they arrived on site the following morning. And they would've carried on all night had it not been for an unexpected eclipse of the Moon."

Le Sterc glanced at the dolmen builder, who was standing with Pierre de Lecq and Sylvia d'Arass just outside the enclosure, but did not follow up the magician's suggestion. "How did that stop them?"

T'loch shrugged his shoulders: "I presume they thought that people might come up from Gor to get a better view of the eclipse and so they decided to leave rather than stay and risk being discovered." He paused. "But even if they had stayed and continued looking, they wouldn't have found it."

"Oh? And why not?"

"Because it wasn't there. I had already removed it! In fact, I didn't put it back until later."

His remarks were greeted by a further eruption from the crowd and much muttering from the Elders. What had T'loch been up to? Planting the evidence?

That, of course, was precisely what he had done, and for a very good reason, as he explained once Le Sterc had yet again restored order.

"I knew that Clychard La Cloche was involved in all of this, but I needed to know the extent of his involvement and how far he'd go to help Grosnez."

"I have not been involved," said La Cloche matter-of-factly.

Some members of the crowd laughed disparagingly and the union chief glared angrily at them.

"Go on," Le Sterc prompted T'loch. "What happened next?" Behind him, his fellow Elders nodded their heads vigorously, whilst outside the onlookers leaned forward attentively, those in the front being pressed against the stones of the enclosure by those to their rear, every last person keen to learn more.

"As I was saying," said T'loch, looking at Clychard La Cloche, "there was no doubt in my mind that our dear union chief was in league with Grosnez. I would now like to share with you the part he played in the, er, proceedings."

La Cloche's piggy eyes returned his gaze in a cold, fixed stare that challenged him to do his worst while at the same time trying to give nothing away.

"First of all, there is the question of the meetings you had with Grosnez," T'loch reminded him.

"There were no meetings," said the union chief emphatically.

"Girard!" called T'loch, looking over to the multitude assembled outside the enclosure.

La Cloche and Grosnez' faces both fell as a stocky, ruddy-faced individual emerged from the crowd and made his way into the enclosure to stand before the Elders. After bowing so low that he almost doubled himself in two, he explained how he had gone to Grosnez' home one evening recently to collect his rente of one goatskin of cider.

"When I went in," he said, "*that* was there, talking with Grosnez." He pointed a finger accusingly at the union chief, who looked at him with the expression of one who had just come across a decomposing carcass washed up on a beach.

"Go on," prompted T'loch.

"I got the distinct impression that they weren't best pleased to see me – that I'd interrupted something important."

"So much for no meetings," said T'loch, permitting himself a slight smirk of satisfaction.

"Well, La Cloche," said Gaetan Le Sterc, "what have you to say?"

The union chief held his composure. "I'd forgotten about that." He shrugged his shoulders. "It wasn't anything important – despite what that fool Girard thinks. He's just poking his nose into things that don't concern him."

"That's as maybe," said T'loch. "But we have now established that you met with Grosnez on at least one occasion, despite what you told us. I wonder how many others there were." He stroked his chin pensively with long, bony fingers. "You must have met with him to arrange the concealing of the slush fund." He watched the other closely to gauge his reaction.

La Cloche appeared unmoved. "As I told you before, there is no slush fund. Therefore as it does not exist, there is nothing to conceal."

"Nothing to conceal?" repeated T'loch, smiling sardonically. He turned to the Elders: "I think you'll find that there was." He refocused his attention on the union chief: "How do you account for this, then?"

"Account for what?" asked La Cloche innocently.

T'loch snapped his fingers.

Half-a-dozen men duly appeared from the crowd, each carrying a large sack.

"Empty them!" ordered T'loch.

The men did as they were bid, and as the piles of shells accumulated on the ground in front of them so the expressions of astonishment grew on the Elders' faces and those of the populace close enough to get a decent view.

"We found these last night in a cave below Grosnez' home," explained T'loch.

"Well?" demanded Le Sterc.

Of the miscreants, only Piton had reacted upon seeing the sacks disgorge the shells; the colour had drained from his face faster than a speeding arrow. The other two had realised what they had contained as soon as they had been brought into the enclosure and maintained the air of nonchalance they had been doing their best to exhibit all along.

"Never seen them before in my life," stated La Cloche matter-of-factly.

Grosnez shrugged his shoulders: "They're sea shells. That cave is a sea cave. Shells are going to accumulate in it. What d'you expect?"

"I don't expect them to arrange themselves according to type in neat orderly piles in niches in the cave walls," said T'loch, and his words were greeted with hoots of laughter from the crowd.

"Well, I don't know anything about them," insisted La Cloche, while wondering how Grosnez could have been so stupid as to leave them where it had obviously been easy to find them.

Grosnez remained calm. "Well, you've got me there!" he exclaimed sarcastically, then went on: "They're my life savings."

"Oh yes?" Vraicer T'loch went over to one of the piles, which consisted exclusively of ormer shells. "Impressive collection," he said, picking one up at random. He held it up to the light and examined it closely. "Just as I thought." He took it over to Le Sterc. "I think you'll find that this has been tampered with to make it more valuable. Look at the holes." He handed the shell to the chairman.

Le Sterc held it up and nodded slowly: "Yes, it's had some extra holes drilled into it - three, as far as I can tell." He passed the shell up to Cou-Cou La Tanche, who, after peering at it myopically for a few moments, handed it down to Branleur de Bitte seated just in front of him and slightly to his right.

"So," continued T'loch, "if these are indeed your life savings, you sought to increase their value by forgery."

"I did not!" declared Grosnez vehemently. "If that shell has been tampered with, as you claim, I know nothing about it." He then shrugged his shoulders. "Perhaps they've all had extra holes drilled into them - I understand that there's a lot of it about at the moment - but really I haven't examined them closely."

"That's as may be," said T'loch. "But the truth is, these are not your life savings, are they?"

Grosnez gave another shrug of his shoulders. "Think what you like," he said.

"*Are* they, Piton?" demanded T'loch.

Taken completely by surprise, the hapless Le Malin, who had been cowering, head bowed, not daring to look at T'loch or the Elders, or indeed anyone else for that matter, simply could not help himself and just blurted out: "N... no."

Grosnez glared at him. "Shut up!" he hissed.

"Go on, Piton," said T'loch gently. Then, by way of encouragement: "You know, it'll look better for you if you cooperate."

"Don't listen to him, Piton," said Grosnez, a frantic note now creeping into his voice.

"And why shouldn't he?" asked T'loch.

Piton looked from one to the other and back again several times, clearly undecided what to do.

"You're in a lot of trouble," T'loch reminded him.

Piton thought quickly. The dream came back to him, more clearly than ever. He made up his mind. Heart pounding in his chest, he pointed at Clychard La Cloche and said: "*He* brought them."

The union chief went as white as the limpets making up one of the shell piles.

A hubbub of excited chatter erupted from the watching multitude. T'loch motioned for quiet.

"Really?" he said, smiling. "How interesting."

"I had to help sort them out and, er, st.. stash them in the cave."

"And when was this?"

An expectant hush had descended over the crowd. All eyes were on Grosnez' servant. The Elders were leaning forward, watching him intently.

"Over a period of time. A sack would arrive and we'd all take it down to the cave and sort out its contents."

"What about the forged ormers?"

Piton shrugged his shoulders: "Don't know anything about them, but I suppose they must've got in with the others somehow."

T'loch massaged his chin. "Yes, I can accept that," he said, nodding. He turned to Grosnez and La Cloche: "*Now* what do you have to say?"

The miscreants in question looked at each other, their brains working overtime.

"Well," said La Cloche after a few moments, "some of the shells you found were undoubtedly Grosnez' savings, but the rest I have to confess were indeed union funds."

"So you admit to salting away funds belonging to the *Dolmen and Granite Workers' Union?*" said Le Sterc.

"I admit to *moving* the shells to Grosnez' residence," said La Cloche.

"Hiding them there for your own use."

"No, for safe keeping."

"For your own use," reiterated Le Sterc.

"No, for safe keeping," repeated La Cloche. "There had been some thefts from *Levitation House*. We thought we knew who the culprit was, but we couldn't prove anything. We decided to move the shells in stages to Grosnez' cave where we felt they would be safe from the, er, light-fingered."

"Such as yourself," said Vraicer T'loch, smiling.

The union chief glared at him. "You can think what you like," he said. "But if you'd care to offer some *proof* in support of your contention that I was, er, salting the funds away for my own use, then I'd be glad to hear it."

T'loch looked at him, stroking his chin pensively. Le Sterc and his fellow Elders watched the two of them closely, as did everyone else. The silence was such that you could have heard a bone pin drop.

"Well?" demanded La Cloche after a few moments.

T'loch felt the frustration welling up inside him. He knew he was right, but at this juncture he could not prove it, even with Piton Le Malin's co-operation. Furthermore, and it was this that really got to him, he knew that the union chief knew that he could not prove it.

"I cannot at the moment..."

"You see?" stated La Cloche triumphantly, interrupting him. "He can't prove a thing!"

"No, I don't b'lieve he can!" agreed Grosnez, a smug expression on his face.

All eyes were now firmly fixed on Vraicer T'loch. Was this most enigmatic of magicians going to fail them, when the outcome of this trial had seemed so certain?

"Well?" asked Le Sterc, a distinctly acidic tone to his voice. "What have you to say?"

T'loch bowed deferentially. "While it is true that I am unable – at least for the time being - to offer any proof for my contention that our worthy friend La Cloche was salting away union funds for his own personal use, I do not retract the accusation. But if I may be permitted to continue, there is more that you must hear."

He was, of course, allowed to carry on. He proceeded to relate how Grosnez enlisted La Cloche's help in trying to get work on the prize dolmen disrupted so that he could continue his search for the vial.

He told how La Cloche had persuaded Fanigot Le Bétyle and his fellow members of the Geonnais Commune to hold a demonstration at Mont Mado so that Gastelois would be prevented, or at the very least delayed, from getting the requisite stone from the quarry. The union chief hotly denied that it had been anything to do with him, that to help persuade them to go along with his plan, he had in fact offered to supply the commune with quantities of a mind-altering substance of which the group was particularly fond but which was not the easiest to get hold of. Unfortunately for him, it turned out that T'loch had been able to promise its members something even more desirable, the thought of which had loosened Fanigot's tongue very much in T'loch's favour.

To add to La Cloche's chagrin, the priest in charge of Mont Mado, Maître Abatfalaise Le Gripert, came forward and described in graphic detail how disruptive the strike had been to his quarry and the personal insults he had had to endure. Gastelois was then summoned into the enclosure, and told how he had had to make do with a piece of Mont Mado granite no bigger than a bétyle, which had not found favour with the *Pouquelaye and Earthworks Committee* in the guise of Mannequin de Perrelle.

"Ah yes, the bétyle," said T'loch, briefly smoothing his moustache with a thumb and forefinger. "Tell us more about that."

"Gladly," said Gastelois. He then related how the stone in question had vanished from his site overnight, and how the bowl of bread and the jar of cider that had been left by the rhyolite outcrop for the Kerions had been subsequently found empty in the dolmen next to where the bétyle had stood to suggest that they were responsible for its disappearance.

"But it was nothing to do with them, was it?"

"I doubt it very much," replied the dolmen builder.

"You believe it was Grosnez and Piton," said T'loch, leading him on.

"Most certainly!" stated the other emphatically.

"What rubbish!" declared Grosnez. "I had nothing to do with it."

But he had reckoned without his servant's perfidy.

"Piton?" said T'loch, looking at him.

The hapless Le Malin then proceeded, somewhat nervously, to spill the beans, telling how he had accompanied his master to Gastelois' site and what had transpired once there. The expression on his face when he described how he had had to eat the stale bread from the bowl and the state of the cider in the jar drew much laughter from the crowd, as did his description of their attempts to uproot the bétyle.

"But you didn't spend all your time at the site that evening, did you?" prompted T'loch.

"Wh.. what're you saying, you?"

"Grosnez did, but you didn't."

Piton looked at the ground. He knew what T'loch was getting at, but wasn't sure how much he should say.

"Grosnez sent you down to the feast at Gor with a potion with which you were to, er, lace the food or drink of a number of Gastelois' men."

Piton glanced up at Grosnez, who seemed to be idly contemplating his surroundings, a nonchalant expression on his face.

"It's also true, is it not," T'loch went on, "that you gave the potion to five of Gastelois' team?"

Piton stared at T'loch, opened his mouth as if to say something.

"Well?" demanded Le Sterc. "Are you denying it?"

"Er... I..." Another glance at Grosnez. "Yes... I mean, no."

"Yes you're denying it, or no you're not?" pressurised the chairman.

Piton was clearly distracted; his eyes flitted from side to side. He had noticed some of the potion's victims, who had pushed their way forward to the front of the crowd. Mordu Le Tapin in particular was favouring him with an especially thunderous look. He decided that there was no point in beating about the bush any longer; he had better just come clean and be done with it.

"Grosnez made me do it," he said.

His master clicked his tongue irritably and raised his eyes skywards.

"Go on," said T'loch. "Ignore him."

"Well, I was told to take the potion down to the feast and put it in the food or drink of some of Gastelois' men, as you said."

"And?"

"I had to do it. I had no choice."

"I'm sure you're right," said T'loch.

"So you did poison some of Gastelois' men?" said Le Sterc.

"Yes," confessed the unfortunate Le Malin. "Only five of them, though."

"Five too many!" shouted a voice from the crowd. It was Mordu Le Tapin, keen to see justice done.

Piton looked nervously at Le Tapin, fearing that, from the tone of the latter's voice and the expression on his face, he was about to perform some painful act upon his person.

"The reason for the poisoning," T'loch went on, "was to render sufficient of the workforce incapacitated so as to delay work on the dolmen, to give Grosnez and La Cloche more time to look for the vial – they patently didn't care who they hurt in their search for the thing."

"That is evident," said Le Sterc grimly. "Do go on."

"The union chief, however, had another trick up his sleeve. His next move was to offer Gastelois assistance by way of three workers to replace some of those who had been taken ill. Now, on the face of it, this would seem like a helpful thing to have done, but I'm sure it will come as no surprise to any of you if I tell you that these three had been briefed beforehand to disrupt work on the dolmen."

T'loch's eyes swept over the assembled Elders. Amazingly enough, none of them had dropped off, despite the length of the proceedings; they were all leaning forward, watching him intently.

"Well, as all who witnessed it will probably remember for the rest of their lives, the levitation of the dolmen's capstones did not go, er, exactly according to plan."

Again he paused, his eyes studying both the Elders and the crowd outside the enclosure. He had their absolute, undivided attention.

"Maîtres Sottevast and Le Gripert in particular should recall the incident in question." T'loch's eyes fell on the two priests, who returned his gaze with puzzled stares.

"They were struck by stones fired by two of the men La Cloche had brought along – Pelletier de Merde and Armand Le Bricateur."

"So *that's* what it was!" exclaimed Fielebert Sottevast, and involuntarily massaged the spot on his left thigh where de Merde's missile had struck. He muttered something to Griesensacq Le Gripert and then both priests glared at Clychard La Cloche, who did not see them as his attention was focussed on T'loch.

"Indeed so," continued the latter. "The end result was the priests lost control of the capstone they were trying to levitate and it crashed down on to the two side-chamber capstones, breaking in two in the process."

Another pause; another look at his audience.

"It was yet another ploy to disrupt work on Gastelois' dolmen and, I regret to say, this time it worked."

"I've never heard such a load of aurochs' bollocks in my life!" declared Clychard La Cloche, with all the conviction he could muster.

"Really?" queried T'loch. "That's not what Pelletier, Armand and the third member of your, er, plants, Pierre Le Bécheur, told me."

"I can't think what they could have told you," said the union chief loftily. "I was only trying to help Gastelois out by suggesting he take them on. I can't be held responsible if the three of them decide to fire stones at the priests. If I'd known for one moment that..."

"*Three* fired stones?" said T'loch, interrupting him

"Yes," said La Cloche.

"That's very interesting. If you recall, I only mentioned Pelletier and Armand, which, I'm sure you'll all agree," at this point he paused to look at the Elders, "adds up to two."

La Cloche's face fell momentarily, but he quickly recovered his composure. "I just assumed that all three of them..."

"You're quite right, though," said T'loch, interrupting him again. "They all fired at the priests, only Pierre's shot missed. I know you paid them handsomely to do what you wanted, with a bit more on top to keep quiet afterwords. But what *I* was able to offer them quickly loosened their tongues and they became garrulous in the extreme."

"So what happened next?" asked Le Sterc, leaning forward, a hand supporting his chin.

"No sooner had disaster struck than La Cloche wasted no time going off to find Toubib Le Véroleux to tell him what had happened. That worthy duly arrived at the dolmen with two of his assistants from *Health and Safety*. Needless to say, it did not take long for Toubib to close the site down."

"Which was precisely what Grosnez and La Cloche wanted," said Le Sterc.

"Yes – if you mean the cessation of work on Gastelois' dolmen," said T'loch. He scratched his head, glanced up at the still darkening sky. *Soon*, he thought. *Soon*. Out loud: "But it wasn't actually necessary."

"Oh? Why?" queried the chairman.

"Because Grosnez already had the vial," explained T'loch.

"What d'you mean?"

"One evening, after everyone had left the site, I hid it in the mound," T'loch went on. "Then, a couple of days later, poor Escogriffe managed to get himself blocked up in a recess in the mound where he had decided to take a nap. His plaintive cries were heard by Gastelois' men and he was duly released from his prison. When he emerged, he was clutching the vial, which he had found in the recess where I had concealed it."

"Bit of a coincidence, that," commented Le Sterc. "I mean, him just happening to decide to take his nap in the same spot where you had hidden the vial."

"Well, I suppose he did have some subtle guidance from yours truly."

"Thought as much," remarked the chairman. "Do continue."

"Escogriffe thought he could keep it, on the basis of finders keepers, and set off for home with it. But he had reckoned without Piton Le Malin, who had been spending his time hiding in a nearby tree watching the site. He saw everything, followed the unfortunate Le Manquais and, when the coast was clear, attacked him and relieved him of the vial. He then wasted no time in taking it to Grosnez."

"Is this true, Piton?" demanded Le Sterc.

The hapless Le Malin nodded, averting his eyes to avoid the chairman's piercing gaze and hanging his head in an attitude of shame.

T'loch glanced at Piton and then went on: "Grosnez had had the vial for some time before La Cloche engineered the disaster with the capstone, but La Cloche didn't know this. I'm sure Grosnez could have told him in time, but evidently he didn't bother."

He paused, massaging his chin with slow, pensive strokes, marshalling his thoughts. His audience waited, the majority patiently, but some impatiently, for him to continue.

"Of course, it's my belief that friend Grosnez never intended to tell his, er, compatriot that he had the vial."

"What're you saying, you?" cried the union chief in a tone of some surprise.

"Well, once Grosnez had the vial, you were surplus to requirements. All he then needed was the turtle shell, and his plans to acquire that were, by that stage, well advanced – he could get it from Mauger's cave with or without your help while the dragon was otherwise engaged in the contest.

"He would go on pretending that he didn't have the vial for as long as was necessary. He let you go on with the sabotaging of the dolmen so that you would, in the end, be blamed for that and suffer the consequences, rather than him."

La Cloche's face had gone a vivid shade of purple and he was making peculiar gurgling noises.

"How interesting," remarked Le Sterc. "But I can't say I'm surprised." He glanced at the union chief, who was now favouring Grosnez with a look of the deepest suspicion.

The latter ignored him, choosing instead to regard Vraicer T'loch with a sardonic leer.

"Of course," resumed T'loch, "the worthy La Cloche was equally intent on relieving his partner of the shell and, once it'd been found, the vial as well. What he planned to do with them once he'd got hold of them is anyone's guess, him being no magician – except, that is, in his ability to make union funds disappear, which, I must say, does have a touch of magic about it. My guess is that he intended to sell them to the highest bidder."

Now it was Grosnez' turn to bestow on La Cloche a look deep with the suspicion.

The union chief merely shrugged his shoulders. "I don't know what he's talking about," he said nonchalantly.

Le Sterc looked at him and his co-accused for a moment before turning to mutter something to the High Elder. Then he said to T'loch: "Time is getting on. Perhaps you would now be good enough to conclude so that we can decide what to do with the, er, prisoners."

"Certainly," said T'loch, with a slight bow. He glanced up at the still darkening sky before continuing: "You are all doubtless wondering why Grosnez should have been so keen to gain possession of the turtle shell.

"As I told you yesterday, all such shells have a number of lines criss-crossing the inside surface. These can be read by those with the right skills and used for divination. The application of a small amount of sea-dragon milk renders the lines clearer and thus easier to read and interpret.

"Each member of the Order to which I belong possesses one of these shells along with a vial of the milk. It goes without saying that we only use them for the highest of moral purposes and the general good."

These words were greeted with approving noises from both the Elders and the onlookers outside the enclosure. Vraicer T'loch bowed to show his appreciation.

"Grosnez stated yesterday that the shell belonged to his father, who had lost it while on a visit here a long time ago, and that he was only retrieving what is rightfully his.

"One part of what he said is, you might be surprised to learn, completely true. The shell did indeed belong to his father, who was a highly esteemed member of our Order."

Much muttering broke out amongst his audience and he raised his right hand to request quiet. As the chatter died down, he resumed his monologue: "It is a tradition of our Order that the first-born son follows his father into it, should that son show the requisite abilities. As Grosnez fulfilled the first condition, it was natural that he should be groomed to succeed his father on the latter's demise. At first he showed great promise, but gradually some undesirable traits in his character began to emerge which caused those entrusted with his training to have grave doubts as to his suitability for admission to the Order."

"What sort of traits?" asked Le Sterc.

"In particular, a markedly selfish streak," replied T'loch. "Absolute selflessness is expected of all members of our Order. Considering the powers at our disposal, it can be no other way.

"As time went on, the young Grosnez increasingly showed his own interests to be more important than those of others. It wasn't blatant – he's far too intelligent for that – but it was noticeable nonetheless, in spite of his efforts to conceal it.

"Our problem was what to do with him. At first, his father refused to accept that his son could be the way we believed him to be, but gradually he saw what the rest of us saw.

"Fortunately for us, one day Grosnez took matters into his own hands and informed us that, as he felt that there was no more that we could teach him and that it would evidently be some time before his father joined the ancestors, he was leaving to broaden his horizons. We wished him well and expressed our hope that one day he would return to complete his training."

T'loch paused briefly to glance up at the sky. By now quite a few of the assembled multitude had also noticed what was happening and were periodically casting anxious glances heavenwards. However, the pull of the magician's monologue ensured that their attention was dragged back from the developing celestial phenomenon to him.

"As Grosnez' father grew older and it became clear that his time here was drawing to a close, we became increasingly concerned about what to do with his turtle shell and his vial of sea-dragon milk. It was deemed imperative that under no circumstances must they be allowed to fall into Grosnez' hands – ever.

"After much deliberation, it was decided to conceal it on this island. Not only did I know Angur well, but your dragon, Old Mauger, and I go back a very long way. I felt as certain as I could that the shell would be safe with him. The vial I decided to keep in my own possession. Grosnez is, of course, a native of Angur, but we believed that his home island was the very last place he'd consider looking when, as was inevitable, he began to search for his father's shell and vial.

"His father himself brought the shell to Angur on what turned out to be his last visit here. He entrusted it to Old Mauger's care and then left, never to return."

"How did Grosnez find out that Mauger had it?" asked Le Sterc, and behind him all the Elders nodded to indicate that they would also like to know the answer to this question.

"I'm not sure," confessed T'loch. "But somehow he did. I'd known for some time that he had been looking for it – ever since his father died, in fact. Prior to this, he had already begun to be a thorn in your sides, although none of you probably realised it. Unbeknown to him, I'd been watching his devious dealings and machinations very closely, waiting for the right time to act. When I found out that he had discovered the whereabouts of his father's shell, I decided that that time had arrived.

"I realised that merely apprehending him with the shell wasn't sufficient to expose him for what he is and would most certainly become if things went his way. I had to help him be the author of his own destruction, so to speak.

"I made sure that he found out about the sea-dragon milk, that he would believe that the turtle shell was useless without the 'milk that glows'. I know that that isn't strictly true – you can still use the shells without it, but it makes their lines easier to read, and more accurately too. Grosnez, however, didn't know about that particular use of the milk, as he left us before he reached that part of his training. I was therefore able to use this lack of knowledge to my advantage.

"Once he believed that the sea-dragon milk was essential, I made sure that he would have to go to great lengths to find the vial and obtain some. This would also test how desperate he was to get hold of it.

"I did indeed bury it on the site of the prize dolmen, but I removed it before he and Piton started to look for it there. I then put it back so that poor Escogriffe would find it. I knew that there was a very good chance that Piton, who had been watching the site from his tree, would see him with it, steal it from him and take it back to his master."

At this point, he looked at Gastelois, standing with his friends not very far away just outside the stones of the enclosure: "I am truly sorry about all the grief you've been caused, Gastelois, but it was, I'm afraid, inevitable. I chose the site of the new dolmen because, as the prize for the dragon contest, I knew that to do so would probably produce the best chance of bringing Clychard La Cloche's involvement in all of this out into the open. And, apart from anything else, I wanted to do that because I believed that it was high time your union chief was cut down to size."

He paused for a moment, surveying the crowd. "And in case any of you are thinking otherwise, the idea of the dragon contest had nothing to do with me – I just persuaded Old Mauger to go along with it, for reasons that should by now be obvious. Building a new dolmen for the winner wasn't my idea either."

"But what exactly was Grosnez intending to do with the turtle shell?" asked Le Sterc, and his fellow Elders muttered their desire to know the answer to this question.

T'loch glanced up at the sky. It was by now difficult not to notice the dimming of the sunlight. Several people followed his gaze heavenwards, scratched their heads and frowned. They all wondered why there had been no announcement.

"Once he had mastered the use of the shell," continued T'loch, "which admittedly might have taken him a considerable time, Grosnez would have been able to use it to control and influence people's lives and destinies." He paused to survey his audience for some moments. "Whatever he might tell you to the contrary, be under no illusion that that was not his intention. He wanted absolute power over all of you, so that each and every one of you would do anything – and everything – that he wanted."

He stared hard at the Elders: "And that includes you. His ultimate aim was to become High Elder of Angur." Another pause. "And of Lesur, Sersur and Ortac too. I looked into the future and I saw what would happen."

As he finished speaking, a rumble began to run through the onlookers as the implications of what they had just heard sank in. This quickly grew to a deafening roar as the populace reacted angrily, with much hurling of abuse and invective, to the revelation that Grosnez, this upstart magician, had been scheming and conniving to take over the Assembly of Elders and rule their lives.

As for the Elders themselves, they found it absolutely unbelievable that one of their subjects could behave in such a way. They were highly embarrassed by that fact that this could have been going on under their noses without them realising it. In particular, they felt quite stupid at having been duped over the dragon contest. They gave vent to their feelings in a prolonged outburst of enraged jabbering.

Despite the seriousness of the occasion, Vraicer T'loch watched the Elders with not a little amusement. He could not recall when he had last seen them so animated.

"Bastard!" A stentorian voice suddenly bellowed above the general din. "Let me get at the bastard!"

Forgetting where he was, Tchiard des Ne Touchepas pushed his way through the crowd, vaulted over one of the quartz stones of the enclosure and charged, grunting and snorting, at Grosnez.

Not wanting to get in the way of this aurochs in human form, the two burly individuals who had been guarding Grosnez stepped smartly aside. The colour drained from the latter's face. Quickly grabbing Piton, he held him in front of him as a shield. Desperately trying to free himself from Grosnez' grip as Ne Touchepas' bulk lumbered threateningly towards them, the hapless Le Malin bobbed about like the flotation sac of an *Iberian battle-coracle* jellyfish being tossed around on the surface of a rough sea.

At the last moment, Grosnez flung his servant roughly aside and tried to flee. But he had left it too late. Ne Touchepas caught up with him before he had taken more than a few steps and, taking hold of him with both hands, lifted him high above his head to the accompaniment of much cheering from the watching crowd outside the enclosure.

"Put me down!" squawked Grosnez.

"You got a good view from up there, you?" shouted someone in the crowd, to peals of laughter.

"Throw him as far away as you can, Tchiard!" yelled another.

"Enough!" cried Gaetan Le Sterc.

Either Tchiard did not hear him above the shouting and cheering or he chose to ignore him; either way, he gave no indication that he had heard.

"I said enough!" shouted Le Sterc, so loudly that his voice went hoarse under the strain. "Put him down!"

"As you wish." With that, Ne Touchepas emitted a blood-curdling bellow and launched Grosnez at Clychard La Cloche. The magician's lanky form connected with the union chief's rotund one and they both collapsed to the ground in a sprawling, undignified heap.

The crowd roared with laughter at this display, clapping and cheering enthusiastically.

"Don't they make a lovely couple!" yelled Clarry Le Brocq. More laughter greeted his words, along with whistles and catcalls.

"Get off me!" wheezed La Cloche.

"Gladly!" said Grosnez between gritted teeth. Freeing himself from the union chief, he got to his feet and, glaring at all and sundry, wiped the dust from his clothes with his hands.

Le Sterc shouted repeatedly for order, straining to make himself heard above the continuing tumult. He was supported in his endeavours by a number of the Elders including Branleur de Bitte, who stood up and waved his stick threateningly at the masses.

When order eventually was restored, the chairman turned to mutter something to the High Elder. Then he addressed the prisoners: "I think we've now heard enough. We will consider this sorry saga very carefully and decide what to do with you. You will not have to wait long for our decision."

Grosnez, who had recovered his composure after his encounter with Tchiard des Ne Touchepas, made an audible clicking noise with his tongue.

"Yes?" queried Le Sterc impatiently.

"Don't we get a chance to say anything?"

The chairman frowned, looked at Cou-Cou La Tanche, who nodded slowly.

"Oh all right, if you must," relented Le Sterc. "But keep it brief."

Murmurs of expectation ran through the onlookers. Grosnez regarded everyone through narrowed eyes. His audience returned his gaze, the hostility towards him now silent, but just as palpable as before.

"First of all, I would like to say that, while it is certainly true that Clychard La Cloche assisted me in some of my endeavours, I am not responsible for some of the things he got up to. I do not know what other motives he may have had over and above helping me retrieve what is rightfully mine. And *that*, I can assure you was my *only* motive, despite what you've been told by *him*!"

He glared briefly at T'loch, and then his piercing gaze again swept over his audience, his face set in an expression of unrepentant defiance.

"As T'loch has told you, my father was a member of the same order of magicians as he himself is. As his first-born son, I was indeed being trained to succeed him when he became one with the ancestors. But being the eldest son is not sufficient in itself – one must show certain abilities if one's training is to be successful."

At this point he puffed out his chest in a display of arrogant self-importance: "Needless to say, *I* showed those abilities, and, I might add, in no small measure."

There were some titters from the audience. Grosnez glared in the direction of those responsible. T'loch permitted a faint smile to cross his features, while slowly shaking his head.

"After a while, I realised that I would not achieve my full potential if I continued my training with my father's Order. I therefore decided to leave and seek instruction elsewhere, and I am pleased to say that, after much searching, I found a suitable tutor."

He paused and once again surveyed everyone with his piercing gaze. "It seems, however, that there were those who were jealous of my skills," he went on, looking at T'loch, "and desired to prevent my admission to the Order upon my father's death."

T'loch again shook his head; what he was hearing was coming as no surprise to him.

The accusation that followed was blunt in its directness: "I now know that *he*, Vraicer T'loch, led the conspiracy against me and, it seems, turned my own father against me, his only son. It was only relatively recently, long after I'd left the Order and indeed long after my father died, that I found out what had been going on. I am now certain that, had I stayed, I would have been expelled from the Order. My abilities made me a threat to T'loch and he wanted me out of the way."

He paused again, to allow these words time to sink in. T'loch continued to shake his head.

"So, my father's turtle shell was hidden where it was hoped I would never find it. As for his vial of sea-dragon milk, you heard T'loch admit that he kept it.

"As I said after the dragon contest, I understood that my father lost his shell while on a visit here many years ago. I believed that because that's what he told me just before he died and I had no reason to doubt him. It now seems that, under T'loch's malign influence, he was lying to me.

"Once I discovered the truth, I resolved to retrieve what was rightfully mine. I managed to find out that Old Mauger had the shell in his cave, but I had no idea how it got there.

"When I found out about the vial, I was determined to get that as well; after all, I was its rightful owner. I cannot believe that I actually asked that thing standing there for his help in finding it." He glanced at T'loch. "But I didn't at that stage know about his involvement in the plot against me.

"As for this nonsense about using the shell to control your lives, that's what it is – absolute nonsense. I never intended to do anything of the sort. I would only ever use such a thing for the benefit of my fellow man."

"You finished now?" asked Gaetan Le Sterc, whose patience, like that of most, if not all, of his colleagues, was exhausted.

"Er... yes," replied Grosnez, somewhat taken aback by the abruptness of the question.

"Vraicer, have you anything to add?"

T'loch shook his head: "No." He stared at Le Sterc: "You can choose to believe me or you can choose to believe him. It's up to you."

The chairman nodded slowly. "We will now consider everything that we have heard. You will have our decision shortly."

As Le Sterc turned to consult with Cou-Cou La Tanche and the other Elders, the crowd outside the enclosure began to chatter excitedly, hotly debating the most likely fate of the three miscreants in the arena.

Grosnez stroked his chin pensively. He knew what the outcome would be. Glancing up at the sky, he smiled sardonically.

Hacquebuttier Le Grandin would soon have some explaining to do, which should prove quite amusing.

Clychard La Cloche thought about protesting that he had not been given a chance to say anything, but decided against it as it seemed to him that there was probably very little point.

As for Piton Le Malin, he sat down, cross-legged, on the ground and began to rock backwards and forwards, moaning to himself about how his life had come to this.

* * *

After the Elders had finished their deliberations, which took them hardly any time at all, Gaetan Le Sterc turned to face the prisoners and then, in the gathering gloom, addressed them in weighty tones: "We have considered the evidence and we find that it makes for a totally convincing case against you. You have been found guilty of heinous crimes against the Elders and people of Angur."

Each of the faces of those to whom his words were addressed wore a different expression. Grosnez' was one of downright defiance as he glared at the chairman, while Piton's was the exact opposite – his head lowered on to his chest, only he appeared to be genuinely contrite. As for La Cloche, the union chief was displaying his customary arrogant pomposity. From the self-important look gracing his podgy features, the indication was that he wasn't expecting anything particularly dire to happen to *him*, whatever he may really have been feeling.

"Grosnez," went on Le Sterc, "yours is without question the most serious case. Your father was indeed very wise to have denied you access to his turtle shell – he clearly knew the evil use to which you would put it. Your sole reason for acquiring the shell and the sea-dragon milk was not to benefit your fellows as you claim, but to gain control of this august Assembly and through it the people of this island."

He paused momentarily before continuing: "And would it have stopped there? Probably not. We could envisage you attempting to take over Lesur and after that the other islands, as indeed Vraicer T'loch has suggested.

"As to a fitting punishment, well, in certain circumstances your execution would have been mandatory, and I have to tell you that such a sentence was indeed considered. However, as no lives have actually been lost, we have decided on banishment from this island.

"Grosnez Chatel, we accordingly banish you from Angur for the remainder of your natural life. You will forfeit all your possessions and all rights you had as a resident."

Apart from the defiant glare, Grosnez showed no other emotion as his sentence was pronounced. It was as he had expected. The mention of the possibility of his execution had not particularly fazed him – he had been certain that they would at the very least have considered it, but he had been equally certain that he would not, in the end, have been condemned to death.

The sky was growing increasingly dark as the eclipse progressed. The birds and indeed all of nature seemed to be lapsing into silence, believing night to be falling. Both those watching outside the enclosure and those inside it were casting occasional anxious glances skywards, most viewing it as an ominous portent and some thinking that, under the circumstances, there was something rather appropriate about it.

Hacquebuttier Le Grandin was clearly more than a little embarrassed. An eclipse had indeed been predicted, but not on this particular day. Words would be had with certain priests: those at both centres entrusted with the task of making the relevant observations.

Le Sterc, who had briefly paused to look up at the eclipse, returned his attention to the matter in hand: "You will be taken forthwith from this place back to the *Chambre des Dames*, where you will be held while preparations are made for your departure.

"You will be placed in a coracle which will be towed out to sea. And I'm sure that we will not be short of volunteers to man the towboat."

A chorus of "Hear! Hear!" went up from the crowd, the stentorian voices of Messrs. Le Brocq and Ne Touchepas clearly audible above those of their compatriots.

"I thought as much," said the chairman. "When the coracle is a sufficient distance from these shores, it will be set adrift and you will thenceforth have to fend for yourself. This should not prove too difficult for a man of your wiles, but to assist you on your way, the coracle will be supplied with both a sail and a set of oars, fishing equipment and bait, and a quantity of food and water.

The DRAGON of ANGUR

"Where you go is up to you – and the vagaries of wind and tide." He paused for a moment before concluding: "But if you are ever seen in these parts again and you are apprehended, I can assure you that we will have no hesitation in ordering your immediate execution."

Grosnez, who had been glaring unremittingly during all of the foregoing at the Elders in general and their chairman in particular, now favoured them with a sardonic smile. He glanced up at the sky. The Sun's disc was almost completely covered. *How appropriate*, he thought wryly.

"Do you have anything to say before you are taken away?" asked Le Sterc.

At that moment, the Moon completely covered the Sun. The gloom was accompanied by an eerie stillness; nature hushed as if in humble reverence. Awe-struck eyes gazed heavenwards. Then a gasp arose from the crowd as the corona flashed into view like a celestial ring of fire. For some, the experience was too much, and they dropped to their knees, mumbling prayers to the ancestors.

The Elders and priests were likewise struck dumb by the spectacle, the annoyance of the former and the embarrassment of the latter at its surprise appearance pushed into the background by what they were seeing.

The Moon gradually cleared the solar disc and as the sky brightened, birdsong began to fill the air once more. A hubbub of excited chattering broke out amongst the gathering as everyone discussed what they had just been privileged to witness.

Le Sterc called for order and, once this had been restored, repeated his question to Grosnez.

All eyes were now upon the latter as everyone wondered what he would say.

"I can assure you," he began, "that all of you – every single one of you – will rue the day that you crossed me. You fools have no idea of what you are doing or whom you are dealing with. I may be going, and I may not be back in person, but there are other ways. I will have my revenge in the fullness of time."

Le Sterc glared at him for a few brief moments. "Oh, get him out of my sight!" he ordered irritably.

As Grosnez was marched out of the enclosure by his two guards, his ears were assaulted by the claps, cheers and cat-calls of the watching multitude. Objecting to the way he was being manhandled, he struggled to free himself from his escort, but soon gave up, realising that resistance was futile. He would bide his time...

Once Grosnez was out of sight and the din accompanying his departure had died down, Le Sterc resumed the task of handing down the sentences.

Piton Le Malin was next. As his name was called out, he stood with bent head, eyes downcast, quivering with dread at the imminent pronouncement of his fate. The crowd, now hushed, waited in eager anticipation.

"Piton Le Malin. If it were not for your co-operation, you would be sharing the same fate as your master. We are of the opinion that you are an exceptionally weak individual, who was easily influenced by a particularly evil man, and from whose control you found it impossible to escape.

"We have therefore decided not to banish you from the island, although you will not, in fact, be staying on it."

Piton glanced up at the chairman, wondering what he meant. Then, as the latter continued, he lowered his head again.

"As much for your own good as for any other reason, it has been deemed appropriate that you no longer remain on this island. You will therefore go to live on Sersur..."

Piton looked up, eyes suddenly wide with terror at the prospect.

"...with Verman Clouet," continued Le Sterc, "for whom you will work." He paused, noticing the expression on the other's face with wry amusement. "Of course, if you don't want to, we can always send you off with Grosnez and you can remain as *his* servant."

"No! No!" cried Piton, the expression on his palid features growing even more fearful. "Sersur fine. I live there with Verman."

"I thought as much," said Le Sterc, nodding slowly. "Verman has agreed to it and La Dame has sanctioned it. And you can thank Vraicer T'loch – it was his idea."

Piton mumbled his appreciation, glancing briefly at T'loch.

"Don't mention it," said that worthy. "It was thought that if you were removed from Grosnez' influence and placed with a good teacher, you might with time come to realise the error of your ways to date."

"Indeed so," said Le Sterc. "With time, also, you may one day be able to return here to live. But for now it is better that you stay away – there are those here who would make your life somewhat uncomfortable were you to remain on Angur." He looked over to the crowd, his eyes falling on Clarry Le Brocq and Tchiard des Ne Touchepas, amongst others. "Verman!"

The venerable Sersurian magician stepped forward from where he had been standing next to one of the uprights encircling the enclosure, a short quartz one upon whose top he had been resting his right hand, soaking up the energy rising through it.

"We entrust this sorry person to your care," continued the chairman. "We hope he serves you well." He turned to Piton. "And r'member, misbehave and you will be sent on your way – for good!"

The tone of voice in which this was said left Piton in no doubt as to where he stood. He nodded his head vigorously to show that he comprehended. He would behave himself. He had no desire to be banished like his erstwhile master.

"And as for you, La Cloche," Le Sterc went on as Verman Clouet led Piton to one side, "we had thought about banishing you like Grosnez, but after giving the matter careful consid'ration and taking into account the help you have on occasion given to the workers of this island, we have decided not to."

La Cloche was visibly relieved.

"But we cannot ignore the fact that you have flagrantly abused your position as head of the *Dolmen and Granite Workers' Union*," continued Le Sterc, "nor can we let it go unpunished. You will therefore be r'moved from the post, stripped of all union-related powers and imprisoned in the Chambre for three months, which should give you ample time to reflect upon the sorry situation in which you find yourself. Furthermore, as thanks partly to you we don't have a finished dolmen to award as a prize, *Levitation House* will be confiscated from the union and given to the winner."

La Cloche's face fell.

"I'm not having some union's cast-off!" declared Hugo de Hambye, who had been listening intently from just outside the enclosure. Ignoring the protocol that required him to stay where he was unless specifically invited in, he strode into the restricted area and stood in front of Le Sterc and the Elders, hands planted firmly on hips, mouth pouting defiantly.

"What do you think you're doing?" demanded the chairman, glaring at him. Behind Le Sterc, the Elders were muttering in a mixture of surprise and anger at this unwarranted intrusion.

"It's bad enough, having won the competition, to find that one's prize hasn't even been finished," said de Hambye between gritted teeth, "but now you're suggesting that I accept a second-hand dolmen."

"It's better then nothing," retorted Le Sterc. "In fact, it's a partic'larly fine example and most people would be more then happy to accept it as a prize."

"It's not yours to give," interjected a voice from the crowd.

Le Sterc wheeled round to see a thin-faced man of medium build and no especially distinguishing features emerge from the throng, having pushed his way through from the back. He peered questioningly at the new arrival.

"I said, it's not yours to give," repeated the latter.

"*What?* What're you saying, you?"

Bertholet Le Tubelin glared at Le Sterc: "That dolmen is mine. *He* pinched it!" He favoured Clychard La Cloche with a withering stare of quite exceptional intensity.

"This is ridiculous!" said an exasperated de Hambye. "You're actually trying to fob me off with a dolmen that belongs to someone else."

"But Bertholet," said Gastelois, cutting in, "the Tubelin dolmen was given to the union by your father to use as its headquarters."

"That's true, that," said someone in the front row of the crowd. "I distinctly r'member old Bartholomé handing it over for that very purpose."

"He was diddled!" declared Bertholet emphatically, as if it were incontrovertible fact.

"Look," said de Hambye between gritted teeth, more exasperated than ever. "I don't care about any of that. I was persuaded to come over here to take part in some half-baked competition against a geriatric, half-knackered dragon on the basis that the winner would get a nice *new* dolmen as the prize. I won the competition and I want my dolmen!" He then stamped the ground with his right foot as if to emphasise his claim.

At that point, the High Elder, who had been paying more attention to what had been going on than you might have realised, leaned forward in his chair, which responded to this movement by wobbling alarmingly, and demanded to be helped to the ground. Branleur de Bitte and Etienne de Crochenolle went to his aid and he was soon standing, albeit rather shakily, on terra firma. Pushing downwards on his stick, he then walked unsteadily to the front of the Assembly, occasionally jabbing at the Elders with the stick when he thought that they weren't moving aside fast enough to allow him through.

"W.well," he croaked once he had positioned himself next to Le Sterc, "it s.seems to us that there is, er, only one solution to this problem."

All eyes were on him as he massaged his bony chin with equally bony fingers. What words of wisdom was the old fool going to utter? Le Sterc stared hard at him, dreading what might come next.

What did come next was as generous as it was unexpected. La Tanche's wizened features seemed to be on the verge of cracking apart as he beamed benevolently at the gathering.

"We have decided," he announced, "that we do not wish to keep our own dolmen in the country."

Everyone stared at him incredulously. *What was he talking about? Give up his country residence?*

"Yes," he continued, nodding slowly, "the *Hougue La Tanche*[13] will have a new owner."

"That is, er, a very generous offer," said Le Sterc, looking at the High Elder, a puzzled frown on his face, "and one that you should accept without question," he added, addressing Hugo de Hambye.

Hugo hesitated, looking doubtful.

"It... it's a very fine, er, dolmen," said Cou-Cou La Tanche by way of encouragement.

"Indeed it is!" agreed Le Sterc emphatically.

"I may well accept, then," said de Hambye. He paused, then said: "But only on condition that I can see it first."

The chairman favoured Hugo with a look of distaste. Was there no pleasing the fellow? He looked at the High Elder for guidance.

La Tanche nodded slowly.

"Well," said Le Sterc, "that appears to be settled then." From the tone of his voice, he was clearly far from pleased that the High

---

[13] Hougue – a local name for the mound or cairn covering a passage-dolmen.

Elder had acquiesced to the contest winner's demands. "But we will finish here first and then the Assembly will repair to *The Granite Cabbage* for refreshments before we go anywhere else."

"So when, exactly, are you going to show me this dolmen?" demanded de Hambye. He had grown to dislike the Elders' chairman as much as the latter had him.

"Oh, sometime this afternoon," said Le Sterc vaguely. "You can meet us there."

"And how am I going to find it? I have no idea where it is."

"Oh for goodness sake!" exclaimed Le Sterc irritably. "Ask someone. *Everyone* knows where it is."

"I'll show him," offered Gastelois, who had been within earshot.

"Excellent!" said the chairman. "Now perhaps we can get back to business."

As Hugo de Hambye left the enclosure, Le Sterc turned back to La Cloche: "As I was saying, the union will forfeit *Levitation House*, which it seems, will now be returned to its rightful owner." He inclined his head towards Bertholet Le Tubelin, who acknowledged him with a curt nod.

"If the union wants somewhere as its headquarters," the chairman continued, "it can have Gastelois' unfinished dolmen, which, we have decided, it *will* complete at its own expense."

"And subject to our requirements," interposed Branleur de Bitte.

This drew a bout of cheering from the crowd. La Cloche glared at the Planning chief, but there was nothing he could do.

"There is one further thing," said Le Sterc, motioning with his hand for the crowd to be quiet. "It is high time that poor Escogriffe had a decent home, so we have decided that he will live in the dolmen when it has been completed."

This was too much for La Cloche who, forgetting the predicament he was in, began to object vociferously: "You can't expect us to have *that* living in our headquarters."

"That is enough!" declared Le Sterc. "Furthermore, Escogriffe will become an honourary member of the union."

More cheering from the crowd. Escogriffe, squatting on the ground next to one of the enclosure's granite uprights and busily stuffing a strand of seaweed into his left ear, beamed vacuously at everyone. La Cloche had gone puce with rage and was making incoherent gurgling noises.

"This all seems eminently fair," observed Vraicer T'loch. "And I have something else for friend Escogriffe."

With that, he walked over to the afflicted one, bent down and tapped him gently on the shoulder. "I have a present for you," he said softly.

Escogriffe looked up at him: "A present? For me?"

T'loch nodded, then reached inside his cloak and withdrew a small vial, which he handed to the Le Manquais.

The latter's eyes lit up as they took in the yellowy-green glow from the vial. "My light!" he exclaimed, snatching it from T'loch's hand. "My pretty light! You've found my pretty light!"

"Is that wise?" queried Le Sterc, looking concerned. "I mean, is it a good idea giving him that?"

"Oh, there won't be a problem," replied T'loch, adding: "As long as nobody tries to relieve him of it." This remark was directed at Piton, who lowered his eyes guiltily to the ground.

Escogriffe had jumped to his feet and, to the delight of the crowd who were cheering him on, was running around the enclosure holding the vial aloft and crying over and over: "My light! Look! I've got my light!"

"Oh, somebody calm him down!" ordered Le Sterc, shouting to make himself heard above the racket.

"Let him be!" said T'loch. "He's not doing any harm."

"That's as may be," said the chairman. "But this sort of display is most unseemly, especially here."

T'loch frowned and then looked at Escogriffe, who promptly ceased his antics and went back to squatting in front of the granite upright where he gently stroked the vial while making soft, cooing noises.

T'loch turned to Le Sterc: "Satisfied?"

The other grunted. "Thank you," he said. "Now, I think we can conclude our business here. Take the union, I mean ex-union, chief away. He and Grosnez can enjoy each other's company for one last time."

EPILOGUE

A HOUGUE FOR HUGO

That afternoon, Gastelois de Bois, Sylvia d'Arass, Pierre de Lecq and Hugo de Hambye were making their way along the dusty track that led to the *Hougue La Tanche*, the High Elder's country retreat. The weather continued bright and sunny, the air crowded with birdsong and the hedgerows bordering the path buzzing with insects. It was as though nature, revitalised, was celebrating a new dawn after the eclipse. Only the great central forest, whose eastern perimeter was visible across the fields to the west of the track, seemed reluctant to join in the general feeling of well-being, its brooding mass as sinister as ever.

En route from the Green Motte, they had thrown caution to the wind and had partaken of a meal in *The White Dragon*. The quality of the fare – a selection of shell fish and something that passed for bread – had been variable at best, and had required the drinking of copious quantities of cider to encourage its passage down the gullet. Despite the amount consumed, the cider was having little effect on them, doubtless due to its strength having been diluted, quite literally, by Harpagon Le Grigou who, true to habit, had watered it down.

They were all now feeling slightly queasy, with the odd gripey pain assailing their guts, which suggested that their stopover in *The White Dragon* had not been the wisest of moves.

"Is that it?" asked Hugo, pointing to a large, two-tiered, grass-topped tumulus that had just come into view some distance ahead of them as they rounded a bend in the track.

"Yes," confirmed Gastelois, then grimaced and began to rub his stomach. "Excuse me," he said and disappeared behind a nearby thicket.

The others stopped and waited, listening to the sounds of evident distress emanating from the bushes and wondering if, or more to the point when, they were going to succumb themselves.

"You all right?" queried Sylvia when Gastelois duly emerged, looking somewhat pale.

He nodded, wiping his mouth with the back of his hand. "Yes, but I don't think I'll risk that place again.

His companions agreed. The way they were all feeling, it was highly unlikely that they would ever want to eat in *The White Dragon* again. Harpagon could serve his culinary delights on other unfortunates, but not on them.

They walked on. A few moments later, however, they stopped again when Pierre suddenly shouted: "What's *that*?"

"What's what?" asked Sylvia.

"*That!*" He pointed to the west, towards the great forest.

The others followed the direction of his outstretched arm. Hovering above the arboreal expanse was what at first sight appeared to be a large black bird, but which they quickly realised could not possibly be. For one thing, it was the wrong shape – the neck too long, the body too elongated and the wings not exactly bird-like – and for another, it was just too big.

"Of course!" said Gastelois suddenly. "You know what that is: it's that dragon – Otis, or whatever he's called – that brought those two over from Piltdown. T'loch told me that they're all staying with him as his guests."

"He's carrying something on his back," observed Sylvia, screwing up her eyes.

"Looks like two people," said Hugo, holding his hand above his eyes to shield them from the afternoon sun.

"Probably the two Piltdowners," said Gastelois. "Maybe they're all on a sight-seeing expedition."

"That sounds a reasonable enough explanation," said Pierre, nodding. "If I hadn't been here before – and I presume they haven't – I'd want to have a look around too."

"I'm surprised, though, that Otis isn't with Old Mauger," remarked Sylvia.

"Oh, you can be sure they'll be spending some time together," said Gastelois.

They then continued on their way. All eyes, especially Hugo de Hambye's, were on the grass-topped tumulus ahead of them.

"It certainly looks big," observed Hugo as they approached the mound. "Did you build it, Gastelois?"

"Yes, sort of."

"What do you mean, sort of?"

"My father started it. I just finished it."

"Come on," interjected Pierre. "You did most of it."

"That's as maybe, but it was his design and he did all the groundwork, along with his friend Rutual from Armor. They drew up the plan and decided the shapes and sizes of the stones between them. I merely realised their conception."

"I get the impression you think it's rather special," said Hugo.

"Anything his father was connected with is special," said Pierre, looking at Gastelois. "To the extent that he's too modest about his own achievements. Isn't that so, Gastelois?"

The latter shrugged, but did not comment.

"What *that*?" Hugo had suddenly noticed something atop the hougue, something he thought should not have been there.

"What?" asked the other three, almost in unison.

"That thing, lying on the summit." Hugo waved an outstretched arm at the object in question.

Gastelois was the first to realise what it was. "It's Old Mauger," he said, laughing.

"The dragon?" queried de Hambye, frowning.

"Yes, Hugo, the dragon."

"What *he* doing up there?"

"Maybe he thinks the mound's an egg," suggested Pierre with a wicked grin, winking at Sylvia. "And he's trying to hatch it."

"Don't be ridiculous!" said Hugo tetchily. He was not renowned for his sense of humour. "If that place is going to be mine, he won't be staying, that's for sure!"

The three Angurians looked at one another. They knew very well that if Mauger had got it into his head to use the summit of the *Hougue La Tanche* for the odd nap – for that's what he seemed to be doing – there was very little that Hugo would be able to do about it. If it were a problem for him, he always had the option of not accepting the High Elder's offer.

They duly reached their destination, following the track around the twenty-five-foot-high mound to the entrance in its eastern side. Hugo de Hambye looked up at it, clearly rather impressed. Like the *Hougue du Tubelin*, the erstwhile *Levitation House*, each of the two tiers was fronted by large blocks of pink granite, in this case obtained from the foreshore just to the west of Ang-Lenn, their smooth, sea-worn faces glowing in the afternoon sunlight.

"You could do a lot with those," remarked Hugo, nodding towards them.

"How do you mean?" asked Pierre.

"Well, you could paint nice designs on them. I think it would really enhance the place."

"Sylvia could do that for you," offered Gastelois, smiling.

"Really?" Hugo looked at her with interest.

Sylvia smiled and nodded.

"Excellent!"

They reached the forecourt of the mound and stood staring at the impeccably-finished granite façade that framed the megalithic trilithon of the entrance to the passage-dolmen within. The façade curved around to either side of the entrance, partially encircling the forecourt, and rose up almost to the top of the first tier.

"Not bad," said Hugo de Hambye. "Not bad at all!"

"Glad you like it," said Gastelois.

"I haven't seen inside yet."

"Well, you will soon."

Just then, a loud snort followed by a fit of coughing emanated from the top of the mound. They all looked in that direction.

"I can see them," announced Old Mauger.

The others could not see what the dragon could, but he did have the advantage of height. Gastelois climbed up to join him.

"Over there," said Mauger, pointing with his snout. From the nostrils of this, smoke drifted lazily upwards, its course occasionally disrupted by the slight breeze that tugged at it from time to time.

Gastelois looked in the direction the dragon was indicating. Sure enough, perambulating somewhat unsteadily along the same path he and the others had recently trod on their way to the *Hougue La Tanche*, came the Elders. At their head was Cou-Cou La Tanche, seated astride an aurochs which was being led by a remarkably thin-looking individual. Even at this distance, you could see that there was an air of sonambulance about them all, totally at odds with the vibrancy of nature around them.

Gastelois could see that quite a few of the Elders were missing from this procession. He concluded that the absent ones had probably overdone it at lunchtime and had decided to stay put to sleep off their excesses. He descended the mound to tell the others that the Elders were on their way.

"Thank goodness for that!" declared Hugo de Hambye. He planted his hands firmly on his hips. "Honestly!" he went on. "I feared that we would be here all day."

After what seemed like an eternity, the Elders duly arrived at the mound.

"Greetings!" said Gaetan Le Sterc.

"Greetings!" returned Gastelois, and he and his companions bowed respectfully to the new arrivals.

As she inclined her body with the others, Sylvia's hazelnut eyes scanned the Elders in front of her. To her intense relief, she saw that her husband, Albert de Richolet, was not amongst them. He had evidently decided that his time was better spent elsewhere. She was only too aware of how much he disapproved of her friendship with Gastelois. If only he knew just how friendly the two of them were!

The thin one, who turned out to be the beanpole-like attendant from the Elders' Assembly Hall, helped the High Elder dismount from his aurochs. The animal was much like its burden – particularly decrepit and long in the dotage – and should have been put out to pasture years ago. But a replacement would involve expenditure, and was therefore being put off for as long as possible.

"Wh... Where is the, er, winner of the contest?" asked La Tanche once he was safely on terra firma and Beanpole had handed him his two walking sticks. He peered myopically at Gastelois, Sylvia, Pierre and Hugo.

The latter stepped forward: "I am here – Hugo de Hambye."

"Ah yes," said the High Elder. "So you are." He turned to Le Sterc: "Gaetan, your arm!"

The chairman walked over and took hold of La Tanche's right arm.

"Right," said the High Elder, looking at Hugo, "if you care to accompany me, we will go inside. Gastelois, I should be, er, grateful if you would join us."

"Certainly," said the dolmen builder. "My pleasure!"

The DRAGON of ANGUR

While the others remained outside in the forecourt, Cou-Cou La Tanche, supported by Gaetan Le Sterc and his walking sticks, walked with unsteady gait towards the entrance to his dolmen, followed by Hugo and Gastelois.

"Well," said Pierre to Sylvia once the High Elder and the three with him had disappeared inside, "all we can do now is wait and hope for the best."

"Supposing Hugo doesn't like it, what then?"

"Don't even go there!"

The Elders decided that they would be more comfortable waiting sitting down and so one by one they positioned their honourable behinds on the dusty, reddish-orange clay surface of the forecourt. Once they had all sat down, Sylvia and Pierre did likewise. For the two of them to have done so before any of the Elders would have been disrespectful.

Time passed. Some of the more elderly of the Elders dozed off and began to snore loudly, as did Old Mauger atop the mound, and, if asked, you would have been hard pressed to choose which was making the greater noise. Sylvia traced spirals and other designs in the clay soil with a forefinger, creating intricate interlinking designs from the large repertoire in her mind. Pierre watched her admiringly, and not for the first time found himself wishing that it was him and not his friend she was attracted to.

Eventually, there were sounds of movement from the dolmen's entrance and Gastelois came out grinning from ear hole to ear hole. "I think he's going to take it," he said.

"Thank the Teus for that!" Pierre breathed a sigh of relief. "Imagine if he'd turned it down."

"I'd prefer not to!"

A few moments later, the High Elder, Gaetan Le Sterc and Hugo de Hambye emerged from the dolmen into the forecourt. From the expressions on their faces, it was clear that all had indeed gone well. The Elders all scrambled to their feet.

Cou-Cou La Tanche faced them and raised both arms: "I am, er, pleased to say that Hugo, er…"

"De Hambye," whispered Le Sterc in his ear.

"Yes. That, er, Hugo de Hambye has agreed to accept my country residence as his prize for winning the, er, dragon contest in, er, lieu of the dolmen that should have been his prize."

Some of the more elderly of the Elders dozed off and began to snore

The other Elders applauded noisily and there were shouts of "Hear! Hear!" and similar utterances.

Awakened by the racket below, Old Mauger listened for a few moments, debating whether to add his two limpets' worth, but in the end he decided not to bother.

Cou-Cou motioned for quiet by waving one of his walking sticks in the air. "So," he said, turning to Hugo, "the *Hougue La Tanche* will be yours."

"I am honoured to be given such a fine dolmen," said Hugo, bowing to the High Elder. "I hope you won't mind if I rename it."

"Not at all," said La Tanche. "What do you, er, intend to call it?"

"Mauger's Mound!" boomed the dragon from above and then gave a hearty laugh, which was cut short by a sudden bout of coughing.

Hugo glared in his direction.

"He's only joking," said Gastelois.

"I hope he is!" declared Hugo, adding emphatically: "I'm not having him staying up there!"

"Mmm," mumbled La Tanche, peering up at the summit. "So, have you, er, thought of a name for it?" he asked, returning his attention to Hugo.

"I have decided to call it the *Hougue Hambye*, after my home town."

"Excellent choice!" declared the High Elder, and there were mutterings of approval from the majority of his colleagues.

"One moment!" said Le Sterc. "Just one moment!"

Everyone looked at him.

"Before it can officially become his, we will have to hold a *Ouïe de Pouquelaye* to transfer ownership."

"A *what*?" queried Hugo.

"A *Ouïe de Pouquelaye*," repeated Gastelois, glancing at Le Sterc. "It's a special hearing in front of select witnesses during which seller and purchaser pass a binding contract transferring ownership of a property such as a dolmen from the former to the latter."

"I see," said Hugo. "When is that likely to happen?"

"Oh, quite soon, I would have thought."

"Ah! And who will organise it?"

"We will," said Le Sterc. "Where are you staying?"

"Er, in Ang-Lenn, at *The Old Coracle* or something."

"*The Old Vraic and Coracle.*"

"That's the one."

"Fine. We'll leave word there when we're ready to hold the *Ouïe.*"

Shortly after that, Cou-Cou La Tanche was remounted on his aurochs and the Elders slowly followed him from the forecourt and away from the newly-named *Hougue Hambye.*

"Well, that worked out all right," said Pierre, after watching the departing sages for some moments.

"Yes, it certainly did," agreed Gastelois. He looked at the others: "This calls for a celebration. *The Old Vraic*, everyone?"

"Suits me," said Hugo. "I'm going back there anyway."

"Excellent!" said Gastelois. "At least there we won't get food poisoning!"

With that, he took Sylvia by the arm and, humming a cheery tune, walked purposefully towards the track that led away from the mound and headed in the general direction of Ang-Lenn.

Behind them, Pierre was bombarding Hugo with questions about his new acquisition: what he really thought of it, what plans he had for it.

As for Hugo, he was only half listening. The other half of his mind was contemplating how pleasant life was going to be as a resident of the Island of Angur. He felt very fortunate. Yes, very fortunate indeed.

From his vantage point, Old Mauger watched them leave through half-opened eyes. He found himself wondering what fresh adventures were in store for them for the future. He yawned and shut his eyes. He would lie here for a little while longer, enjoy the warmth of the afternoon, and then go home.

* * *

On a stone bench abutting one of the tall granite megaliths forming the walls of Vraicer T'loch's home reposed the turtle shell, its intricate pattern of lines reflecting the yellowy-green glow from the vial of liquid lying next to it.

It was the following day and T'loch was swinging gently over his seaweed fire, watching the sea-dragon and its baby cavorting in the waves far out to sea. He found himself wondering where they would end up and what would become of them. Whatever their fate, he felt certain that they were not destined for misfortune.

Closer to Angur, he could see a coracle with its flotilla escort being borne northwards by a strong southerly wind. Every passing moment was taking Grosnez further away from the island. T'loch smiled a satisfied smile. The islanders were well shot of him - that was for certain.

His mind then homed in on the unfinished dolmen in the east of Angur, where a solitary figure was squatting near the broken capstone in its main chamber, playing contentedly with a vial of yellowy-green liquid. Escogriffe was happy. T'loch felt glad.

He withdrew his mind from the dolmen and opened his eyes to look at the stone bench where the yellowy-green glow from the vial of real sea-dragon milk showed up the intricate pattern of lines on the turtle shell lying next to it.

All had gone well. Yes, all had gone very well indeed.

* * *

Old Mauger lay on his belly at the edge of the marsh, smoking contentedly in the shade of an ancient tree. The sound of breakers reached his ears from a not-too distant shore, accompanied intermittently by the screeching of seagulls wheeling overhead.

He yawned and shut his eyes. Rich green and soft golden light filtered through the gently waving leafy canopy of the nearby tree and wove intricate patterns on his eyelids, some of it seeping through to register on his sleepy brain. He rolled on to his back and listened to the sounds around him for a while, but gradually these became fainter and more distant as he slowly drifted off into a peaceful slumber, smoke rising lazily from his broad nostrils.

Around him, the marsh muttered its way through the hot afternoon, fanned by a cool, leisurely breeze from the sea.

THE END